OUTER DARKNESS

**CREATED BY
JOHN LAYMAN
AFU CHAN**

™

44.61348 -113.23677 1.97937 34.436598 -45.69123 13.67433 BANISHMENT 2.052345 -9.9953326 -87.56649 1.0345167 7.
-4.32983 55.435928 9.384758 57.62323522 152.07075 3.49 6.69716 -72.84844 1.01 37.66841 15.08234 -21.00382 -108.98404 1.15

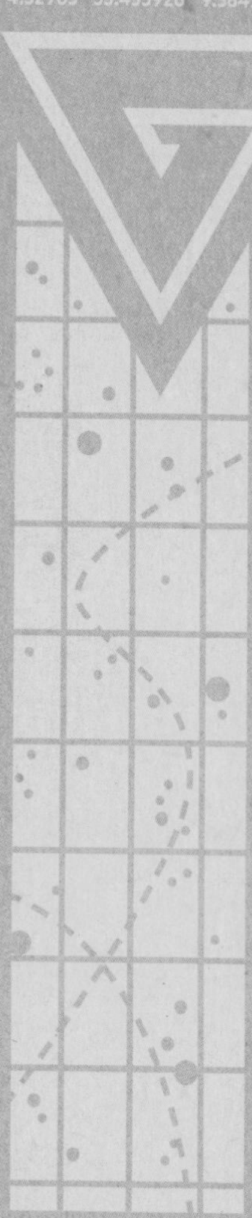

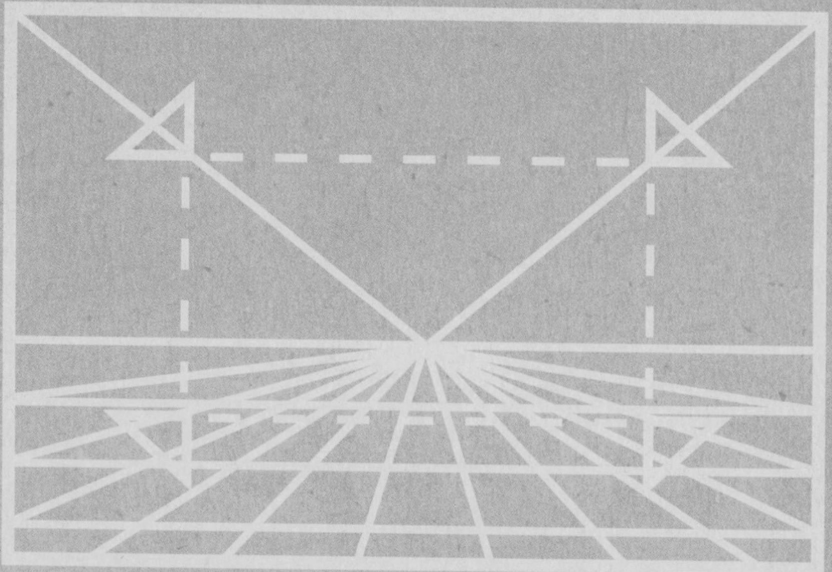

-4.32983 55.435928 9.384758 57.623235 152.07075 3.49 6.69716 -72.84844
1.01 37.66841 15.08234 -21.00382 -108.98404 1.15 -22.03528 -2.72653 1.16
MATHEMATICS FAILED >>>_ NEW ATTEMPT .0349SEC >_ -4.32983 6.32383

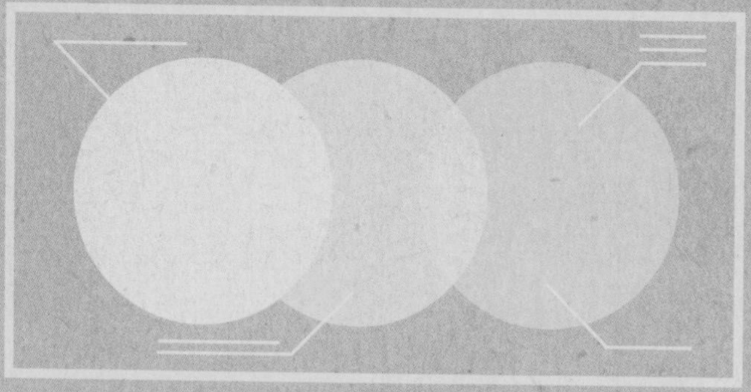

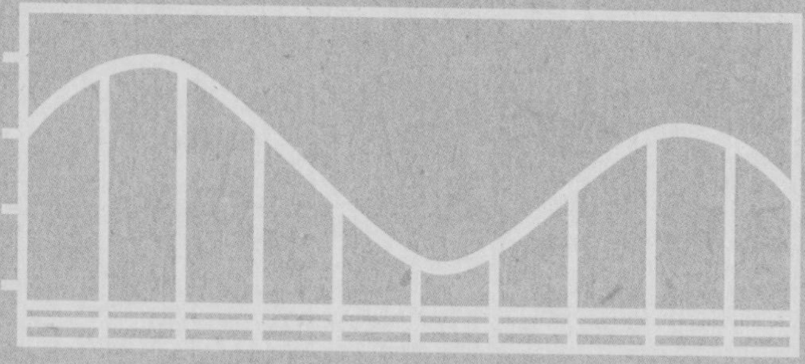

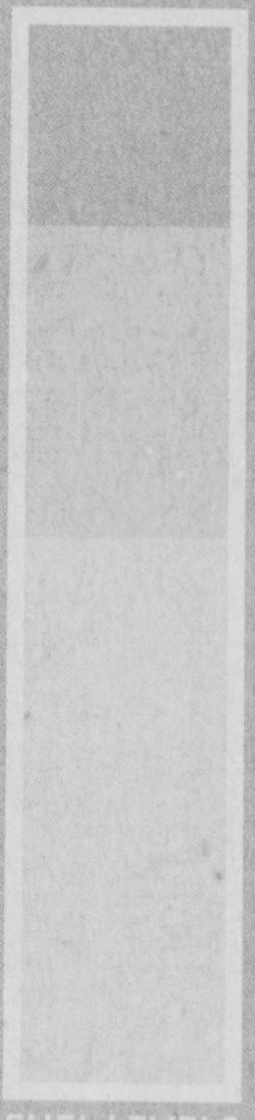

FUEL LEVELS

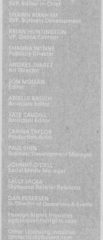

FOR SKYBOUND ENTERTAINMENT

ROBERT KIRKMAN Chairman
DAVID ALPERT CEO
SEAN MACKIEWICZ SVP, Editor-in-Chief
SHAWN KIRKHAM SVP, Business Development
BRIAN HUNTINGTON VP, Online Content
SHAUNA WYNNE Publicity Director
ANDRES JUAREZ Art Director
JON MOISAN Editor
ARIELLE BASICH Associate Editor
KATE CAUDILL Assistant Editor
CARINA TAYLOR Production Artist
PAUL SHIN Business Development Manager
JOHNNY O'DELL Social Media Manager
SALLY JACKA Skybound Retailer Relations
DAN PETERSEN Sr. Director of Operations & Events

Foreign Rights Inquiries ag@sequentialrights.com

Other Licensing Inquiries contact@skybound.com

SKYBOUND.COM

IMAGE COMICS, INC.

ROBERT KIRKMAN Chief Operating Officer
ERIK LARSEN Chief Financial Officer
TODD MCFARLANE President
MARC SILVESTRI Chief Executive Officer
JIM VALENTINO Vice President
ERIC STEPHENSON Publisher / Chief Creative Officer
COREY HART Director of Sales
JEFF BOISON Director of Publishing Planning & Book Trade Sales
CHRIS ROSS Director of Digital Sales
JEFF STANG Director of Specialty Sales
KAT SALAZAR Director of PR & Marketing
DREW GILL Art Director
HEATHER DOORNINK Production Director
NICOLE LAPALME Controller

IMAGECOMICS.COM

OUTER DARKNESS VOLUME 1. FIRST PRINTING. May 2019. Published by Image Comics, Inc. Office of publication: 2701 NW Vaughn St., Ste. 780, Portland, OR 97210.

ISBN: 978-1-5343-1210-4

4758 >>>_ QUANTUM WARDS ALPHA 37.239753 88.19483 -120.69952 -168.454783 2.1478663 EXORCISM SUCCESSFUL
2653 -97.53299 1.16 RESURRECTION FAILED >>>_ NEW ATTEMPT .0349SEC >_ 39.19273 -4.32983 55.435928 9.384758 -46.90415

V1: EACH OTHER'S THROATS

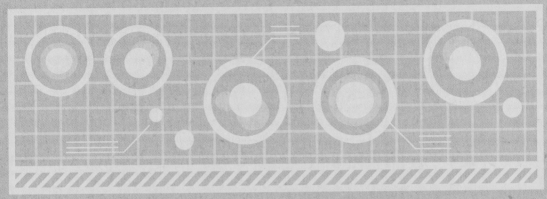

15.08234 -21.00382 -108.98404 1.15 -22.03528 -2.72653 1.16 ANALYSIS >>>_ .0349SEC >_ -4.32983 55.435928 9.384758 -46.90415
44.61348 -113.23677 34.4598 -45.69123 -4.32983 55.435928 9.384758 57.62323S 152.07075 3.49 6.69716 -72.84844 1.01 37.66841
-4.32983 55.435928 9.384758 57.623235 152.07075 3.49 6.69716 -72.84844 1.01 37.66841 15.08234 -7.32513 55.435928 9.384758
57.623235 152.07075 3.49 6.69716 -72.32556 1.01 37.66841 15.08234 -21.00382 -108.98404 1.15 -22.03528 -2.72653 1.1 BATTLE
AUTHORIZATION >>>_ SUCCESSFUL ATTEMPT .0349SEC >_ -4.32983 55.435928 9.384758 -46.90415 44.61348 -113.23677 -45.69123

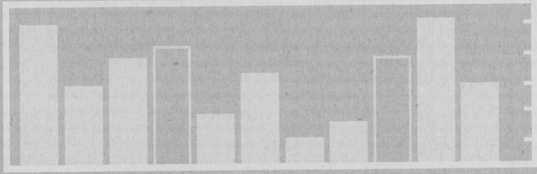

-72.84844 1.01 37.66841 15.08234 -21.00382 -108.98404 1.15 -22.03528 -2.72653 1.16
.0349SEC >_ -4.32983 55.435928 9.384758 -46.90415 44.61348 -113.23677 34.4598 -45.69123
55.435928 9.384758 57.623235 152.07075 3.49 6.69716 -72.84844 1.01 37.66841 15.08234
71.393884 3.021 5.73942 -4.32983 55.3554832 9.384758 57.623235 152.0749 6.69716

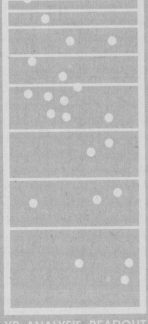

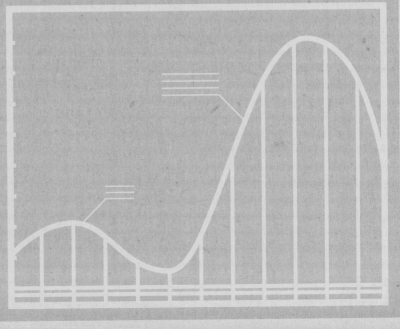

XR ANALYSIS READOUT

PART 1

CAPTAIN ON THE BRIDGE

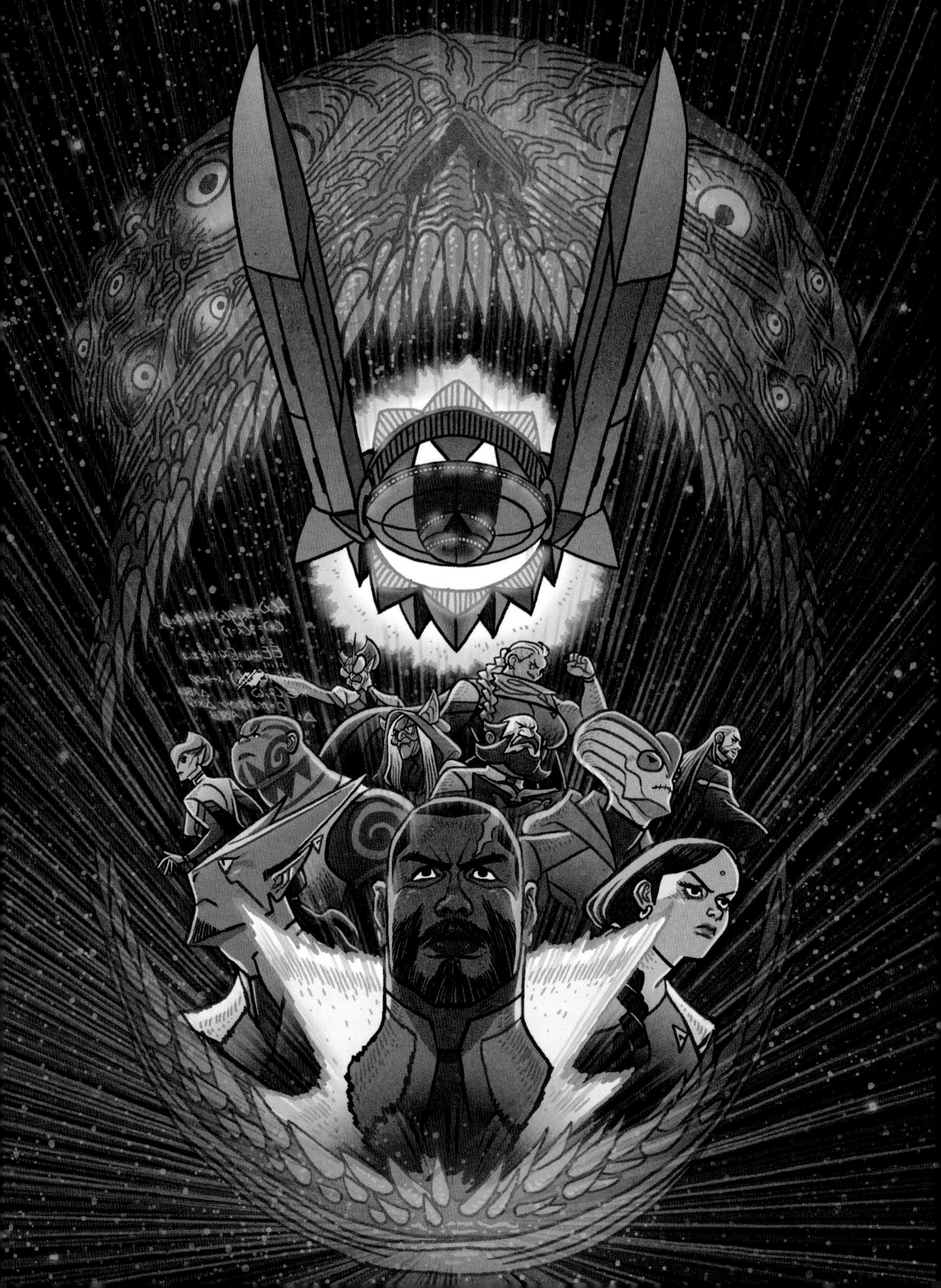

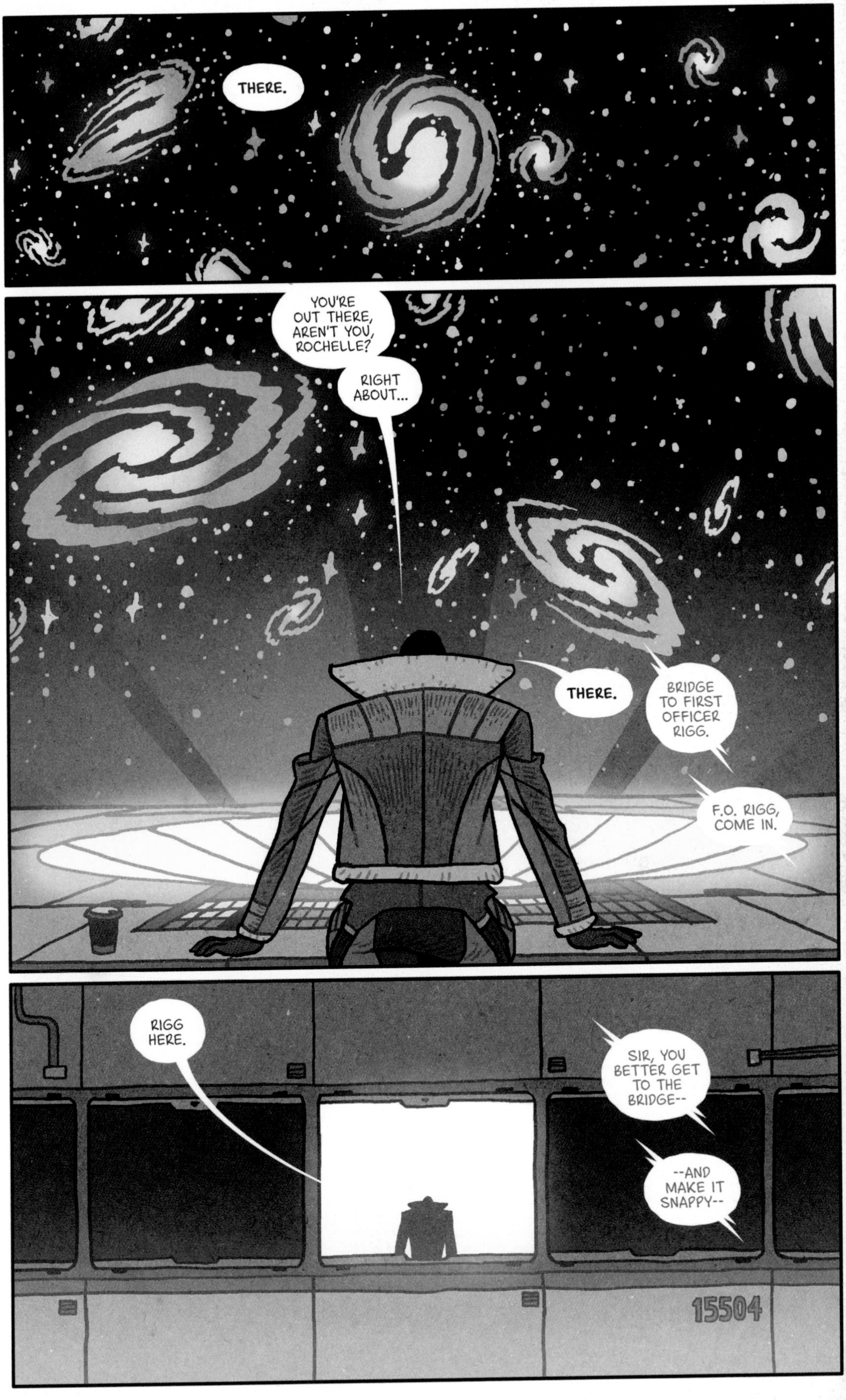
THERE.
YOU'RE OUT THERE, AREN'T YOU, ROCHELLE?
RIGHT ABOUT...
THERE.
BRIDGE TO FIRST OFFICER RIGG.
F.O. RIGG, COME IN.
RIGG HERE.
SIR, YOU BETTER GET TO THE BRIDGE--
--AND MAKE IT SNAPPY--
15504

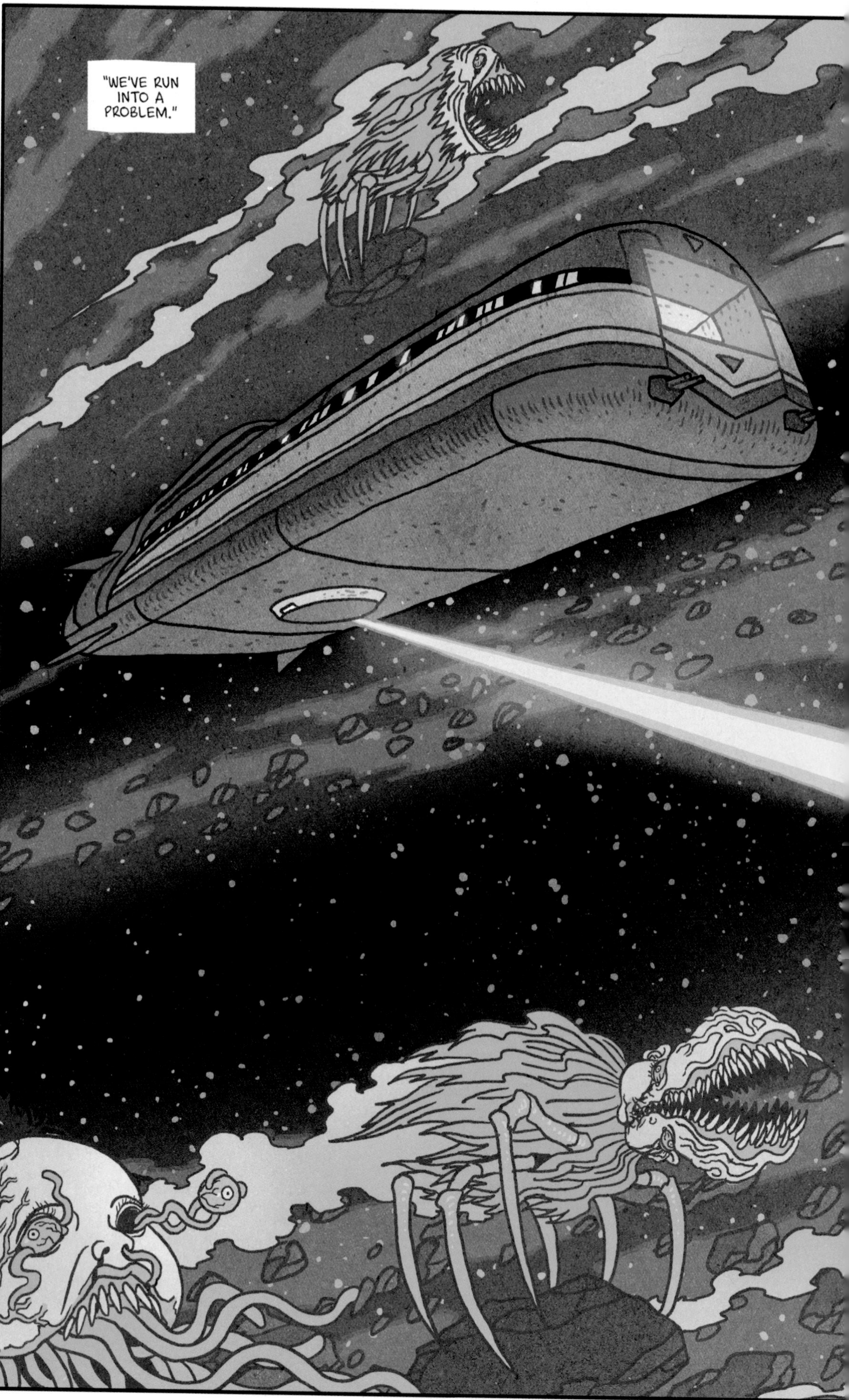
"WE'VE RUN
INTO A
PROBLEM."

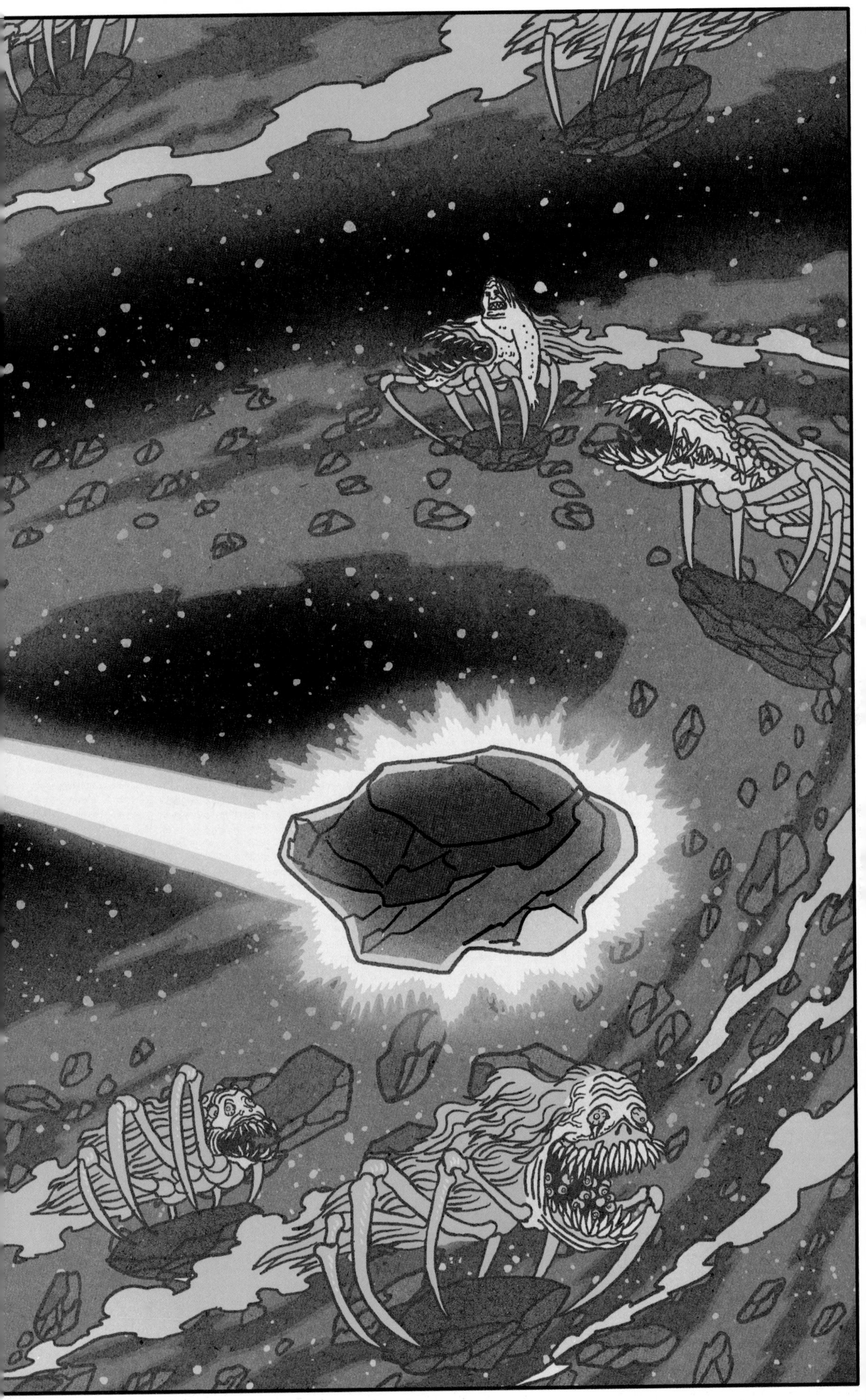

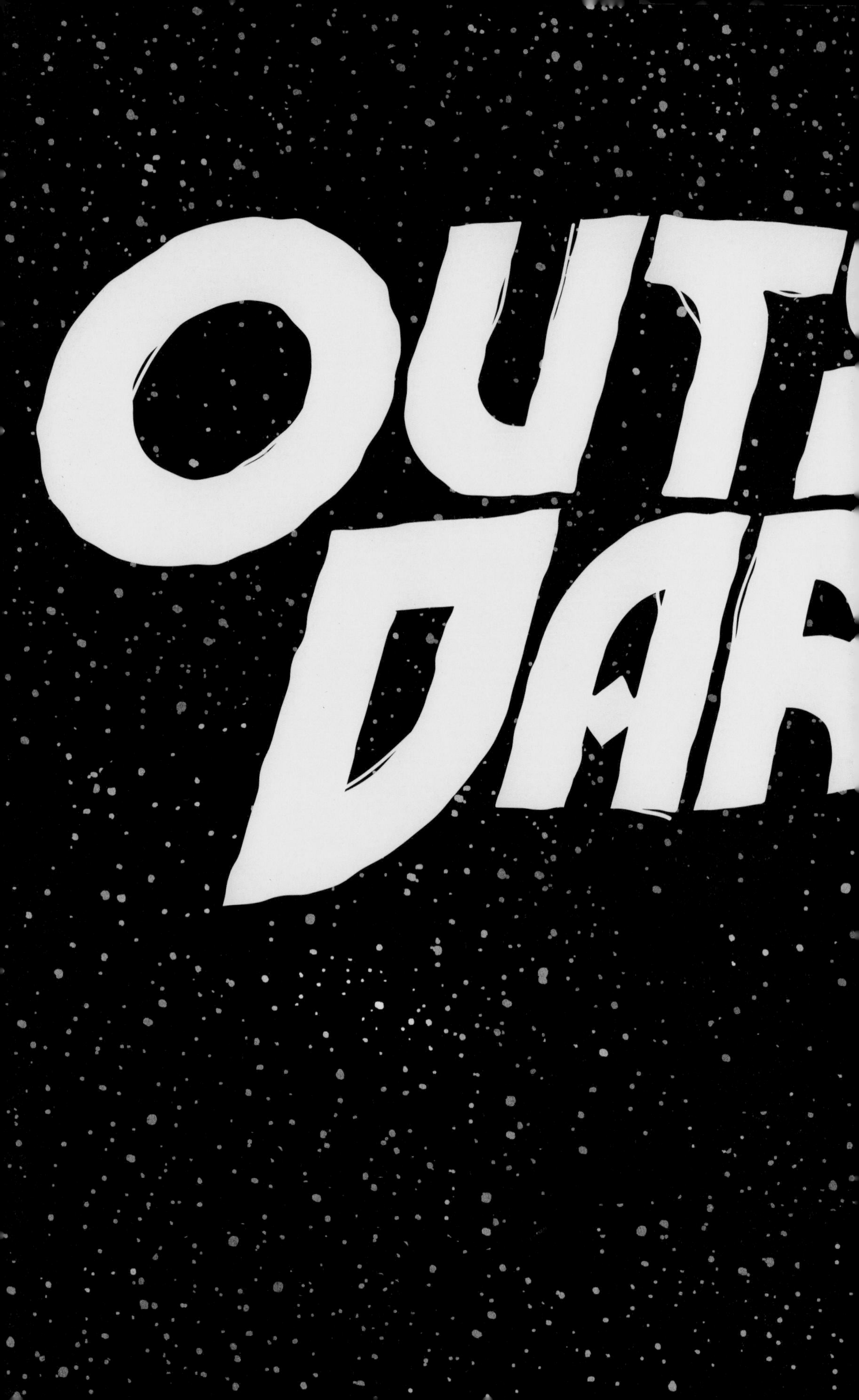

"AND CAST THE WORTHLESS SERVANT INTO THE OUTER DARKNESS. IN THAT PLACE THERE WILL BE WEEPING AND GNASHING OF TEETH."
MATTHEW 25:30

JOHN LAYMAN
CREATOR/WRITER

AFU CHAN
CREATOR/ARTIST

PAT BROSSEAU
LETTERER

JON MOISAN
EDITOR

AFU CHAN
COVER ARTIST

ANDRES JUAREZ
LOGO DESIGN

CARINA TAYLOR
PRODUCTION DESIGN

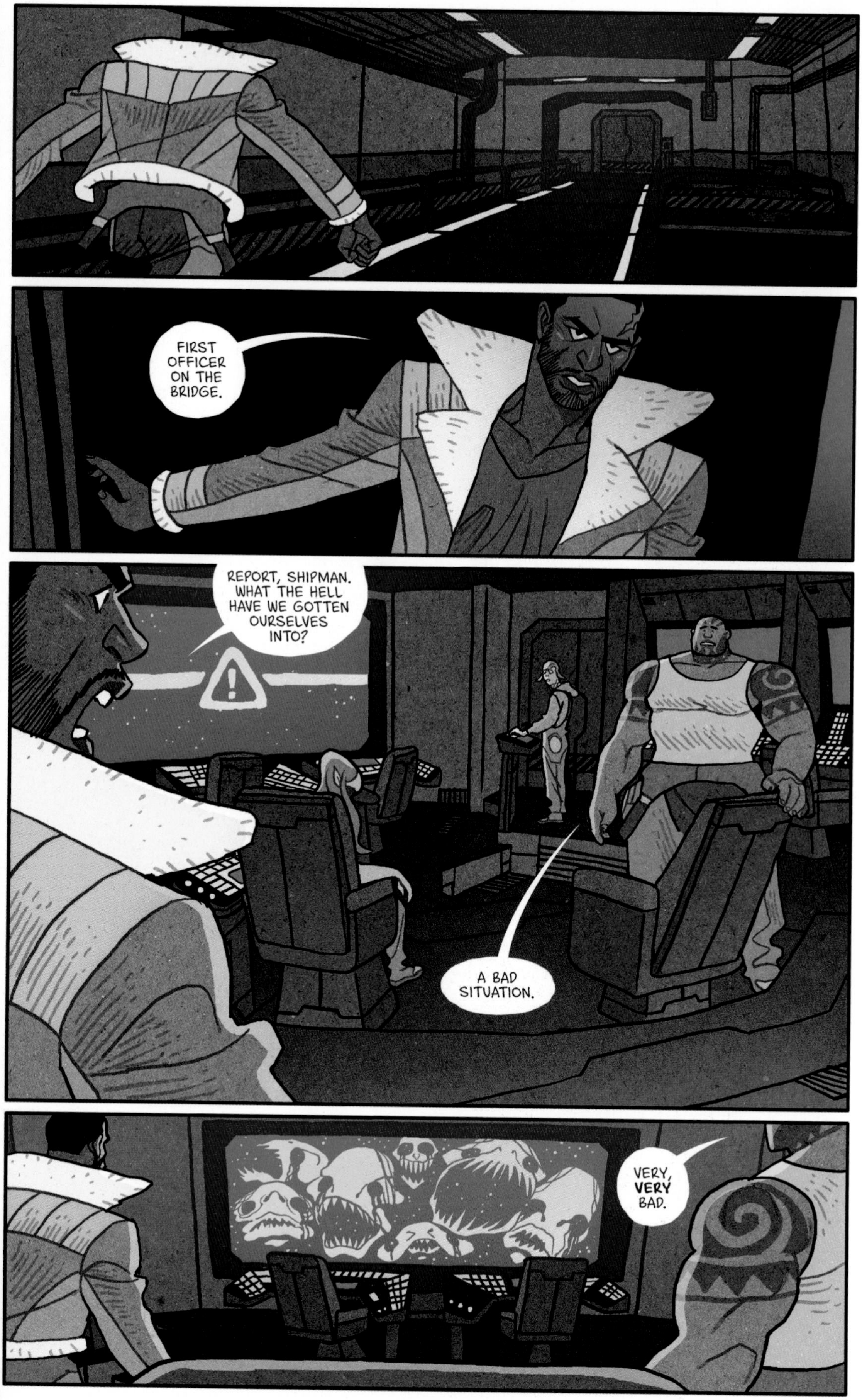
FIRST OFFICER ON THE BRIDGE.
REPORT, SHIPMAN. WHAT THE HELL HAVE WE GOTTEN OURSELVES INTO?
A BAD SITUATION.
VERY, **VERY** BAD.

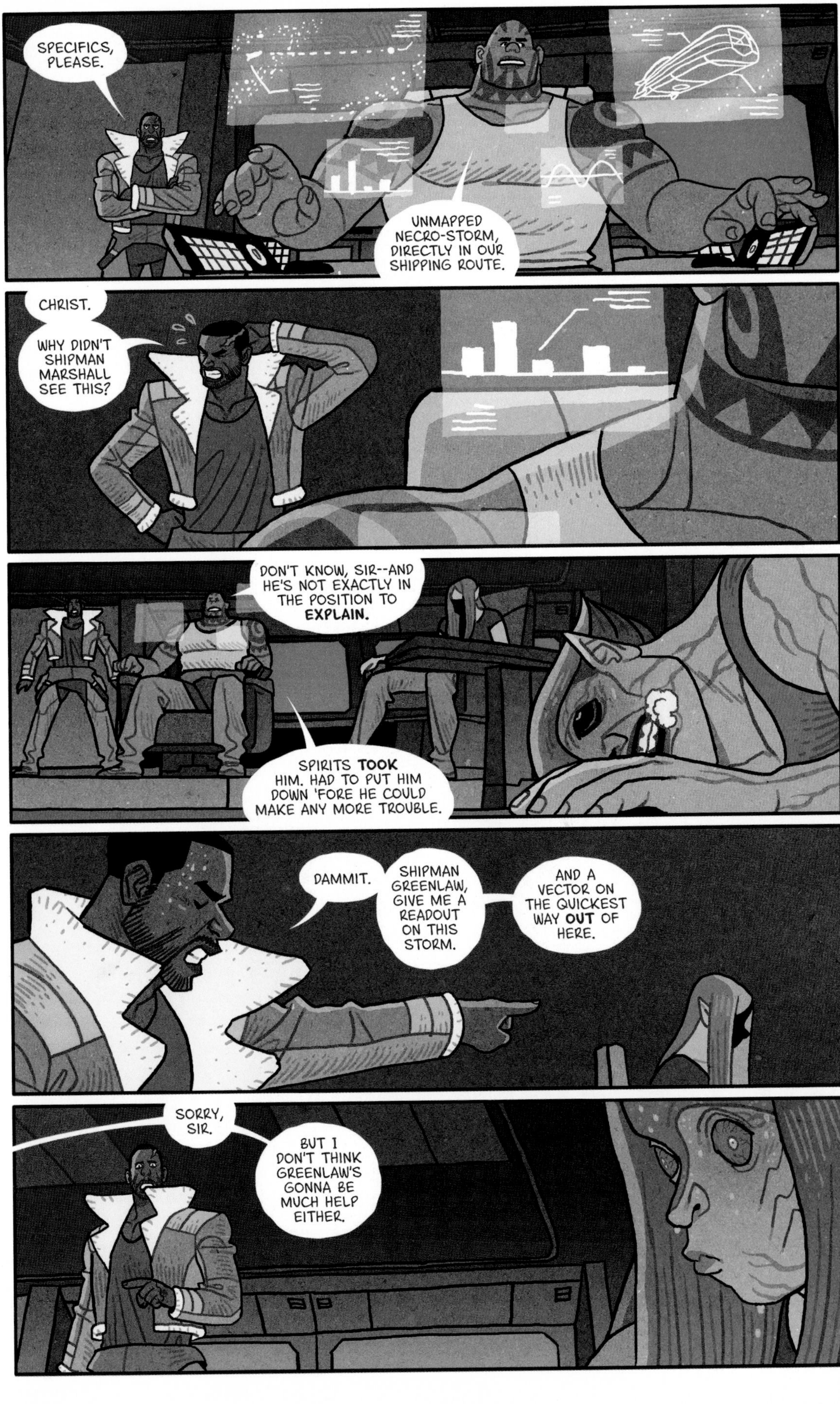
SPECIFICS, PLEASE.
UNMAPPED NECRO-STORM, DIRECTLY IN OUR SHIPPING ROUTE.
CHRIST.
WHY DIDN'T SHIPMAN MARSHALL SEE THIS?
DON'T KNOW, SIR--AND HE'S NOT EXACTLY IN THE POSITION TO **EXPLAIN.**
SPIRITS **TOOK** HIM. HAD TO PUT HIM DOWN 'FORE HE COULD MAKE ANY MORE TROUBLE.
DAMMIT.
SHIPMAN GREENLAW, GIVE ME A READOUT ON THIS STORM.
AND A VECTOR ON THE QUICKEST WAY **OUT** OF HERE.
SORRY, SIR.
BUT I DON'T THINK GREENLAW'S GONNA BE MUCH HELP EITHER.

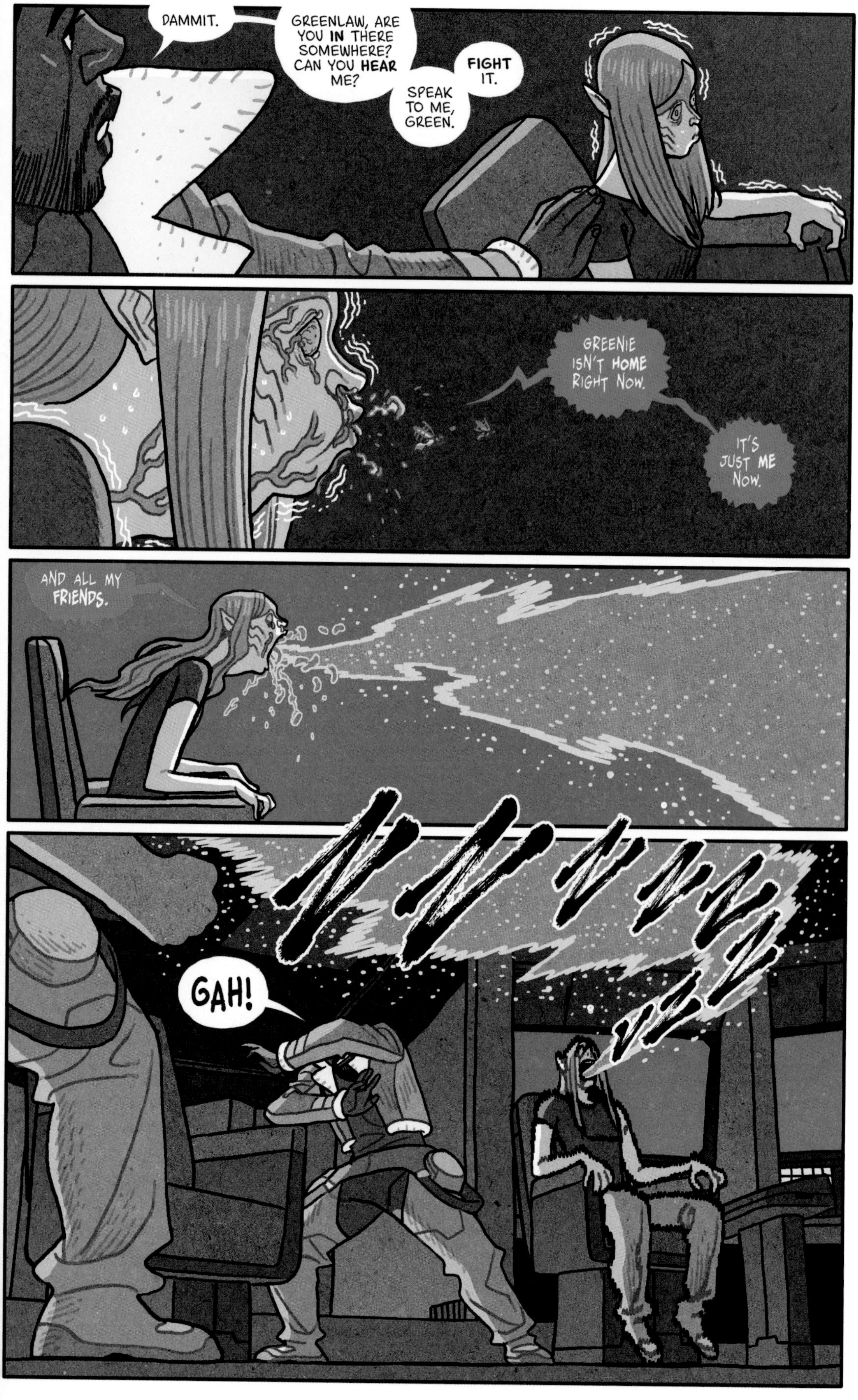
DAMMIT.
GREENLAW, ARE YOU IN THERE SOMEWHERE? CAN YOU HEAR ME?
SPEAK TO ME, GREEN.
FIGHT IT.
GREENIE ISN'T HOME RIGHT NOW.
IT'S JUST ME NOW.
AND ALL MY FRIENDS.
GAH!

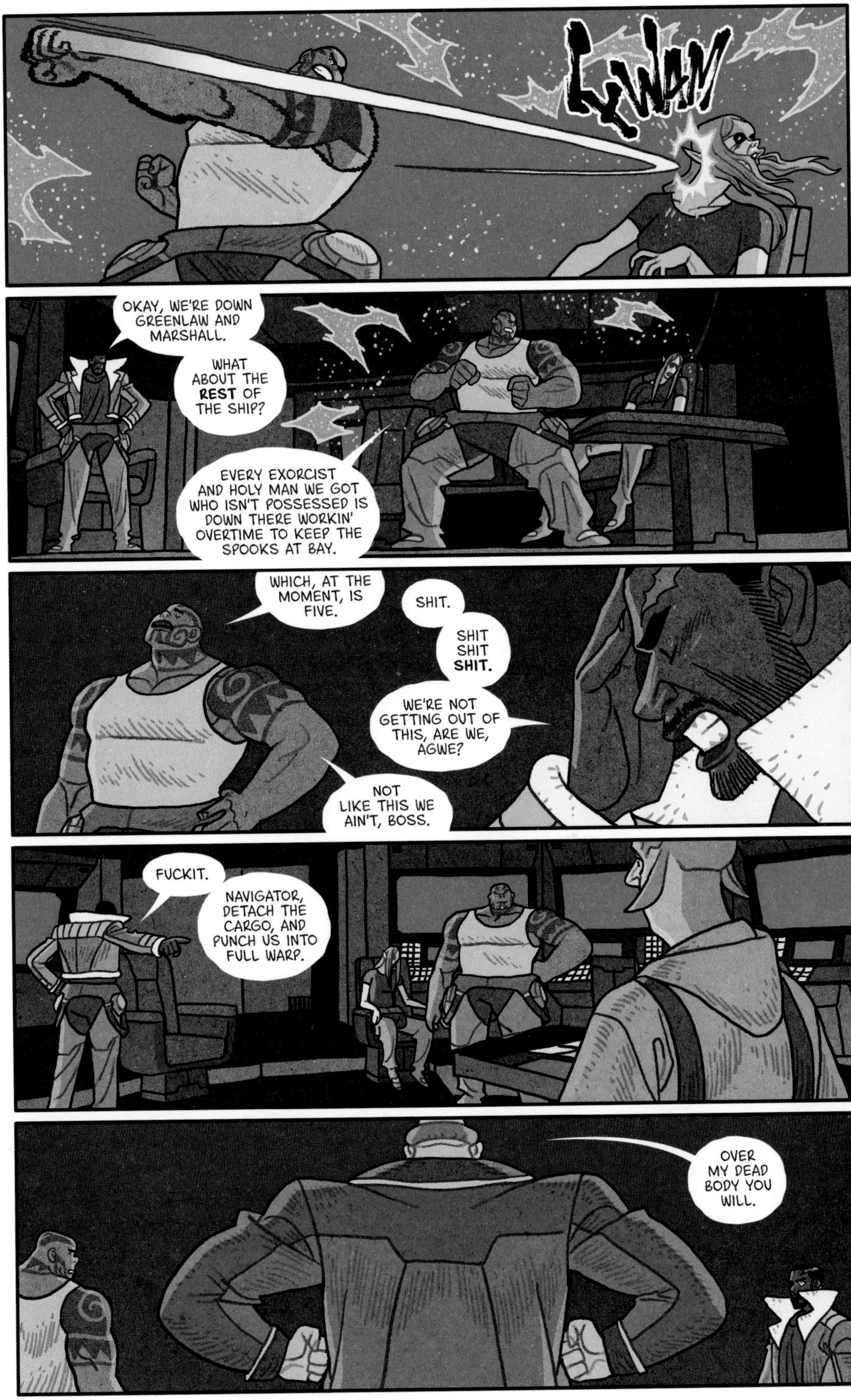

KWAM
OKAY, WE'RE DOWN GREENLAW AND MARSHALL.
WHAT ABOUT THE **REST** OF THE SHIP?
EVERY EXORCIST AND HOLY MAN WE GOT WHO ISN'T POSSESSED IS DOWN THERE WORKIN' OVERTIME TO KEEP THE SPOOKS AT BAY.
WHICH, AT THE MOMENT, IS FIVE.
SHIT.
SHIT SHIT **SHIT.**
WE'RE NOT GETTING OUT OF THIS, ARE WE, AGWE?
NOT LIKE THIS WE AIN'T, BOSS.
FUCKIT.
NAVIGATOR, DETACH THE CARGO, AND PUNCH US INTO FULL WARP.
OVER MY DEAD BODY YOU WILL.

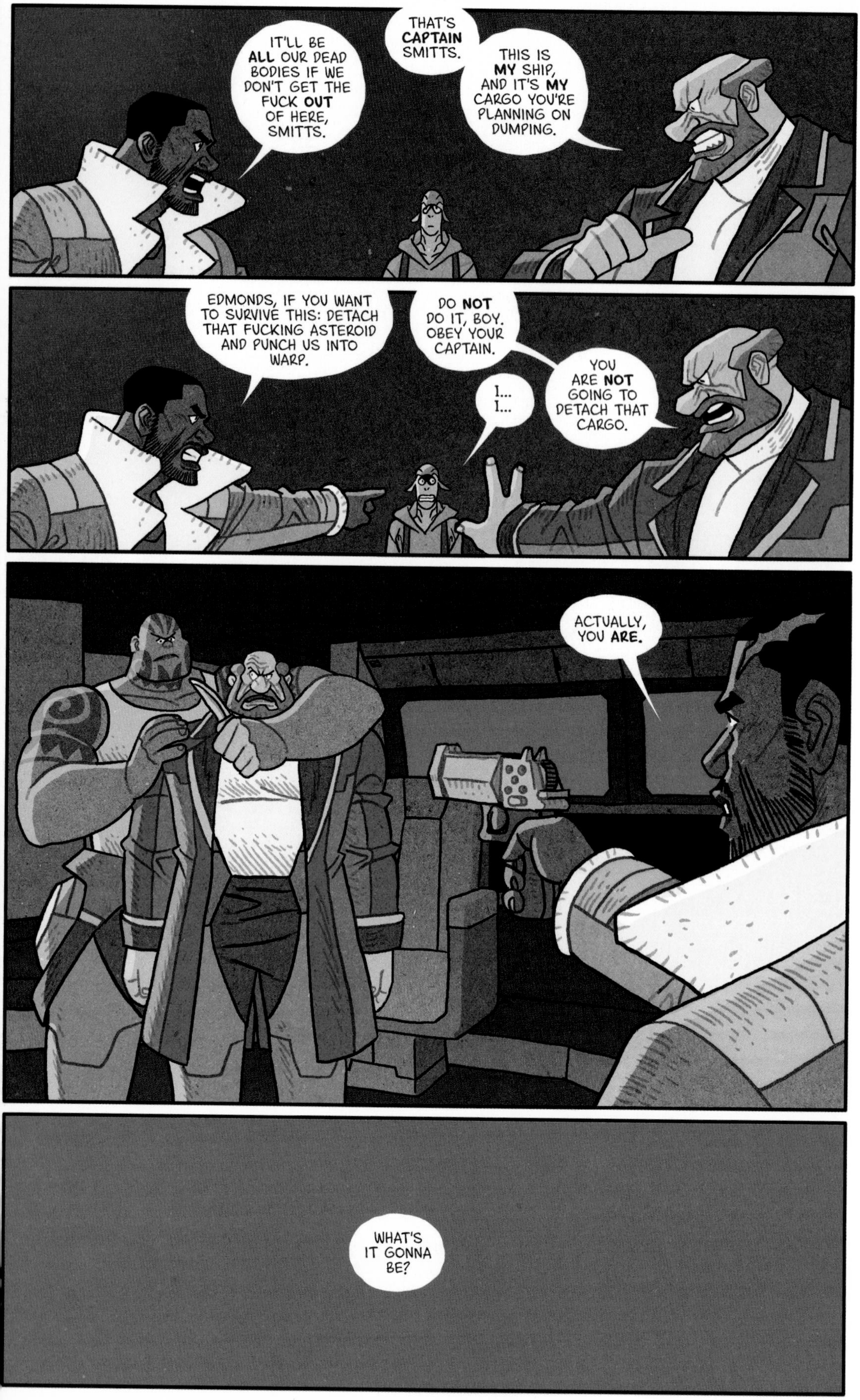
IT'LL BE ALL OUR DEAD BODIES IF WE DON'T GET THE FUCK OUT OF HERE, SMITTS.
THAT'S CAPTAIN SMITTS.
THIS IS MY SHIP, AND IT'S MY CARGO YOU'RE PLANNING ON DUMPING.
EDMONDS, IF YOU WANT TO SURVIVE THIS: DETACH THAT FUCKING ASTEROID AND PUNCH US INTO WARP.
DO NOT DO IT, BOY. OBEY YOUR CAPTAIN.
I... I...
YOU ARE NOT GOING TO DETACH THAT CARGO.
ACTUALLY, YOU ARE.
WHAT'S IT GONNA BE?

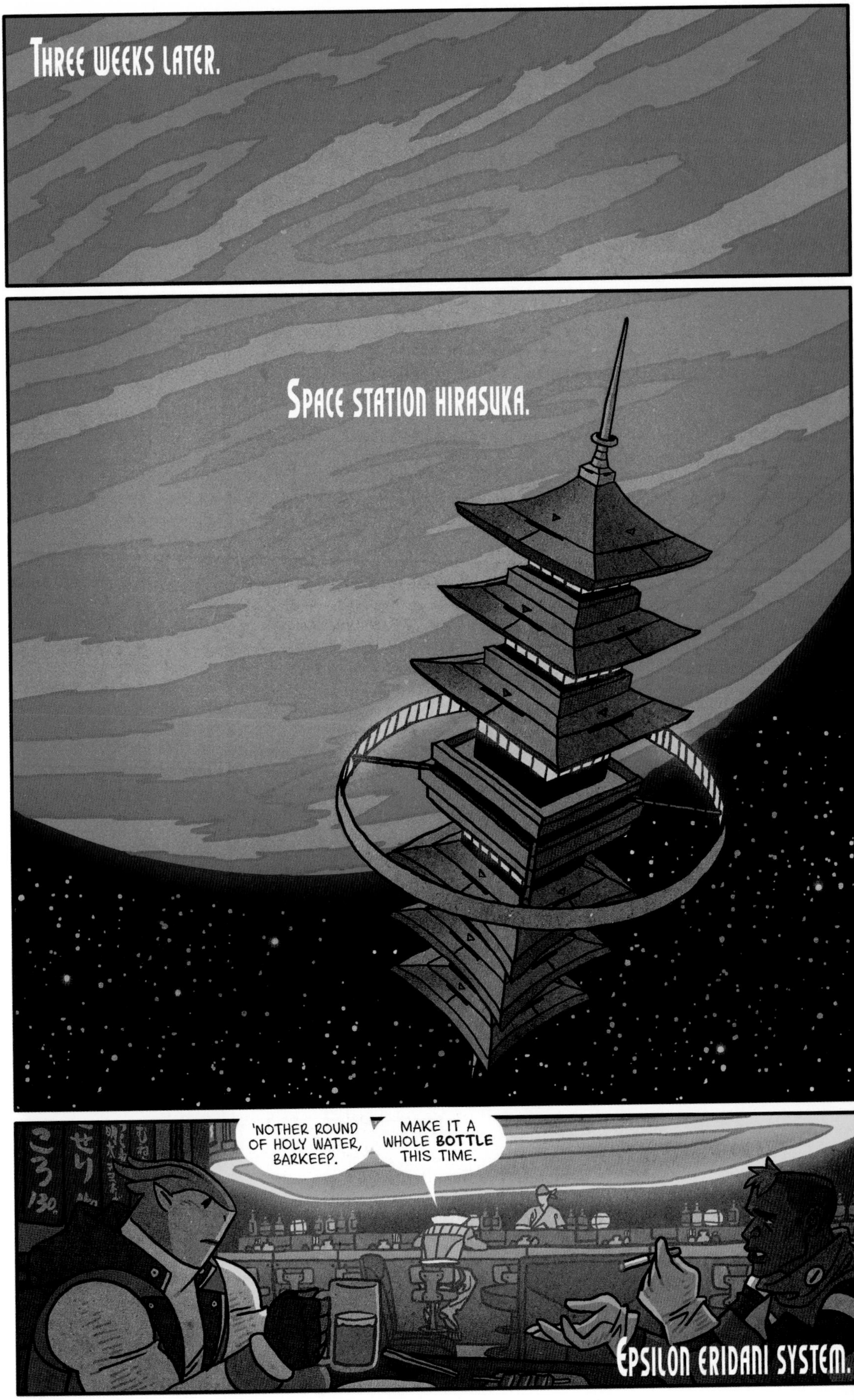
THREE WEEKS LATER.
SPACE STATION HIRASUKA.
'NOTHER ROUND OF HOLY WATER, BARKEEP.
MAKE IT A WHOLE **BOTTLE** THIS TIME.
EPSILON ERIDANI SYSTEM.

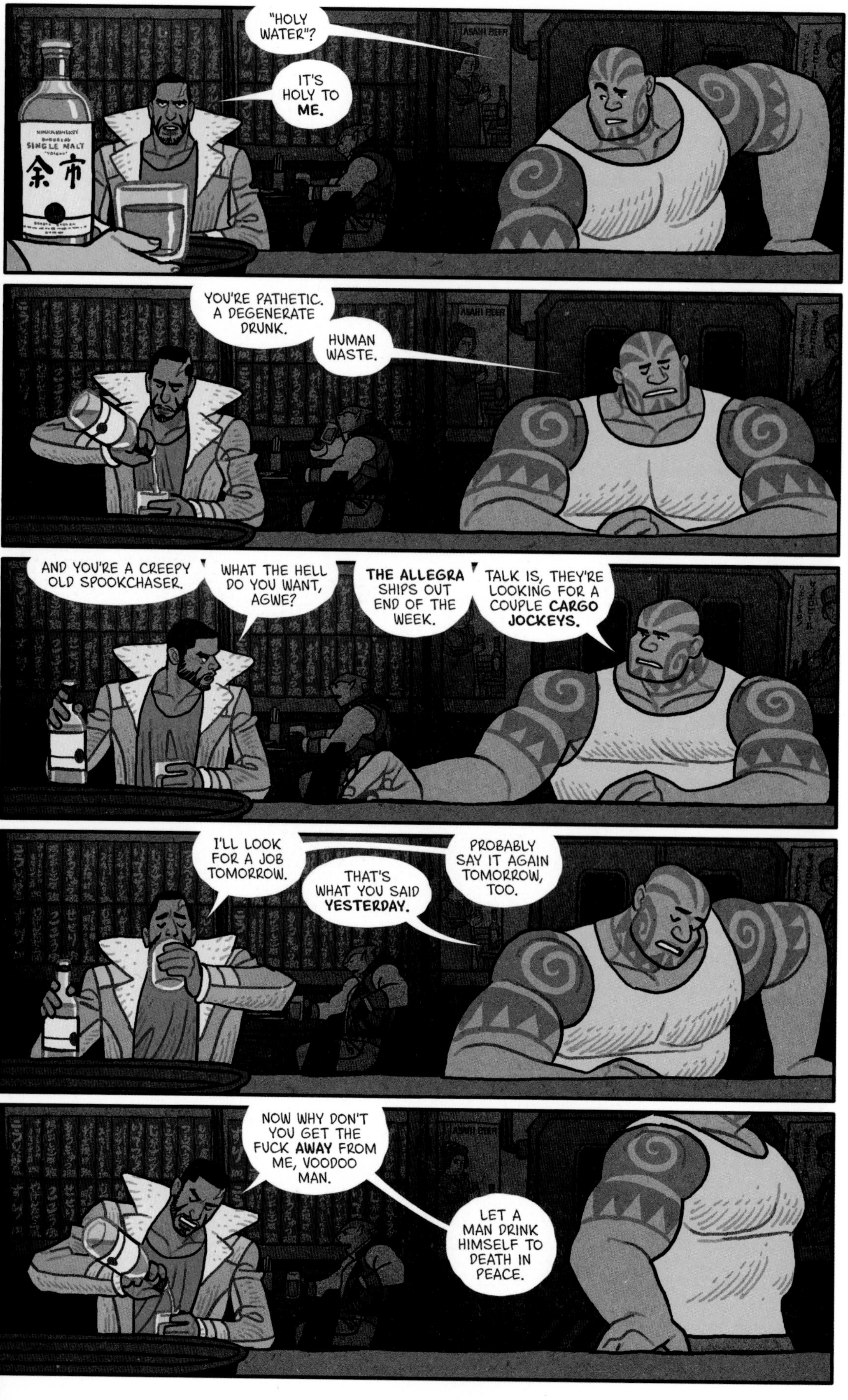
"HOLY WATER"?
SINGLE MALT
余市
IT'S HOLY TO **ME.**
ASAHI BEER
YOU'RE PATHETIC. A DEGENERATE DRUNK.
HUMAN WASTE.
AND YOU'RE A CREEPY OLD SPOOKCHASER.
WHAT THE HELL DO YOU WANT, AGWE?
THE ALLEGRA SHIPS OUT END OF THE WEEK.
TALK IS, THEY'RE LOOKING FOR A COUPLE **CARGO JOCKEYS.**
I'LL LOOK FOR A JOB TOMORROW.
THAT'S WHAT YOU SAID **YESTERDAY.**
PROBABLY SAY IT AGAIN TOMORROW, TOO.
NOW WHY DON'T YOU GET THE FUCK **AWAY** FROM ME, VOODOO MAN.
LET A MAN DRINK HIMSELF TO DEATH IN PEACE.

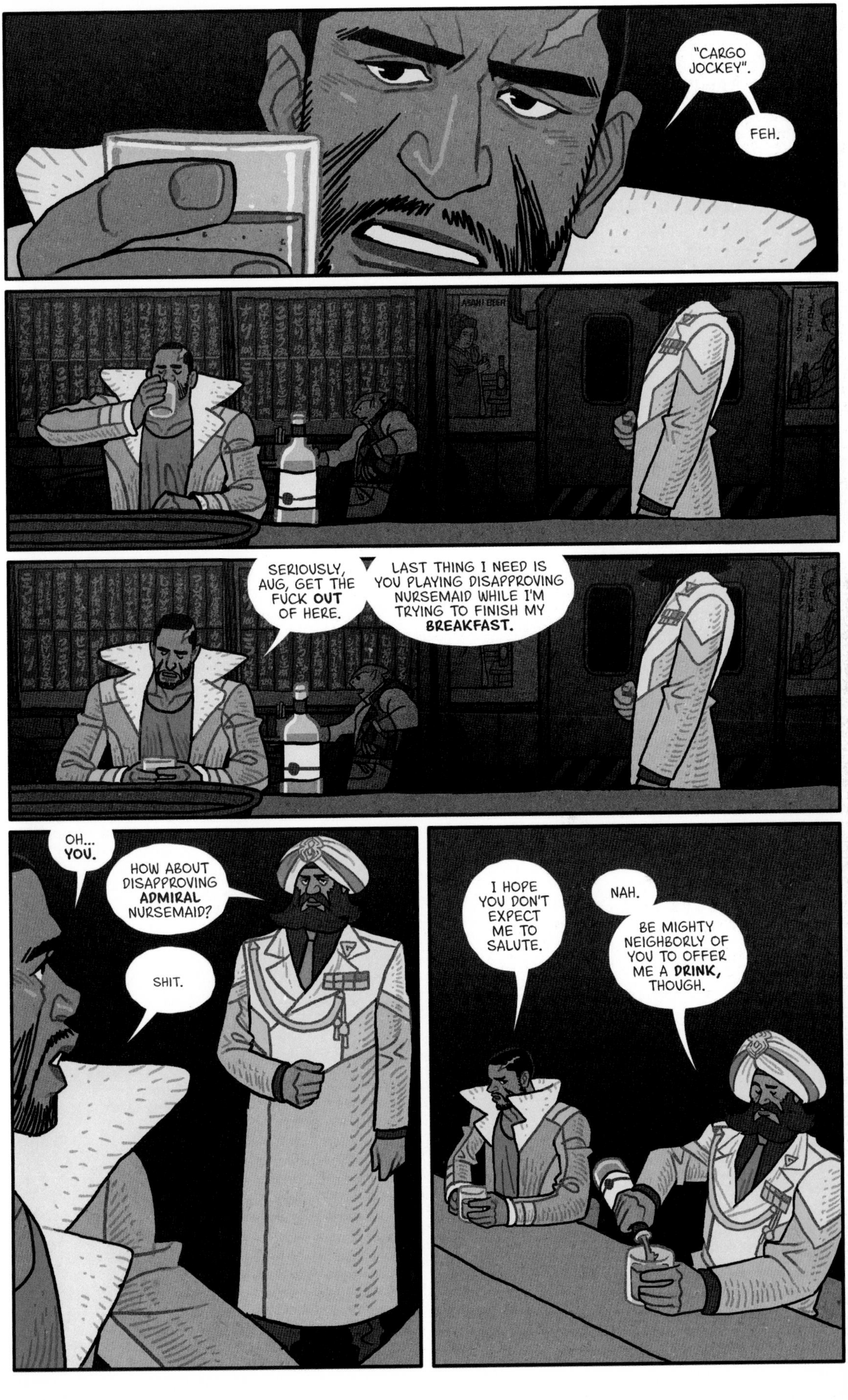
"CARGO JOCKEY".
FEH.
ASAHI BEER
SERIOUSLY, AUG, GET THE FUCK **OUT** OF HERE.
LAST THING I NEED IS YOU PLAYING DISAPPROVING NURSEMAID WHILE I'M TRYING TO FINISH MY **BREAKFAST.**
OH... **YOU.**
HOW ABOUT DISAPPROVING **ADMIRAL** NURSEMAID?
SHIT.
I HOPE YOU DON'T EXPECT ME TO SALUTE.
NAH.
BE MIGHTY NEIGHBORLY OF YOU TO OFFER ME A **DRINK,** THOUGH.

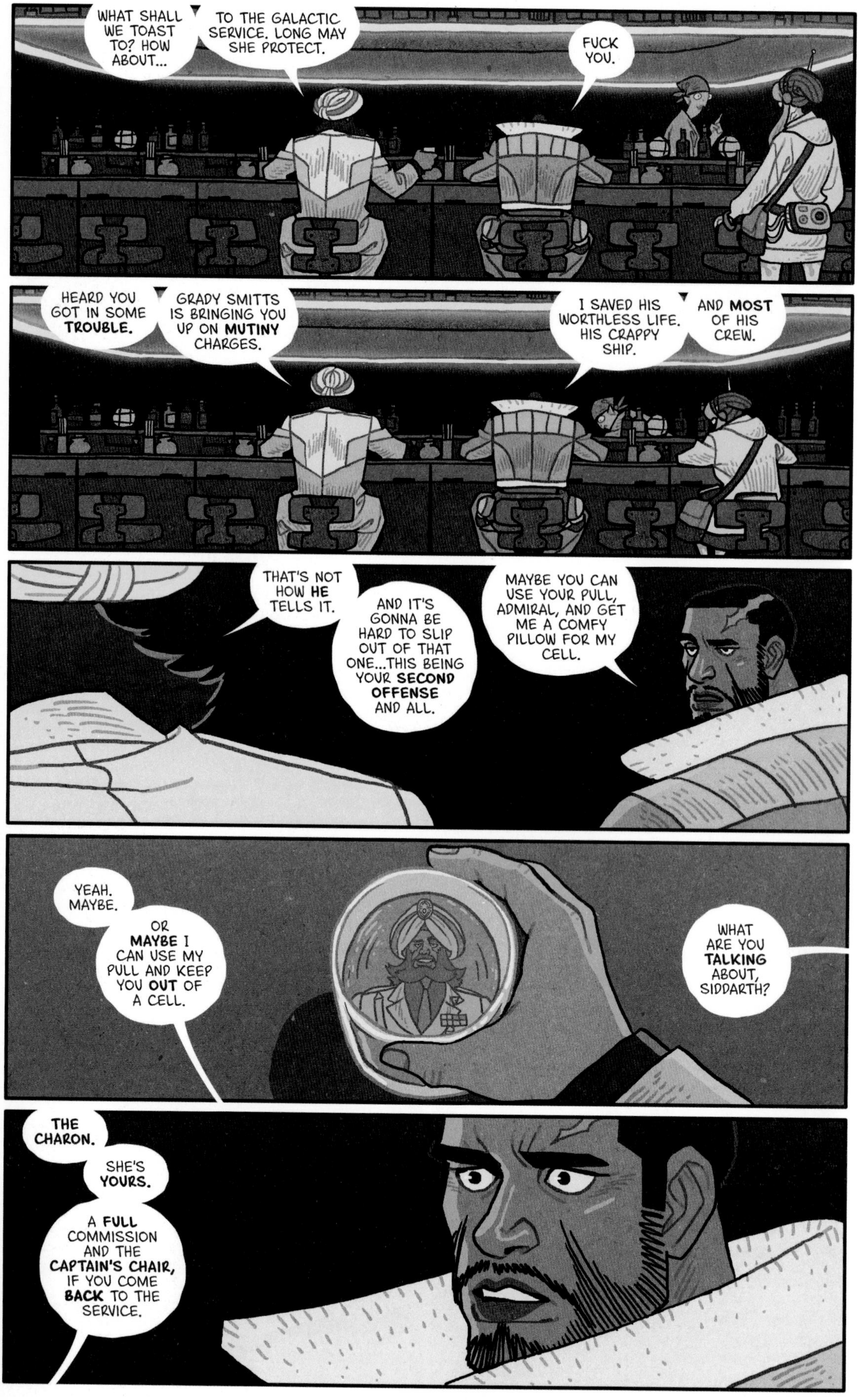
WHAT SHALL WE TOAST TO? HOW ABOUT...
TO THE GALACTIC SERVICE. LONG MAY SHE PROTECT.
FUCK YOU.
HEARD YOU GOT IN SOME **TROUBLE.**
GRADY SMITTS IS BRINGING YOU UP ON **MUTINY** CHARGES.
I SAVED HIS WORTHLESS LIFE. HIS CRAPPY SHIP.
AND **MOST** OF HIS CREW.
THAT'S NOT HOW **HE** TELLS IT.
AND IT'S GONNA BE HARD TO SLIP OUT OF THAT ONE...THIS BEING YOUR **SECOND OFFENSE** AND ALL.
MAYBE YOU CAN USE YOUR PULL, ADMIRAL, AND GET ME A COMFY PILLOW FOR MY CELL.
YEAH. MAYBE.
OR **MAYBE** I CAN USE MY PULL AND KEEP YOU **OUT** OF A CELL.
WHAT ARE YOU **TALKING** ABOUT, SIDDARTH?
THE CHARON.
SHE'S **YOURS.**
A **FULL** COMMISSION AND THE **CAPTAIN'S CHAIR,** IF YOU COME **BACK** TO THE SERVICE.

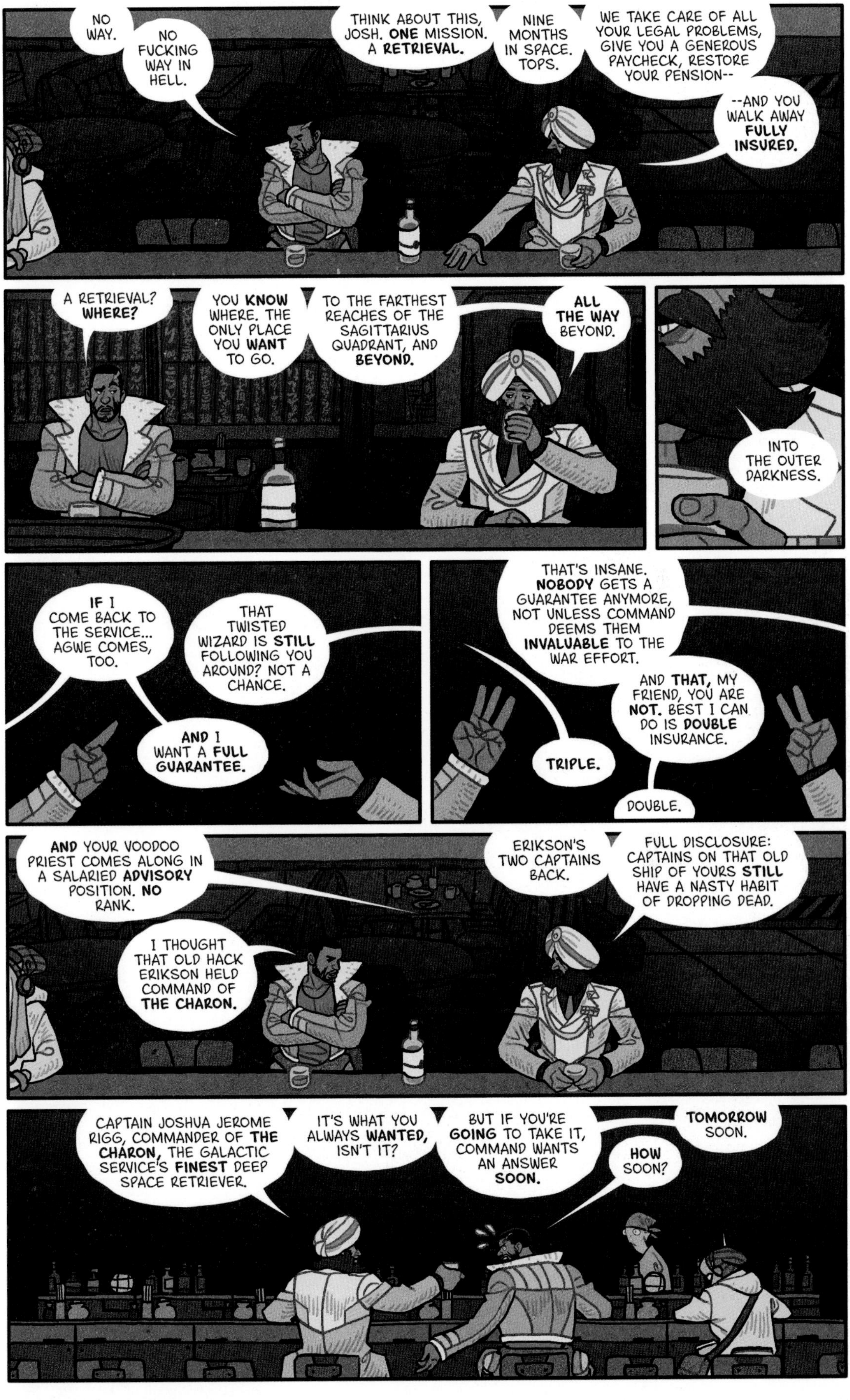
NO WAY.
NO FUCKING WAY IN HELL.
THINK ABOUT THIS, JOSH. ONE MISSION. A RETRIEVAL.
NINE MONTHS IN SPACE. TOPS.
WE TAKE CARE OF ALL YOUR LEGAL PROBLEMS, GIVE YOU A GENEROUS PAYCHECK, RESTORE YOUR PENSION--
--AND YOU WALK AWAY FULLY INSURED.
A RETRIEVAL? WHERE?
YOU KNOW WHERE. THE ONLY PLACE YOU WANT TO GO.
TO THE FARTHEST REACHES OF THE SAGITTARIUS QUADRANT, AND BEYOND.
ALL THE WAY BEYOND.
INTO THE OUTER DARKNESS.
IF I COME BACK TO THE SERVICE... AGWE COMES, TOO.
THAT TWISTED WIZARD IS STILL FOLLOWING YOU AROUND? NOT A CHANCE.
AND I WANT A FULL GUARANTEE.
THAT'S INSANE. NOBODY GETS A GUARANTEE ANYMORE, NOT UNLESS COMMAND DEEMS THEM INVALUABLE TO THE WAR EFFORT.
AND THAT, MY FRIEND, YOU ARE NOT. BEST I CAN DO IS DOUBLE INSURANCE.
TRIPLE.
DOUBLE.
AND YOUR VOODOO PRIEST COMES ALONG IN A SALARIED ADVISORY POSITION. NO RANK.
I THOUGHT THAT OLD HACK ERIKSON HELD COMMAND OF THE CHARON.
ERIKSON'S TWO CAPTAINS BACK.
FULL DISCLOSURE: CAPTAINS ON THAT OLD SHIP OF YOURS STILL HAVE A NASTY HABIT OF DROPPING DEAD.
CAPTAIN JOSHUA JEROME RIGG, COMMANDER OF THE CHARON, THE GALACTIC SERVICE'S FINEST DEEP SPACE RETRIEVER.
IT'S WHAT YOU ALWAYS WANTED, ISN'T IT?
BUT IF YOU'RE GOING TO TAKE IT, COMMAND WANTS AN ANSWER SOON.
HOW SOON?
TOMORROW SOON.

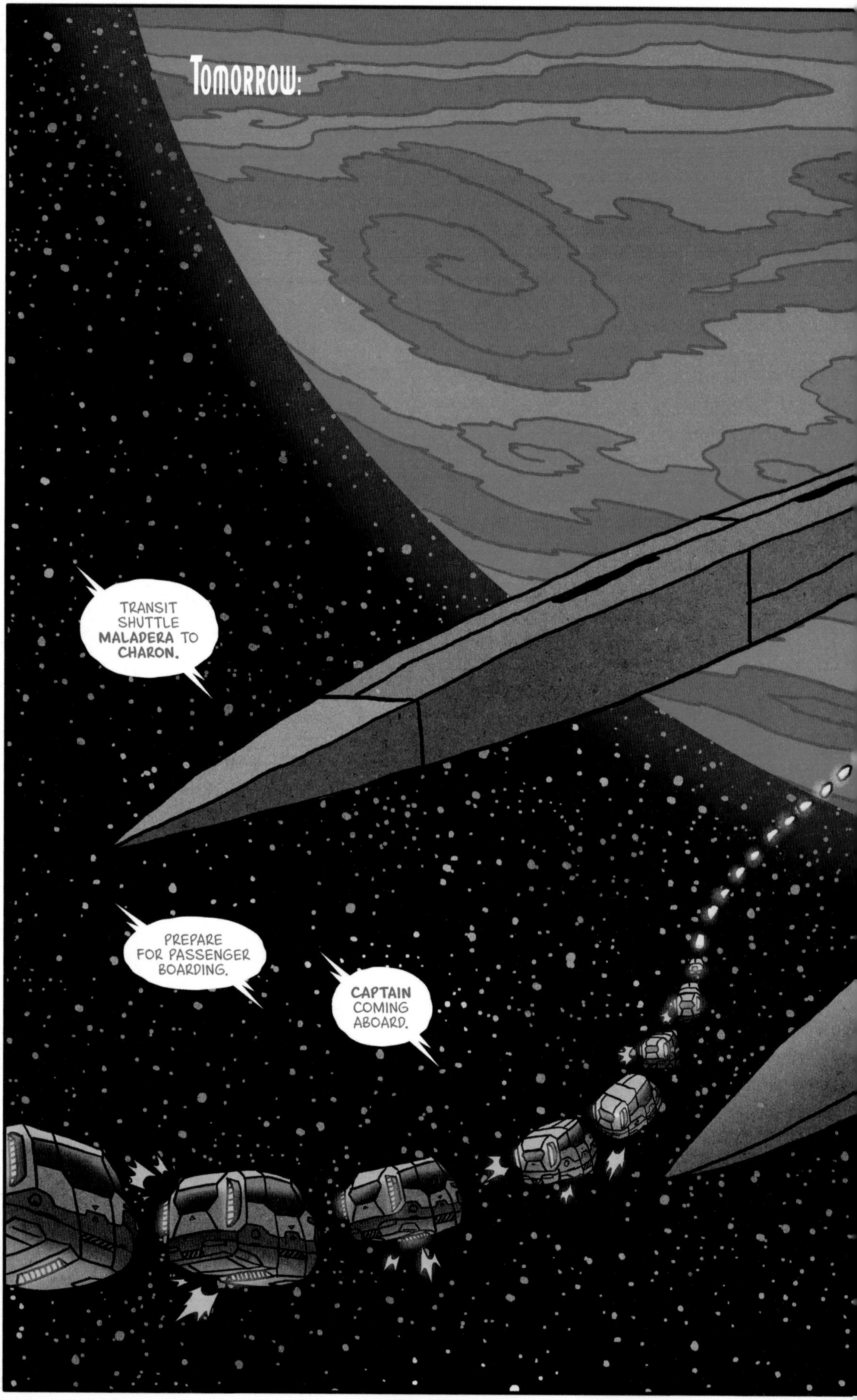
TOMORROW:
TRANSIT SHUTTLE MALADERA TO CHARON.
PREPARE FOR PASSENGER BOARDING.
CAPTAIN COMING ABOARD.

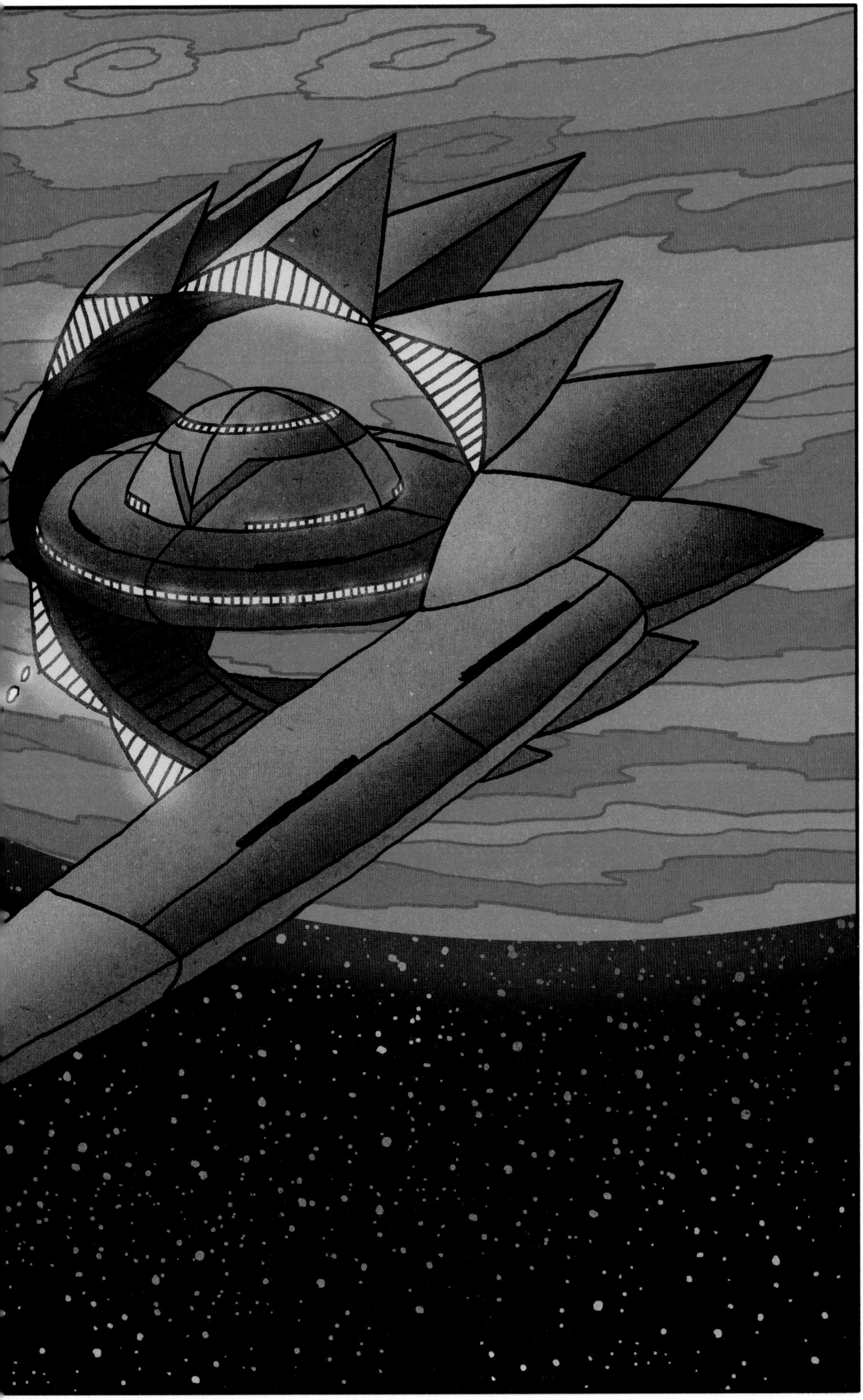

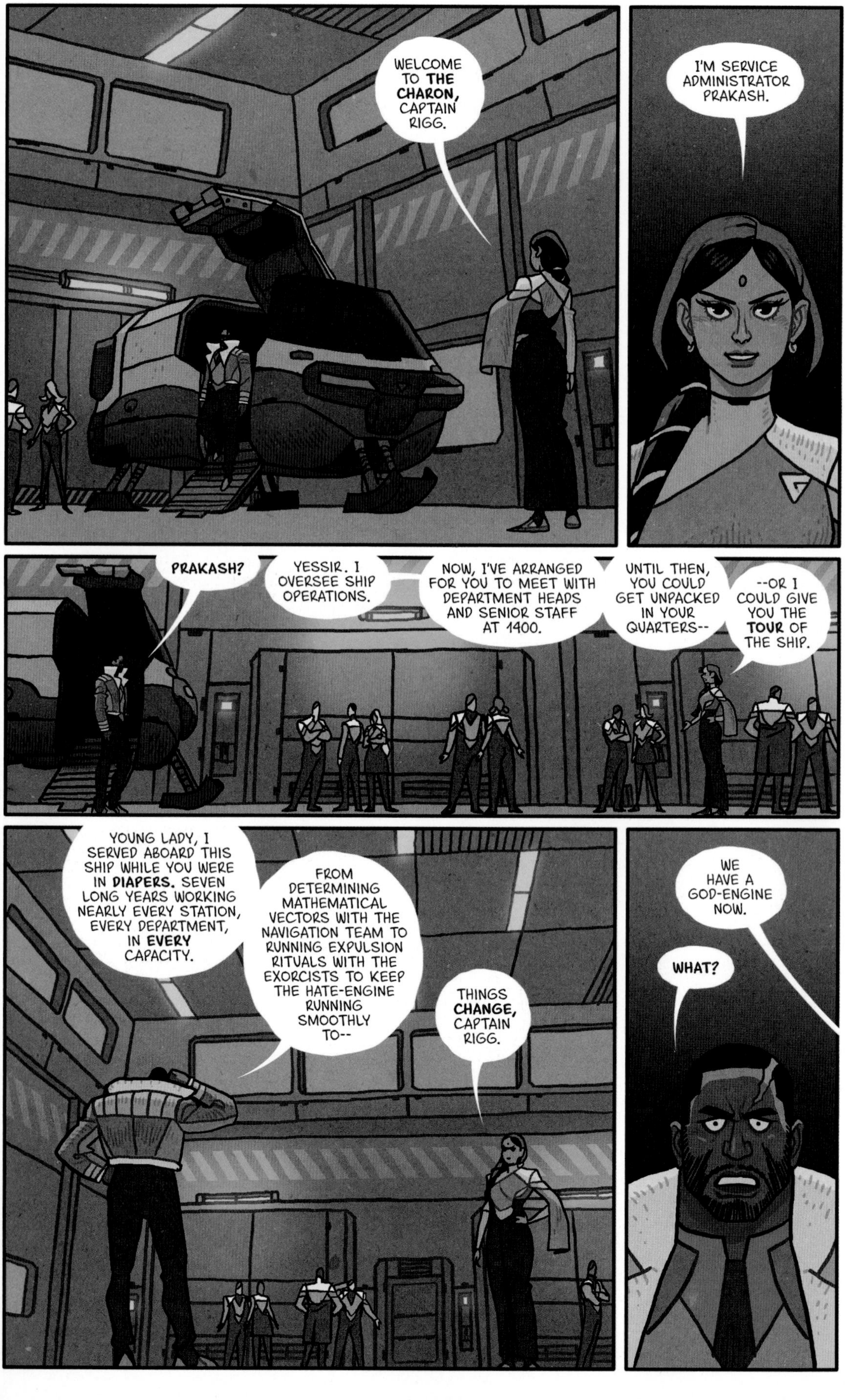
WELCOME TO THE CHARON, CAPTAIN RIGG.
I'M SERVICE ADMINISTRATOR PRAKASH.
PRAKASH?
YESSIR. I OVERSEE SHIP OPERATIONS.
NOW, I'VE ARRANGED FOR YOU TO MEET WITH DEPARTMENT HEADS AND SENIOR STAFF AT 1400.
UNTIL THEN, YOU COULD GET UNPACKED IN YOUR QUARTERS--
--OR I COULD GIVE YOU THE TOUR OF THE SHIP.
YOUNG LADY, I SERVED ABOARD THIS SHIP WHILE YOU WERE IN DIAPERS. SEVEN LONG YEARS WORKING NEARLY EVERY STATION, EVERY DEPARTMENT, IN EVERY CAPACITY.
FROM DETERMINING MATHEMATICAL VECTORS WITH THE NAVIGATION TEAM TO RUNNING EXPULSION RITUALS WITH THE EXORCISTS TO KEEP THE HATE-ENGINE RUNNING SMOOTHLY TO--
THINGS CHANGE, CAPTAIN RIGG.
WE HAVE A GOD-ENGINE NOW.
WHAT?

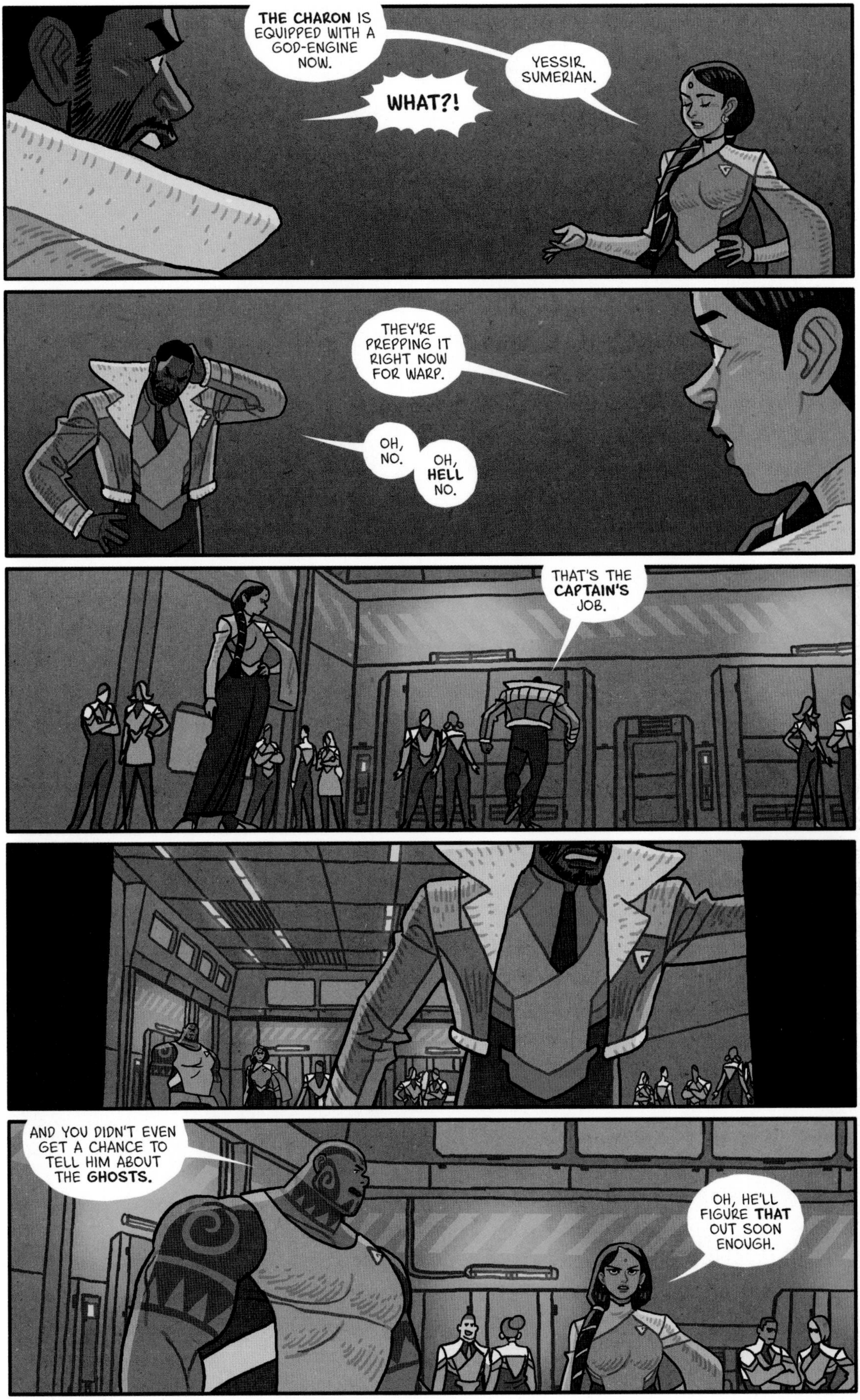
THE CHARON IS EQUIPPED WITH A GOD-ENGINE NOW.
YESSIR. SUMERIAN.
WHAT?!
THEY'RE PREPPING IT RIGHT NOW FOR WARP.
OH, NO.
OH, HELL NO.
THAT'S THE CAPTAIN'S JOB.
AND YOU DIDN'T EVEN GET A CHANCE TO TELL HIM ABOUT THE GHOSTS.
OH, HE'LL FIGURE THAT OUT SOON ENOUGH.

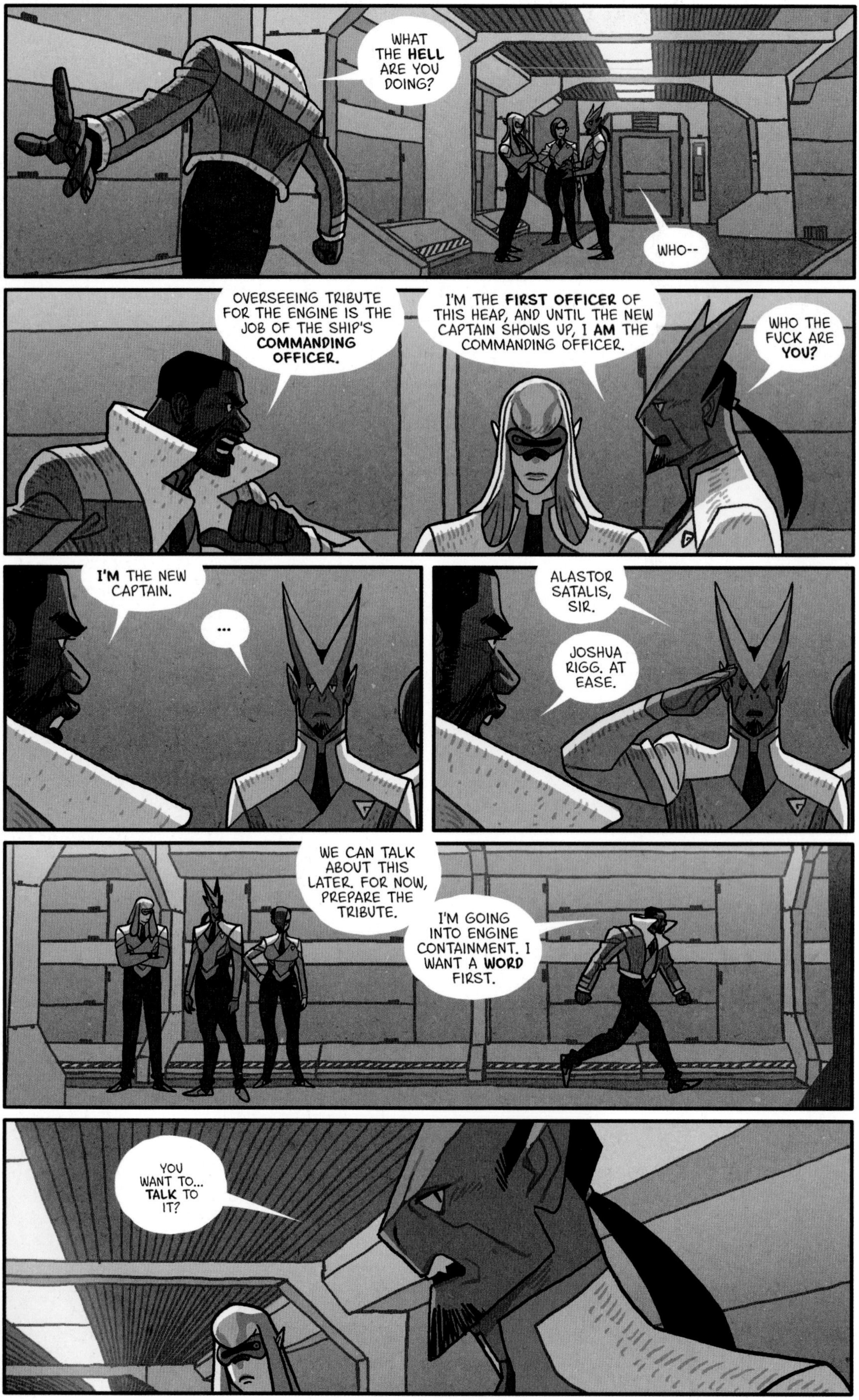
WHAT THE HELL ARE YOU DOING?
WHO--
OVERSEEING TRIBUTE FOR THE ENGINE IS THE JOB OF THE SHIP'S COMMANDING OFFICER.
I'M THE FIRST OFFICER OF THIS HEAP, AND UNTIL THE NEW CAPTAIN SHOWS UP, I AM THE COMMANDING OFFICER.
WHO THE FUCK ARE YOU?
I'M THE NEW CAPTAIN.
...
ALASTOR SATALIS, SIR.
JOSHUA RIGG. AT EASE.
WE CAN TALK ABOUT THIS LATER. FOR NOW, PREPARE THE TRIBUTE.
I'M GOING INTO ENGINE CONTAINMENT. I WANT A WORD FIRST.
YOU WANT TO... TALK TO IT?

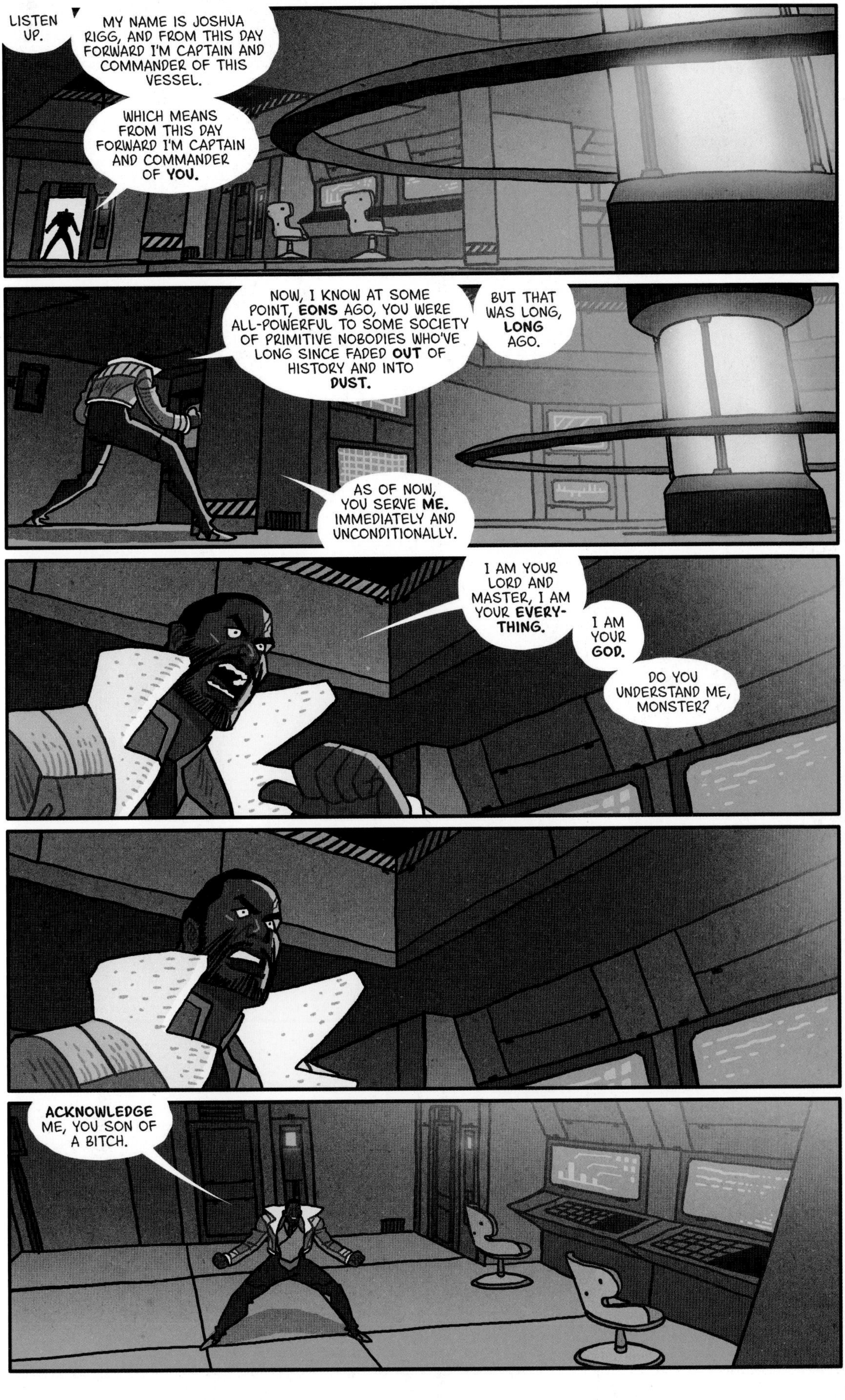
LISTEN UP.
MY NAME IS JOSHUA RIGG, AND FROM THIS DAY FORWARD I'M CAPTAIN AND COMMANDER OF THIS VESSEL.
WHICH MEANS FROM THIS DAY FORWARD I'M CAPTAIN AND COMMANDER OF **YOU.**
NOW, I KNOW AT SOME POINT, **EONS** AGO, YOU WERE ALL-POWERFUL TO SOME SOCIETY OF PRIMITIVE NOBODIES WHO'VE LONG SINCE FADED **OUT** OF HISTORY AND INTO **DUST.**
BUT THAT WAS LONG, **LONG** AGO.
AS OF NOW, YOU SERVE **ME.** IMMEDIATELY AND UNCONDITIONALLY.
I AM YOUR LORD AND MASTER, I AM YOUR **EVERY-THING.**
I AM YOUR **GOD.**
DO YOU UNDERSTAND ME, MONSTER?
ACKNOWLEDGE ME, YOU SON OF A BITCH.

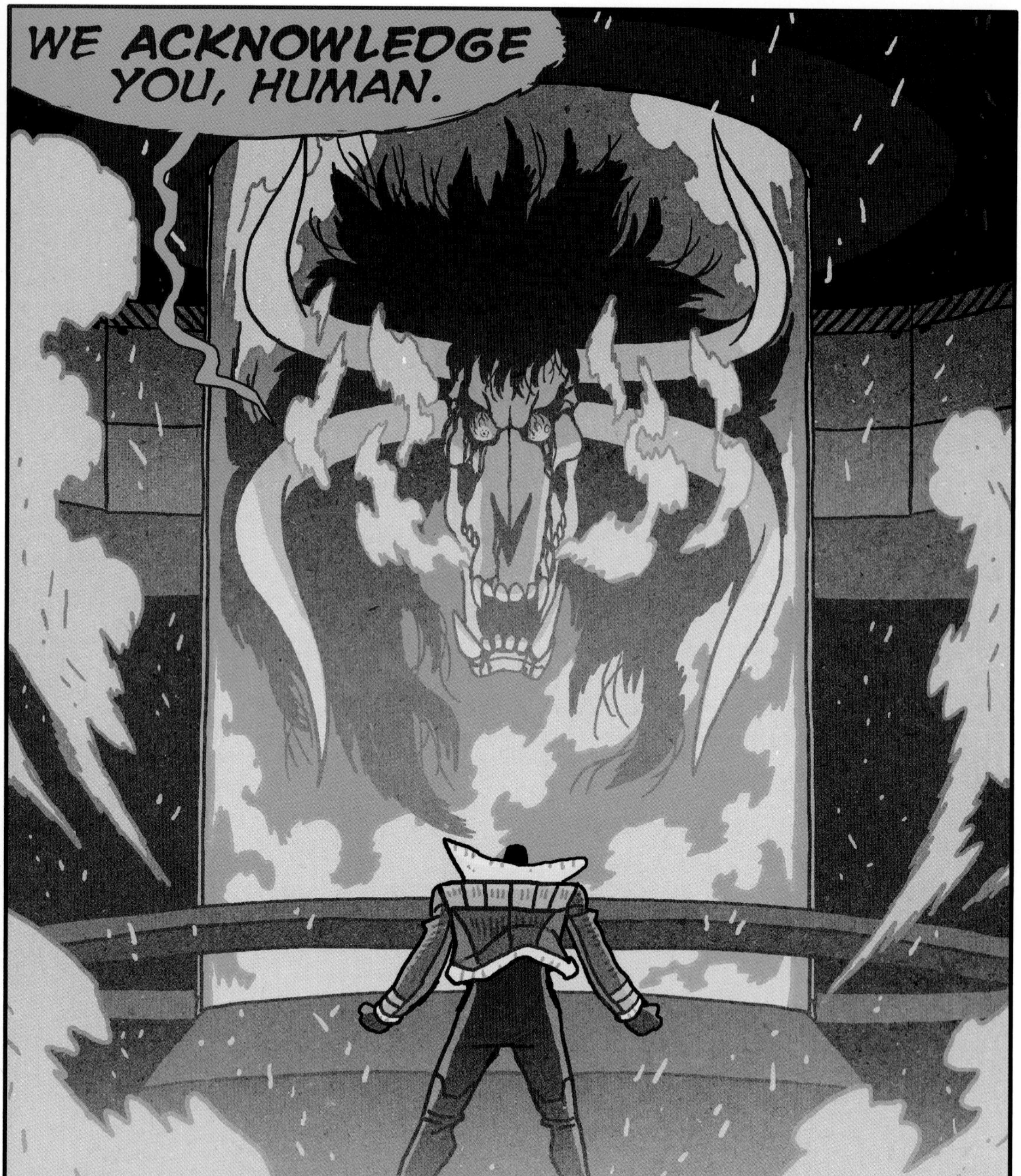
WE ACKNOWLEDGE YOU, HUMAN.

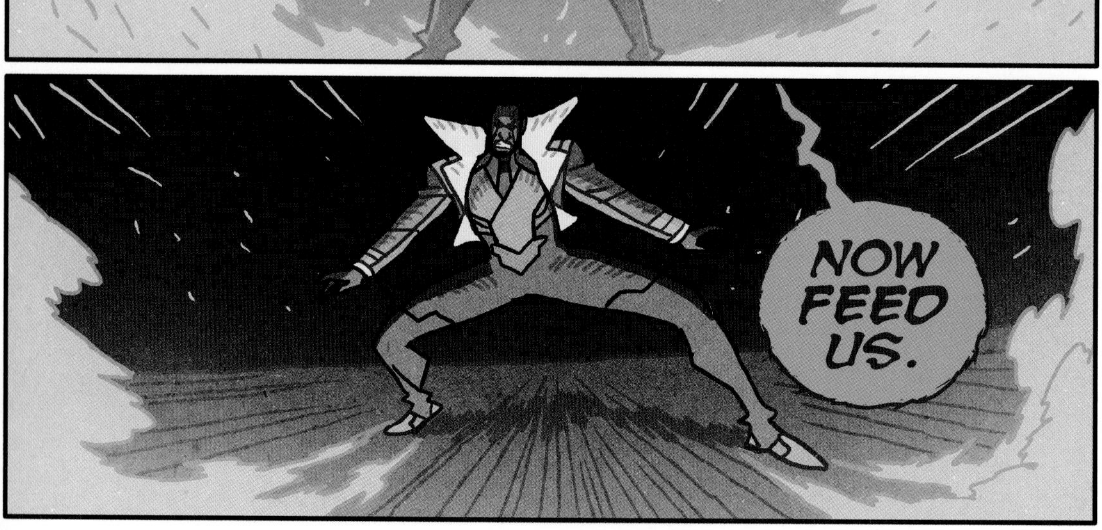
NOW FEED US.

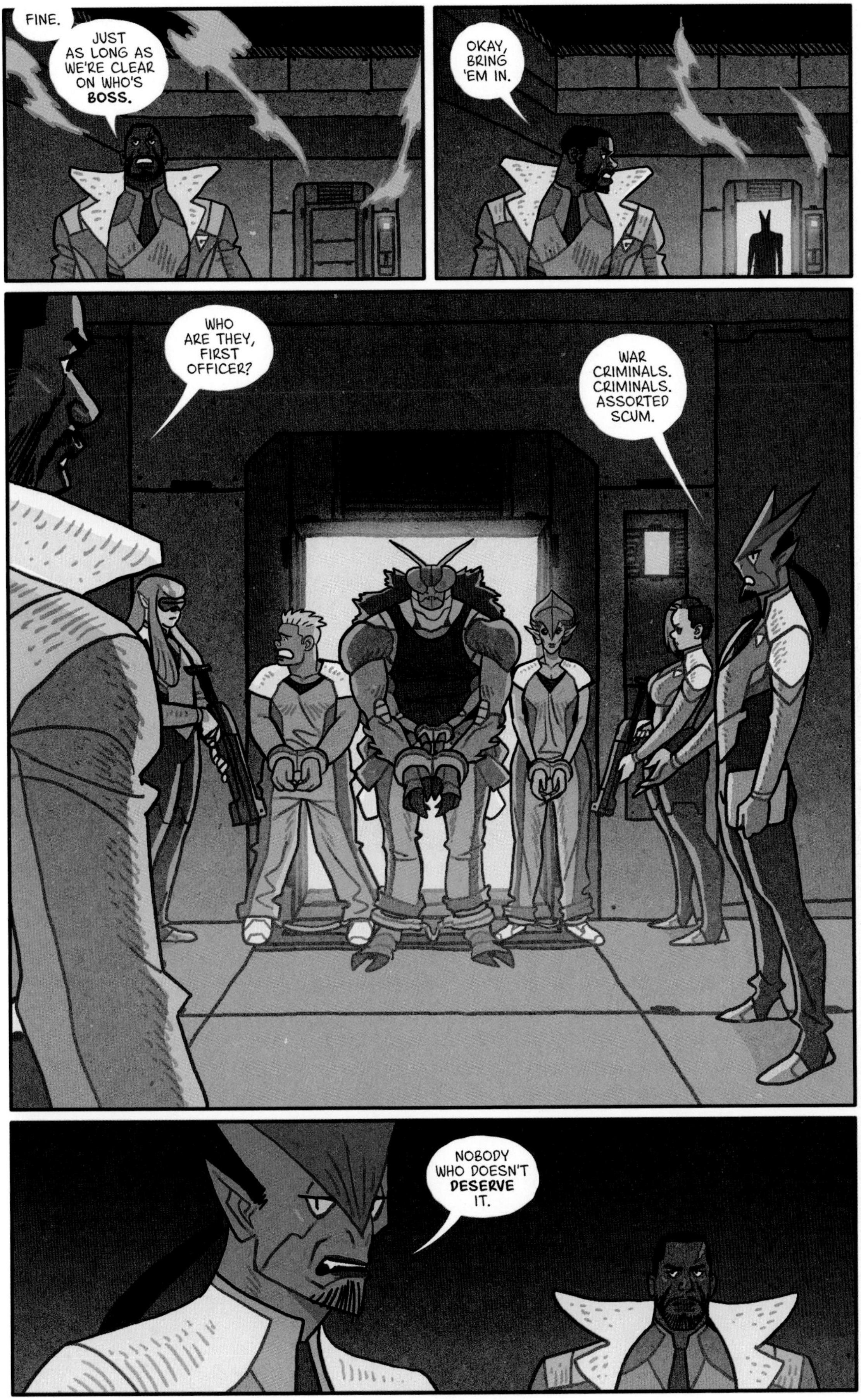
FINE.
JUST AS LONG AS WE'RE CLEAR ON WHO'S **BOSS.**
OKAY, BRING 'EM IN.
WHO ARE THEY, FIRST OFFICER?
WAR CRIMINALS. CRIMINALS. ASSORTED SCUM.
NOBODY WHO DOESN'T **DESERVE** IT.

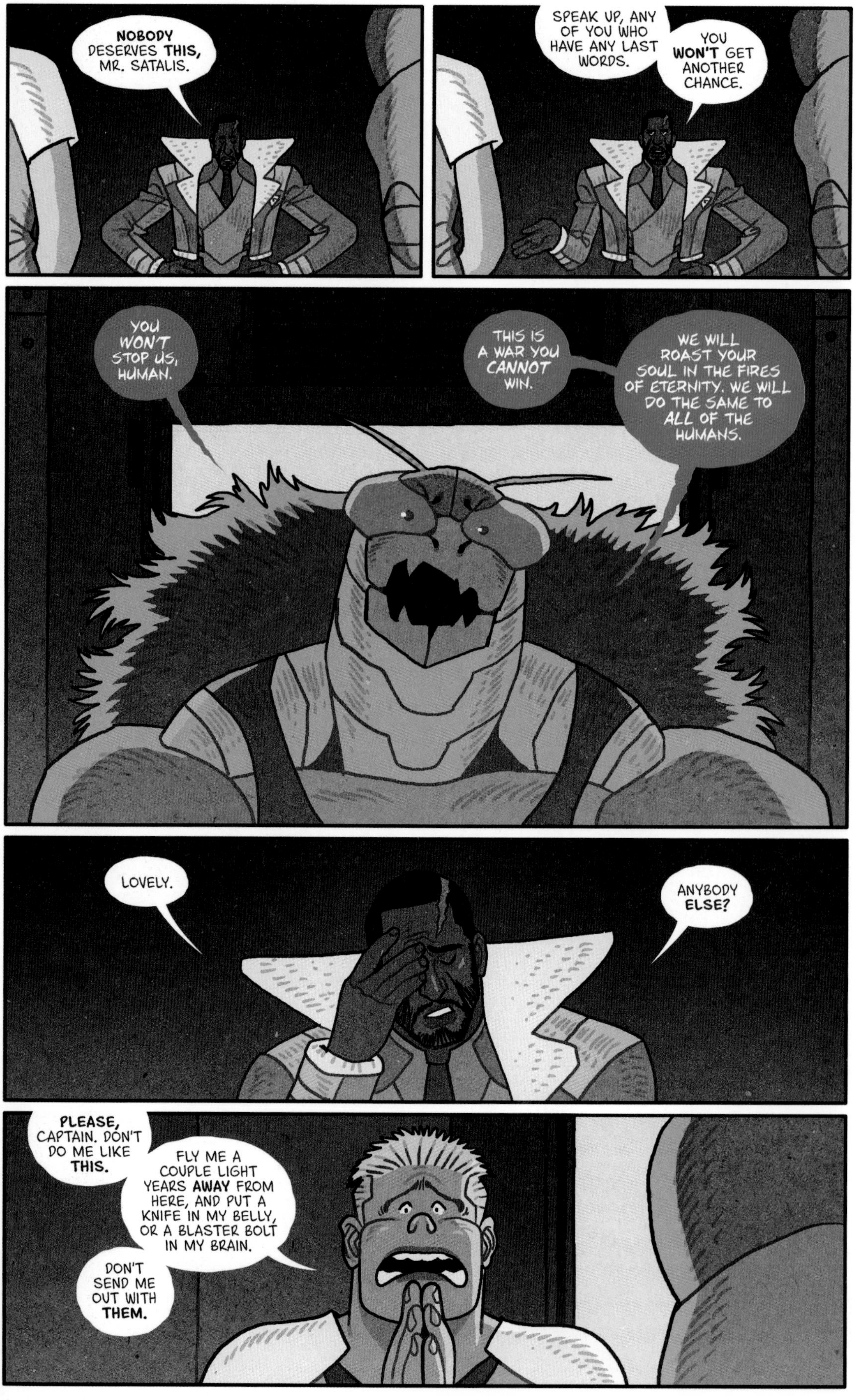
NOBODY DESERVES THIS, MR. SATALIS.
SPEAK UP, ANY OF YOU WHO HAVE ANY LAST WORDS.
YOU WON'T GET ANOTHER CHANCE.
YOU WON'T STOP US, HUMAN.
THIS IS A WAR YOU CANNOT WIN.
WE WILL ROAST YOUR SOUL IN THE FIRES OF ETERNITY. WE WILL DO THE SAME TO ALL OF THE HUMANS.
LOVELY.
ANYBODY ELSE?
PLEASE, CAPTAIN. DON'T DO ME LIKE THIS.
FLY ME A COUPLE LIGHT YEARS AWAY FROM HERE, AND PUT A KNIFE IN MY BELLY, OR A BLASTER BOLT IN MY BRAIN.
DON'T SEND ME OUT WITH THEM.

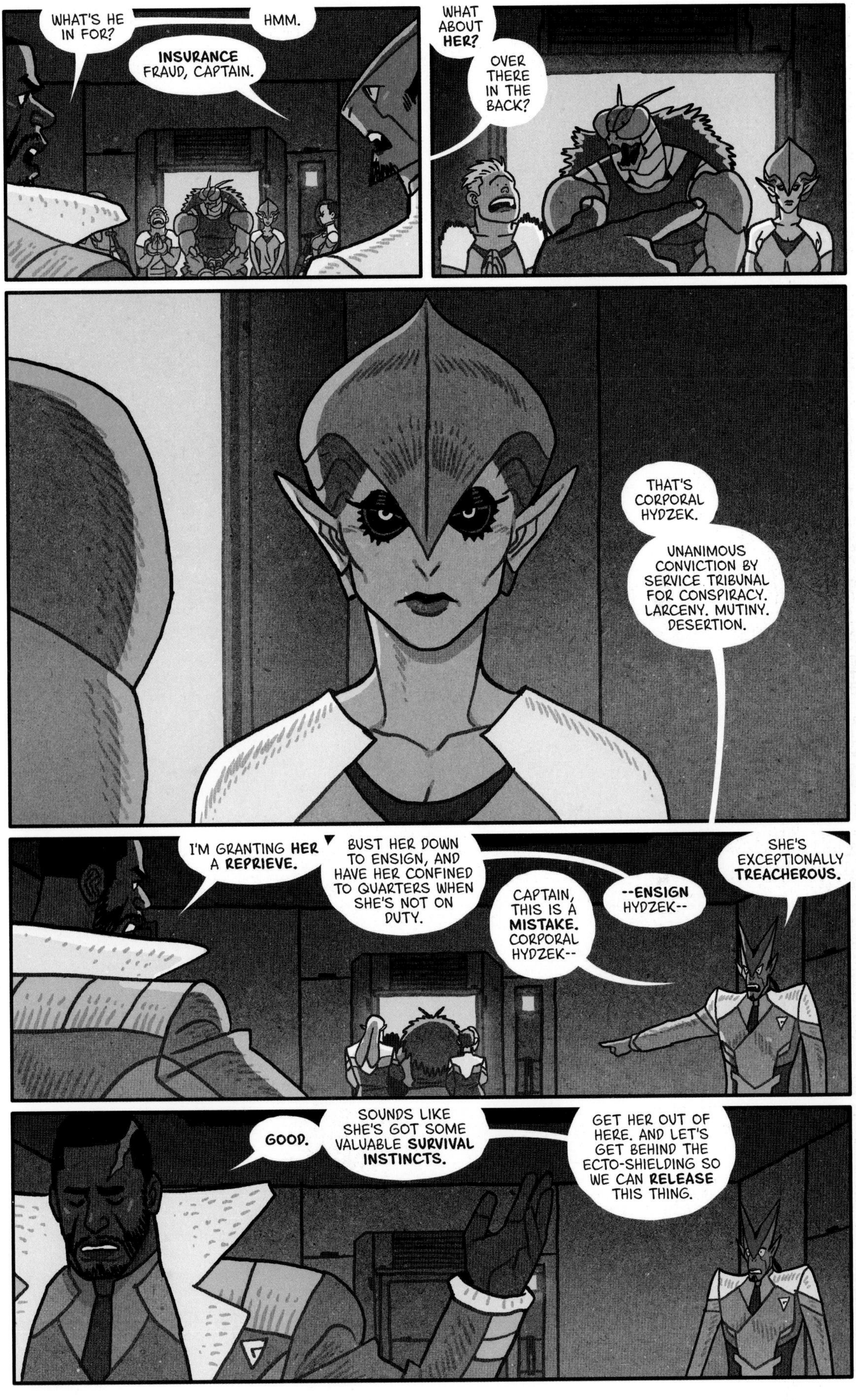
WHAT'S HE IN FOR?
HMM.
INSURANCE FRAUD, CAPTAIN.
WHAT ABOUT HER?
OVER THERE IN THE BACK?
THAT'S CORPORAL HYDZEK.
UNANIMOUS CONVICTION BY SERVICE TRIBUNAL FOR CONSPIRACY. LARCENY. MUTINY. DESERTION.
I'M GRANTING HER A REPRIEVE.
BUST HER DOWN TO ENSIGN, AND HAVE HER CONFINED TO QUARTERS WHEN SHE'S NOT ON DUTY.
CAPTAIN, THIS IS A MISTAKE. CORPORAL HYDZEK--
--ENSIGN HYDZEK--
SHE'S EXCEPTIONALLY TREACHEROUS.
GOOD.
SOUNDS LIKE SHE'S GOT SOME VALUABLE SURVIVAL INSTINCTS.
GET HER OUT OF HERE. AND LET'S GET BEHIND THE ECTO-SHIELDING SO WE CAN RELEASE THIS THING.

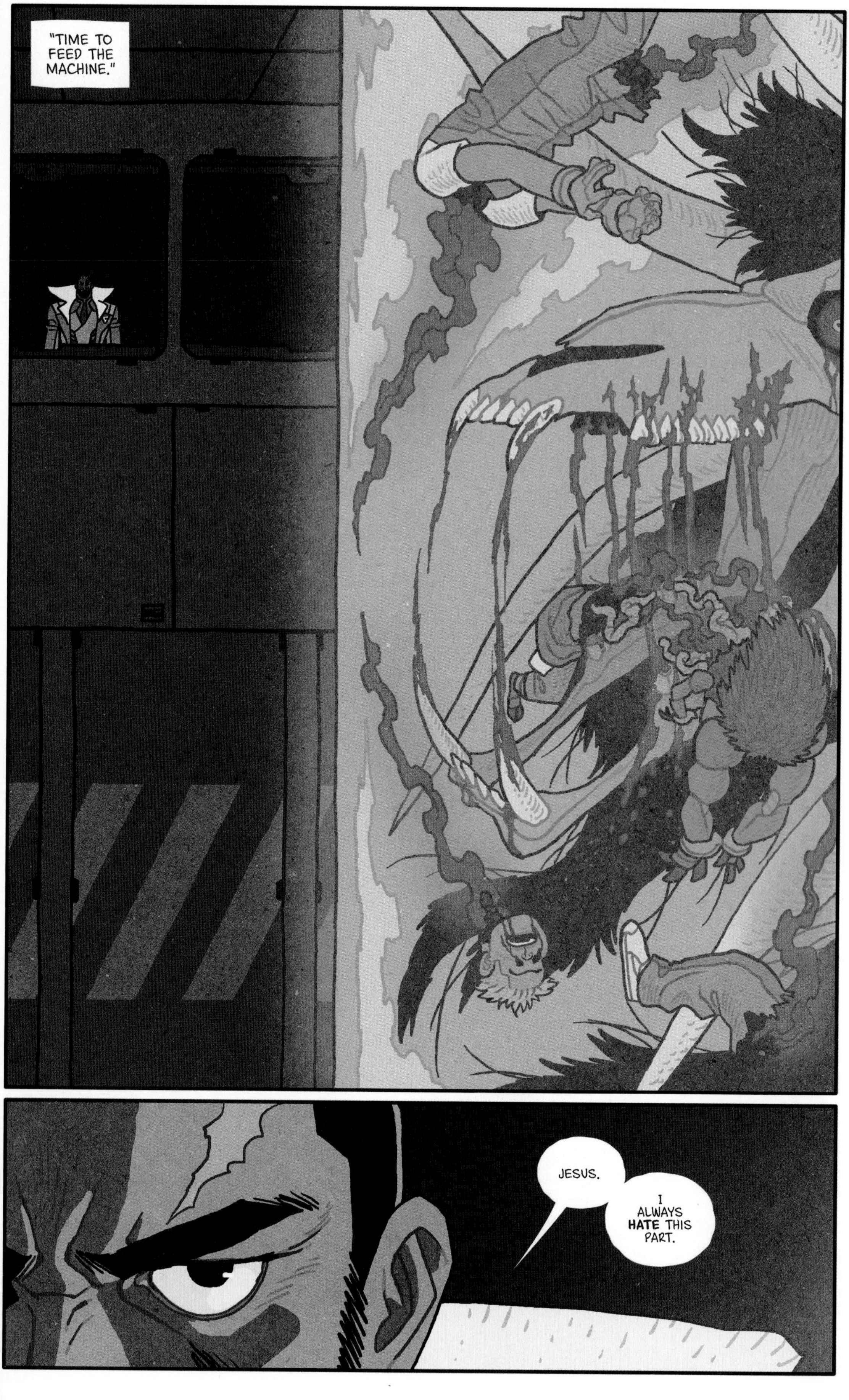
"TIME TO FEED THE MACHINE."
JESUS.
I ALWAYS **HATE** THIS PART.

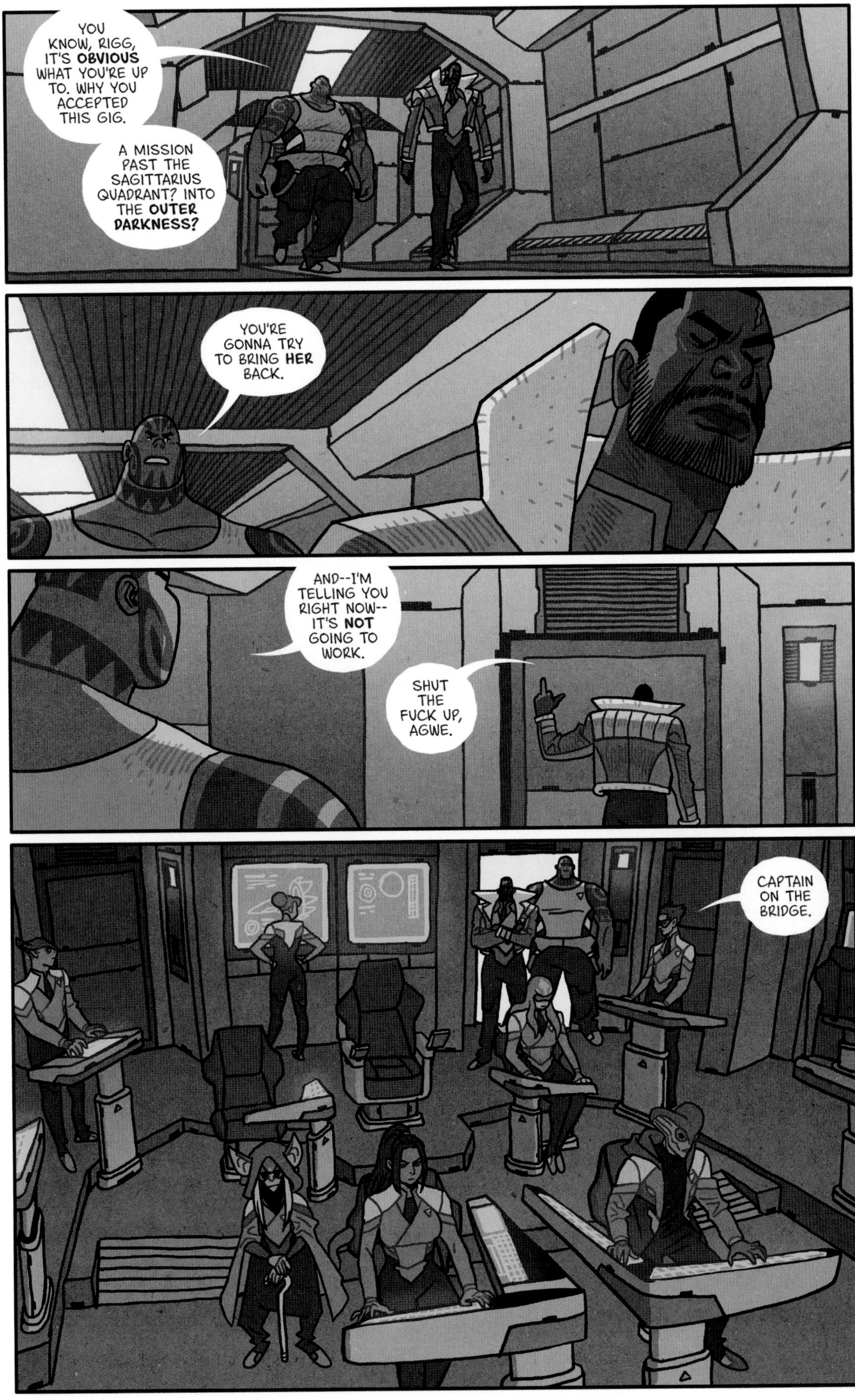

YOU KNOW, RIGG, IT'S **OBVIOUS** WHAT YOU'RE UP TO. WHY YOU ACCEPTED THIS GIG.
A MISSION PAST THE SAGITTARIUS QUADRANT? INTO THE **OUTER DARKNESS?**
YOU'RE GONNA TRY TO BRING **HER** BACK.
AND--I'M TELLING YOU RIGHT NOW--IT'S **NOT** GOING TO WORK.
SHUT THE FUCK UP, AGWE.
CAPTAIN ON THE BRIDGE.

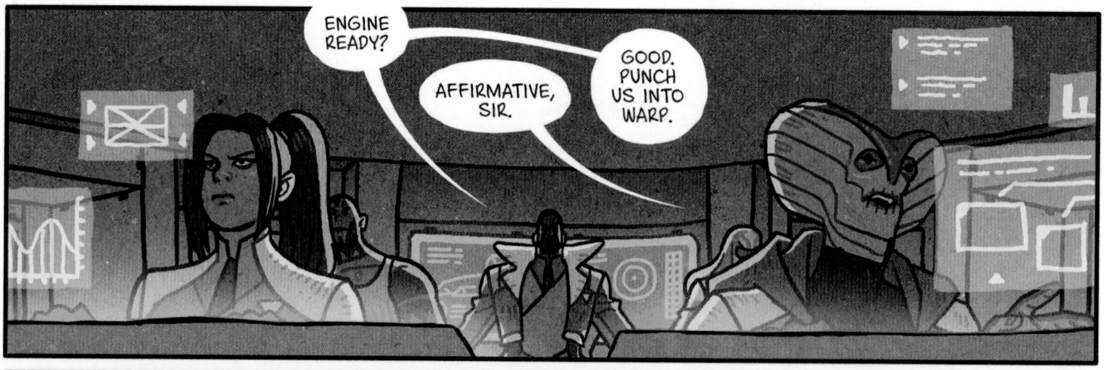
ENGINE READY?
AFFIRMATIVE, SIR.
GOOD. PUNCH US INTO WARP.

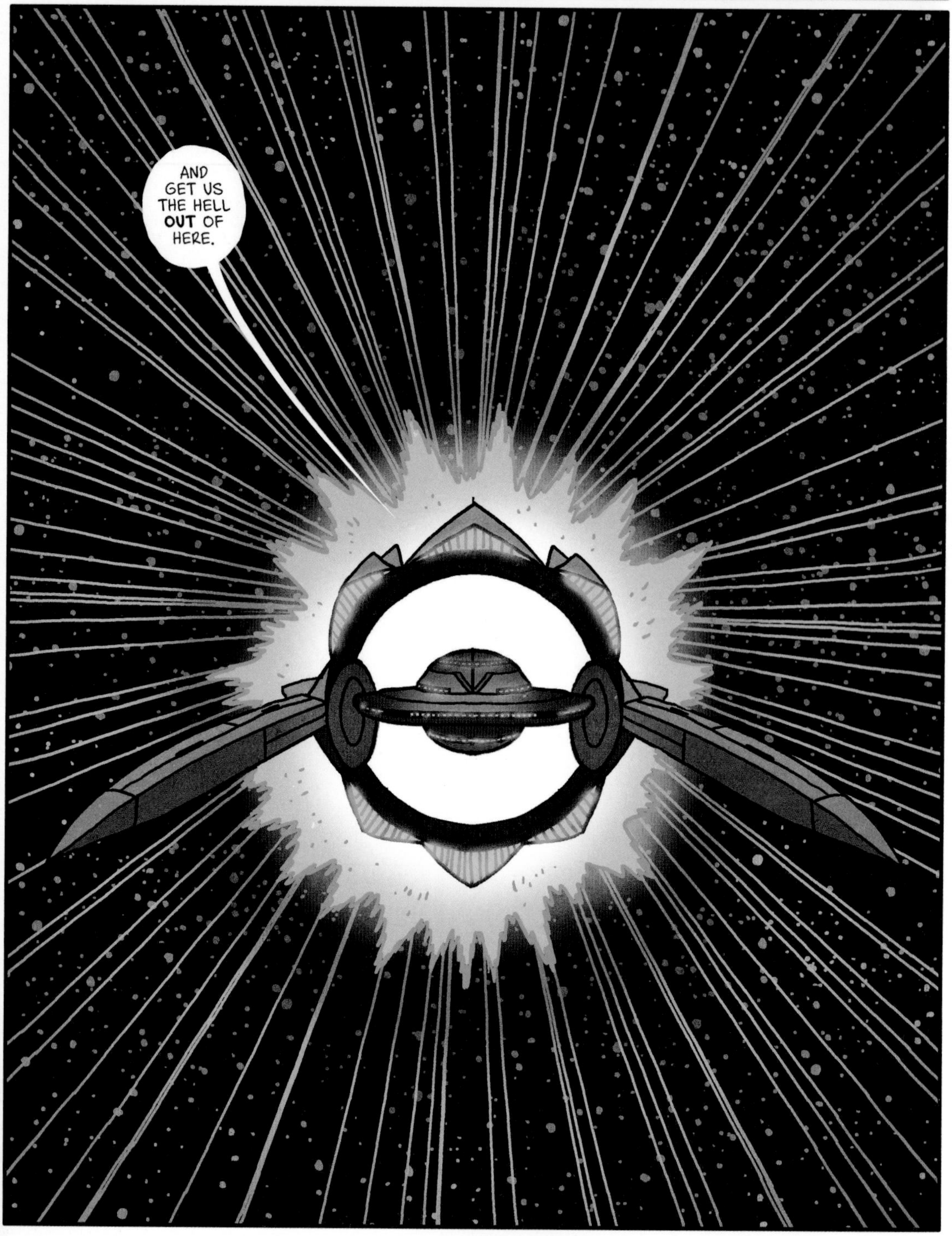
AND GET US THE HELL OUT OF HERE.

PART 2
RED ALERT

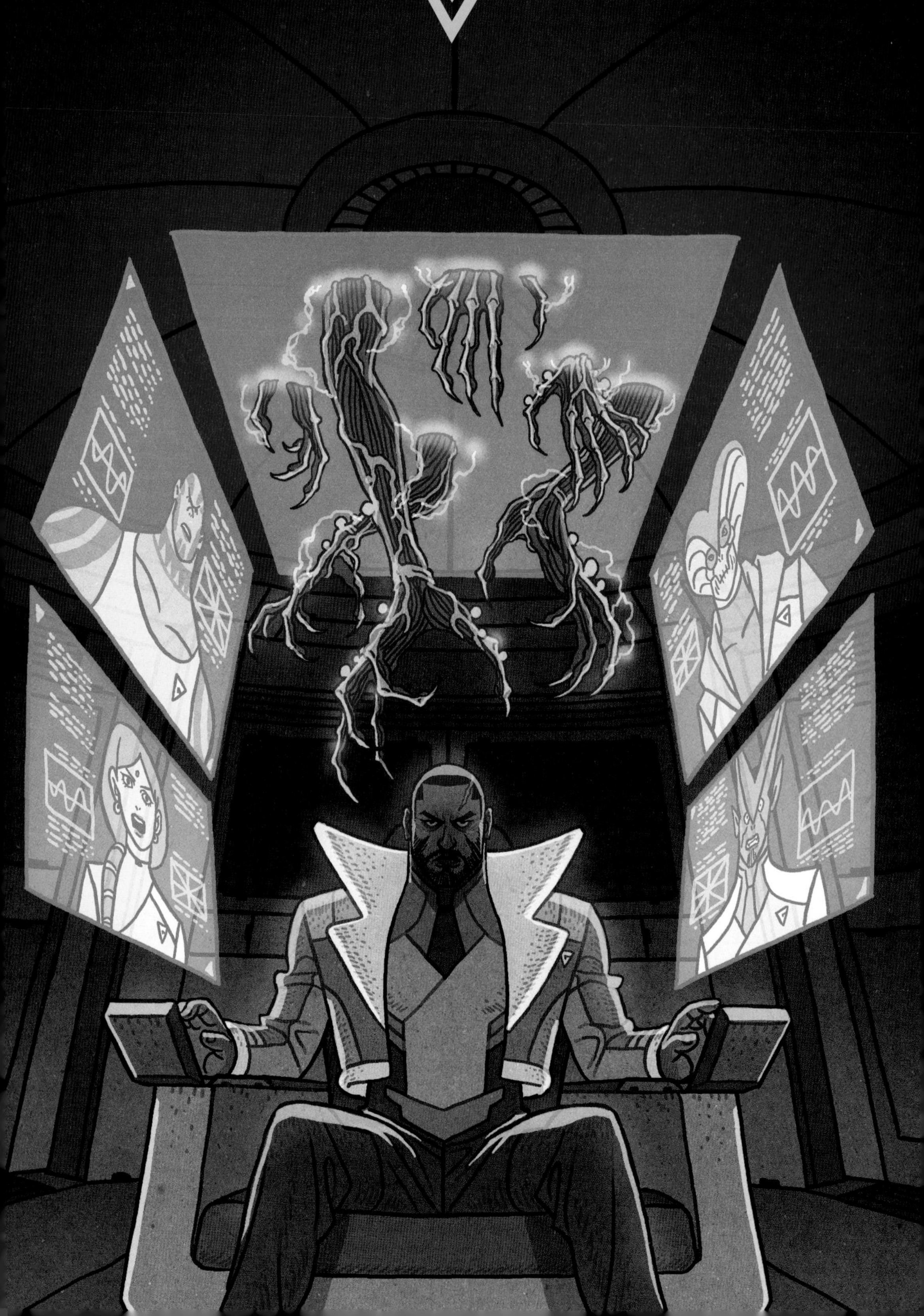

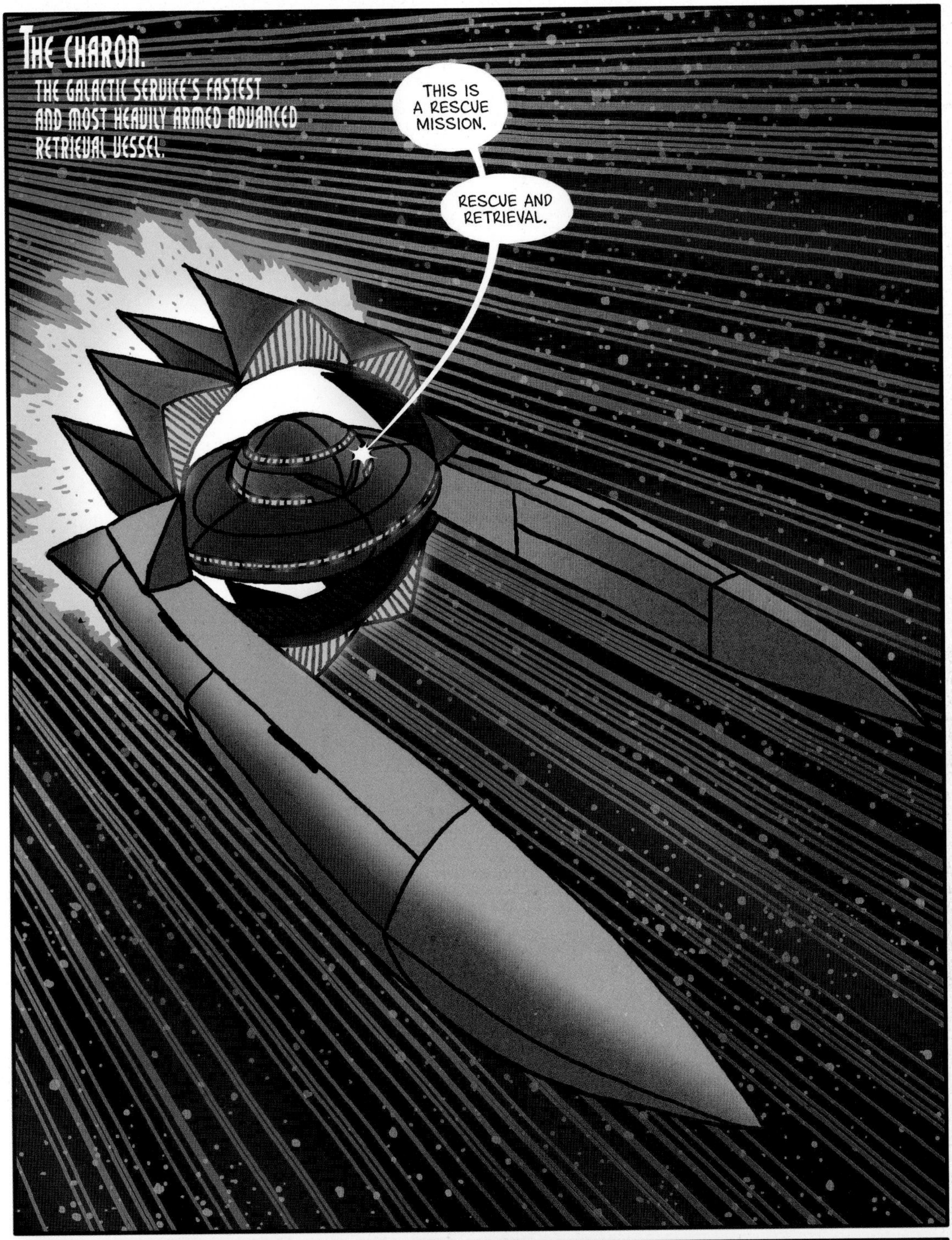
The Charon.
The Galactic Service's fastest and most heavily armed advanced retrieval vessel.
THIS IS A RESCUE MISSION.
RESCUE AND RETRIEVAL.

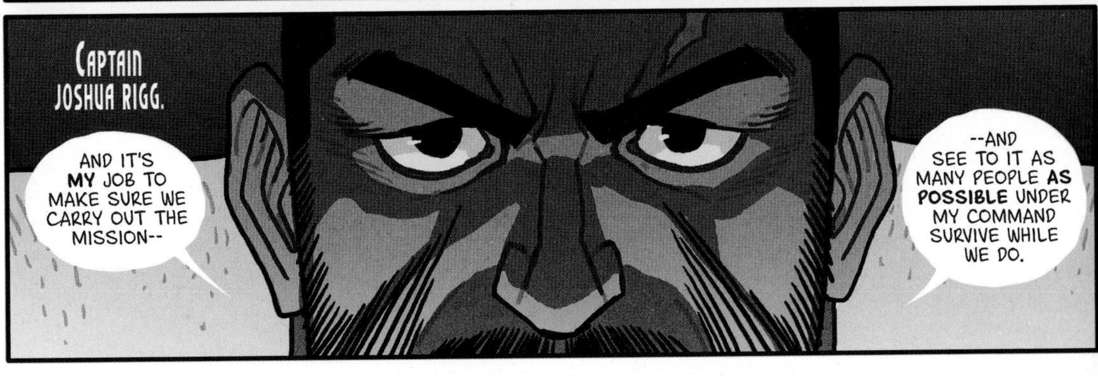
Captain Joshua Rigg.
AND IT'S MY JOB TO MAKE SURE WE CARRY OUT THE MISSION--
--AND SEE TO IT AS MANY PEOPLE AS POSSIBLE UNDER MY COMMAND SURVIVE WHILE WE DO.

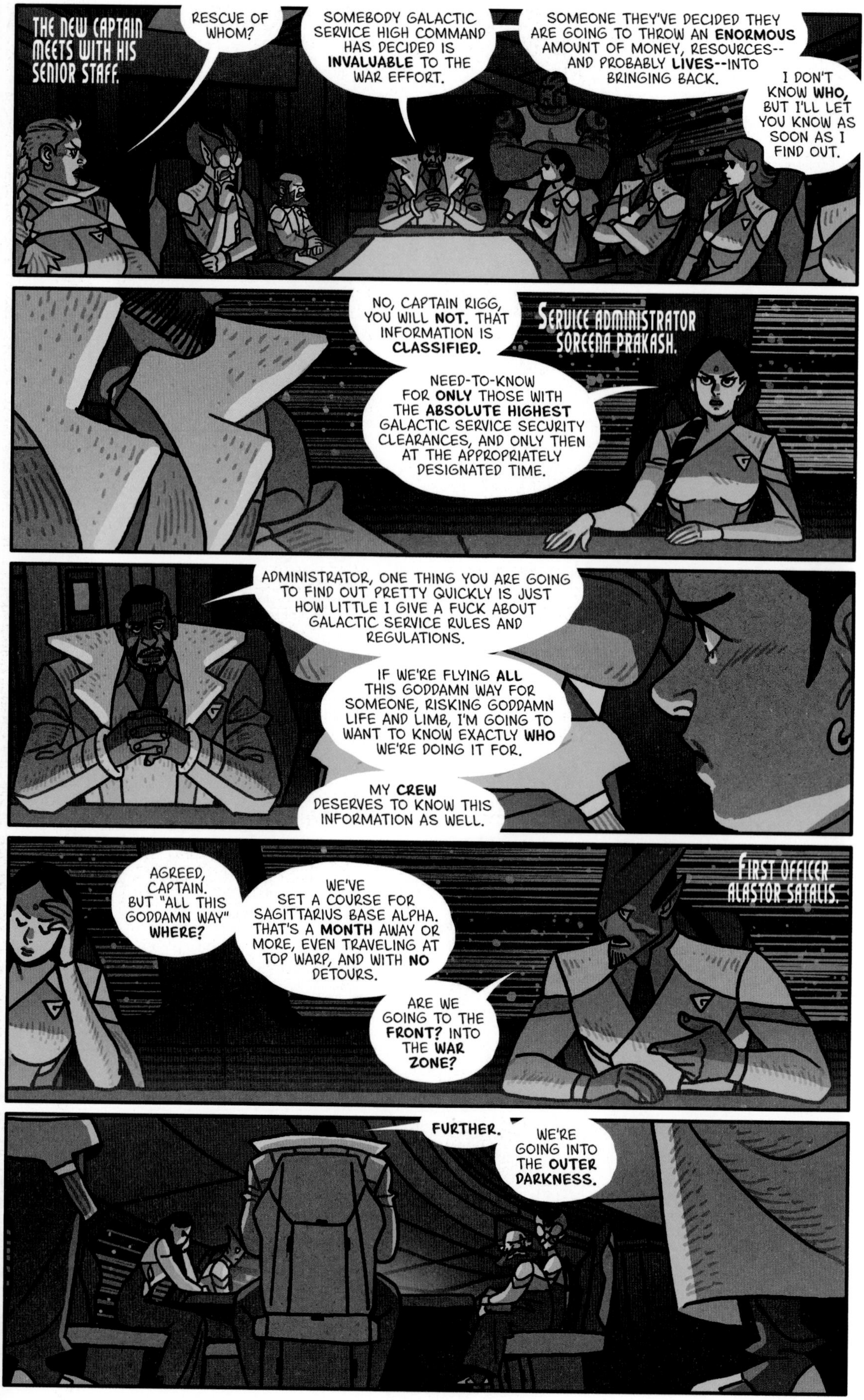
THE NEW CAPTAIN MEETS WITH HIS SENIOR STAFF.
RESCUE OF WHOM?
SOMEBODY GALACTIC SERVICE HIGH COMMAND HAS DECIDED IS **INVALUABLE** TO THE WAR EFFORT.
SOMEONE THEY'VE DECIDED THEY ARE GOING TO THROW AN **ENORMOUS** AMOUNT OF MONEY, RESOURCES-- AND PROBABLY **LIVES**--INTO BRINGING BACK.
I DON'T KNOW **WHO,** BUT I'LL LET YOU KNOW AS SOON AS I FIND OUT.
NO, CAPTAIN RIGG, YOU WILL **NOT.** THAT INFORMATION IS **CLASSIFIED.**
SERVICE ADMINISTRATOR SOREENA PRAKASH.
NEED-TO-KNOW FOR **ONLY** THOSE WITH THE **ABSOLUTE HIGHEST** GALACTIC SERVICE SECURITY CLEARANCES, AND ONLY THEN AT THE APPROPRIATELY DESIGNATED TIME.
ADMINISTRATOR, ONE THING YOU ARE GOING TO FIND OUT PRETTY QUICKLY IS JUST HOW LITTLE I GIVE A FUCK ABOUT GALACTIC SERVICE RULES AND REGULATIONS.
IF WE'RE FLYING **ALL** THIS GODDAMN WAY FOR SOMEONE, RISKING GODDAMN LIFE AND LIMB, I'M GOING TO WANT TO KNOW EXACTLY **WHO** WE'RE DOING IT FOR.
MY **CREW** DESERVES TO KNOW THIS INFORMATION AS WELL.
AGREED, CAPTAIN. BUT "ALL THIS GODDAMN WAY" **WHERE?**
FIRST OFFICER ALASTOR SATALIS.
WE'VE SET A COURSE FOR SAGITTARIUS BASE ALPHA. THAT'S A **MONTH** AWAY OR MORE, EVEN TRAVELING AT TOP WARP, AND WITH **NO** DETOURS.
ARE WE GOING TO THE **FRONT?** INTO THE **WAR ZONE?**
FURTHER.
WE'RE GOING INTO THE **OUTER DARKNESS.**

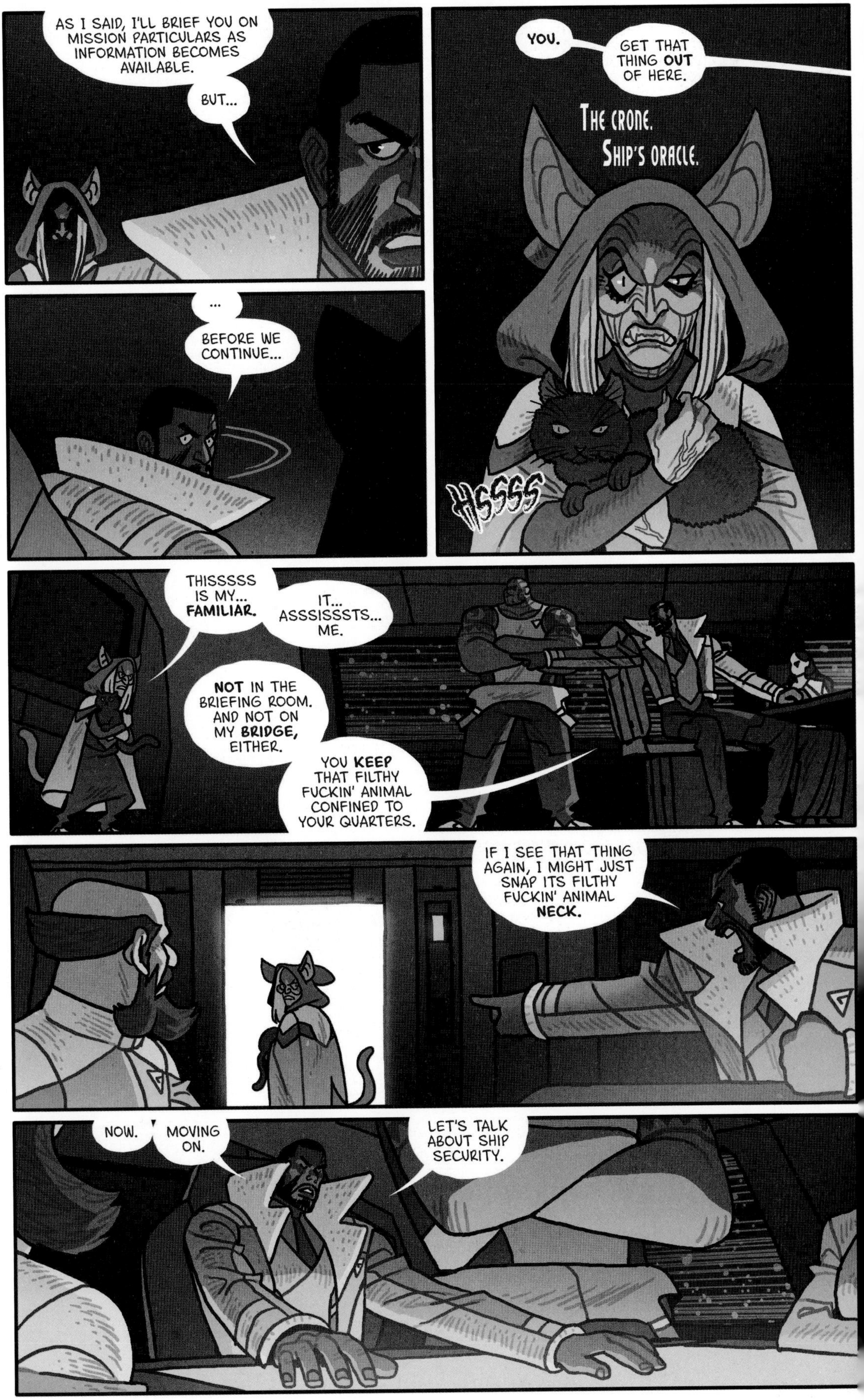

AS I SAID, I'LL BRIEF YOU ON MISSION PARTICULARS AS INFORMATION BECOMES AVAILABLE.
BUT...
...
BEFORE WE CONTINUE...
YOU.
GET THAT THING **OUT** OF HERE.
THE CRONE.
SHIP'S ORACLE.
HSSSS
THISSSSS IS MY... **FAMILIAR.**
IT... ASSSISSSTS... ME.
NOT IN THE BRIEFING ROOM. AND NOT ON MY **BRIDGE,** EITHER.
YOU **KEEP** THAT FILTHY FUCKIN' ANIMAL CONFINED TO YOUR QUARTERS.
IF I SEE THAT THING AGAIN, I MIGHT JUST SNAP ITS FILTHY FUCKIN' ANIMAL **NECK.**
NOW.
MOVING ON.
LET'S TALK ABOUT SHIP SECURITY.

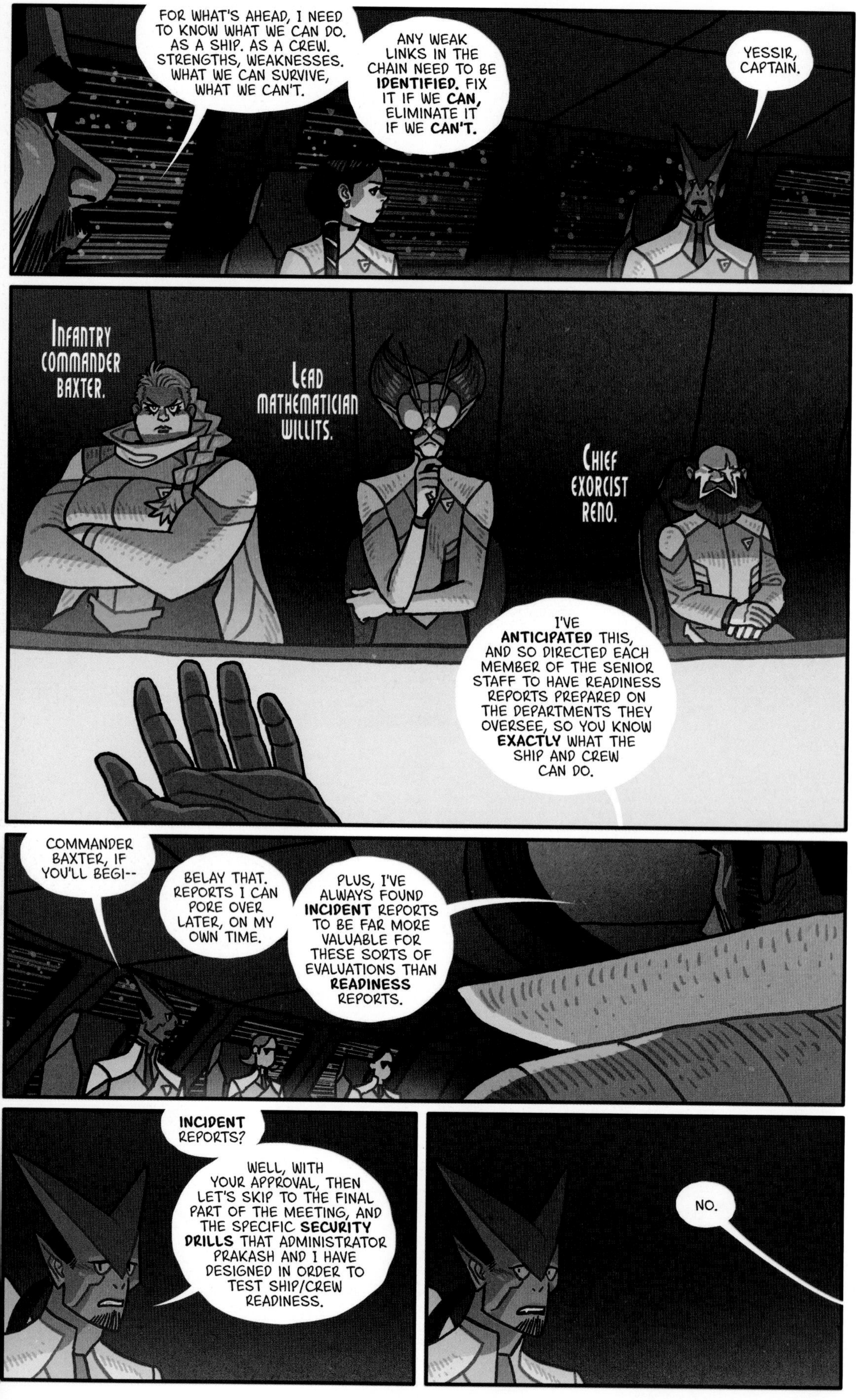
FOR WHAT'S AHEAD, I NEED TO KNOW WHAT WE CAN DO. AS A SHIP. AS A CREW. STRENGTHS, WEAKNESSES. WHAT WE CAN SURVIVE, WHAT WE CAN'T.
ANY WEAK LINKS IN THE CHAIN NEED TO BE **IDENTIFIED.** FIX IT IF WE **CAN,** ELIMINATE IT IF WE **CAN'T.**
YESSIR, CAPTAIN.
Infantry commander Baxter.
Lead mathematician Willits.
Chief exorcist Reno.
I'VE **ANTICIPATED** THIS, AND SO DIRECTED EACH MEMBER OF THE SENIOR STAFF TO HAVE READINESS REPORTS PREPARED ON THE DEPARTMENTS THEY OVERSEE, SO YOU KNOW **EXACTLY** WHAT THE SHIP AND CREW CAN DO.
COMMANDER BAXTER, IF YOU'LL BEGI--
BELAY THAT. REPORTS I CAN PORE OVER LATER, ON MY OWN TIME.
PLUS, I'VE ALWAYS FOUND **INCIDENT** REPORTS TO BE FAR MORE VALUABLE FOR THESE SORTS OF EVALUATIONS THAN **READINESS** REPORTS.
INCIDENT REPORTS?
WELL, WITH YOUR APPROVAL, THEN LET'S SKIP TO THE FINAL PART OF THE MEETING, AND THE SPECIFIC **SECURITY DRILLS** THAT ADMINISTRATOR PRAKASH AND I HAVE DESIGNED IN ORDER TO TEST SHIP/CREW READINESS.
NO.

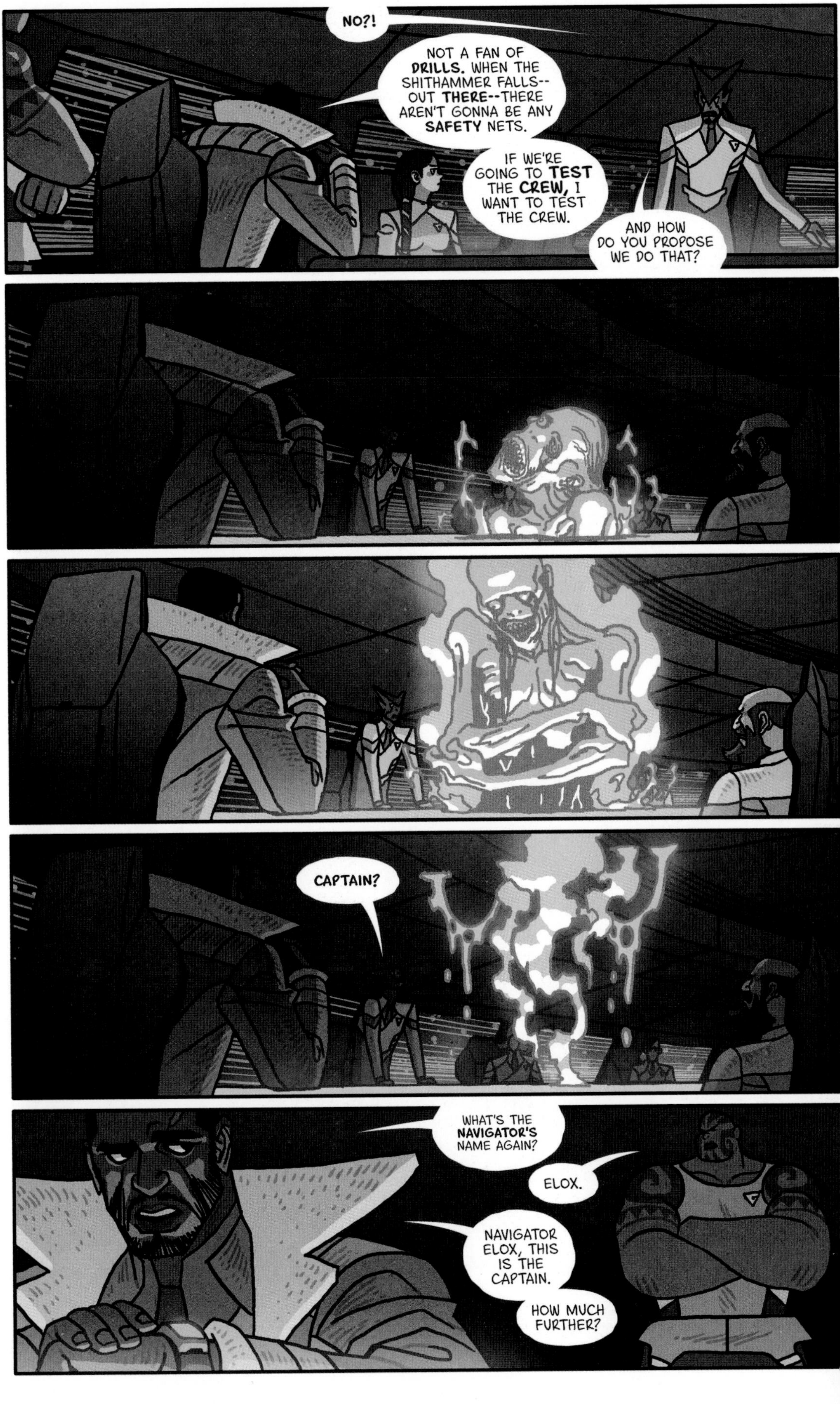
NO?!
NOT A FAN OF DRILLS. WHEN THE SHITHAMMER FALLS-- OUT THERE--THERE AREN'T GONNA BE ANY SAFETY NETS.
IF WE'RE GOING TO TEST THE CREW, I WANT TO TEST THE CREW.
AND HOW DO YOU PROPOSE WE DO THAT?
CAPTAIN?
WHAT'S THE NAVIGATOR'S NAME AGAIN?
ELOX.
NAVIGATOR ELOX, THIS IS THE CAPTAIN.
HOW MUCH FURTHER?

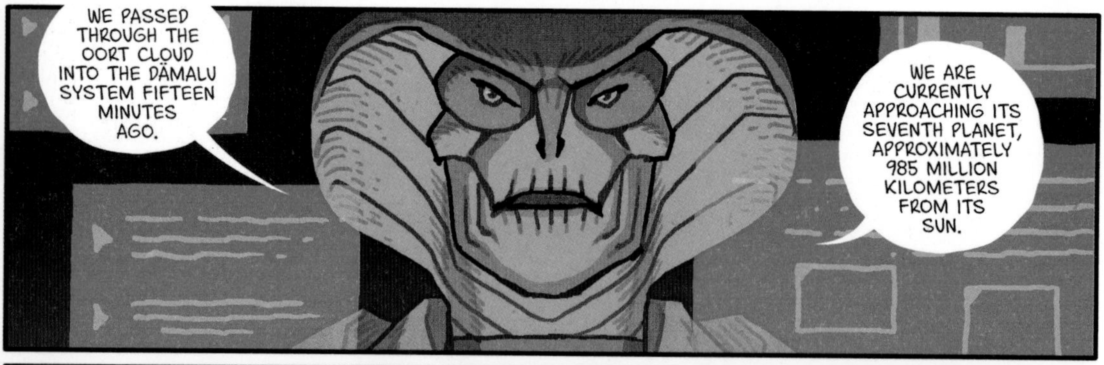
WE PASSED THROUGH THE OORT CLOUD INTO THE DÄMALU SYSTEM FIFTEEN MINUTES AGO.
WE ARE CURRENTLY APPROACHING ITS SEVENTH PLANET, APPROXIMATELY 985 MILLION KILOMETERS FROM ITS SUN.

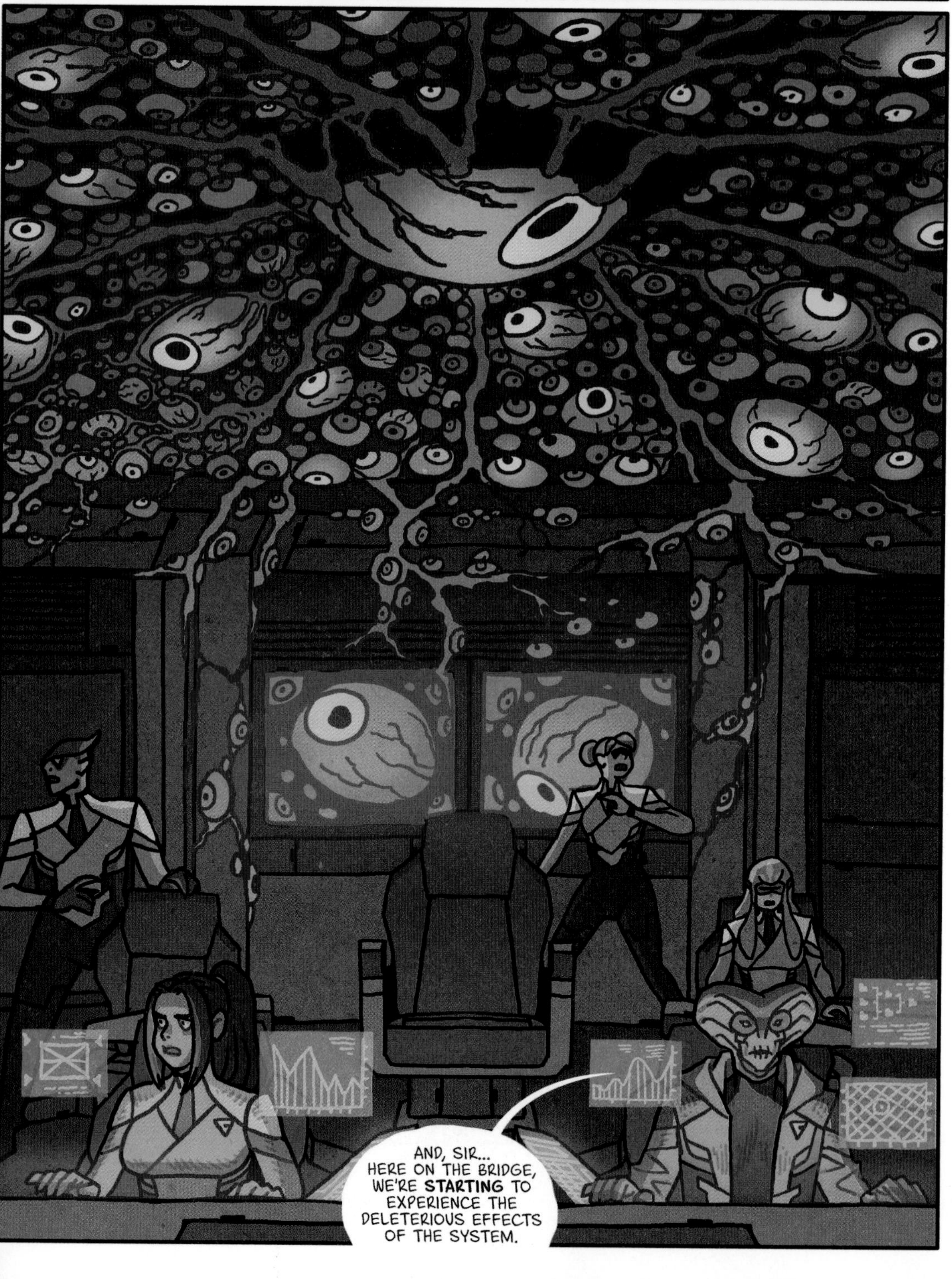
AND, SIR... HERE ON THE BRIDGE, WE'RE **STARTING** TO EXPERIENCE THE DELETERIOUS EFFECTS OF THE SYSTEM.

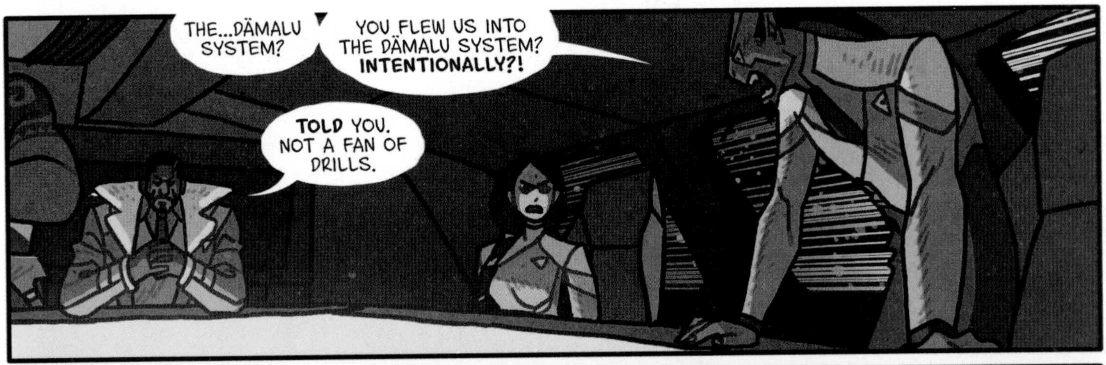
THE...DÄMALU SYSTEM?
YOU FLEW US INTO THE DÄMALU SYSTEM? **INTENTIONALLY?!**
TOLD YOU. NOT A FAN OF DRILLS.

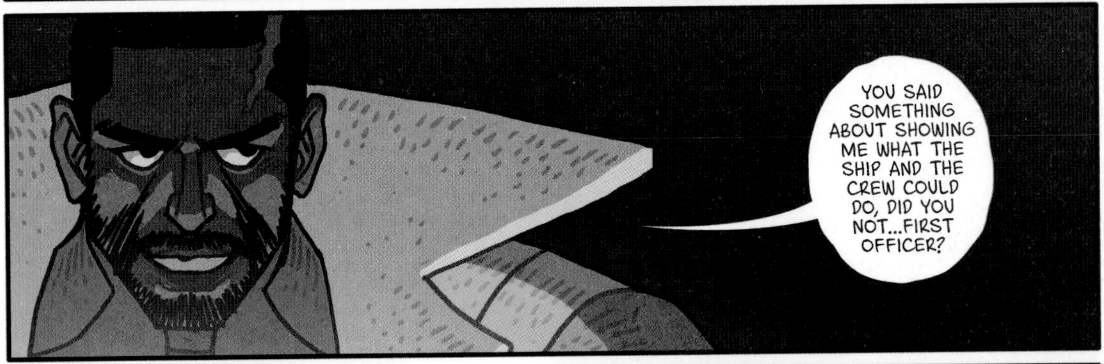
YOU SAID SOMETHING ABOUT SHOWING ME WHAT THE SHIP AND THE CREW COULD DO, DID YOU NOT...FIRST OFFICER?

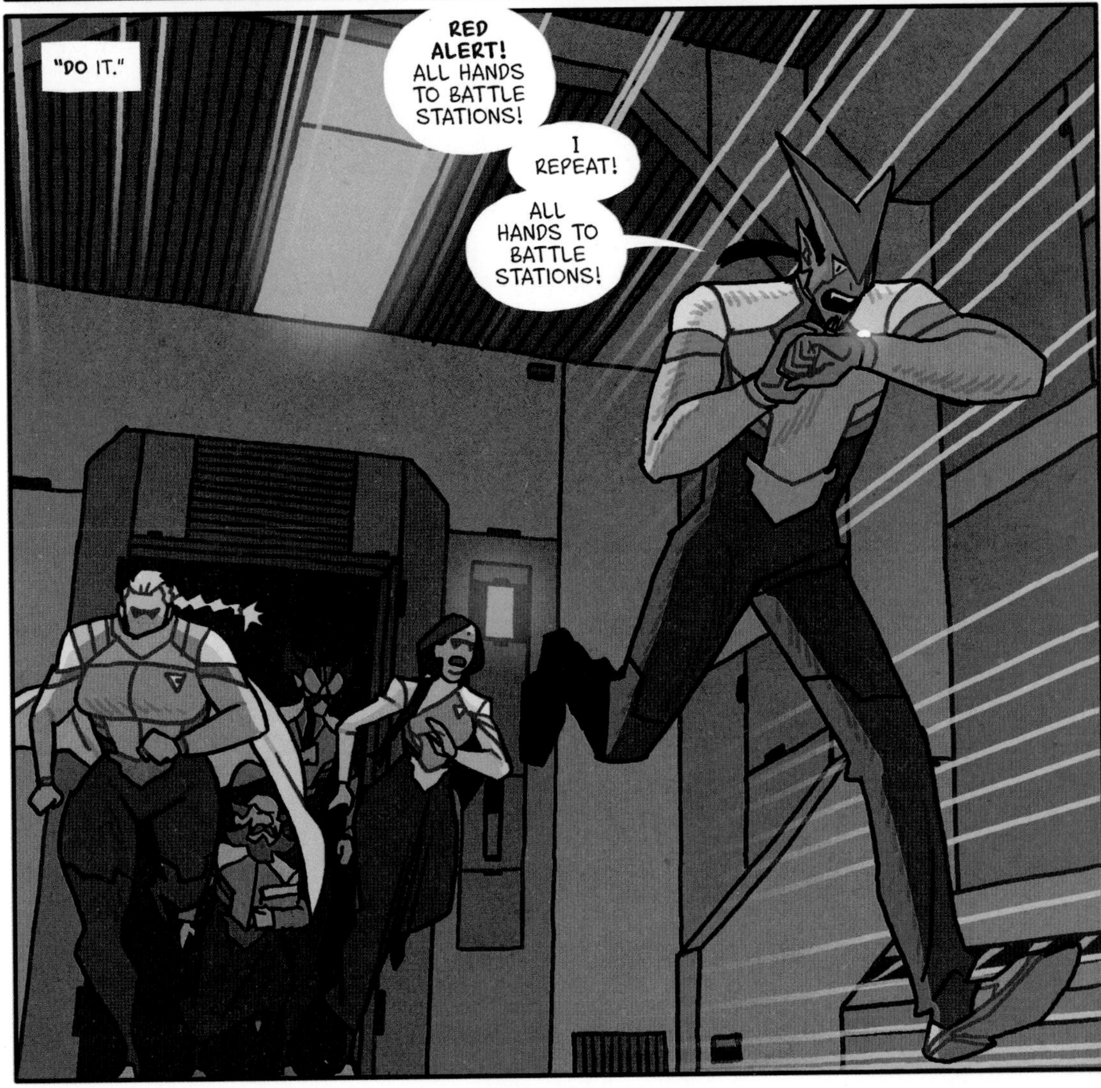
"DO IT."
RED ALERT! ALL HANDS TO BATTLE STATIONS!
I REPEAT!
ALL HANDS TO BATTLE STATIONS!

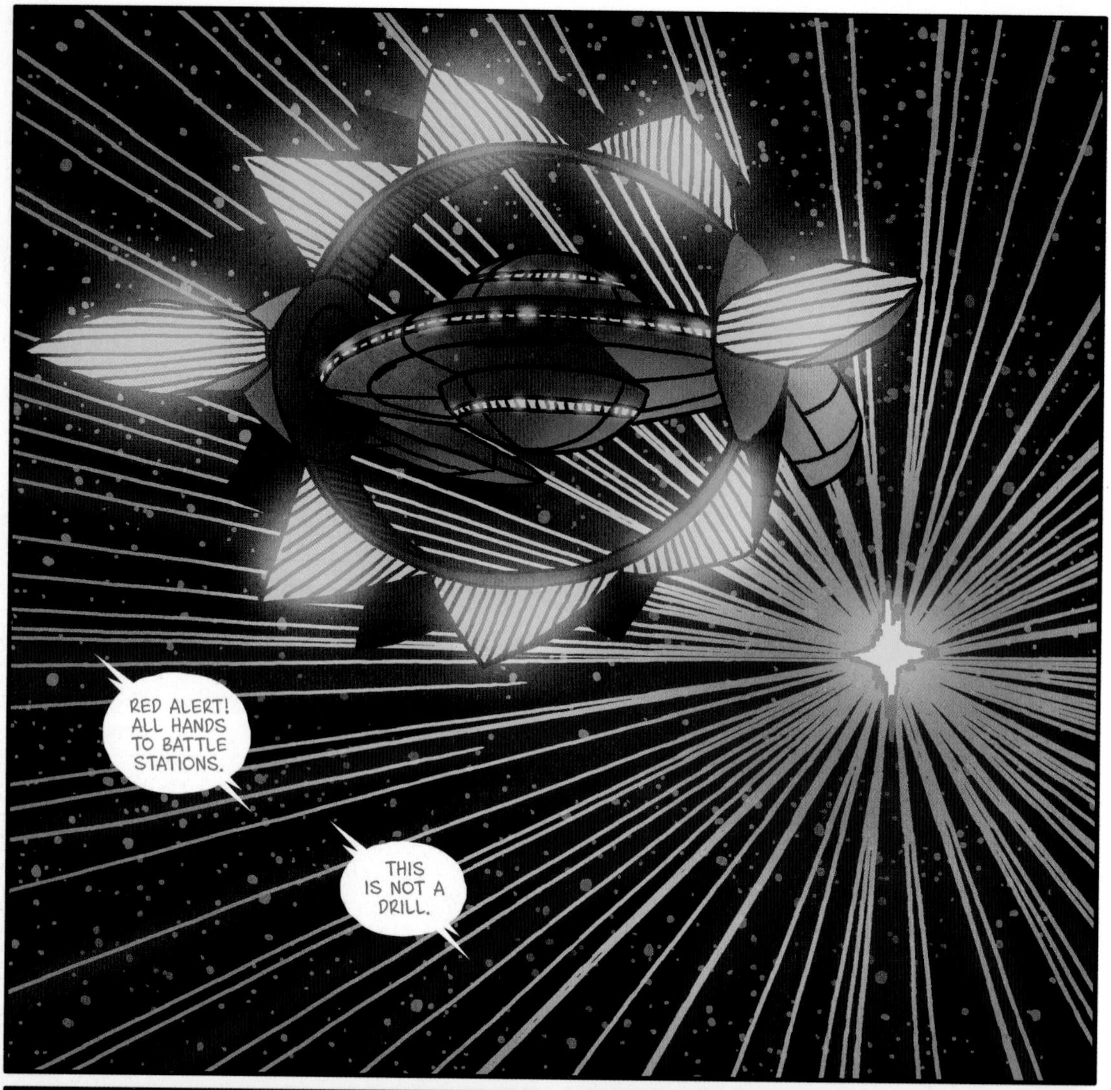
RED ALERT! ALL HANDS TO BATTLE STATIONS.
THIS IS NOT A DRILL.

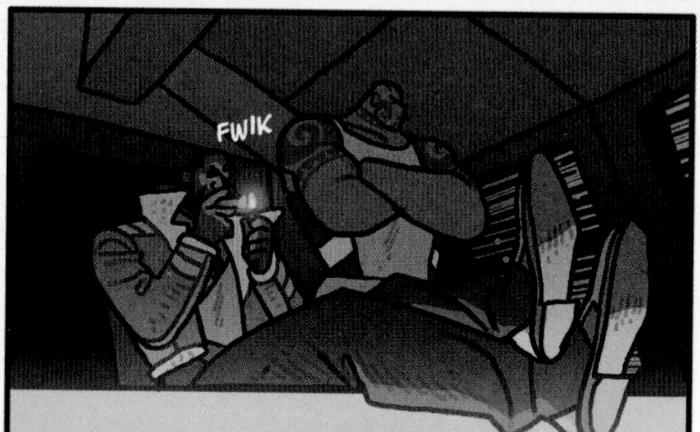
FWIK

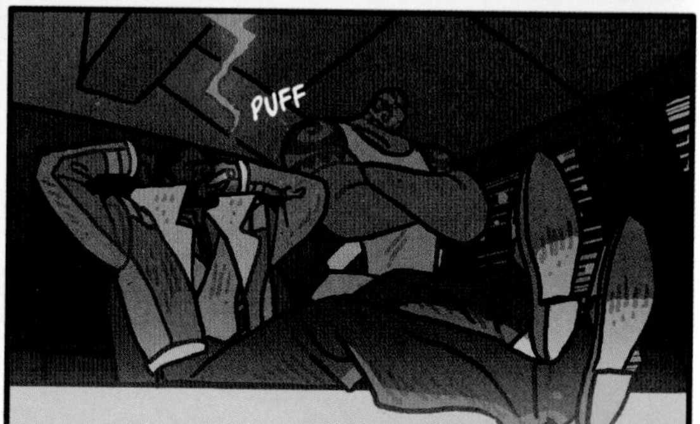
PUFF

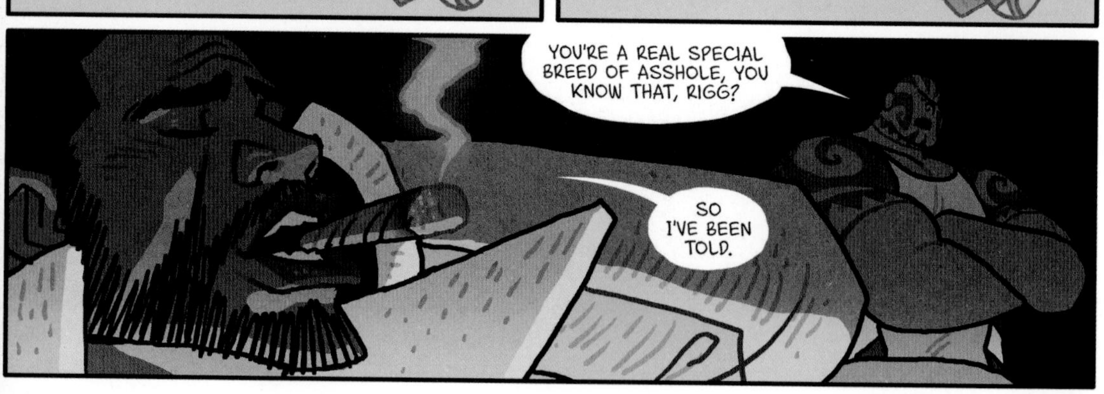
YOU'RE A REAL SPECIAL BREED OF ASSHOLE, YOU KNOW THAT, RIGG?
SO I'VE BEEN TOLD.

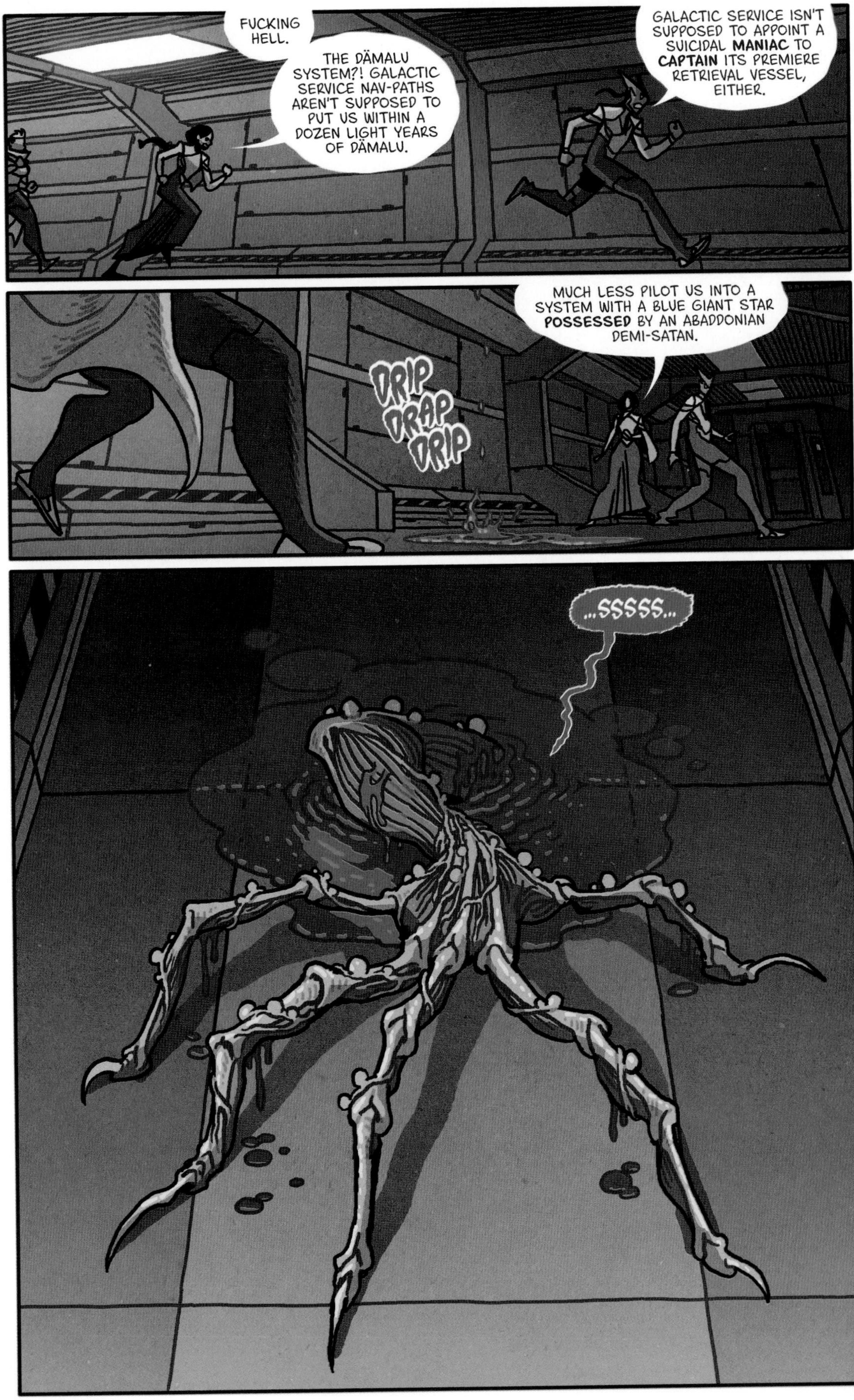
FUCKING HELL.
THE DÄMALU SYSTEM?! GALACTIC SERVICE NAV-PATHS AREN'T SUPPOSED TO PUT US WITHIN A DOZEN LIGHT YEARS OF DÄMALU.
GALACTIC SERVICE ISN'T SUPPOSED TO APPOINT A SUICIDAL **MANIAC** TO **CAPTAIN** ITS PREMIERE RETRIEVAL VESSEL, EITHER.
MUCH LESS PILOT US INTO A SYSTEM WITH A BLUE GIANT STAR **POSSESSED** BY AN ABADDONIAN DEMI-SATAN.
DRIP
DRAP
DRIP
...SSSSS...

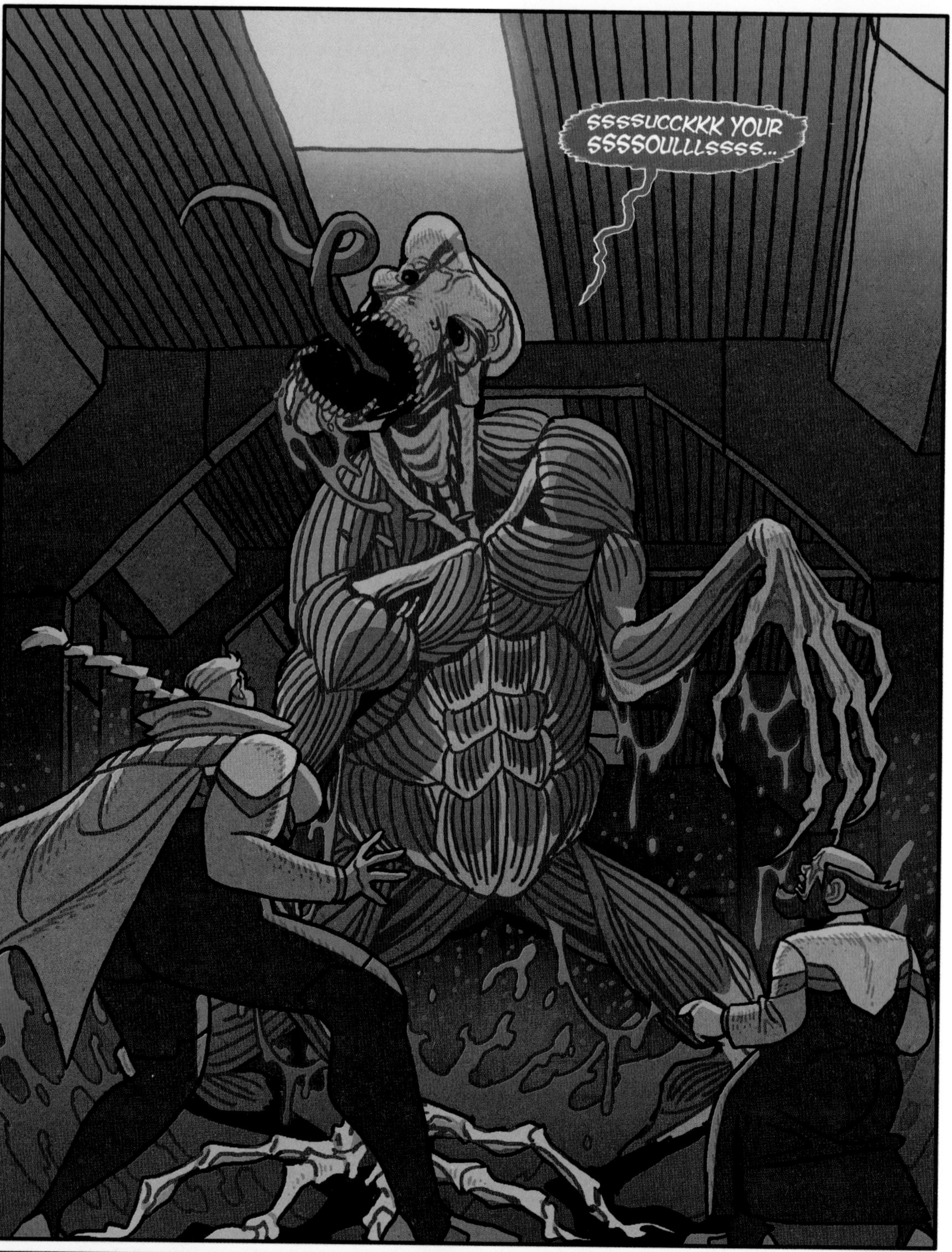
SSSSUCCKKK YOUR SSSSOULLLSSSS...

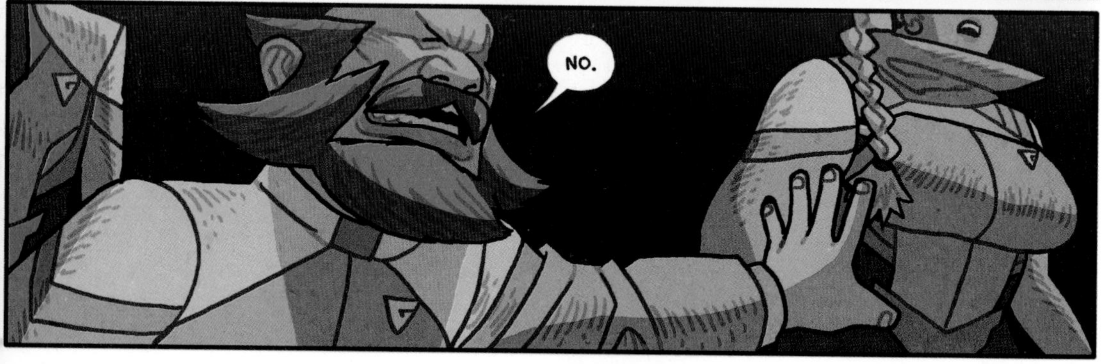
NO.

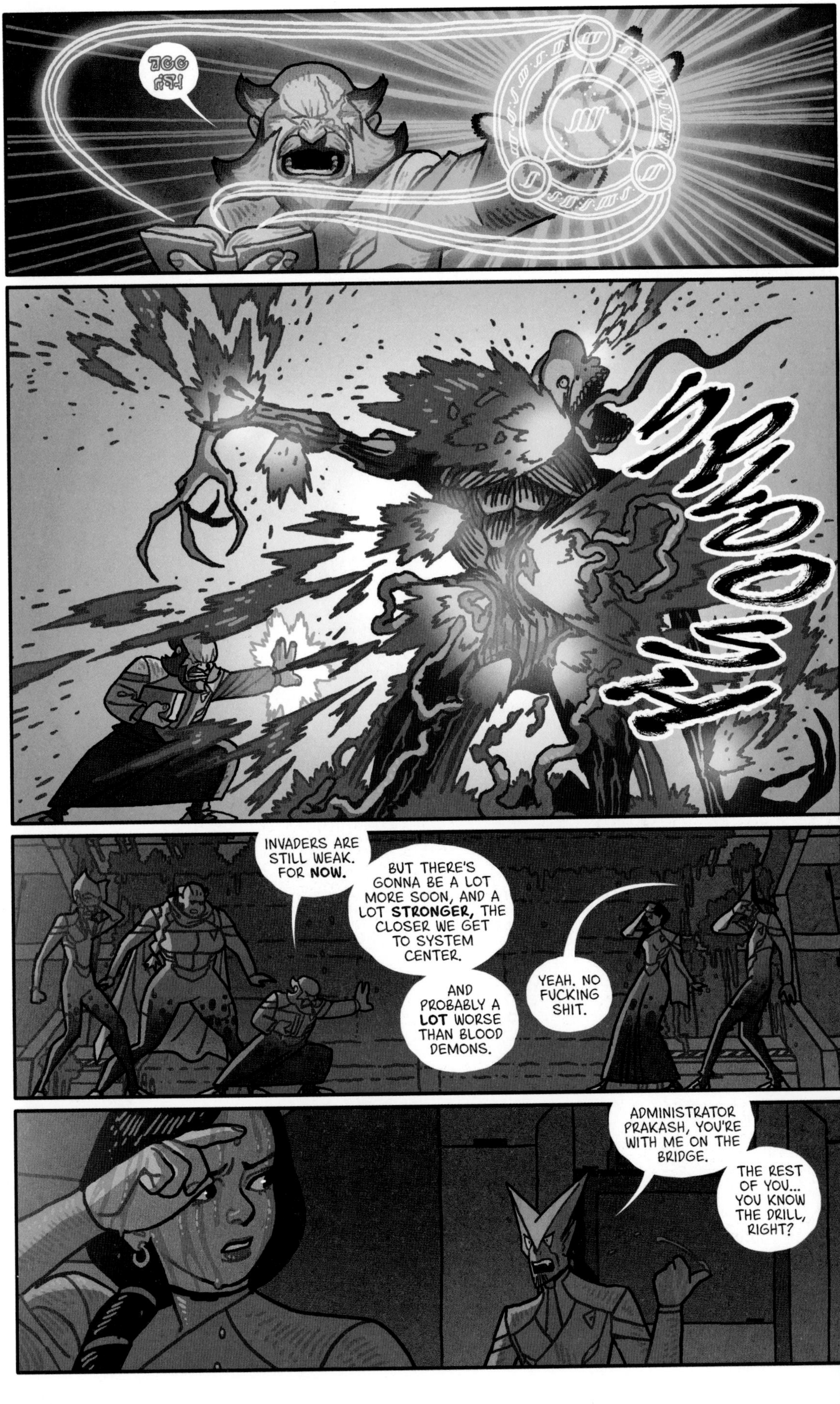

INVADERS ARE STILL WEAK. FOR **NOW.**
BUT THERE'S GONNA BE A LOT MORE SOON, AND A LOT **STRONGER,** THE CLOSER WE GET TO SYSTEM CENTER.
AND PROBABLY A **LOT** WORSE THAN BLOOD DEMONS.
YEAH. NO FUCKING SHIT.
ADMINISTRATOR PRAKASH, YOU'RE WITH ME ON THE BRIDGE.
THE REST OF YOU... YOU KNOW THE DRILL, RIGHT?

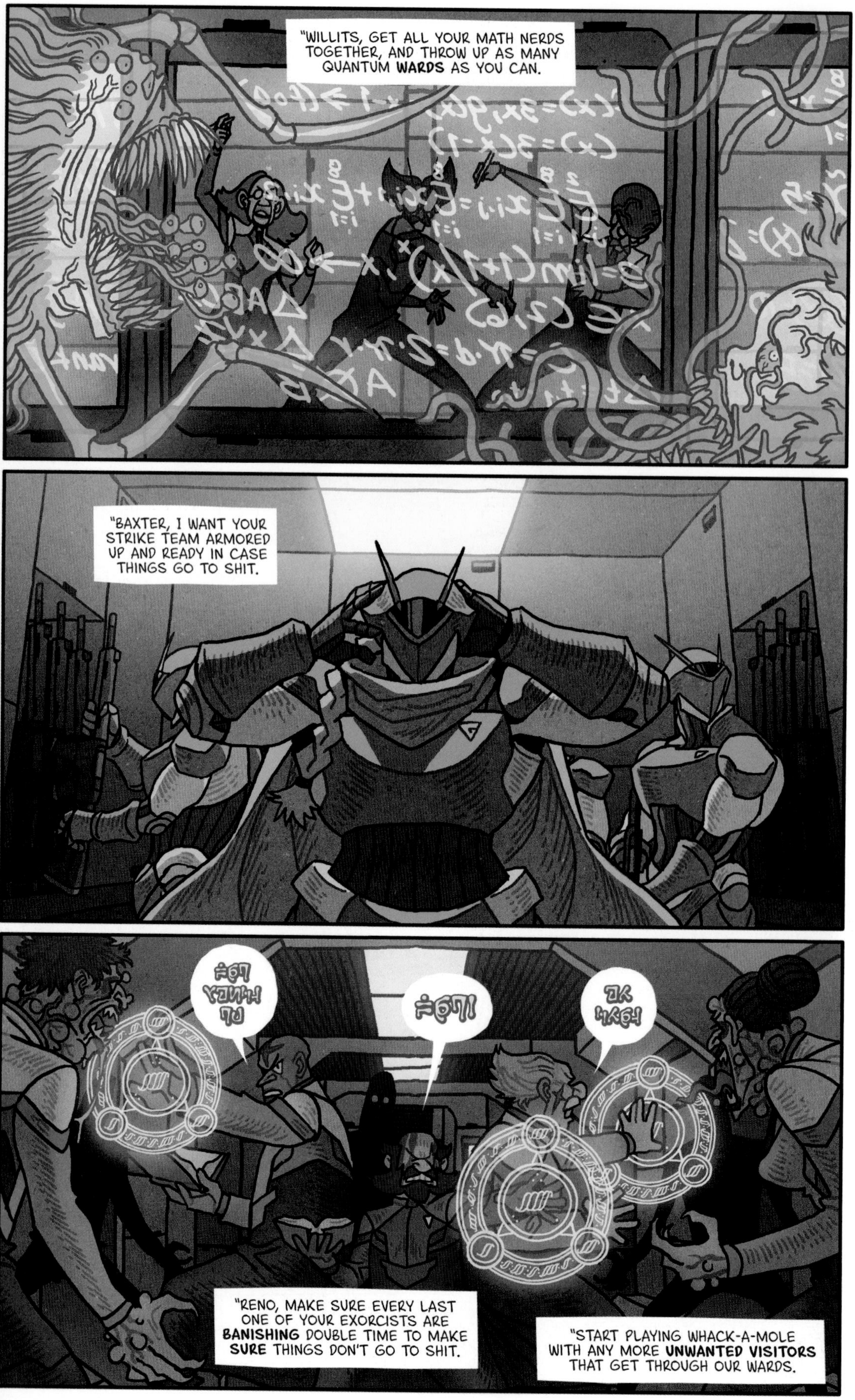
"WILLITS, GET ALL YOUR MATH NERDS TOGETHER, AND THROW UP AS MANY QUANTUM WARDS AS YOU CAN.
"BAXTER, I WANT YOUR STRIKE TEAM ARMORED UP AND READY IN CASE THINGS GO TO SHIT.
"RENO, MAKE SURE EVERY LAST ONE OF YOUR EXORCISTS ARE BANISHING DOUBLE TIME TO MAKE SURE THINGS DON'T GO TO SHIT.
"START PLAYING WHACK-A-MOLE WITH ANY MORE UNWANTED VISITORS THAT GET THROUGH OUR WARDS.

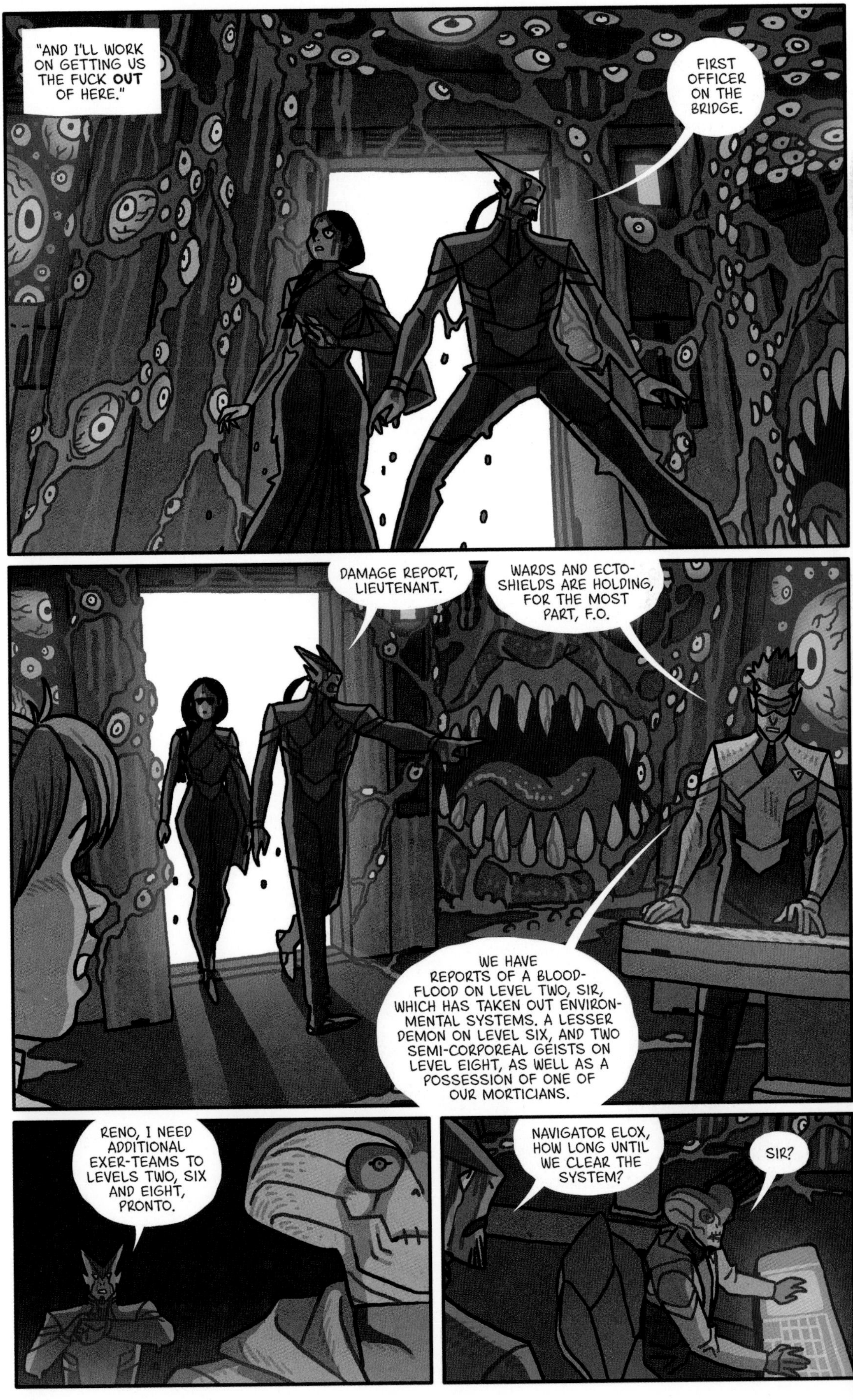
"AND I'LL WORK ON GETTING US THE FUCK **OUT** OF HERE."
FIRST OFFICER ON THE BRIDGE.
DAMAGE REPORT, LIEUTENANT.
WARDS AND ECTO-SHIELDS ARE HOLDING, FOR THE MOST PART, F.O.
WE HAVE REPORTS OF A BLOOD-FLOOD ON LEVEL TWO, SIR, WHICH HAS TAKEN OUT ENVIRONMENTAL SYSTEMS. A LESSER DEMON ON LEVEL SIX, AND TWO SEMI-CORPOREAL GEISTS ON LEVEL EIGHT, AS WELL AS A POSSESSION OF ONE OF OUR MORTICIANS.
RENO, I NEED ADDITIONAL EXER-TEAMS TO LEVELS TWO, SIX AND EIGHT, PRONTO.
NAVIGATOR ELOX, HOW LONG UNTIL WE CLEAR THE SYSTEM?
SIR?

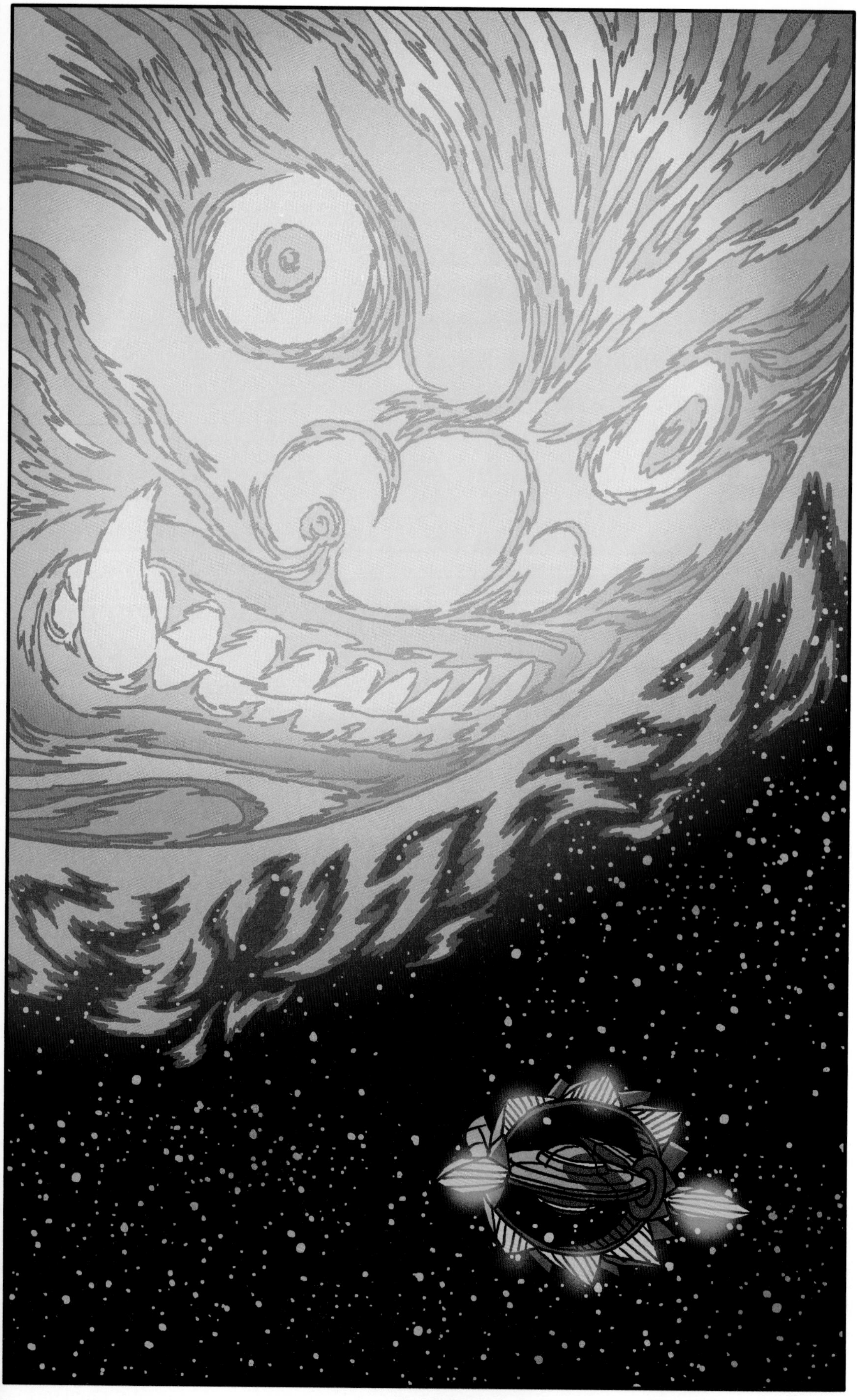

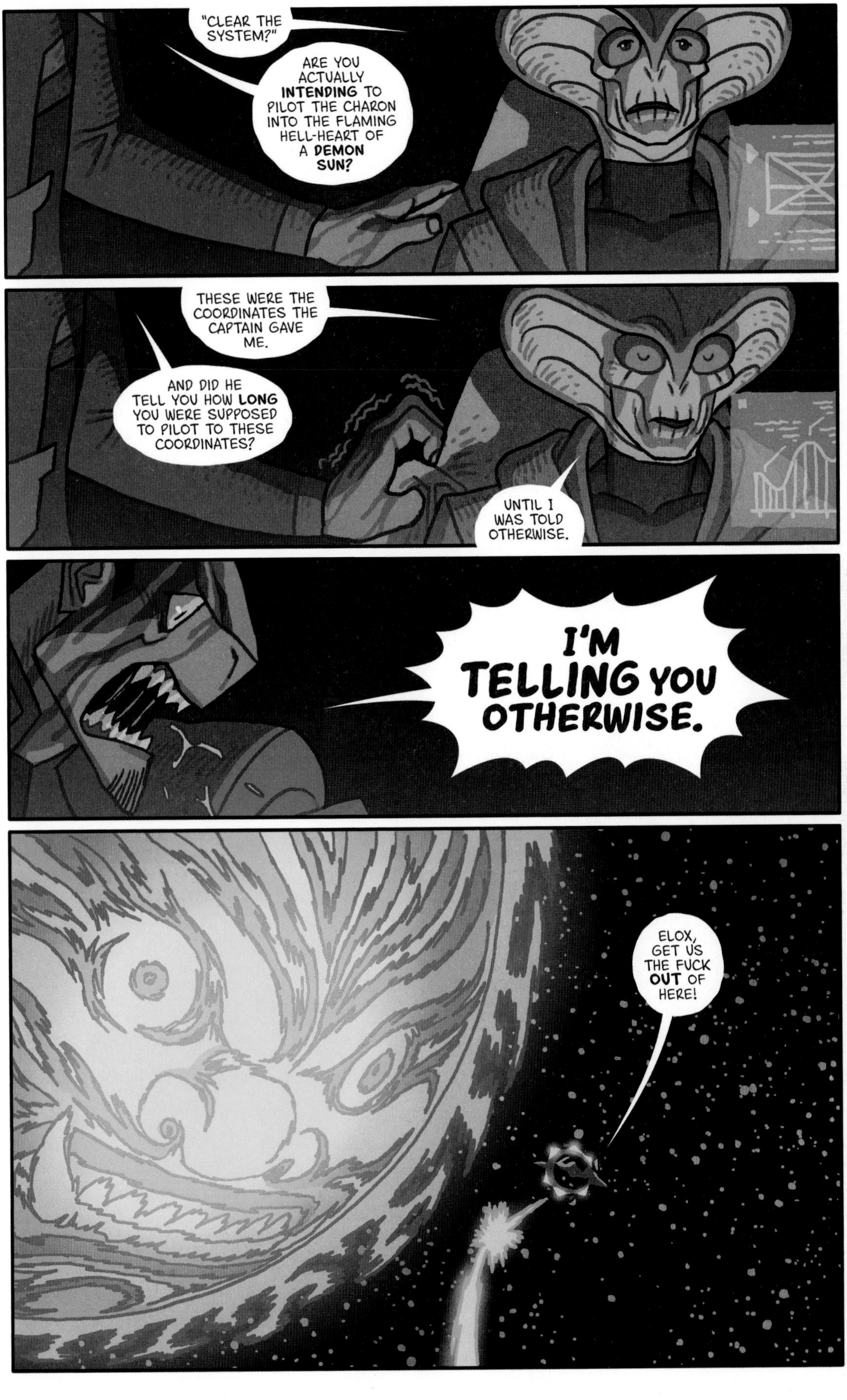
"CLEAR THE SYSTEM?"
ARE YOU ACTUALLY **INTENDING** TO PILOT THE CHARON INTO THE FLAMING HELL-HEART OF A **DEMON SUN?**
THESE WERE THE COORDINATES THE CAPTAIN GAVE ME.
AND DID HE TELL YOU HOW **LONG** YOU WERE SUPPOSED TO PILOT TO THESE COORDINATES?
UNTIL I WAS TOLD OTHERWISE.
I'M **TELLING** YOU OTHERWISE.
ELOX, GET US THE FUCK **OUT** OF HERE!

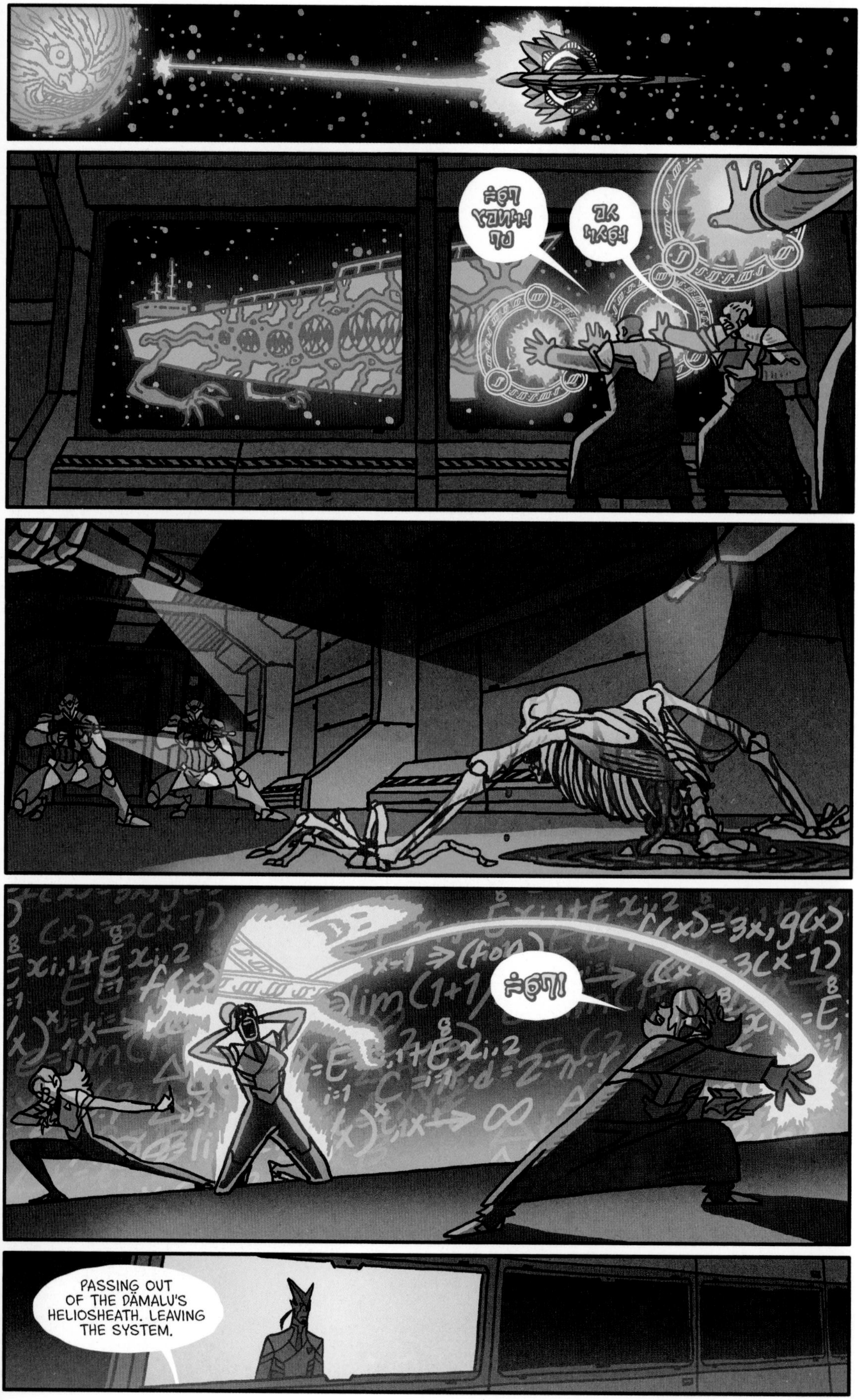
PASSING OUT OF THE DÄMALU'S HELIOSHEATH. LEAVING THE SYSTEM.

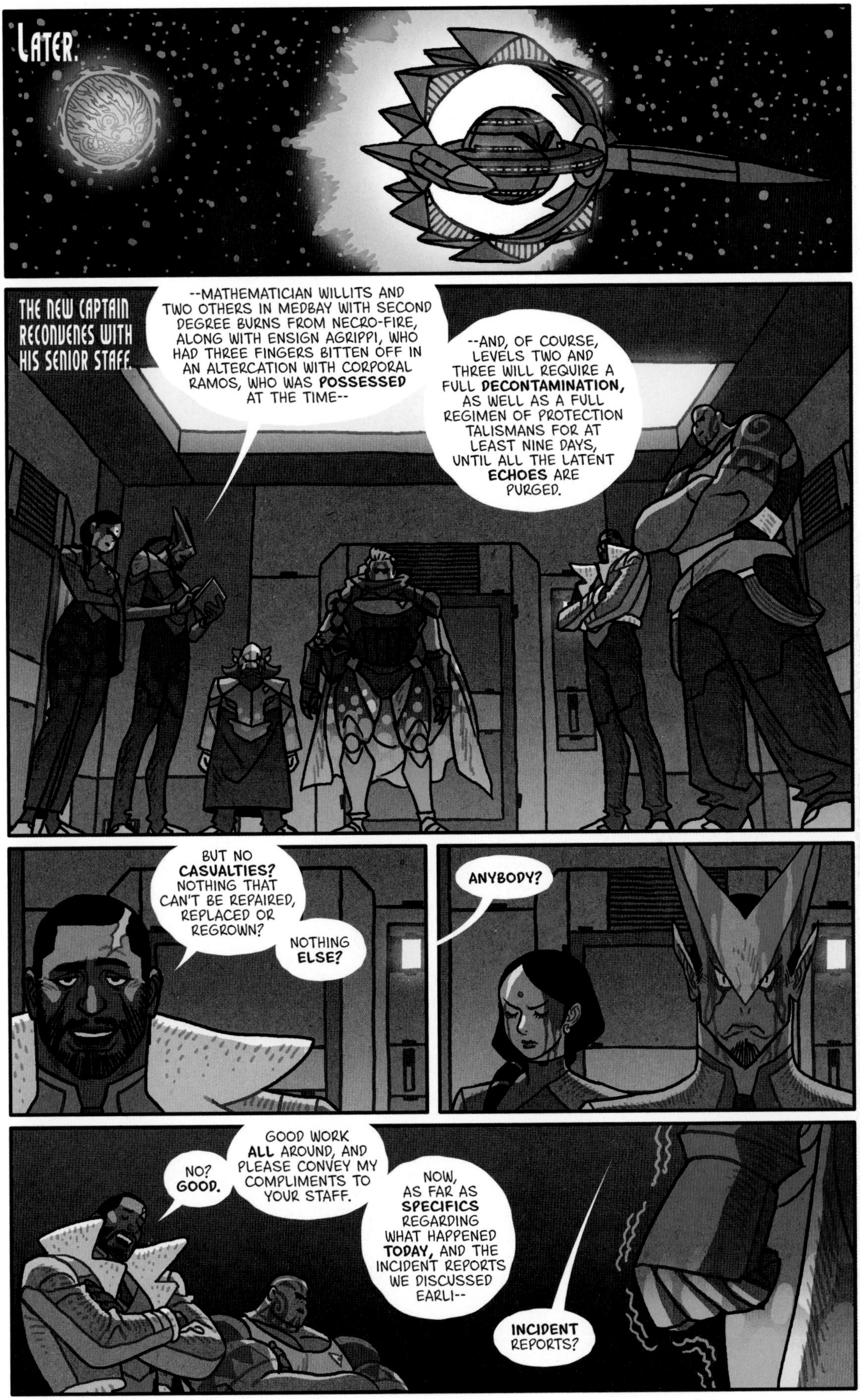
LATER.
THE NEW CAPTAIN RECONVENES WITH HIS SENIOR STAFF.
--MATHEMATICIAN WILLITS AND TWO OTHERS IN MEDBAY WITH SECOND DEGREE BURNS FROM NECRO-FIRE, ALONG WITH ENSIGN AGRIPPI, WHO HAD THREE FINGERS BITTEN OFF IN AN ALTERCATION WITH CORPORAL RAMOS, WHO WAS POSSESSED AT THE TIME--
--AND, OF COURSE, LEVELS TWO AND THREE WILL REQUIRE A FULL DECONTAMINATION, AS WELL AS A FULL REGIMEN OF PROTECTION TALISMANS FOR AT LEAST NINE DAYS, UNTIL ALL THE LATENT ECHOES ARE PURGED.
BUT NO CASUALTIES? NOTHING THAT CAN'T BE REPAIRED, REPLACED OR REGROWN?
NOTHING ELSE?
ANYBODY?
NO? GOOD.
GOOD WORK ALL AROUND, AND PLEASE CONVEY MY COMPLIMENTS TO YOUR STAFF.
NOW, AS FAR AS SPECIFICS REGARDING WHAT HAPPENED TODAY, AND THE INCIDENT REPORTS WE DISCUSSED EARLI--
INCIDENT REPORTS?

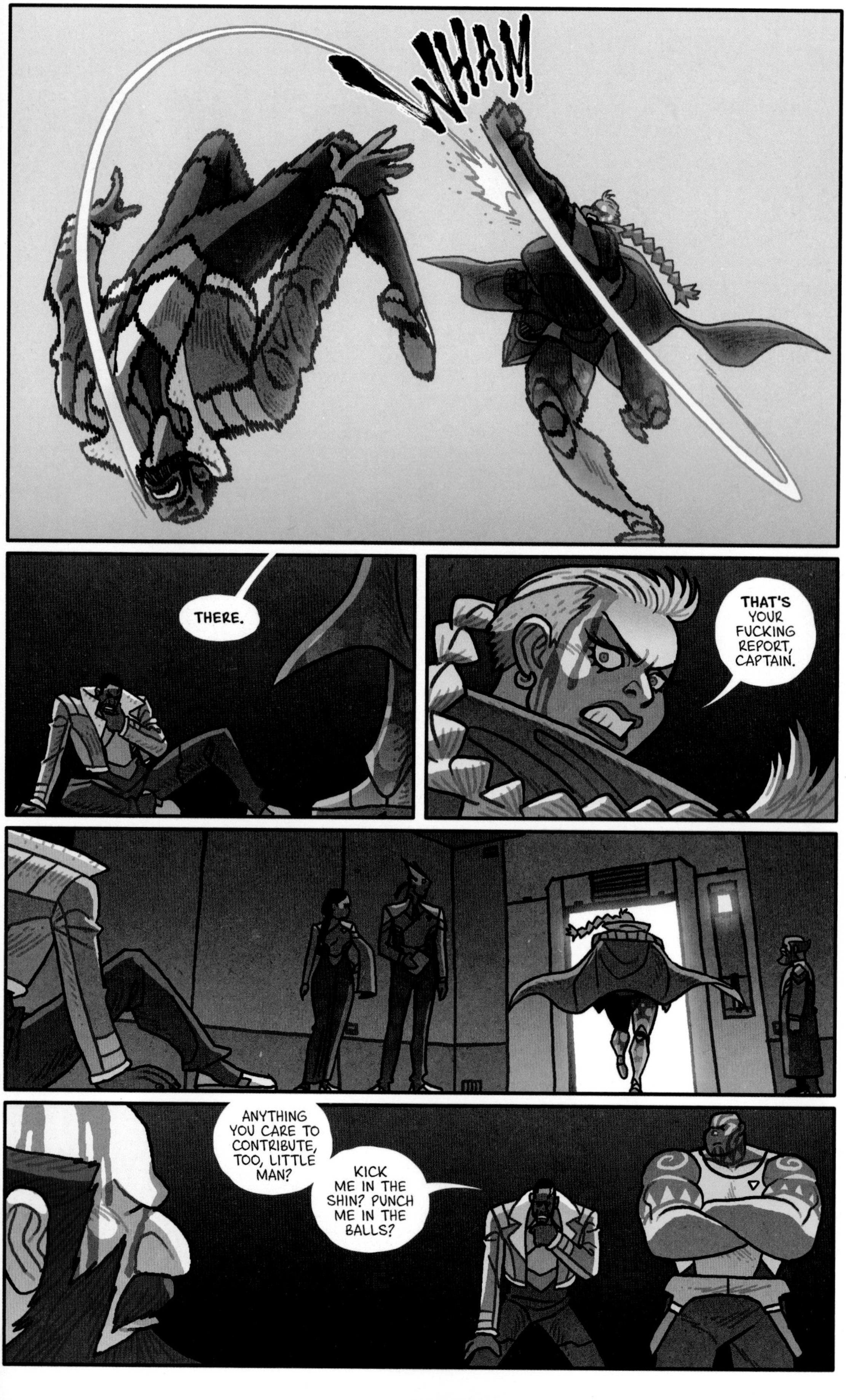
WHAM
THERE.
THAT'S YOUR FUCKING REPORT, CAPTAIN.
ANYTHING YOU CARE TO CONTRIBUTE, TOO, LITTLE MAN?
KICK ME IN THE SHIN? PUNCH ME IN THE BALLS?

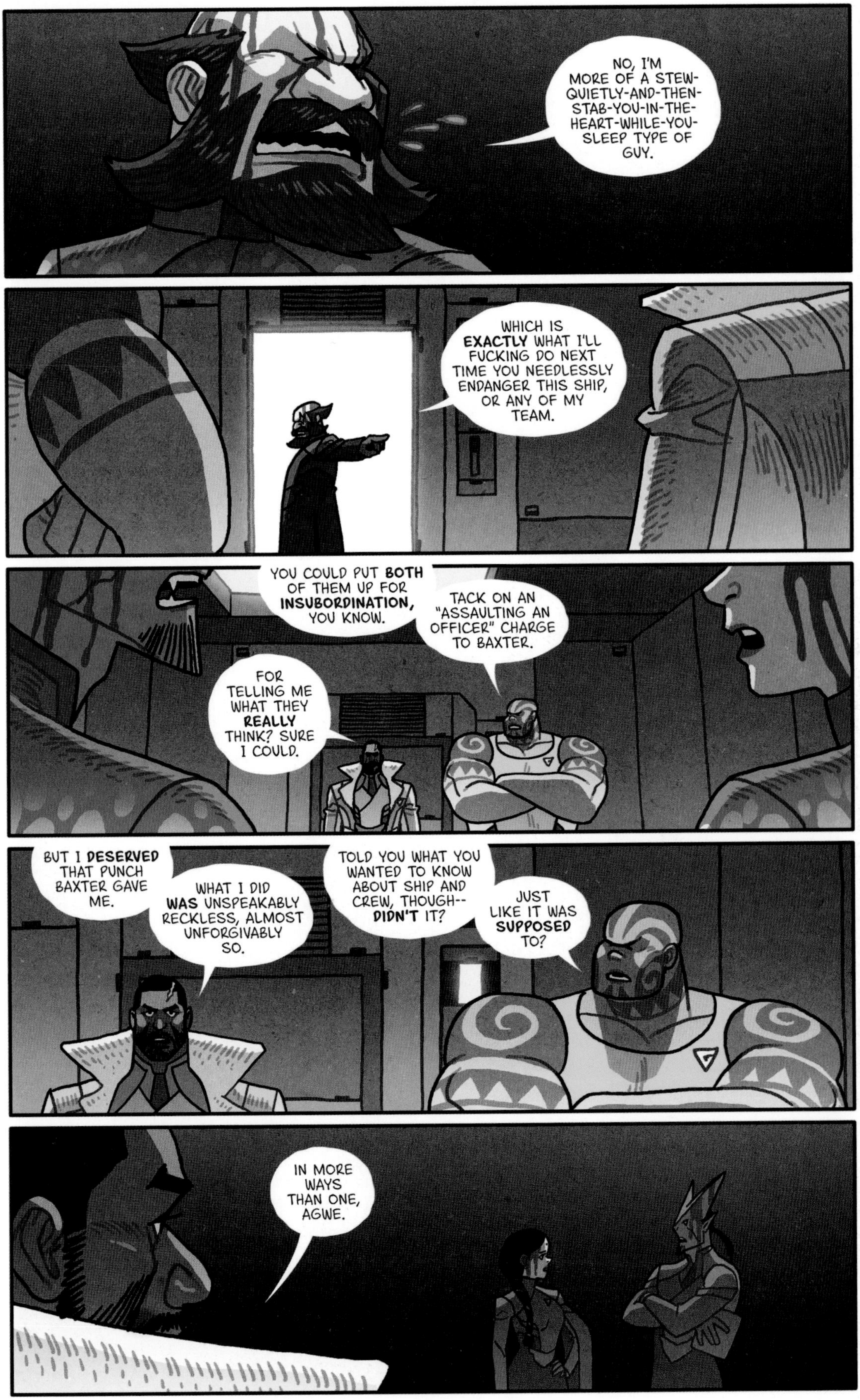
NO, I'M MORE OF A STEW-QUIETLY-AND-THEN-STAB-YOU-IN-THE-HEART-WHILE-YOU-SLEEP TYPE OF GUY.
WHICH IS **EXACTLY** WHAT I'LL FUCKING DO NEXT TIME YOU NEEDLESSLY ENDANGER THIS SHIP, OR ANY OF MY TEAM.
YOU COULD PUT **BOTH** OF THEM UP FOR **INSUBORDINATION,** YOU KNOW.
TACK ON AN "ASSAULTING AN OFFICER" CHARGE TO BAXTER.
FOR TELLING ME WHAT THEY **REALLY** THINK? SURE I COULD.
BUT I **DESERVED** THAT PUNCH BAXTER GAVE ME.
WHAT I DID **WAS** UNSPEAKABLY RECKLESS, ALMOST UNFORGIVABLY SO.
TOLD YOU WHAT YOU WANTED TO KNOW ABOUT SHIP AND CREW, THOUGH-- **DIDN'T** IT?
JUST LIKE IT WAS **SUPPOSED** TO?
IN MORE WAYS THAN ONE, AGWE.

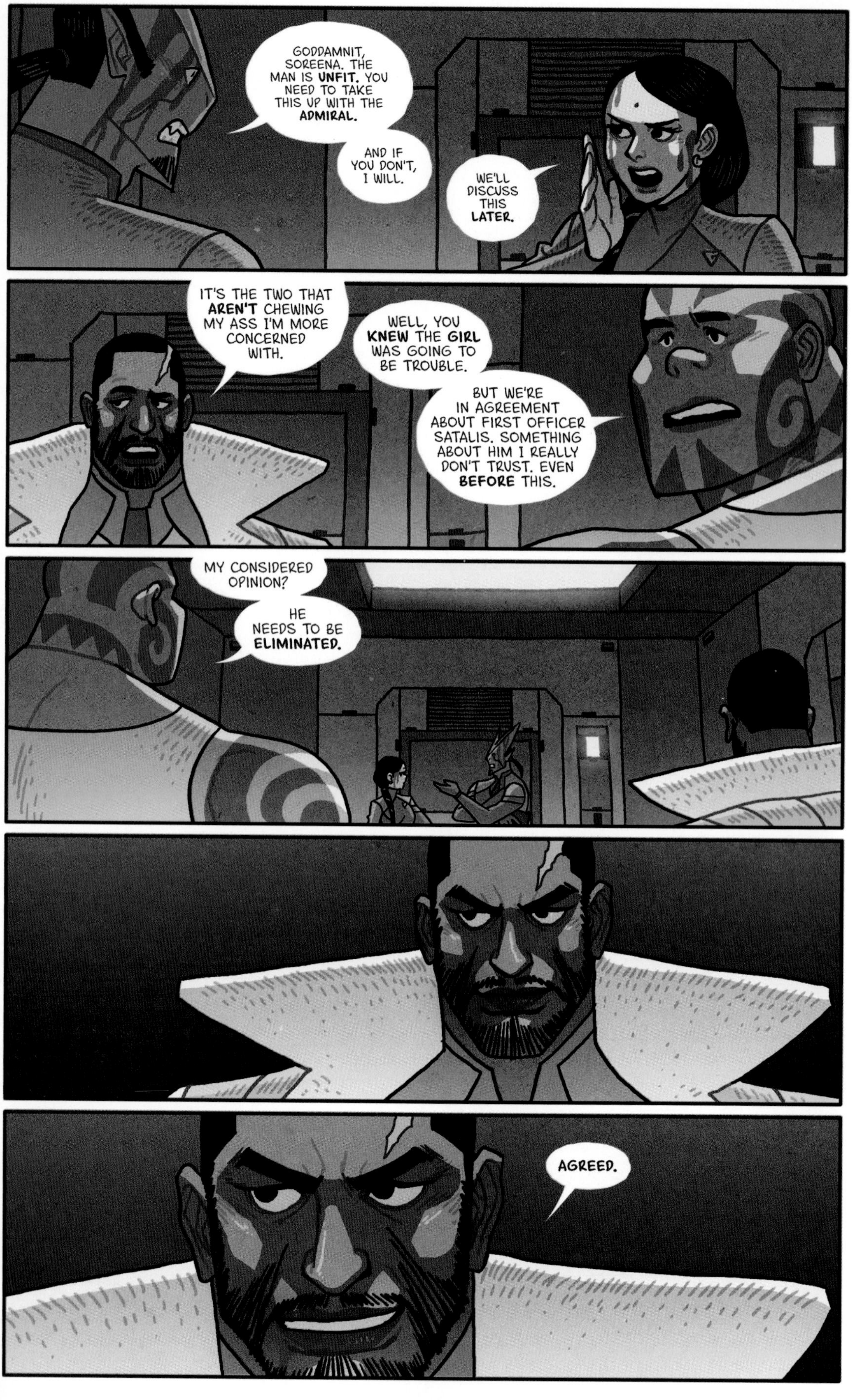
GODDAMNIT, SOREENA. THE MAN IS UNFIT. YOU NEED TO TAKE THIS UP WITH THE ADMIRAL.
AND IF YOU DON'T, I WILL.
WE'LL DISCUSS THIS LATER.
IT'S THE TWO THAT AREN'T CHEWING MY ASS I'M MORE CONCERNED WITH.
WELL, YOU KNEW THE GIRL WAS GOING TO BE TROUBLE.
BUT WE'RE IN AGREEMENT ABOUT FIRST OFFICER SATALIS. SOMETHING ABOUT HIM I REALLY DON'T TRUST. EVEN BEFORE THIS.
MY CONSIDERED OPINION?
HE NEEDS TO BE ELIMINATED.
AGREED.

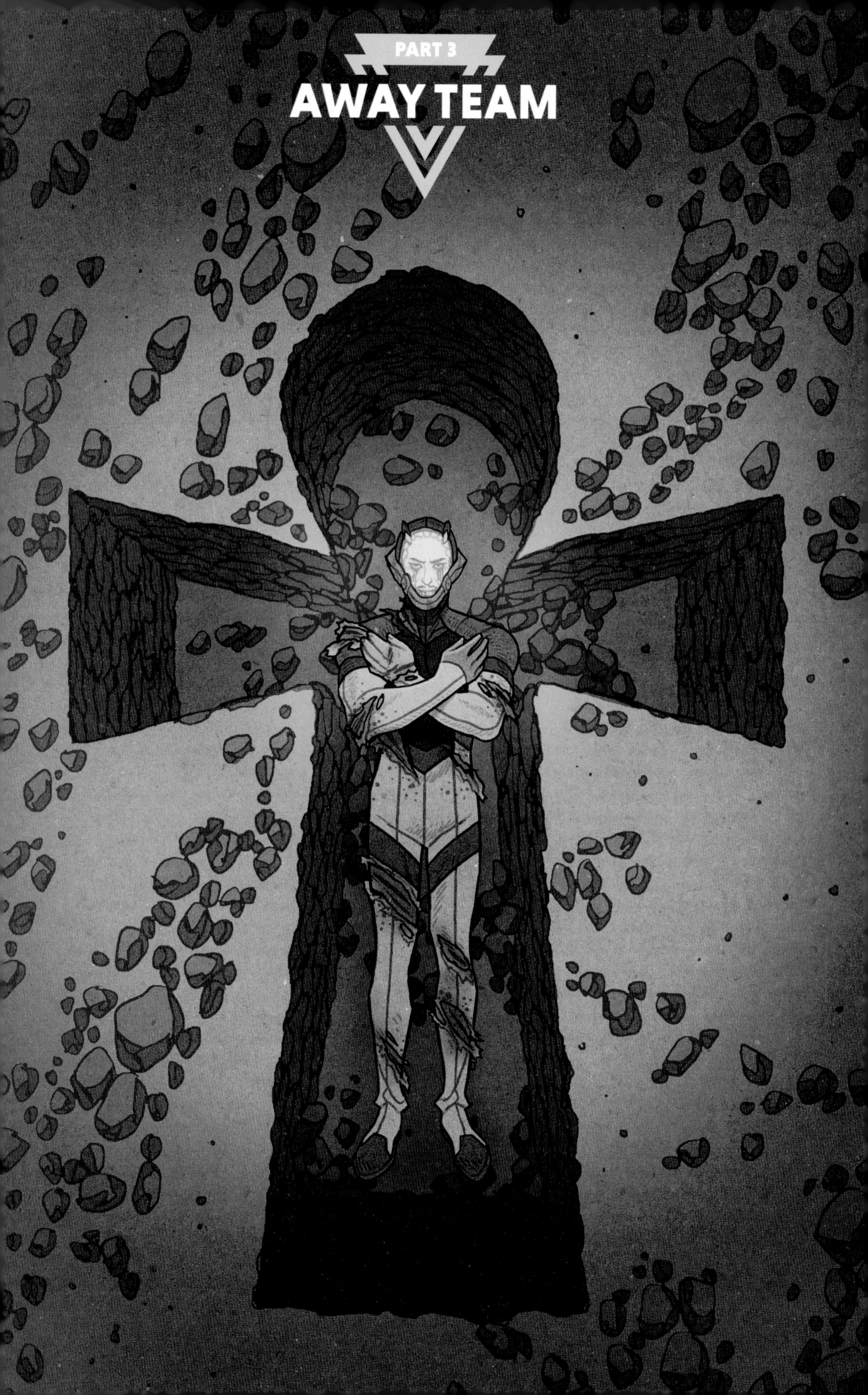
PART 3
AWAY TEAM

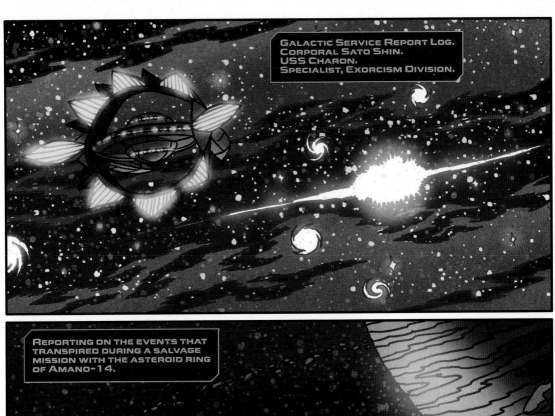

GALACTIC SERVICE REPORT LOG.
CORPORAL SATO SHIN.
USS CHARON.
SPECIALIST, EXORCISM DIVISION.

REPORTING ON THE EVENTS THAT
TRANSPIRED DURING A SALVAGE
MISSION WITH THE ASTEROID RING
OF AMANO-14.

SPECIFICALLY, THE **INCIDENT** THAT
OCCURRED WITH MYSELF AND NEWLY-
ASSIGNED ENSIGN MALONA HYDZEK.

THIS
WAY.

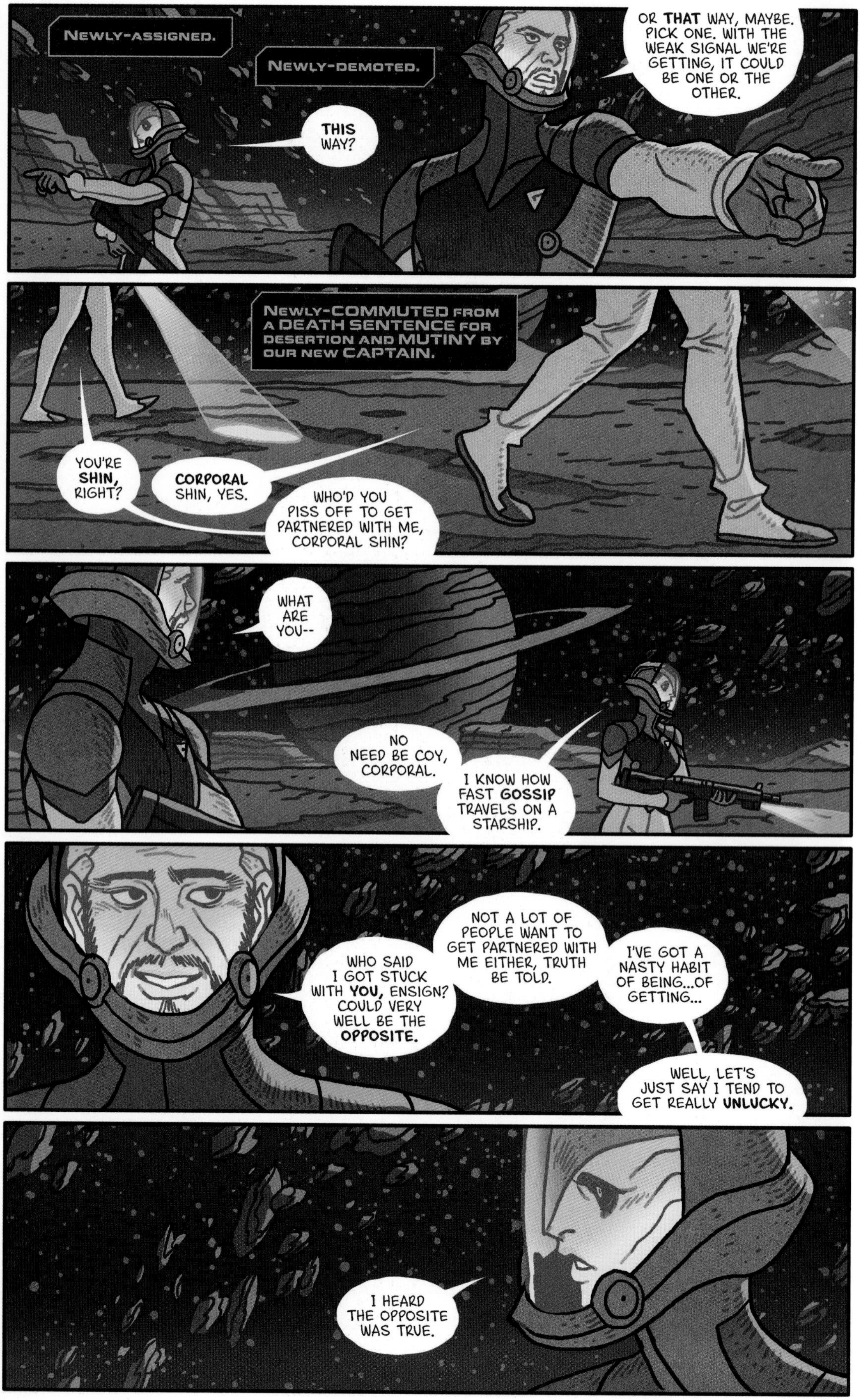
Newly-assigned.
Newly-demoted.
OR THAT WAY, MAYBE. PICK ONE. WITH THE WEAK SIGNAL WE'RE GETTING, IT COULD BE ONE OR THE OTHER.
THIS WAY?
Newly-COMMUTED from a DEATH SENTENCE for desertion and MUTINY by our new CAPTAIN.
YOU'RE SHIN, RIGHT?
CORPORAL SHIN, YES.
WHO'D YOU PISS OFF TO GET PARTNERED WITH ME, CORPORAL SHIN?
WHAT ARE YOU--
NO NEED BE COY, CORPORAL.
I KNOW HOW FAST GOSSIP TRAVELS ON A STARSHIP.
WHO SAID I GOT STUCK WITH YOU, ENSIGN? COULD VERY WELL BE THE OPPOSITE.
NOT A LOT OF PEOPLE WANT TO GET PARTNERED WITH ME EITHER, TRUTH BE TOLD.
I'VE GOT A NASTY HABIT OF BEING...OF GETTING...
WELL, LET'S JUST SAY I TEND TO GET REALLY UNLUCKY.
I HEARD THE OPPOSITE WAS TRUE.

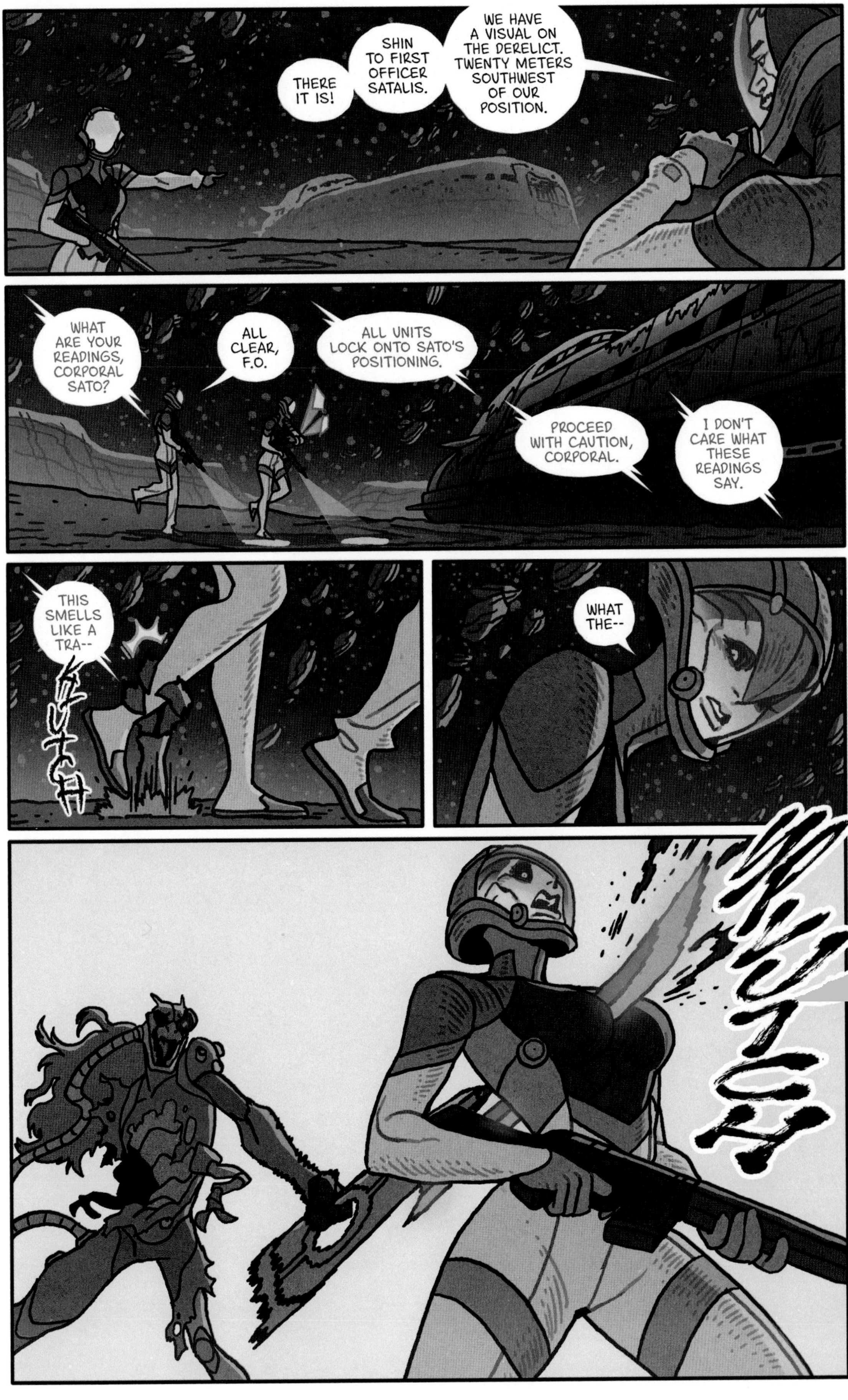
THERE IT IS!
SHIN TO FIRST OFFICER SATALIS.
WE HAVE A VISUAL ON THE DERELICT. TWENTY METERS SOUTHWEST OF OUR POSITION.
WHAT ARE YOUR READINGS, CORPORAL SATO?
ALL CLEAR, F.O.
ALL UNITS LOCK ONTO SATO'S POSITIONING.
PROCEED WITH CAUTION, CORPORAL.
I DON'T CARE WHAT THESE READINGS SAY.
THIS SMELLS LIKE A TRA--
WHAT THE--

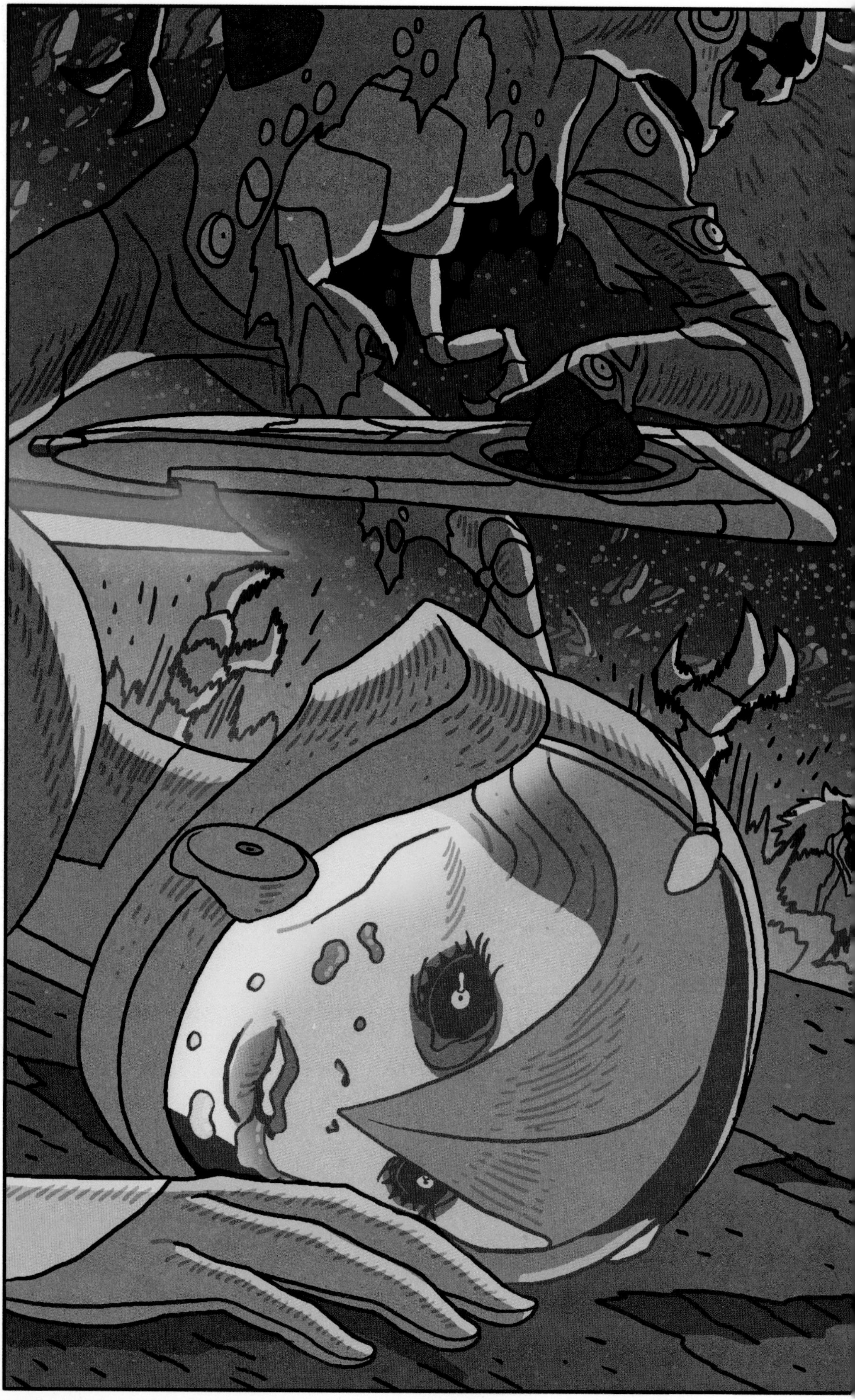

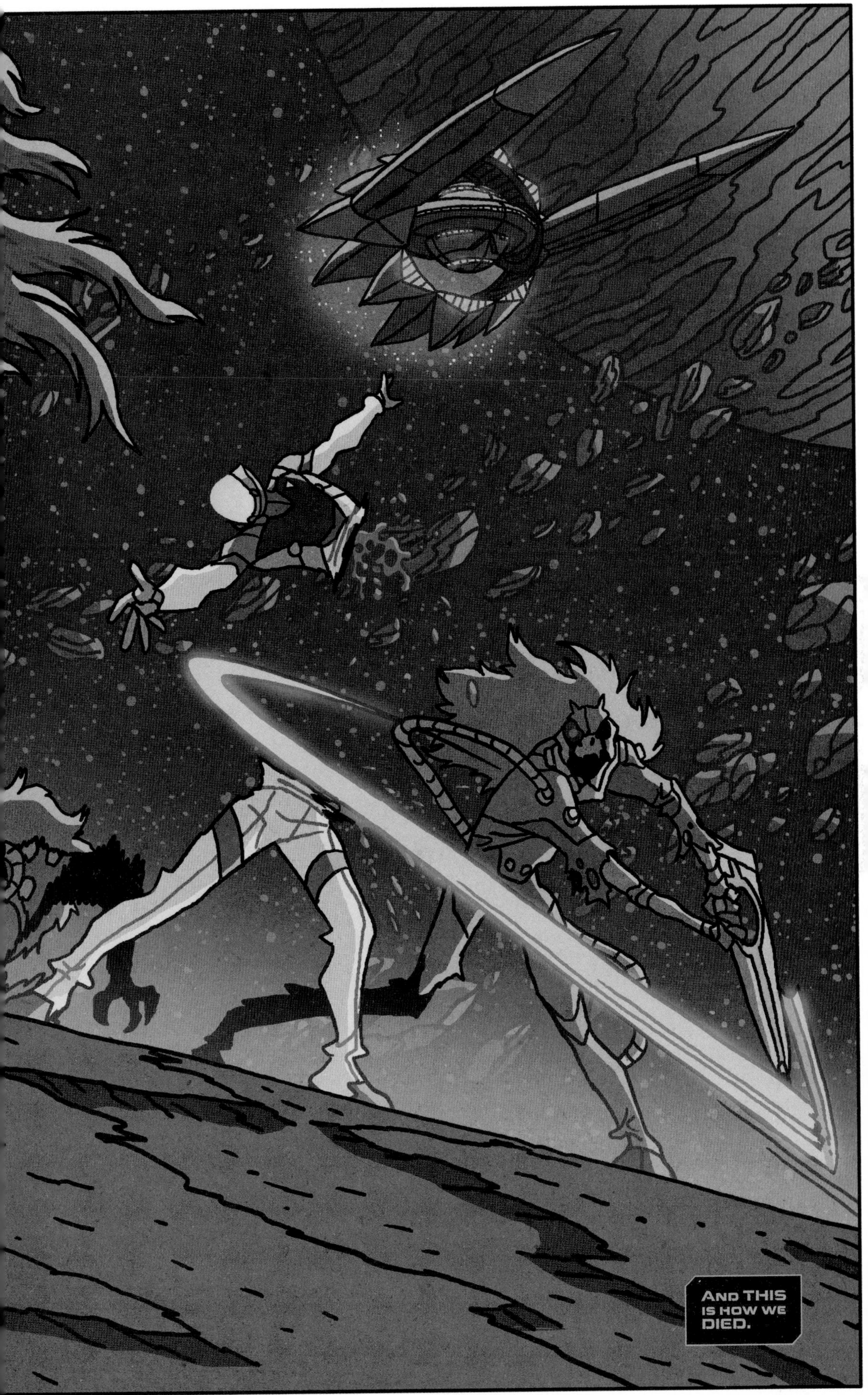
AND THIS IS HOW WE DIED.

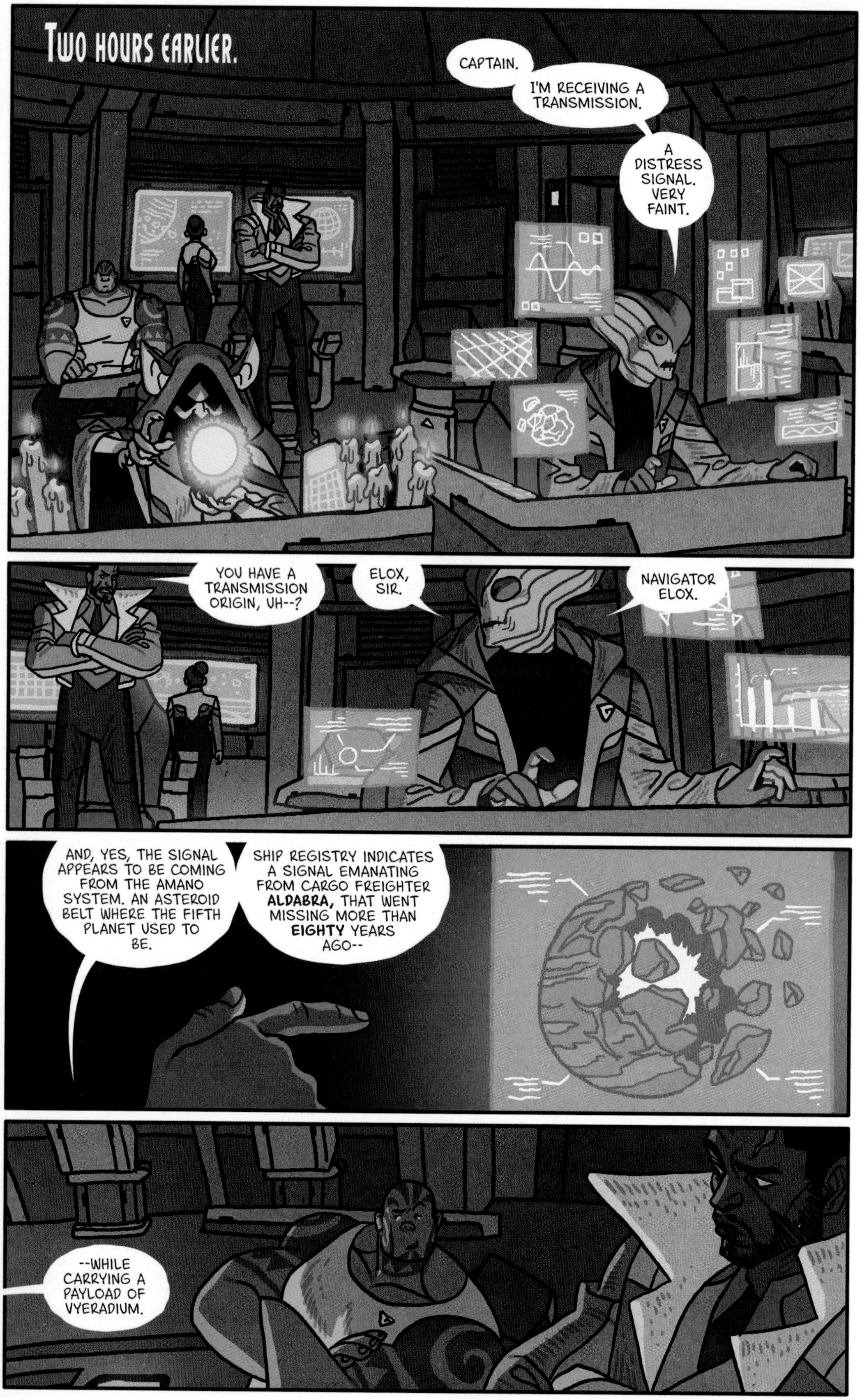
TWO HOURS EARLIER.
CAPTAIN.
I'M RECEIVING A TRANSMISSION.
A DISTRESS SIGNAL. VERY FAINT.
YOU HAVE A TRANSMISSION ORIGIN, UH--?
ELOX, SIR.
NAVIGATOR ELOX.
AND, YES, THE SIGNAL APPEARS TO BE COMING FROM THE AMANO SYSTEM. AN ASTEROID BELT WHERE THE FIFTH PLANET USED TO BE.
SHIP REGISTRY INDICATES A SIGNAL EMANATING FROM CARGO FREIGHTER **ALDABRA,** THAT WENT MISSING MORE THAN **EIGHTY** YEARS AGO--
--WHILE CARRYING A PAYLOAD OF VYERADIUM.

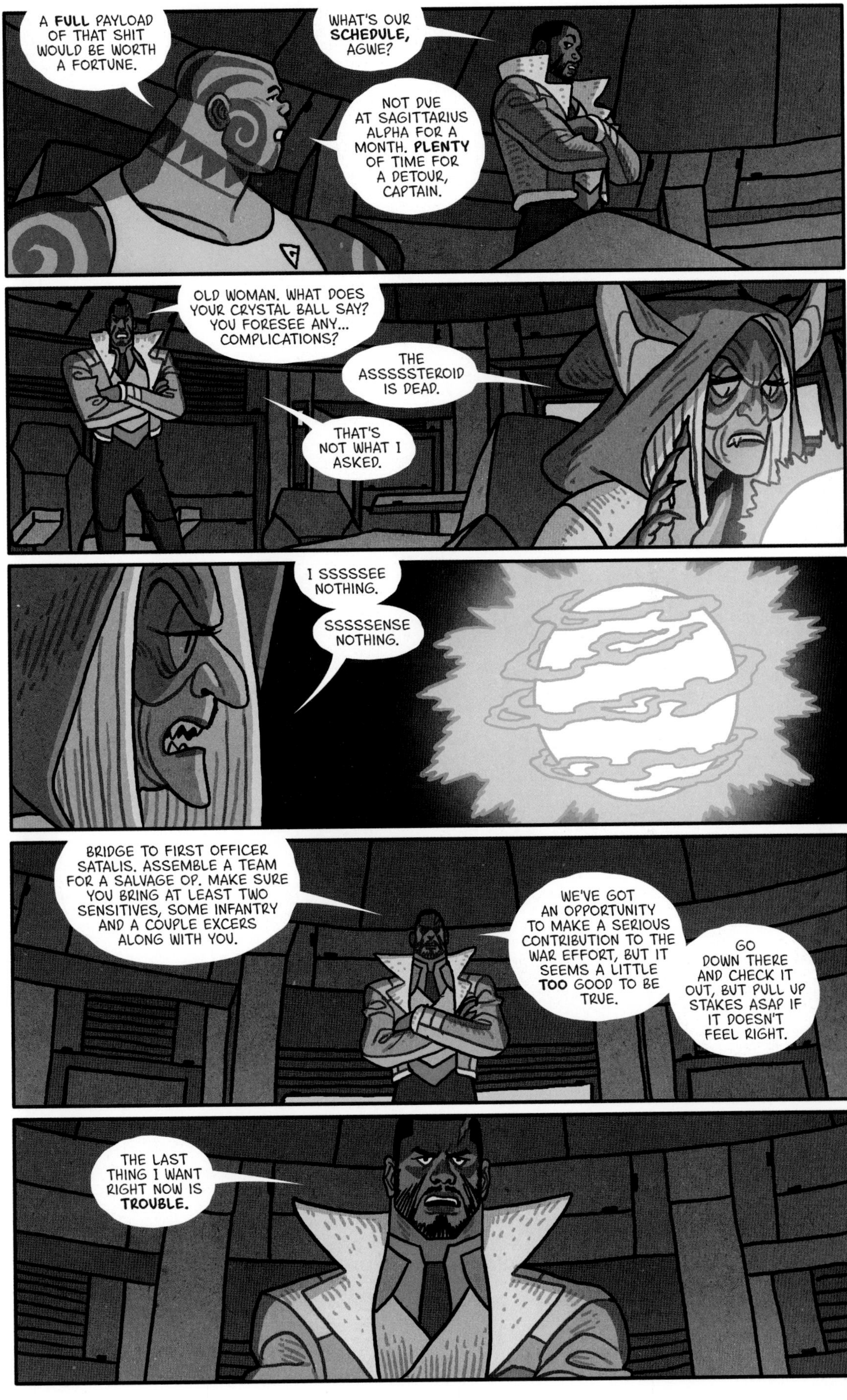
A FULL PAYLOAD OF THAT SHIT WOULD BE WORTH A FORTUNE.
WHAT'S OUR SCHEDULE, AGWE?
NOT DUE AT SAGITTARIUS ALPHA FOR A MONTH. PLENTY OF TIME FOR A DETOUR, CAPTAIN.
OLD WOMAN. WHAT DOES YOUR CRYSTAL BALL SAY? YOU FORESEE ANY... COMPLICATIONS?
THE ASSSSSTEROID IS DEAD.
THAT'S NOT WHAT I ASKED.
I SSSSSEE NOTHING.
SSSSSENSE NOTHING.
BRIDGE TO FIRST OFFICER SATALIS. ASSEMBLE A TEAM FOR A SALVAGE OP. MAKE SURE YOU BRING AT LEAST TWO SENSITIVES, SOME INFANTRY AND A COUPLE EXCERS ALONG WITH YOU.
WE'VE GOT AN OPPORTUNITY TO MAKE A SERIOUS CONTRIBUTION TO THE WAR EFFORT, BUT IT SEEMS A LITTLE TOO GOOD TO BE TRUE.
GO DOWN THERE AND CHECK IT OUT, BUT PULL UP STAKES ASAP IF IT DOESN'T FEEL RIGHT.
THE LAST THING I WANT RIGHT NOW IS TROUBLE.

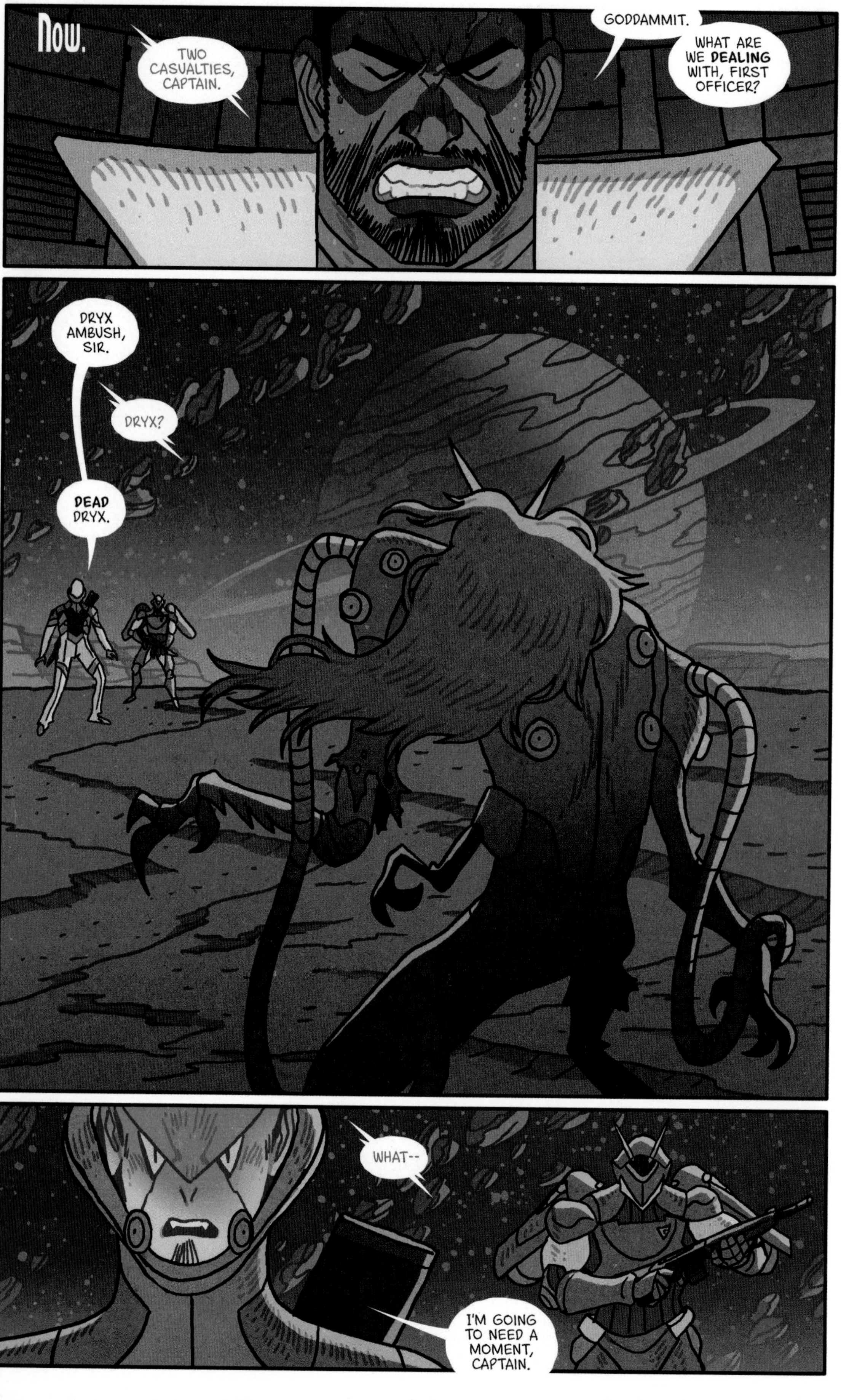
Now.
TWO CASUALTIES, CAPTAIN.
GODDAMMIT.
WHAT ARE WE **DEALING** WITH, FIRST OFFICER?
DRYX AMBUSH, SIR.
DRYX?
DEAD DRYX.
WHAT--
I'M GOING TO NEED A MOMENT, CAPTAIN.

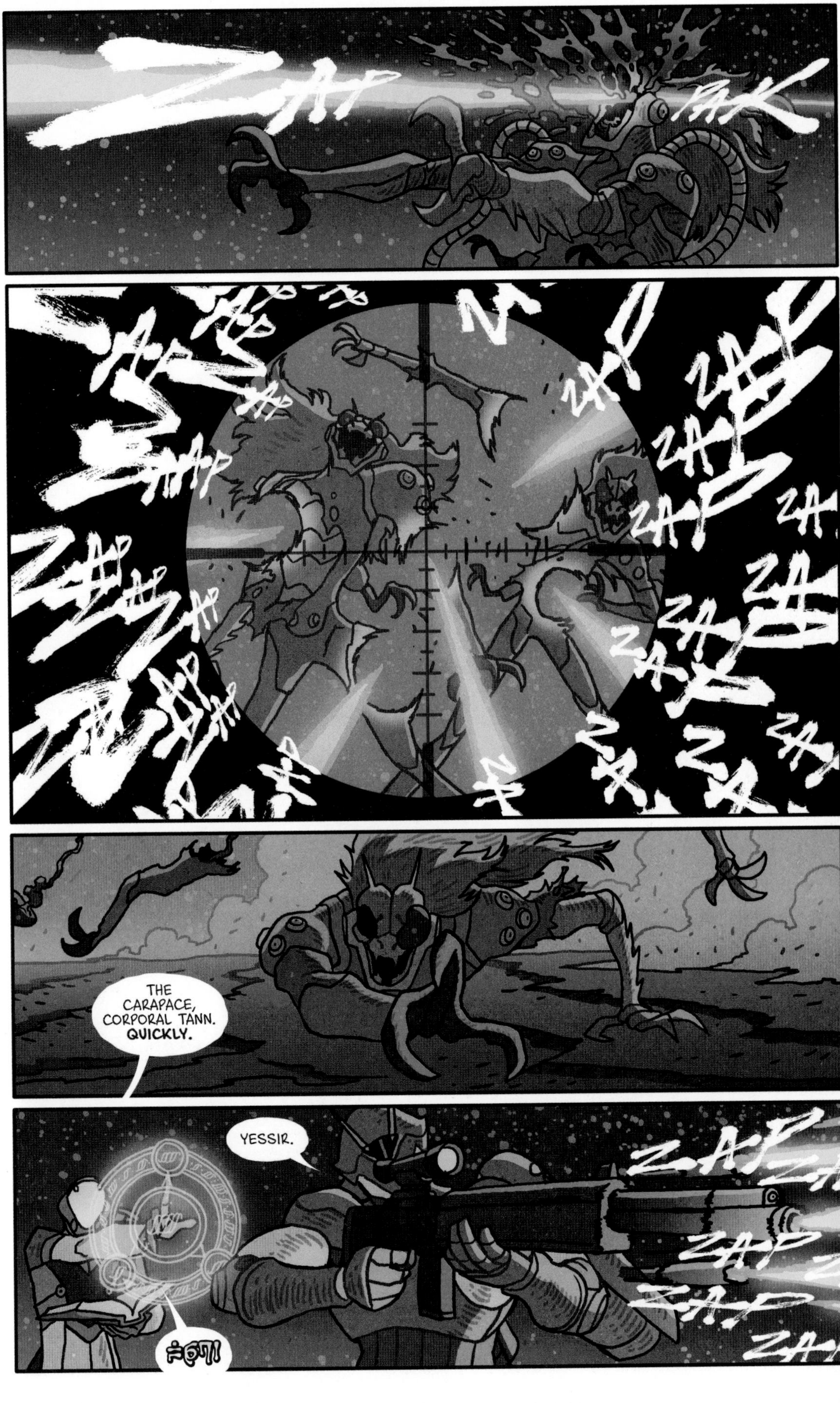
ZAP
PAK
ZAP
ZAP
ZAP
ZAP
THE CARAPACE, CORPORAL TANN. **QUICKLY.**
YESSIR.
ZAP
ZAP
ZAP

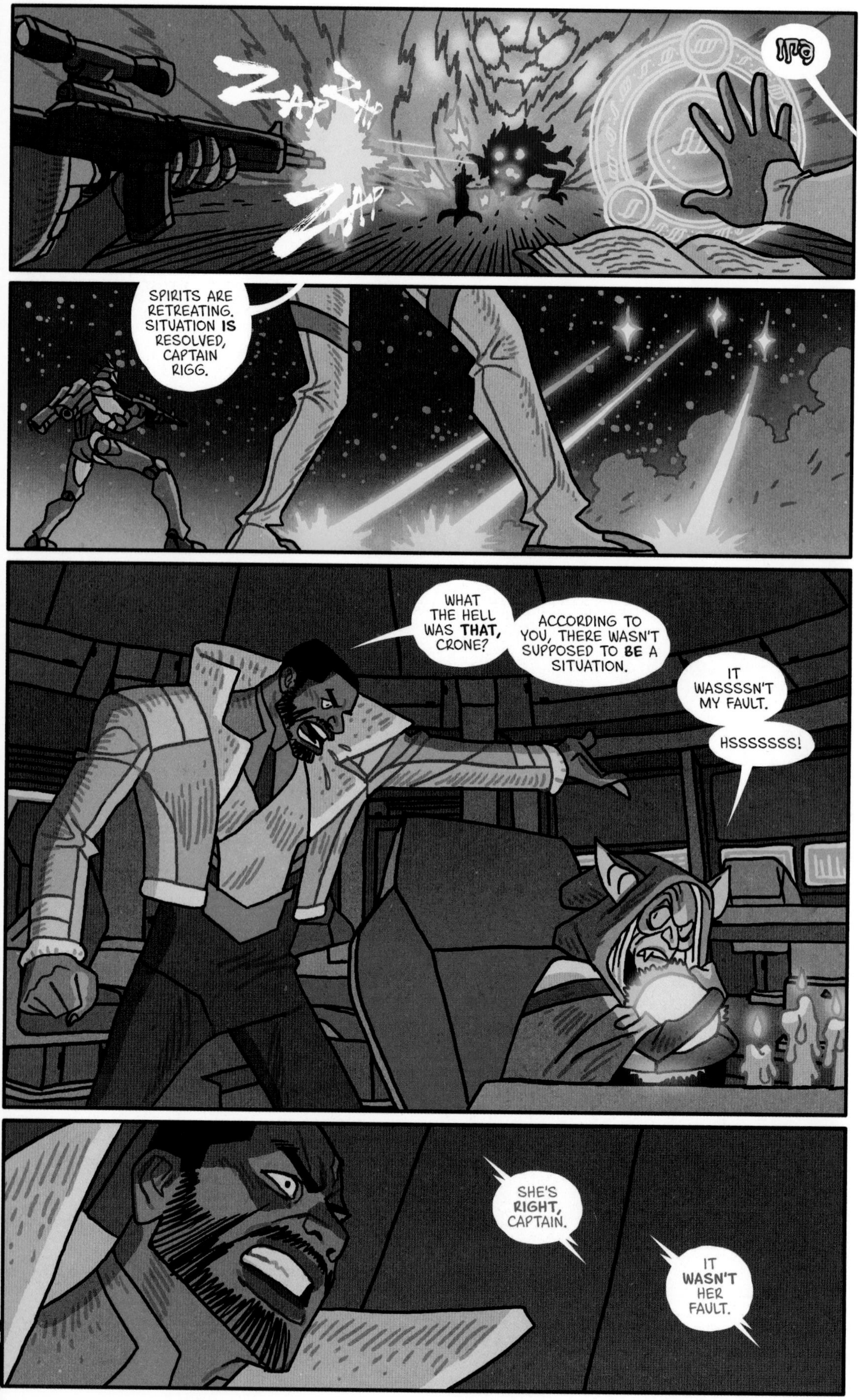
ZAP ZAP
ZAP ZAP
SPIRITS ARE RETREATING. SITUATION IS RESOLVED, CAPTAIN RIGG.
WHAT THE HELL WAS THAT, CRONE?
ACCORDING TO YOU, THERE WASN'T SUPPOSED TO BE A SITUATION.
IT WASSSSN'T MY FAULT.
HSSSSSSS!
SHE'S RIGHT, CAPTAIN.
IT WASN'T HER FAULT.

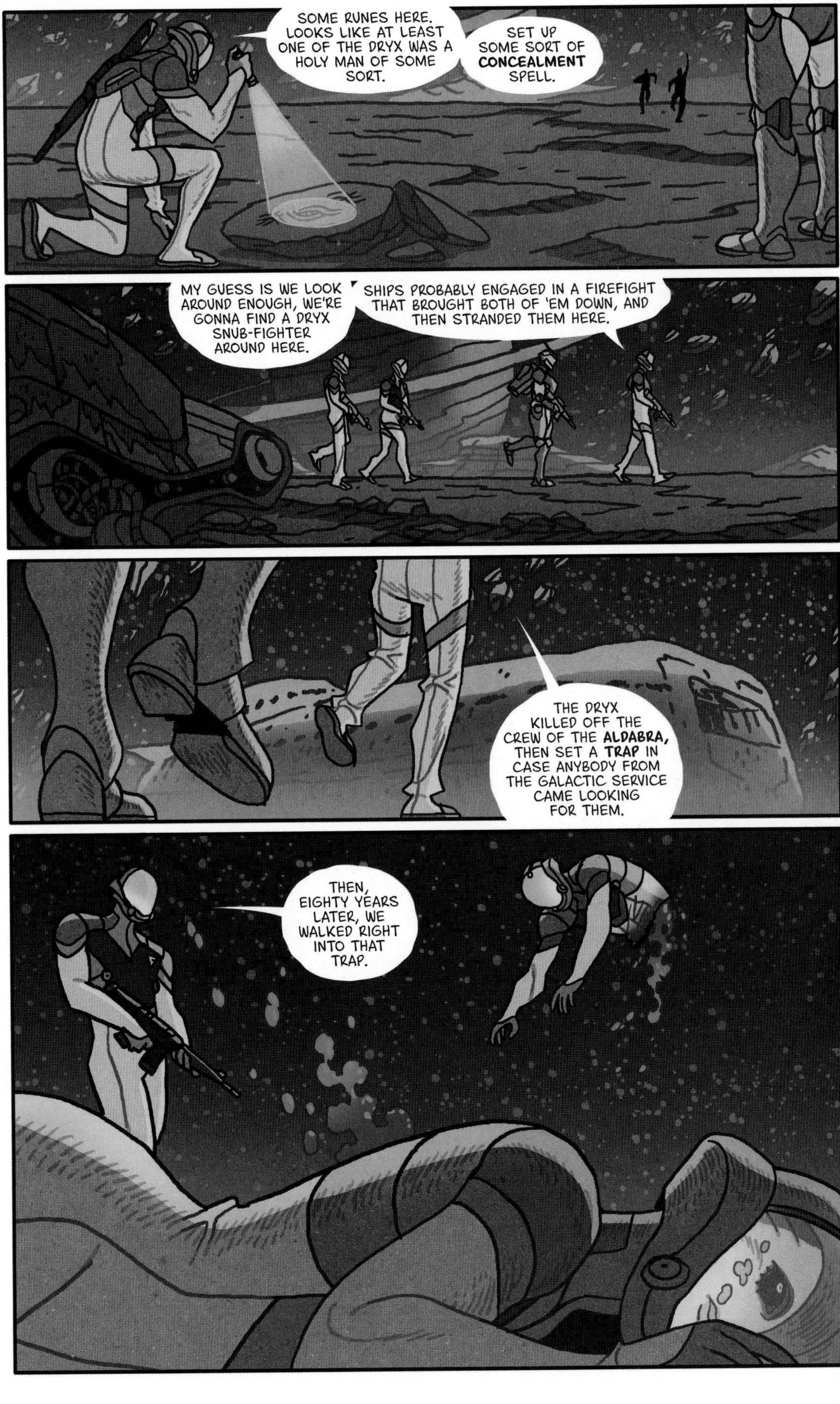
SOME RUNES HERE. LOOKS LIKE AT LEAST ONE OF THE DRYX WAS A HOLY MAN OF SOME SORT.
SET UP SOME SORT OF **CONCEALMENT** SPELL.
MY GUESS IS WE LOOK AROUND ENOUGH, WE'RE GONNA FIND A DRYX SNUB-FIGHTER AROUND HERE.
SHIPS PROBABLY ENGAGED IN A FIREFIGHT THAT BROUGHT BOTH OF 'EM DOWN, AND THEN STRANDED THEM HERE.
THE DRYX KILLED OFF THE CREW OF THE **ALDABRA,** THEN SET A **TRAP** IN CASE ANYBODY FROM THE GALACTIC SERVICE CAME LOOKING FOR THEM.
THEN, EIGHTY YEARS LATER, WE WALKED RIGHT INTO THAT TRAP.

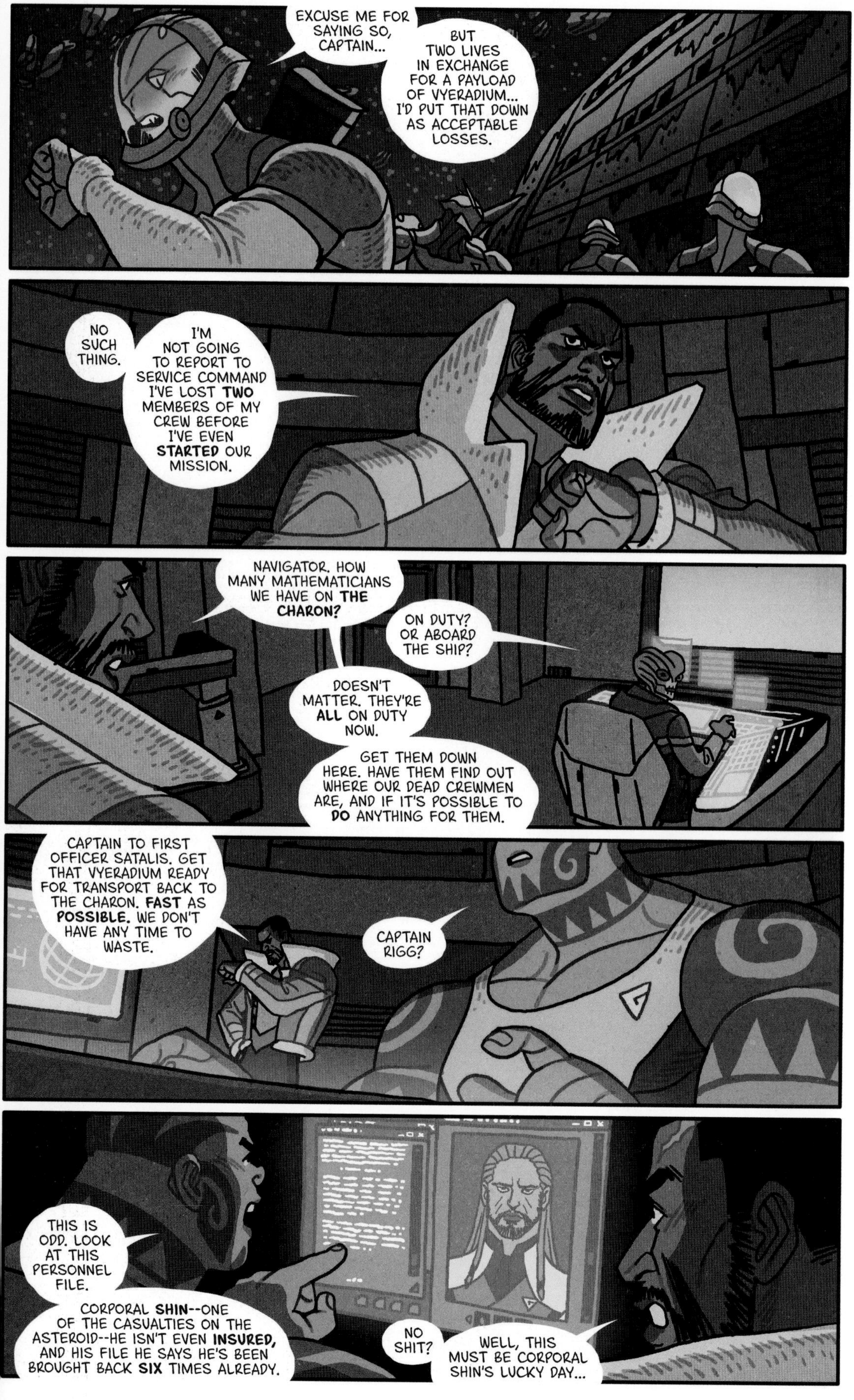

EXCUSE ME FOR SAYING SO, CAPTAIN...
BUT TWO LIVES IN EXCHANGE FOR A PAYLOAD OF VYERADIUM... I'D PUT THAT DOWN AS ACCEPTABLE LOSSES.
NO SUCH THING.
I'M NOT GOING TO REPORT TO SERVICE COMMAND I'VE LOST **TWO** MEMBERS OF MY CREW BEFORE I'VE EVEN **STARTED** OUR MISSION.
NAVIGATOR. HOW MANY MATHEMATICIANS WE HAVE ON **THE CHARON?**
ON DUTY? OR ABOARD THE SHIP?
DOESN'T MATTER. THEY'RE **ALL** ON DUTY NOW.
GET THEM DOWN HERE. HAVE THEM FIND OUT WHERE OUR DEAD CREWMEN ARE, AND IF IT'S POSSIBLE TO **DO** ANYTHING FOR THEM.
CAPTAIN TO FIRST OFFICER SATALIS. GET THAT VYERADIUM READY FOR TRANSPORT BACK TO THE CHARON. **FAST** AS **POSSIBLE.** WE DON'T HAVE ANY TIME TO WASTE.
CAPTAIN RIGG?
THIS IS ODD. LOOK AT THIS PERSONNEL FILE.
CORPORAL **SHIN**--ONE OF THE CASUALTIES ON THE ASTEROID--HE ISN'T EVEN **INSURED,** AND HIS FILE HE SAYS HE'S BEEN BROUGHT BACK **SIX** TIMES ALREADY.
NO SHIT?
WELL, THIS MUST BE CORPORAL SHIN'S LUCKY DAY...

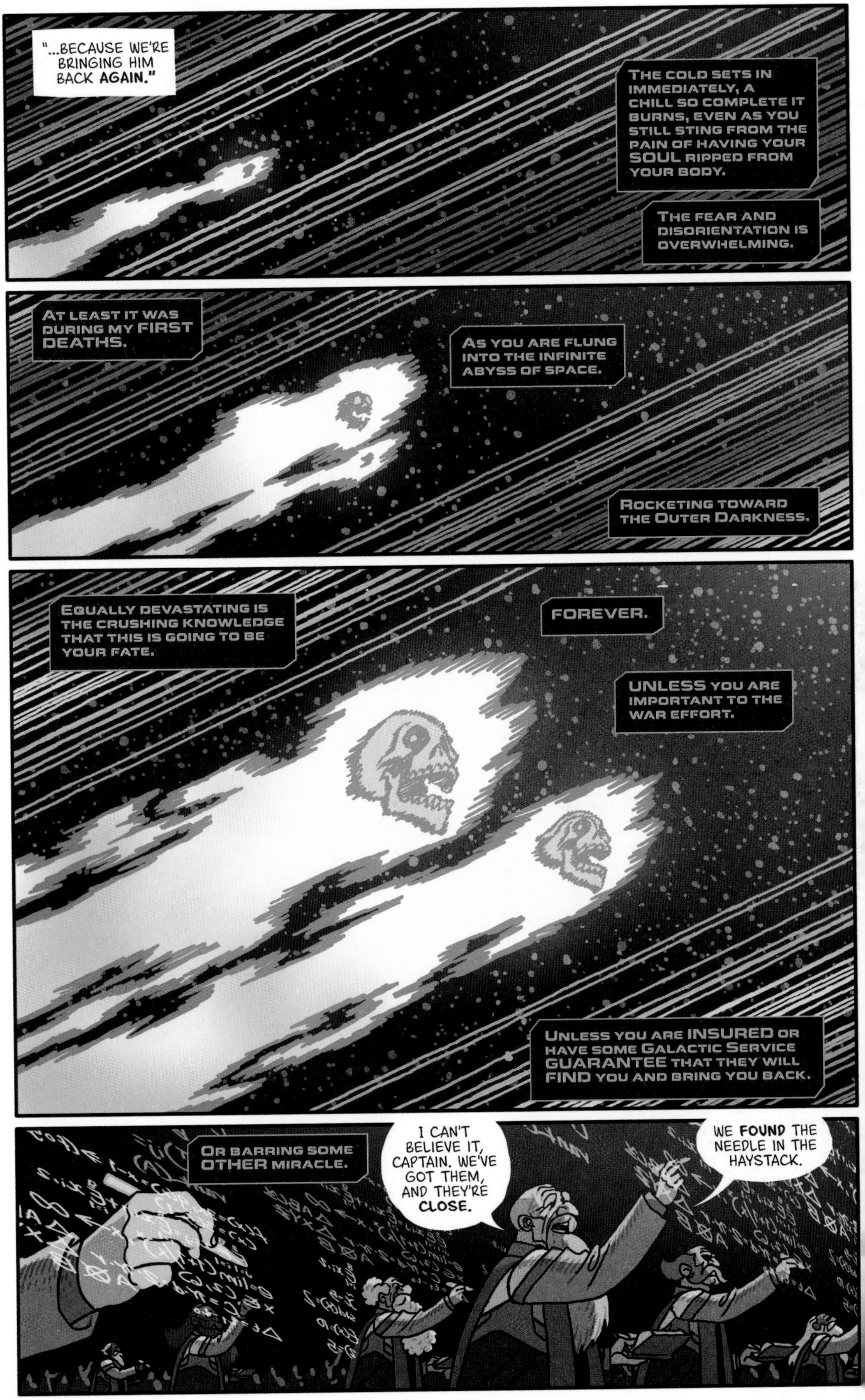
"...BECAUSE WE'RE BRINGING HIM BACK AGAIN."
THE COLD SETS IN IMMEDIATELY, A CHILL SO COMPLETE IT BURNS, EVEN AS YOU STILL STING FROM THE PAIN OF HAVING YOUR SOUL RIPPED FROM YOUR BODY.
THE FEAR AND DISORIENTATION IS OVERWHELMING.
AT LEAST IT WAS DURING MY FIRST DEATHS.
AS YOU ARE FLUNG INTO THE INFINITE ABYSS OF SPACE.
ROCKETING TOWARD THE OUTER DARKNESS.
EQUALLY DEVASTATING IS THE CRUSHING KNOWLEDGE THAT THIS IS GOING TO BE YOUR FATE.
FOREVER.
UNLESS YOU ARE IMPORTANT TO THE WAR EFFORT.
UNLESS YOU ARE INSURED OR HAVE SOME GALACTIC SERVICE GUARANTEE THAT THEY WILL FIND YOU AND BRING YOU BACK.
OR BARRING SOME OTHER MIRACLE.
I CAN'T BELIEVE IT, CAPTAIN. WE'VE GOT THEM, AND THEY'RE CLOSE.
WE FOUND THE NEEDLE IN THE HAYSTACK.

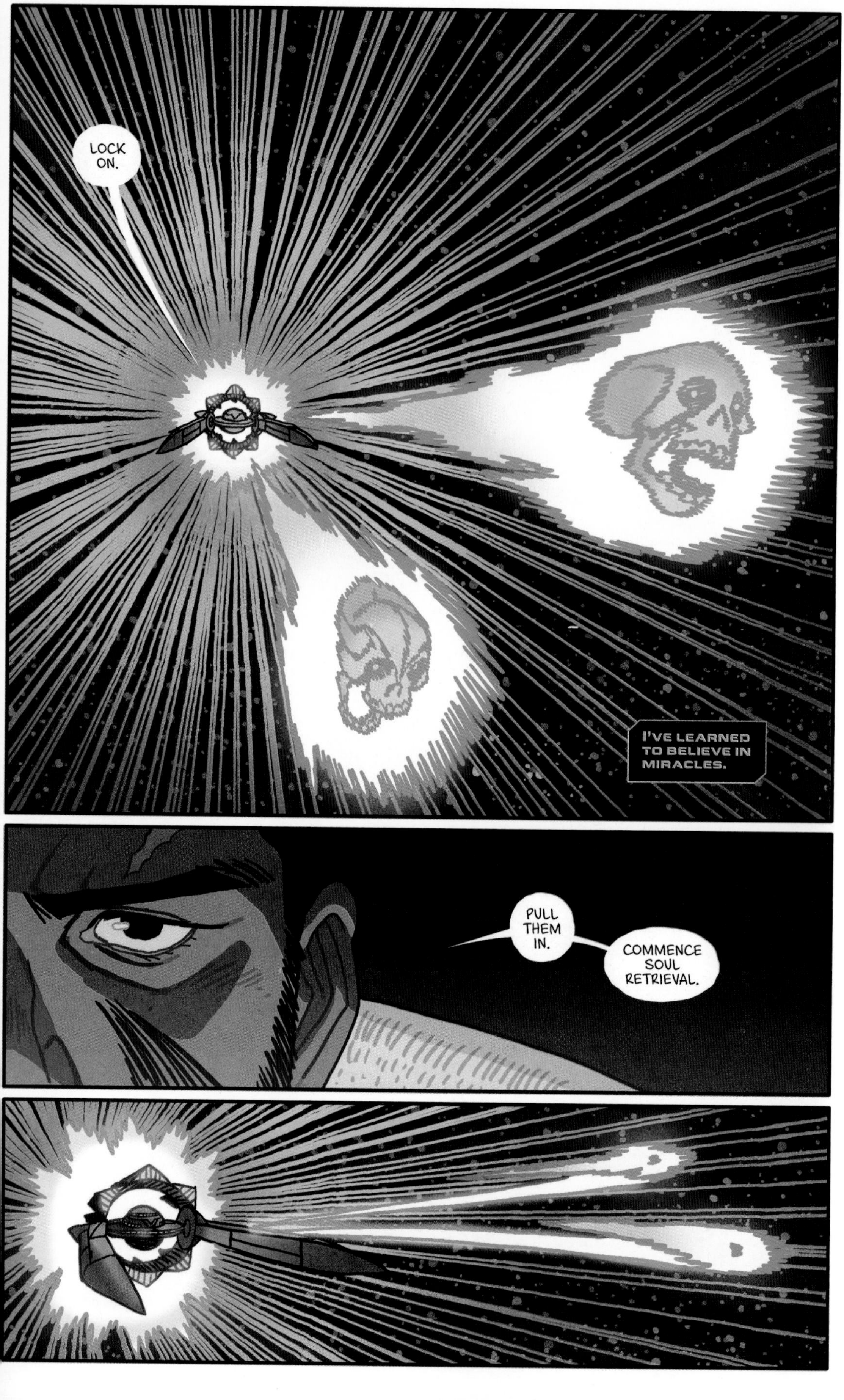
LOCK ON.
I'VE LEARNED TO BELIEVE IN MIRACLES.
PULL THEM IN.
COMMENCE SOUL RETRIEVAL.

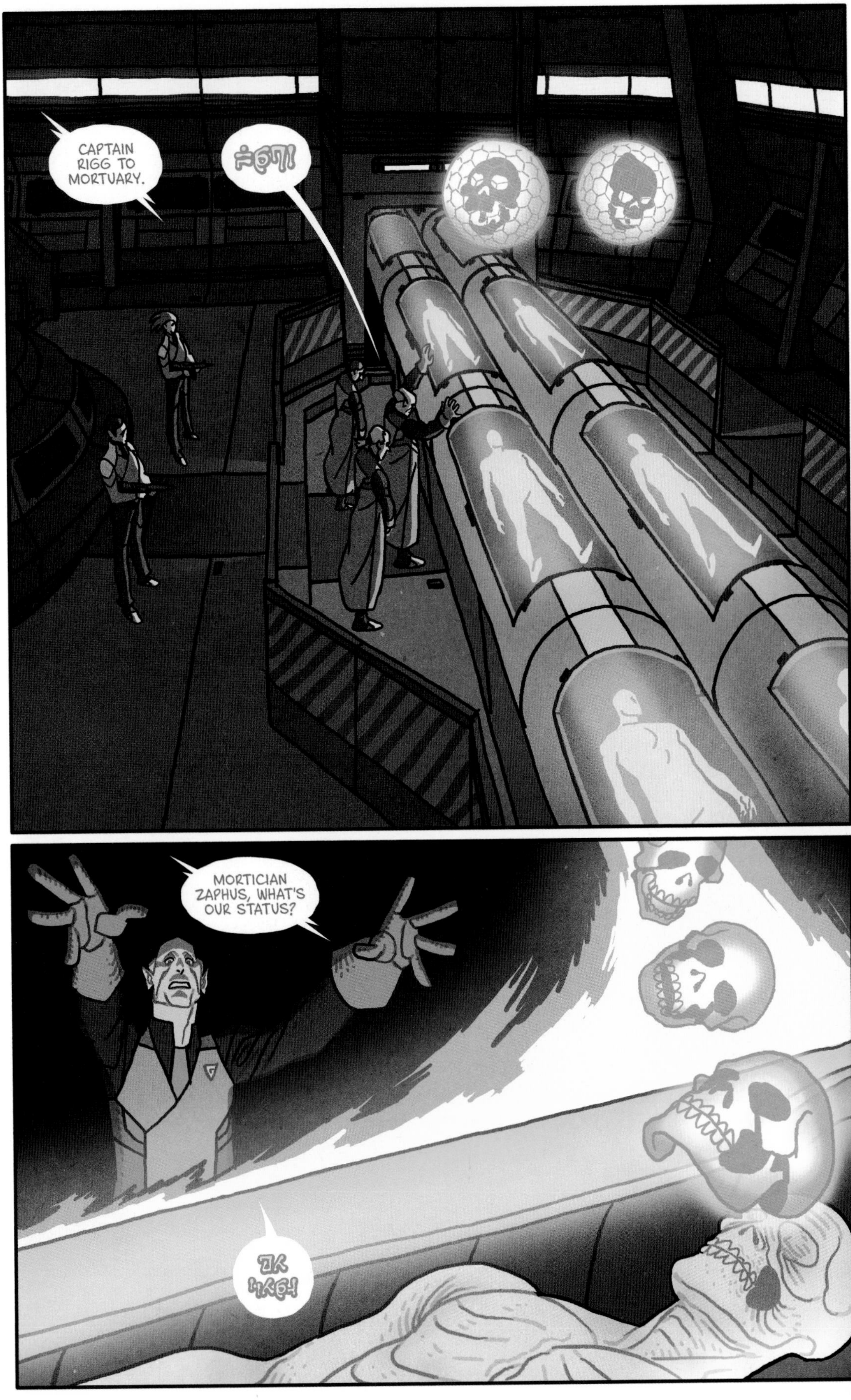
CAPTAIN RIGG TO MORTUARY.
MORTICIAN ZAPHUS, WHAT'S OUR STATUS?

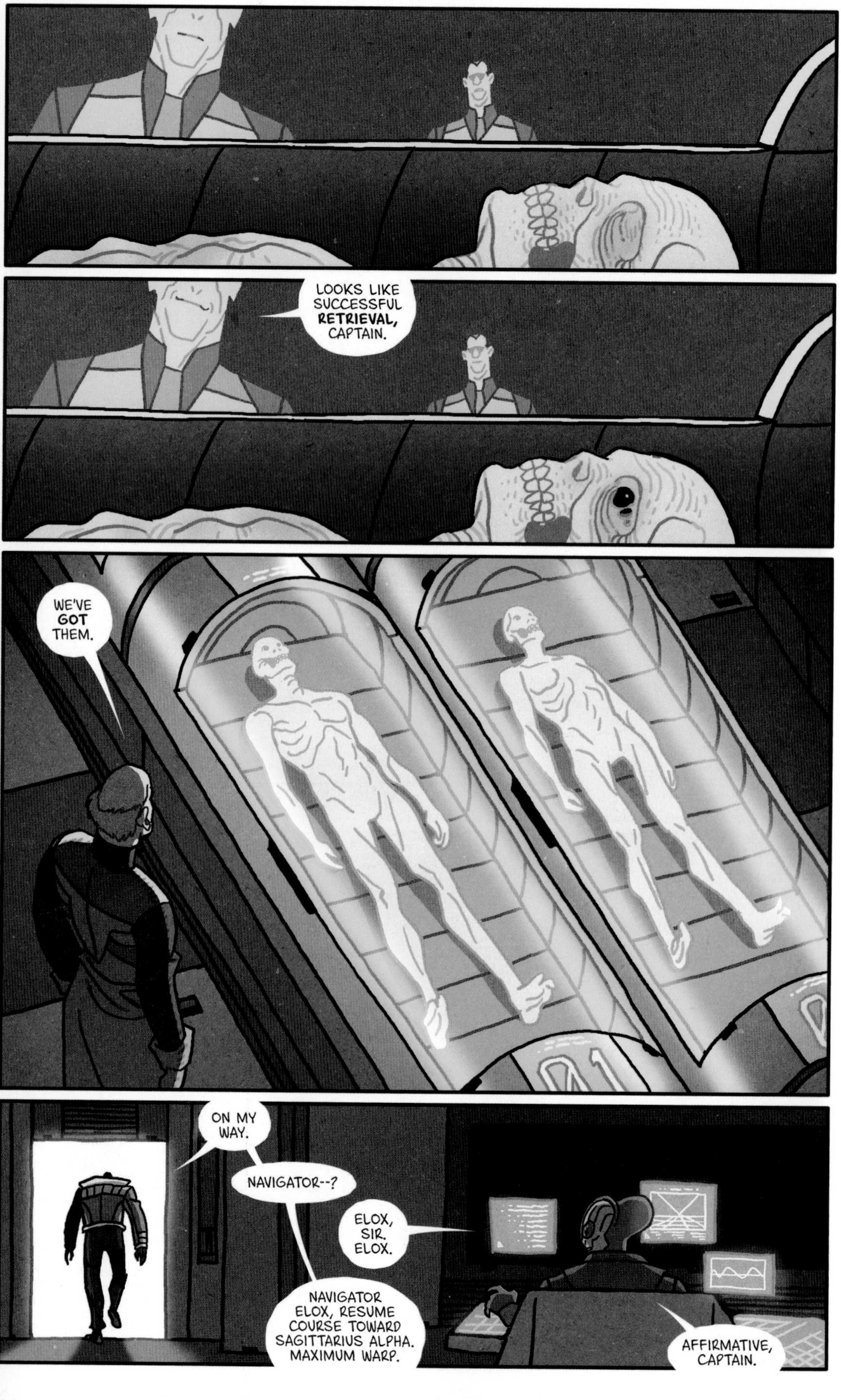
LOOKS LIKE SUCCESSFUL **RETRIEVAL,** CAPTAIN.
WE'VE **GOT** THEM.
01
ON MY WAY.
NAVIGATOR--?
ELOX, SIR. ELOX.
NAVIGATOR ELOX, RESUME COURSE TOWARD SAGITTARIUS ALPHA. MAXIMUM WARP.
AFFIRMATIVE, CAPTAIN.

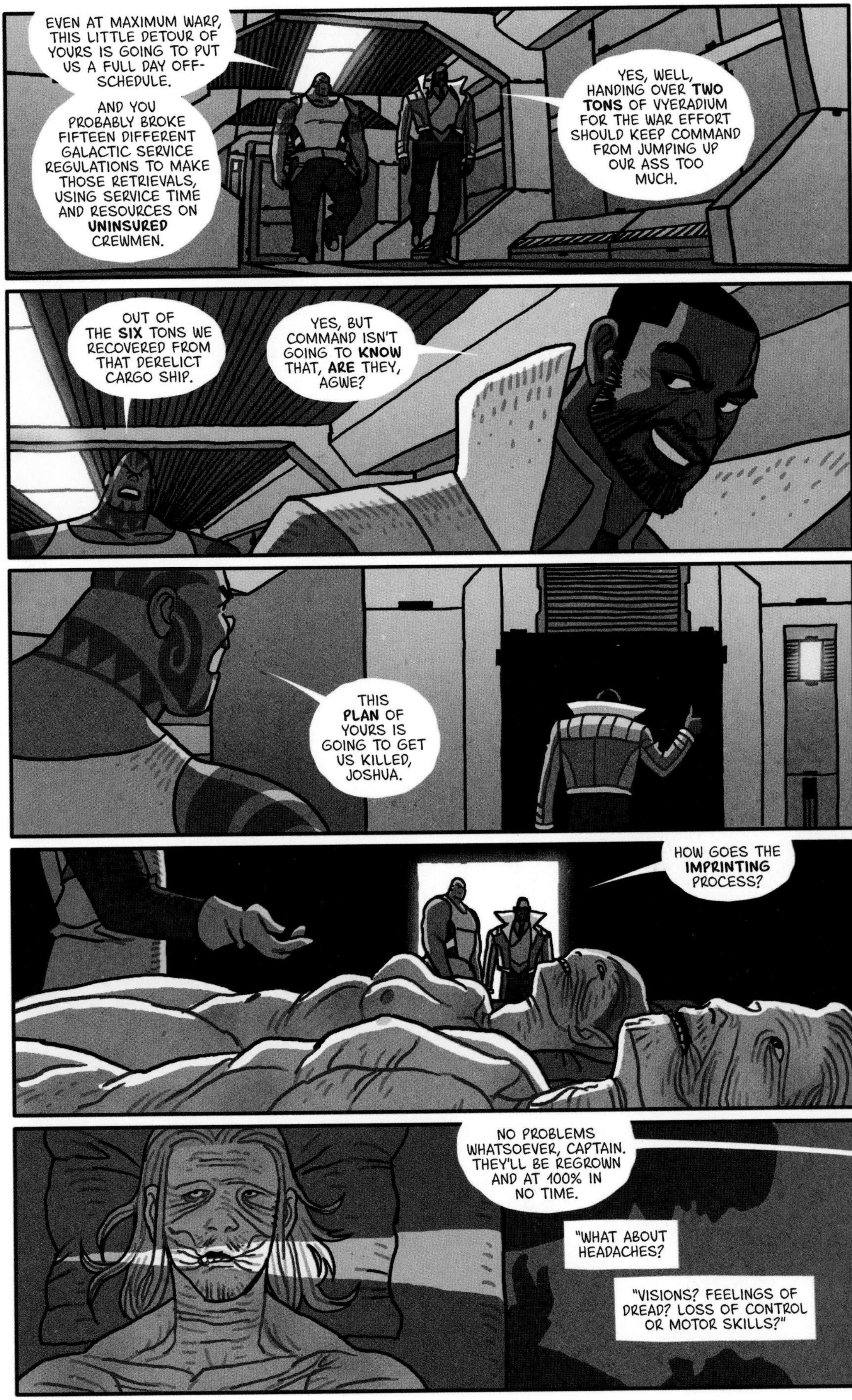

EVEN AT MAXIMUM WARP, THIS LITTLE DETOUR OF YOURS IS GOING TO PUT US A FULL DAY OFF-SCHEDULE.
AND YOU PROBABLY BROKE FIFTEEN DIFFERENT GALACTIC SERVICE REGULATIONS TO MAKE THOSE RETRIEVALS, USING SERVICE TIME AND RESOURCES ON **UNINSURED** CREWMEN.
YES, WELL, HANDING OVER **TWO TONS** OF VYERADIUM FOR THE WAR EFFORT SHOULD KEEP COMMAND FROM JUMPING UP OUR ASS TOO MUCH.
OUT OF THE **SIX** TONS WE RECOVERED FROM THAT DERELICT CARGO SHIP.
YES, BUT COMMAND ISN'T GOING TO **KNOW** THAT, **ARE** THEY, AGWE?
THIS **PLAN** OF YOURS IS GOING TO GET US KILLED, JOSHUA.
HOW GOES THE **IMPRINTING** PROCESS?
NO PROBLEMS WHATSOEVER, CAPTAIN. THEY'LL BE REGROWN AND AT 100% IN NO TIME.
"WHAT ABOUT HEADACHES?
"VISIONS? FEELINGS OF DREAD? LOSS OF CONTROL OR MOTOR SKILLS?"

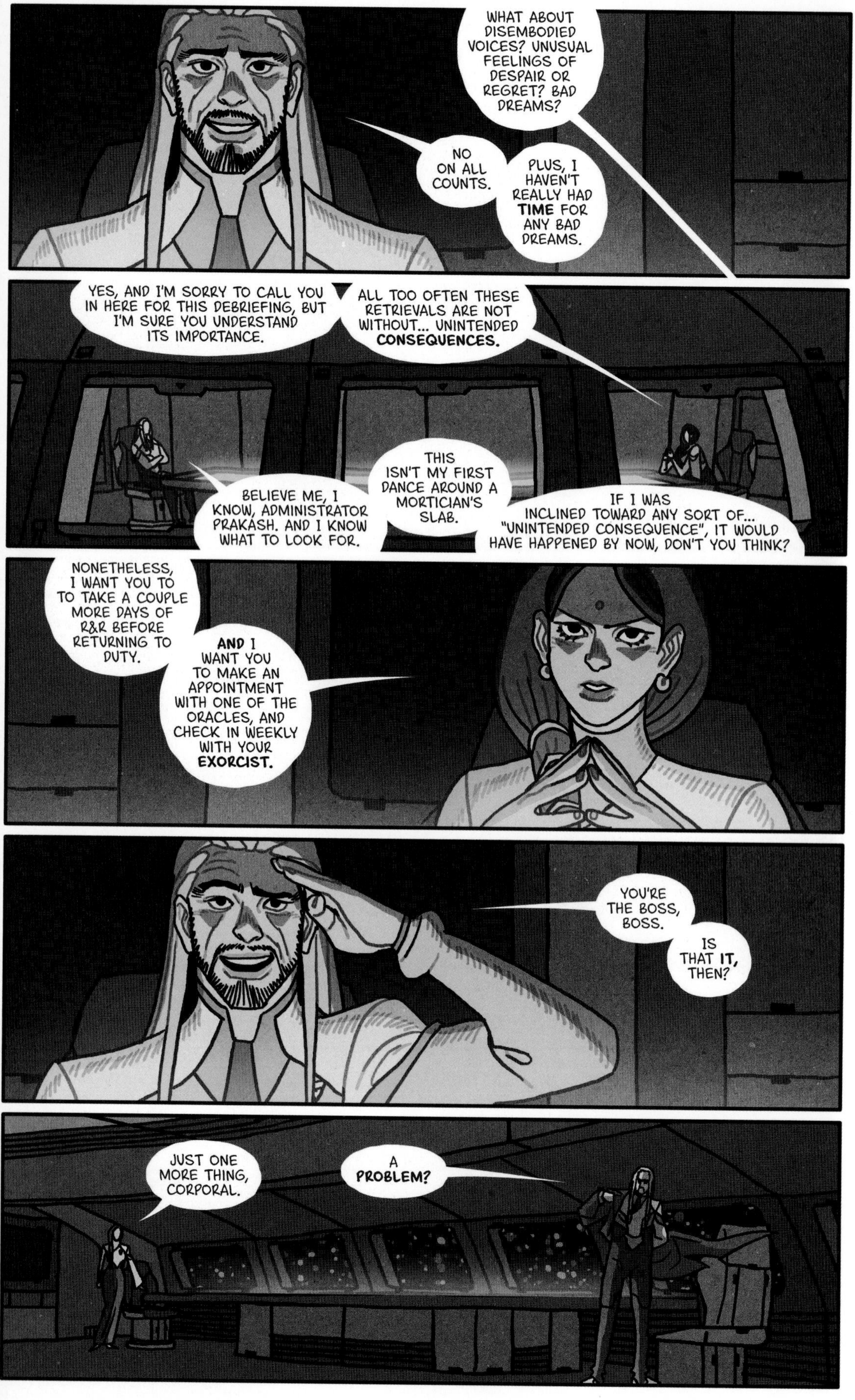
WHAT ABOUT DISEMBODIED VOICES? UNUSUAL FEELINGS OF DESPAIR OR REGRET? BAD DREAMS?
NO ON ALL COUNTS.
PLUS, I HAVEN'T REALLY HAD **TIME** FOR ANY BAD DREAMS.
YES, AND I'M SORRY TO CALL YOU IN HERE FOR THIS DEBRIEFING, BUT I'M SURE YOU UNDERSTAND ITS IMPORTANCE.
ALL TOO OFTEN THESE RETRIEVALS ARE NOT WITHOUT... UNINTENDED **CONSEQUENCES.**
BELIEVE ME, I KNOW, ADMINISTRATOR PRAKASH. AND I KNOW WHAT TO LOOK FOR.
THIS ISN'T MY FIRST DANCE AROUND A MORTICIAN'S SLAB.
IF I WAS INCLINED TOWARD ANY SORT OF... "UNINTENDED CONSEQUENCE", IT WOULD HAVE HAPPENED BY NOW, DON'T YOU THINK?
NONETHELESS, I WANT YOU TO TO TAKE A COUPLE MORE DAYS OF R&R BEFORE RETURNING TO DUTY.
AND I WANT YOU TO MAKE AN APPOINTMENT WITH ONE OF THE ORACLES, AND CHECK IN WEEKLY WITH YOUR **EXORCIST.**
YOU'RE THE BOSS, BOSS.
IS THAT **IT,** THEN?
JUST ONE MORE THING, CORPORAL.
A **PROBLEM?**

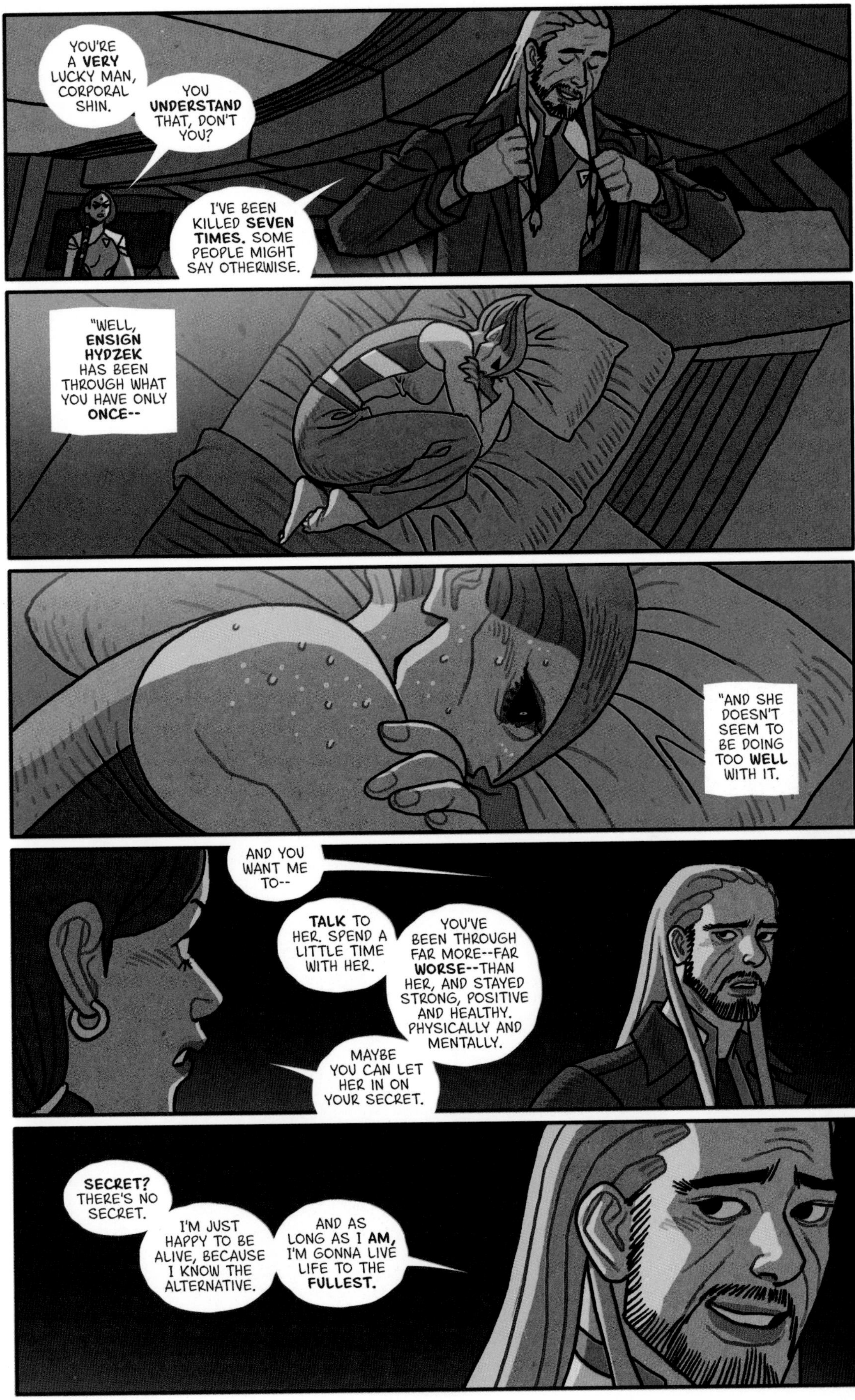
YOU'RE A VERY LUCKY MAN, CORPORAL SHIN.
YOU UNDERSTAND THAT, DON'T YOU?
I'VE BEEN KILLED SEVEN TIMES. SOME PEOPLE MIGHT SAY OTHERWISE.
"WELL, ENSIGN HYDZEK HAS BEEN THROUGH WHAT YOU HAVE ONLY ONCE--
"AND SHE DOESN'T SEEM TO BE DOING TOO WELL WITH IT.
AND YOU WANT ME TO--
TALK TO HER. SPEND A LITTLE TIME WITH HER.
YOU'VE BEEN THROUGH FAR MORE--FAR WORSE--THAN HER, AND STAYED STRONG, POSITIVE AND HEALTHY. PHYSICALLY AND MENTALLY.
MAYBE YOU CAN LET HER IN ON YOUR SECRET.
SECRET? THERE'S NO SECRET.
I'M JUST HAPPY TO BE ALIVE, BECAUSE I KNOW THE ALTERNATIVE.
AND AS LONG AS I AM, I'M GONNA LIVE LIFE TO THE FULLEST.

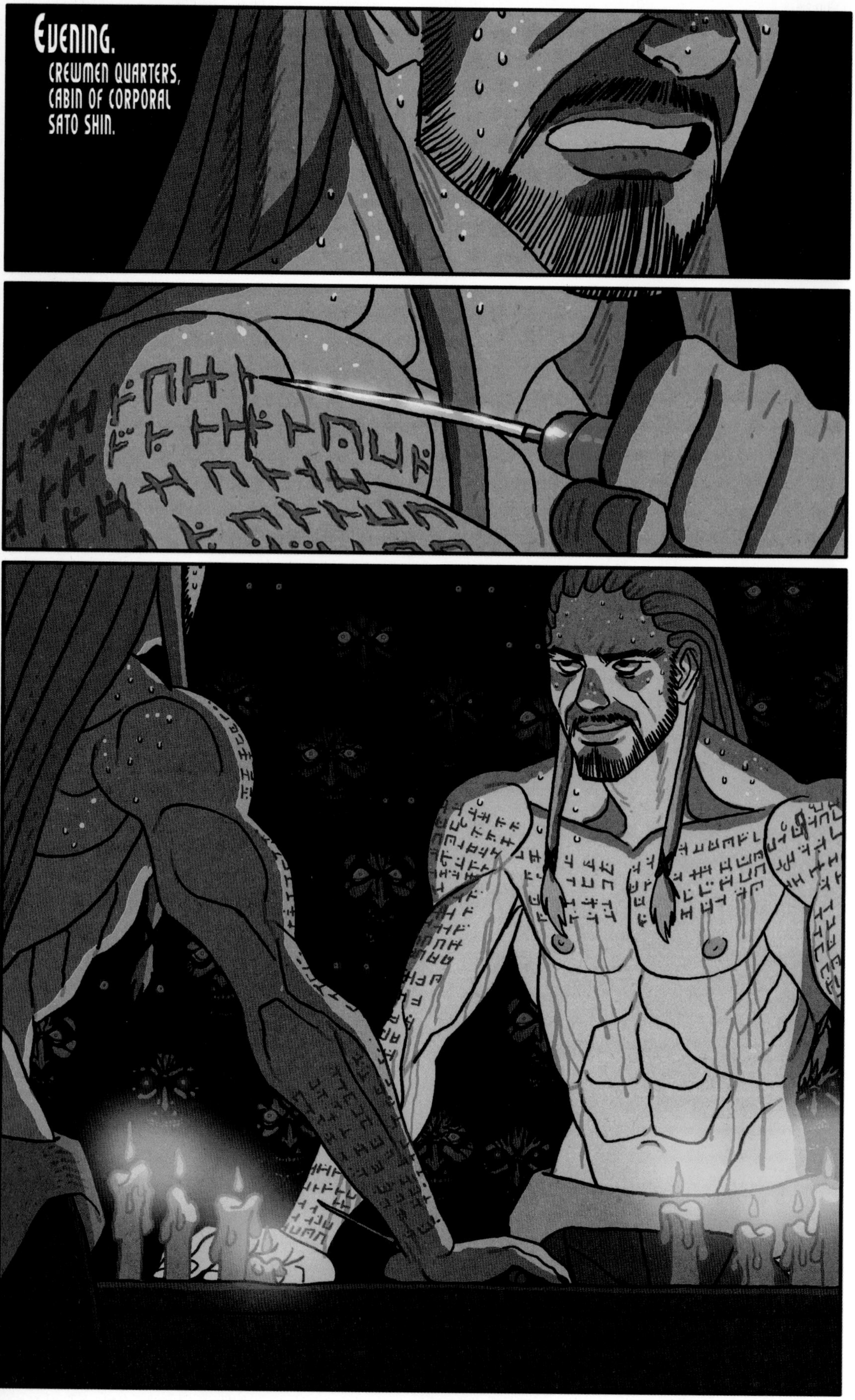
EVENING.
CREWMEN QUARTERS,
CABIN OF CORPORAL
SATO SHIN.

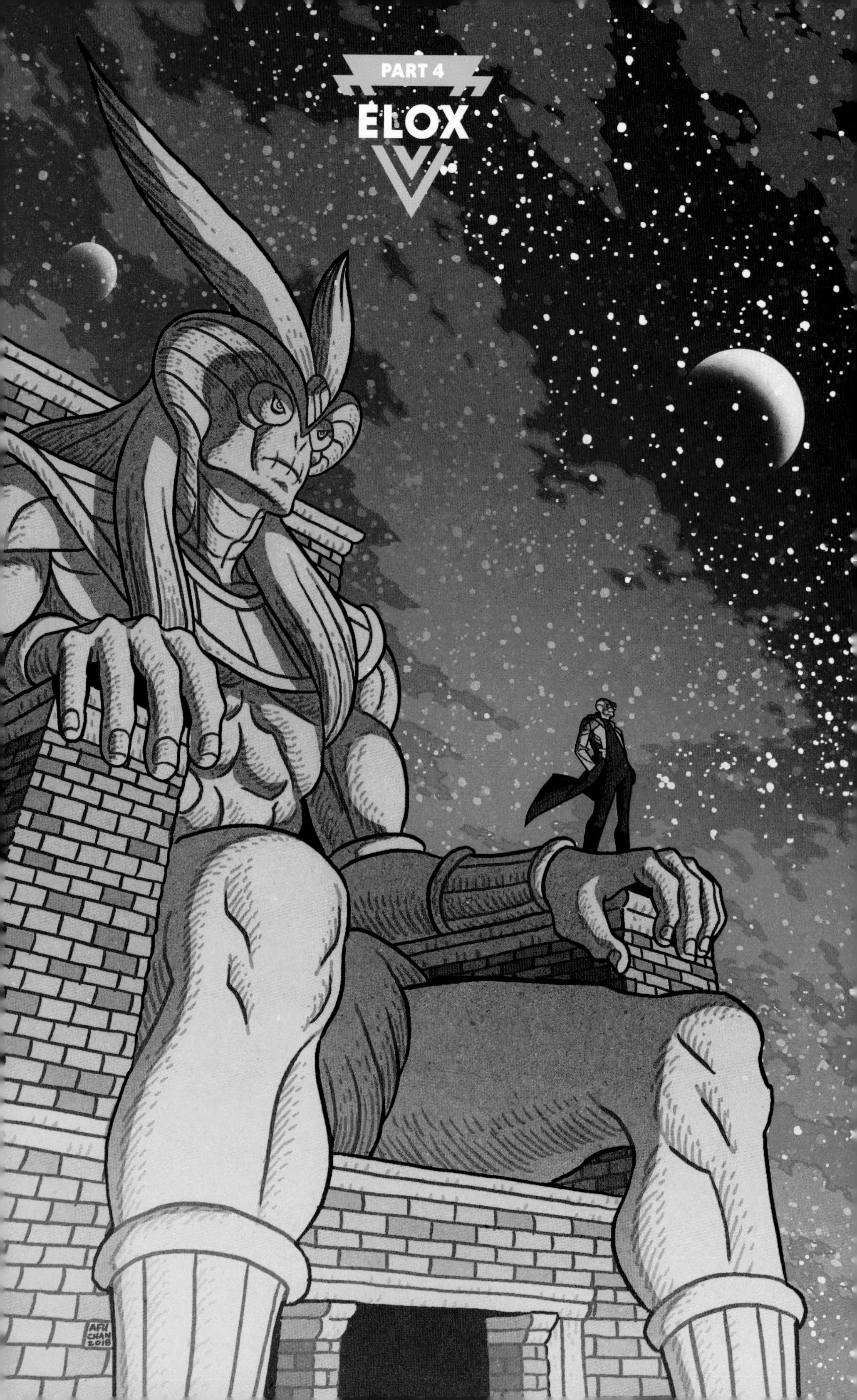
PART 4
ELOX
AFU CHAN 2018

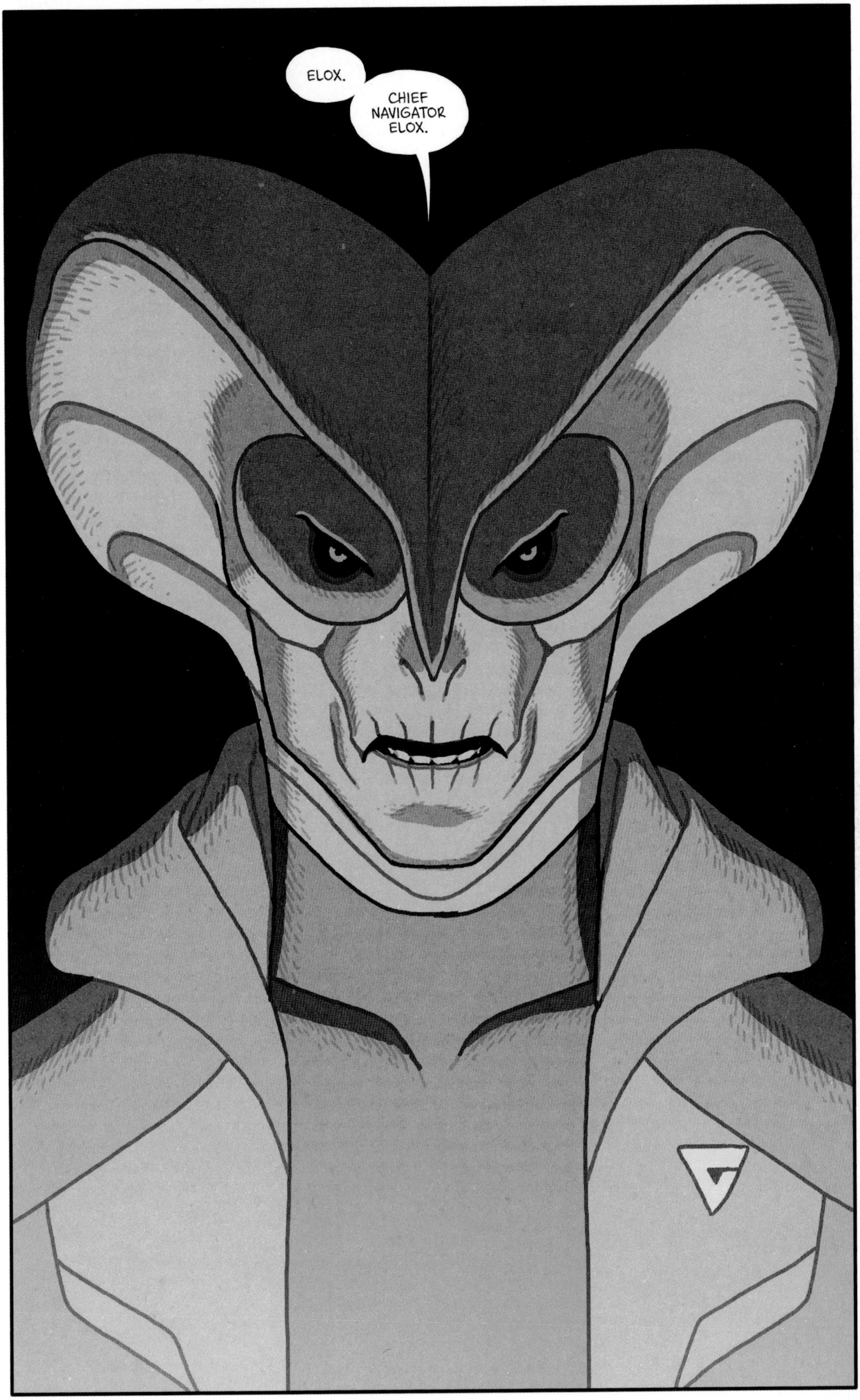
ELOX.
CHIEF NAVIGATOR ELOX.

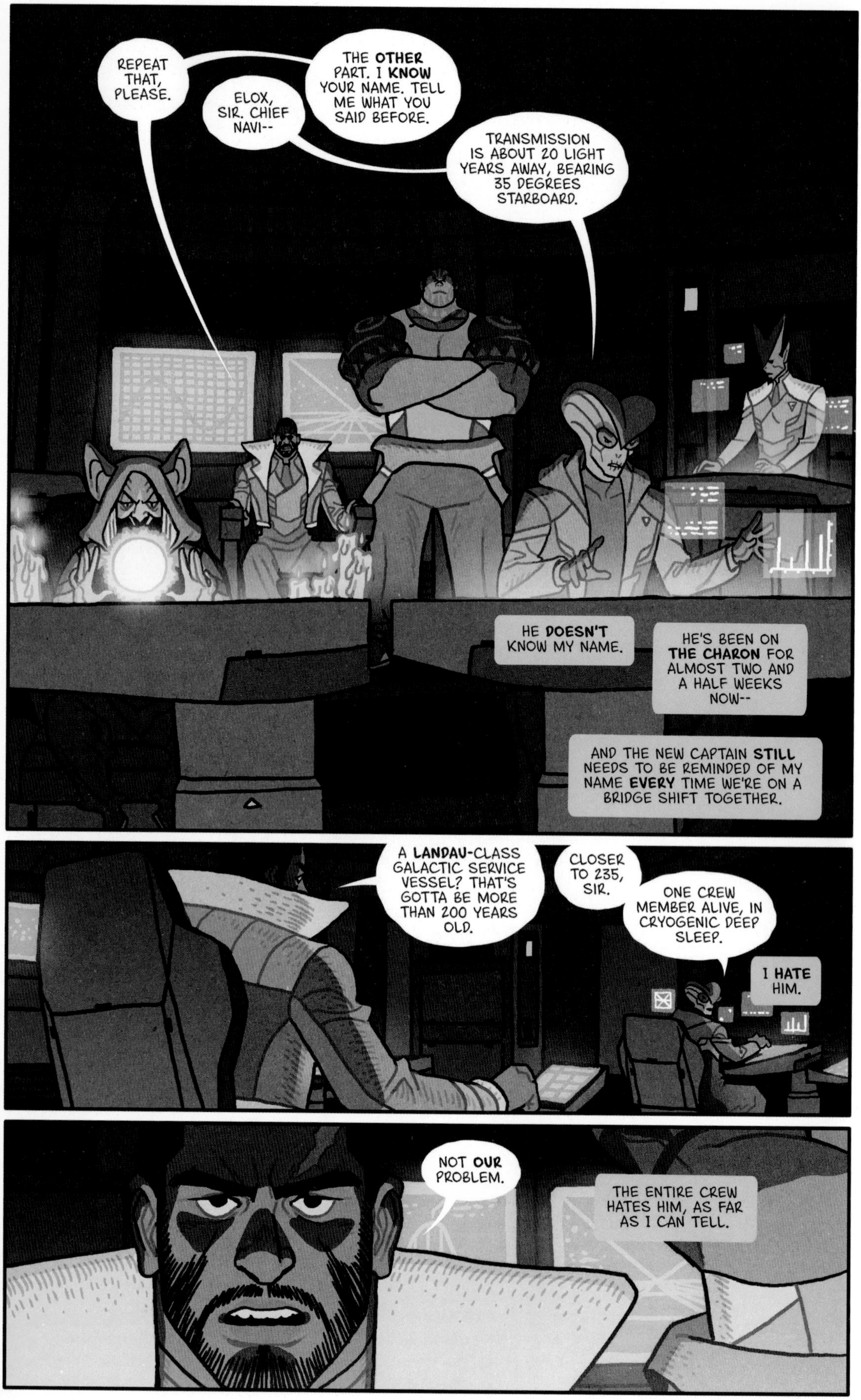
REPEAT THAT, PLEASE.
ELOX, SIR. CHIEF NAVI--
THE OTHER PART. I KNOW YOUR NAME. TELL ME WHAT YOU SAID BEFORE.
TRANSMISSION IS ABOUT 20 LIGHT YEARS AWAY, BEARING 35 DEGREES STARBOARD.
HE DOESN'T KNOW MY NAME.
HE'S BEEN ON THE CHARON FOR ALMOST TWO AND A HALF WEEKS NOW--
AND THE NEW CAPTAIN STILL NEEDS TO BE REMINDED OF MY NAME EVERY TIME WE'RE ON A BRIDGE SHIFT TOGETHER.
A LANDAU-CLASS GALACTIC SERVICE VESSEL? THAT'S GOTTA BE MORE THAN 200 YEARS OLD.
CLOSER TO 235, SIR.
ONE CREW MEMBER ALIVE, IN CRYOGENIC DEEP SLEEP.
I HATE HIM.
NOT OUR PROBLEM.
THE ENTIRE CREW HATES HIM, AS FAR AS I CAN TELL.

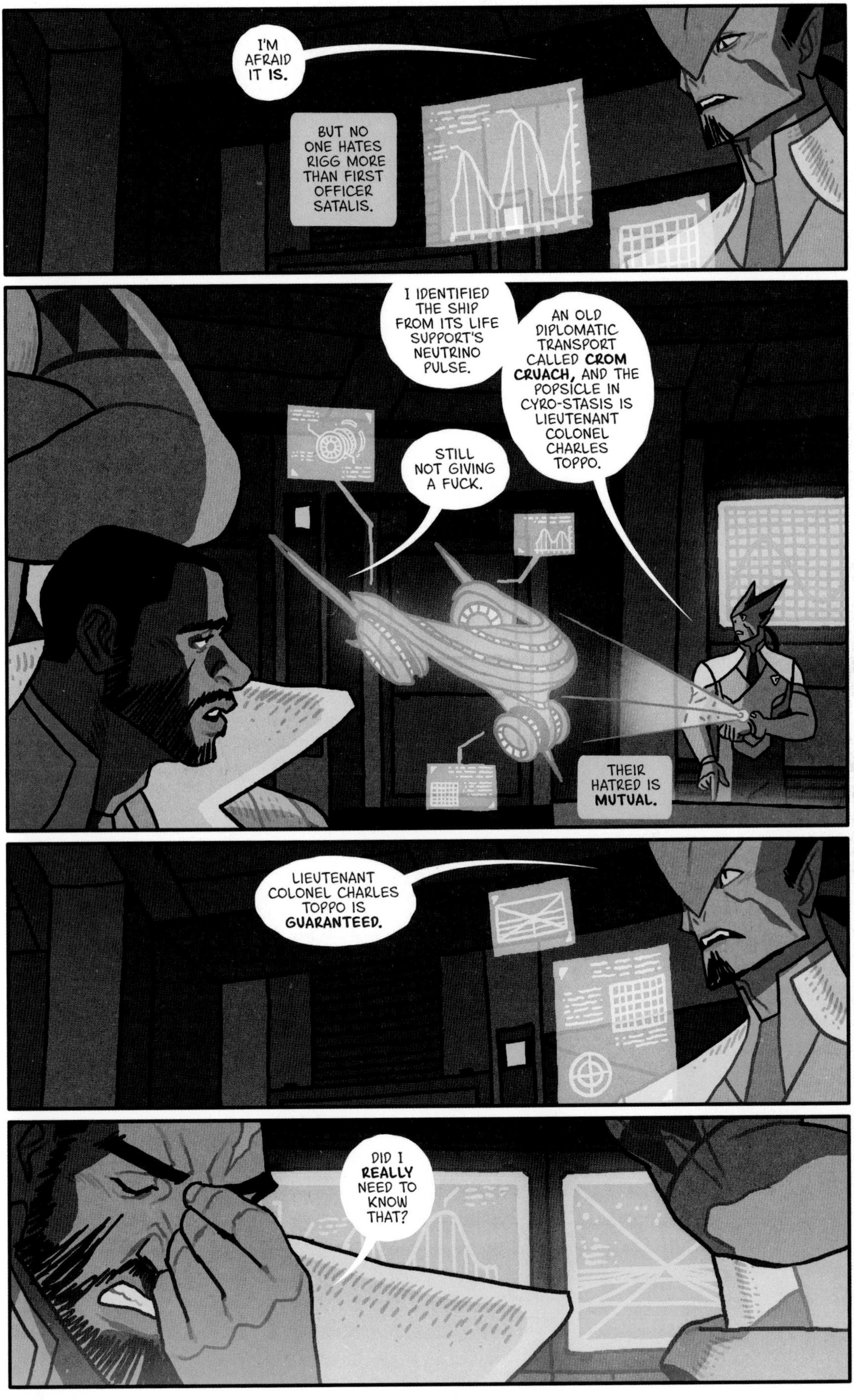
I'M AFRAID IT IS.
BUT NO ONE HATES RIGG MORE THAN FIRST OFFICER SATALIS.
I IDENTIFIED THE SHIP FROM ITS LIFE SUPPORT'S NEUTRINO PULSE.
AN OLD DIPLOMATIC TRANSPORT CALLED CROM CRUACH, AND THE POPSICLE IN CYRO-STASIS IS LIEUTENANT COLONEL CHARLES TOPPO.
STILL NOT GIVING A FUCK.
THEIR HATRED IS MUTUAL.
LIEUTENANT COLONEL CHARLES TOPPO IS GUARANTEED.
DID I REALLY NEED TO KNOW THAT?

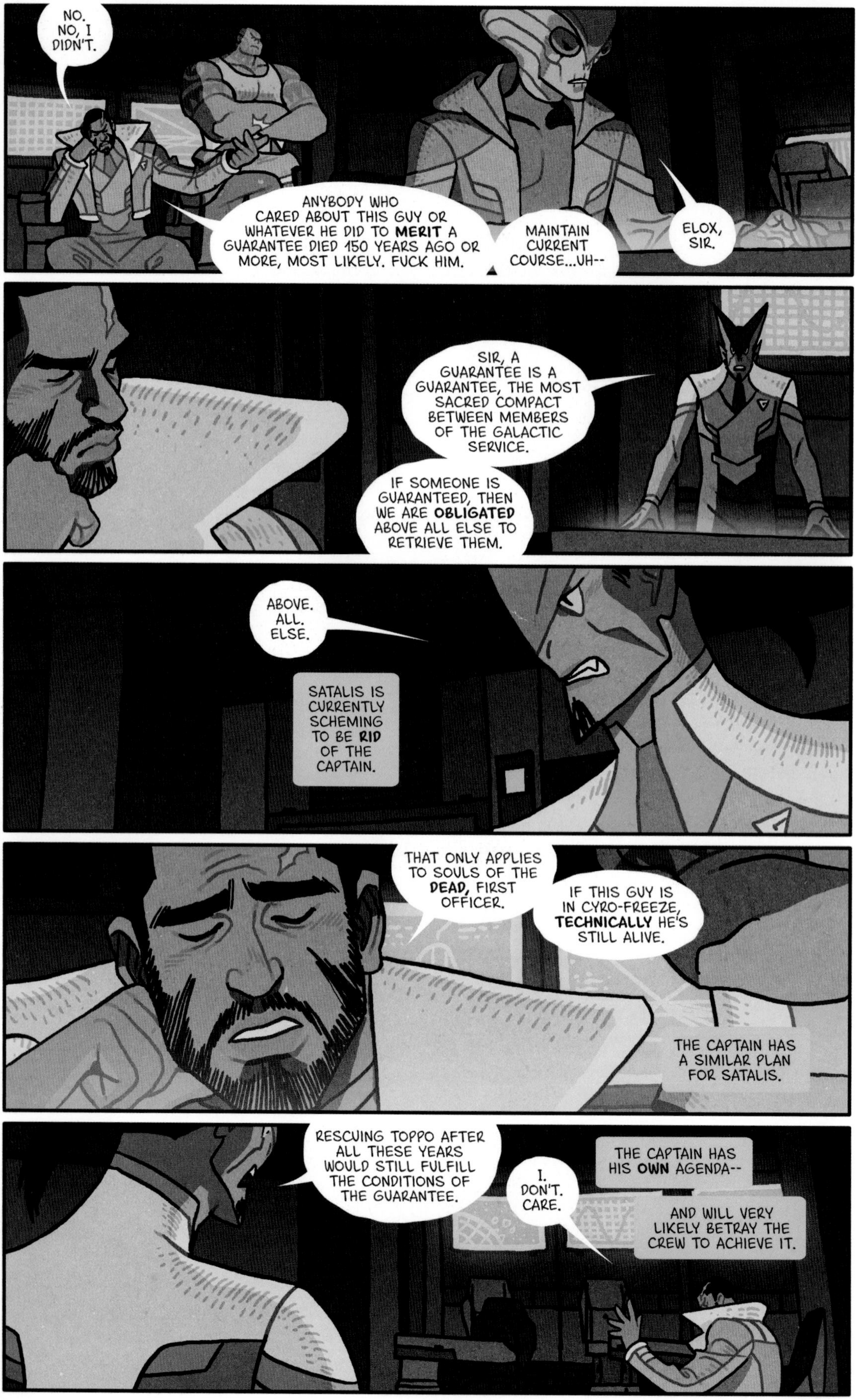
NO. NO, I DIDN'T.
ANYBODY WHO CARED ABOUT THIS GUY OR WHATEVER HE DID TO **MERIT** A GUARANTEE DIED 150 YEARS AGO OR MORE, MOST LIKELY. FUCK HIM.
MAINTAIN CURRENT COURSE...UH--
ELOX, SIR.
SIR, A GUARANTEE IS A GUARANTEE, THE MOST SACRED COMPACT BETWEEN MEMBERS OF THE GALACTIC SERVICE.
IF SOMEONE IS GUARANTEED, THEN WE ARE **OBLIGATED** ABOVE ALL ELSE TO RETRIEVE THEM.
ABOVE. ALL. ELSE.
SATALIS IS CURRENTLY SCHEMING TO BE **RID** OF THE CAPTAIN.
THAT ONLY APPLIES TO SOULS OF THE **DEAD,** FIRST OFFICER.
IF THIS GUY IS IN CYRO-FREEZE, **TECHNICALLY** HE'S STILL ALIVE.
THE CAPTAIN HAS A SIMILAR PLAN FOR SATALIS.
RESCUING TOPPO AFTER ALL THESE YEARS WOULD STILL FULFILL THE CONDITIONS OF THE GUARANTEE.
I. DON'T. CARE.
THE CAPTAIN HAS HIS **OWN** AGENDA--
AND WILL VERY LIKELY BETRAY THE CREW TO ACHIEVE IT.

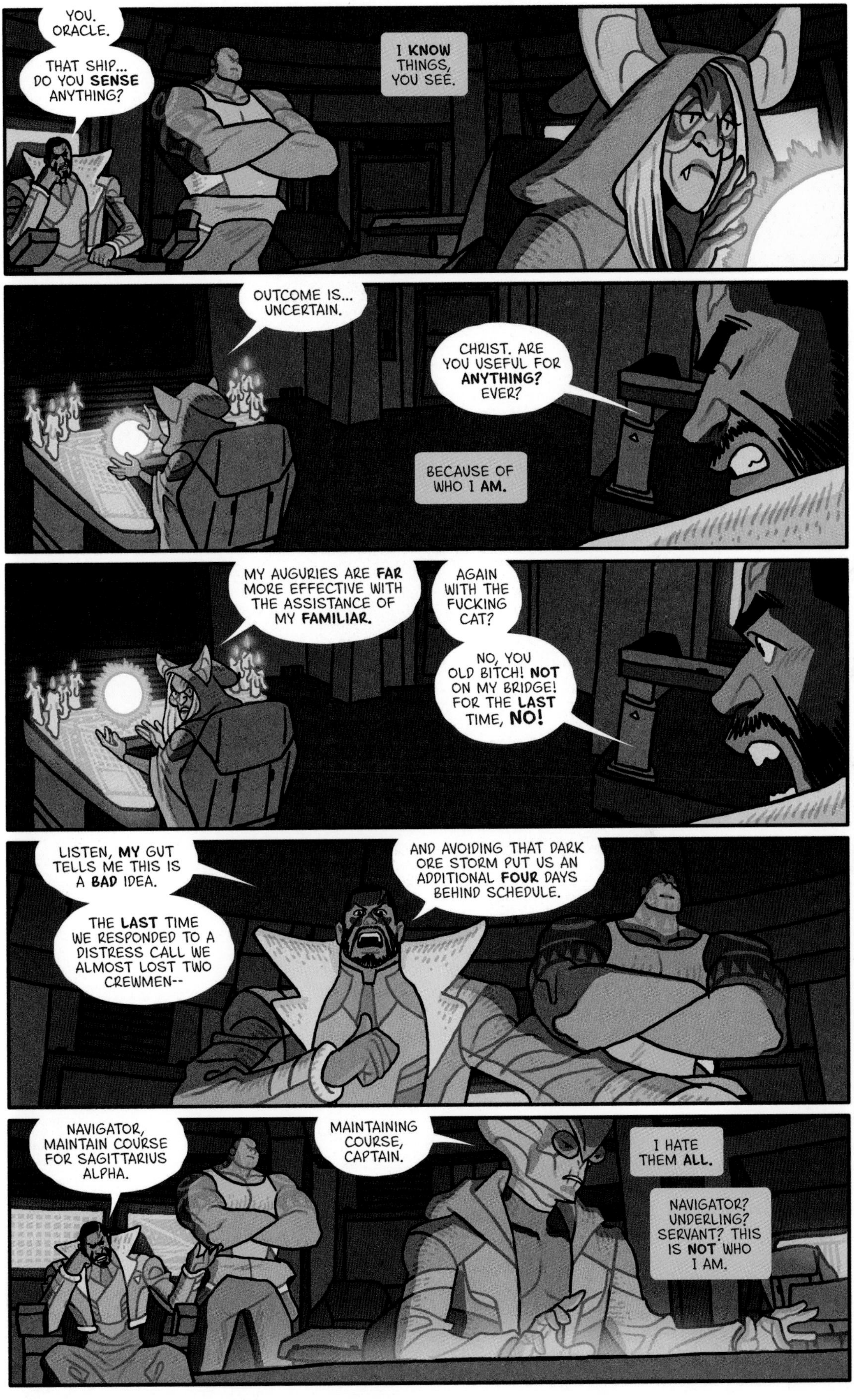
YOU. ORACLE.
THAT SHIP... DO YOU SENSE ANYTHING?
I KNOW THINGS, YOU SEE.
OUTCOME IS... UNCERTAIN.
CHRIST. ARE YOU USEFUL FOR ANYTHING? EVER?
BECAUSE OF WHO I AM.
MY AUGURIES ARE FAR MORE EFFECTIVE WITH THE ASSISTANCE OF MY FAMILIAR.
AGAIN WITH THE FUCKING CAT?
NO, YOU OLD BITCH! NOT ON MY BRIDGE! FOR THE LAST TIME, NO!
LISTEN, MY GUT TELLS ME THIS IS A BAD IDEA.
THE LAST TIME WE RESPONDED TO A DISTRESS CALL WE ALMOST LOST TWO CREWMEN--
AND AVOIDING THAT DARK ORE STORM PUT US AN ADDITIONAL FOUR DAYS BEHIND SCHEDULE.
NAVIGATOR, MAINTAIN COURSE FOR SAGITTARIUS ALPHA.
MAINTAINING COURSE, CAPTAIN.
I HATE THEM ALL.
NAVIGATOR? UNDERLING? SERVANT? THIS IS NOT WHO I AM.

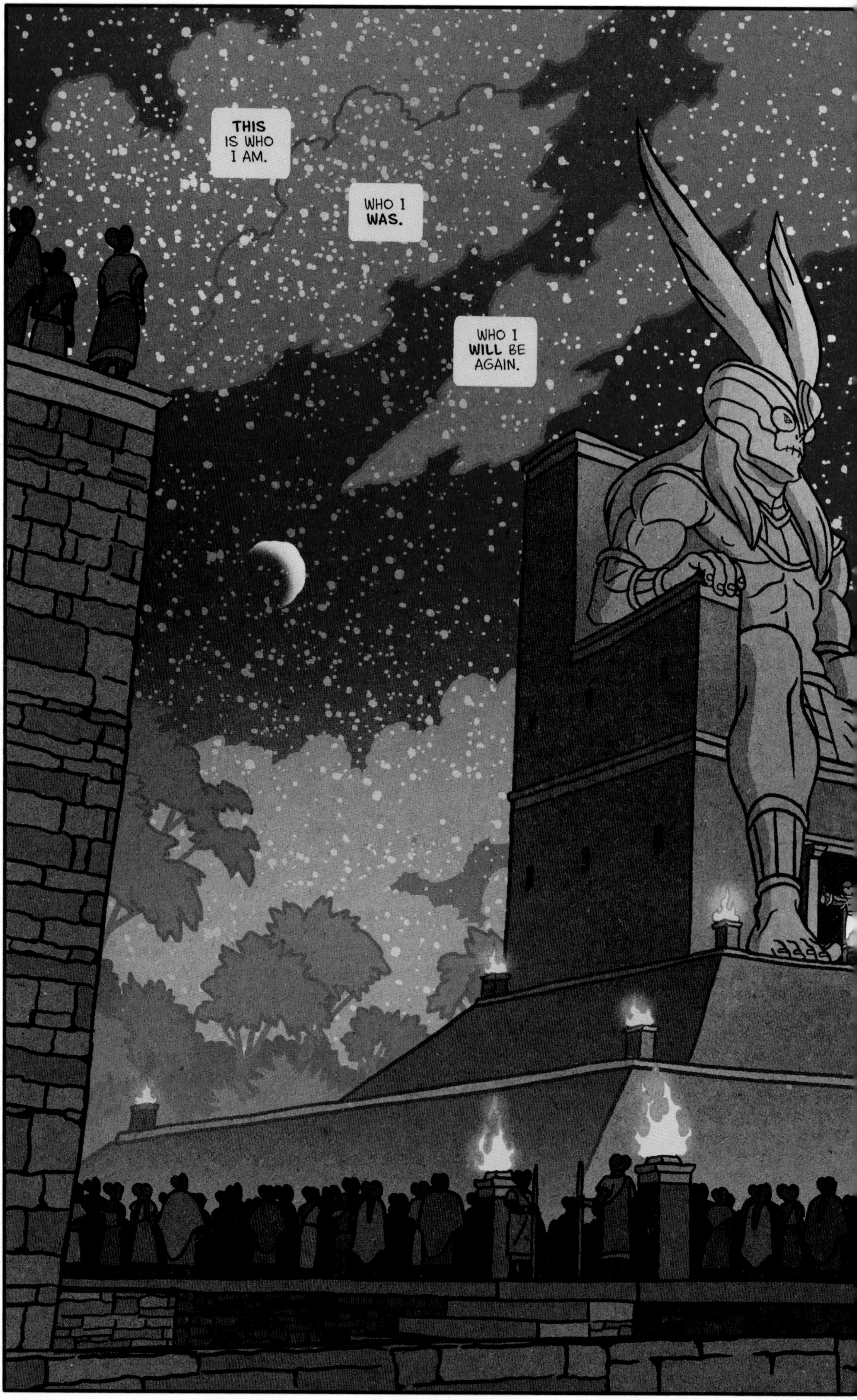
THIS IS WHO I AM.
WHO I WAS.
WHO I WILL BE AGAIN.

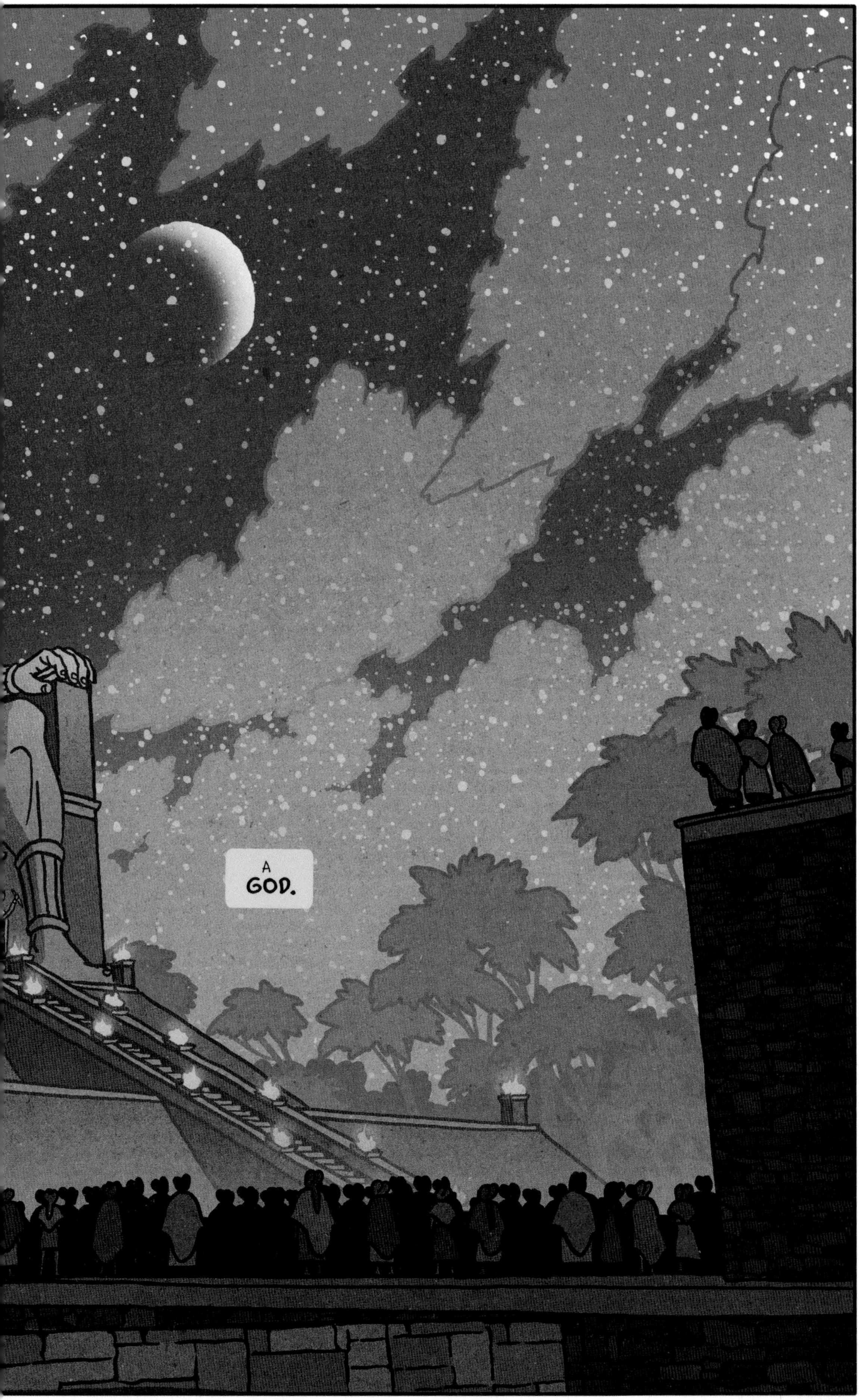
A GOD.

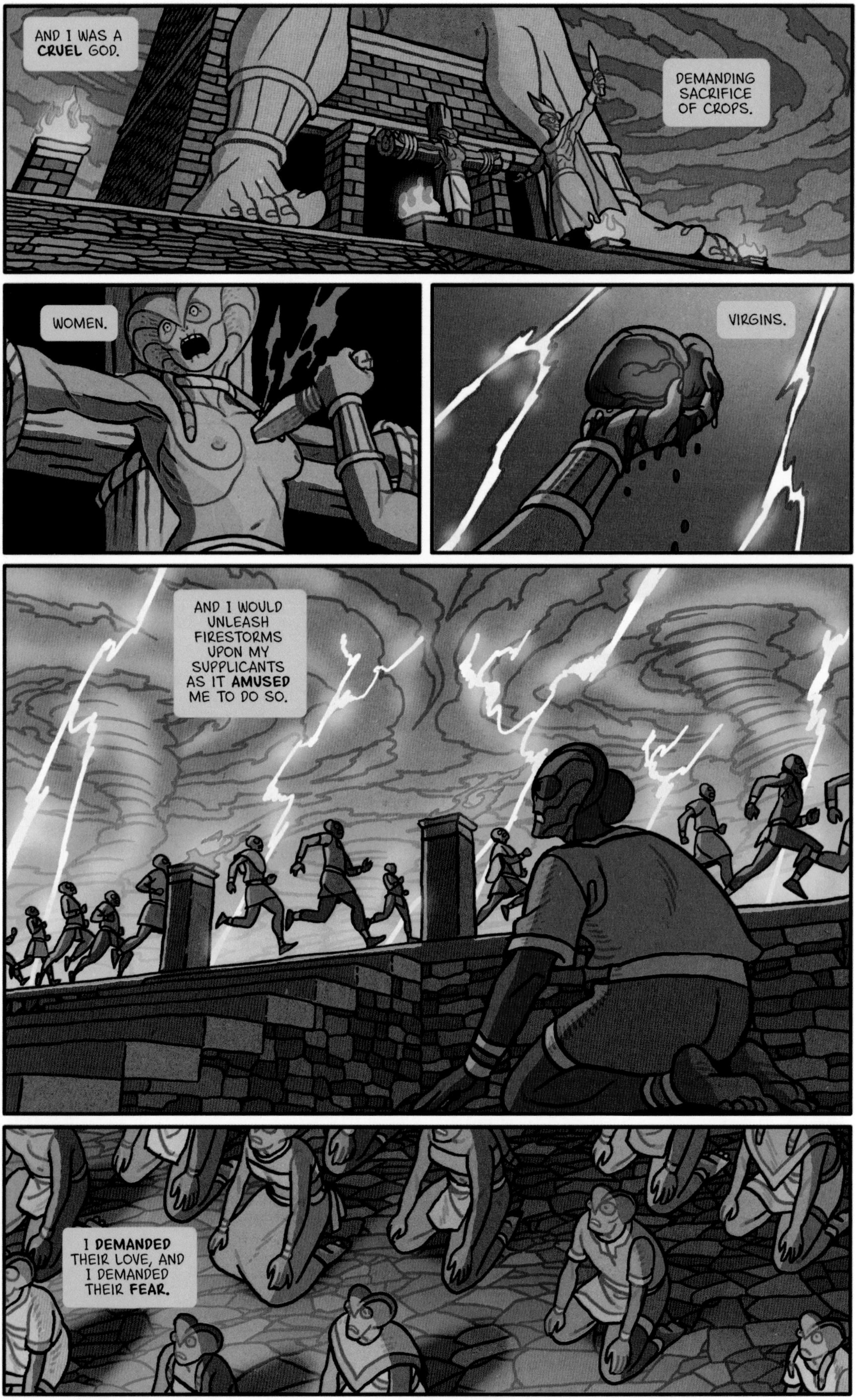
AND I WAS A **CRUEL** GOD.
DEMANDING SACRIFICE OF CROPS.
WOMEN.
VIRGINS.
AND I WOULD UNLEASH FIRESTORMS UPON MY SUPPLICANTS AS IT **AMUSED** ME TO DO SO.
I **DEMANDED** THEIR LOVE, AND I DEMANDED THEIR **FEAR**.

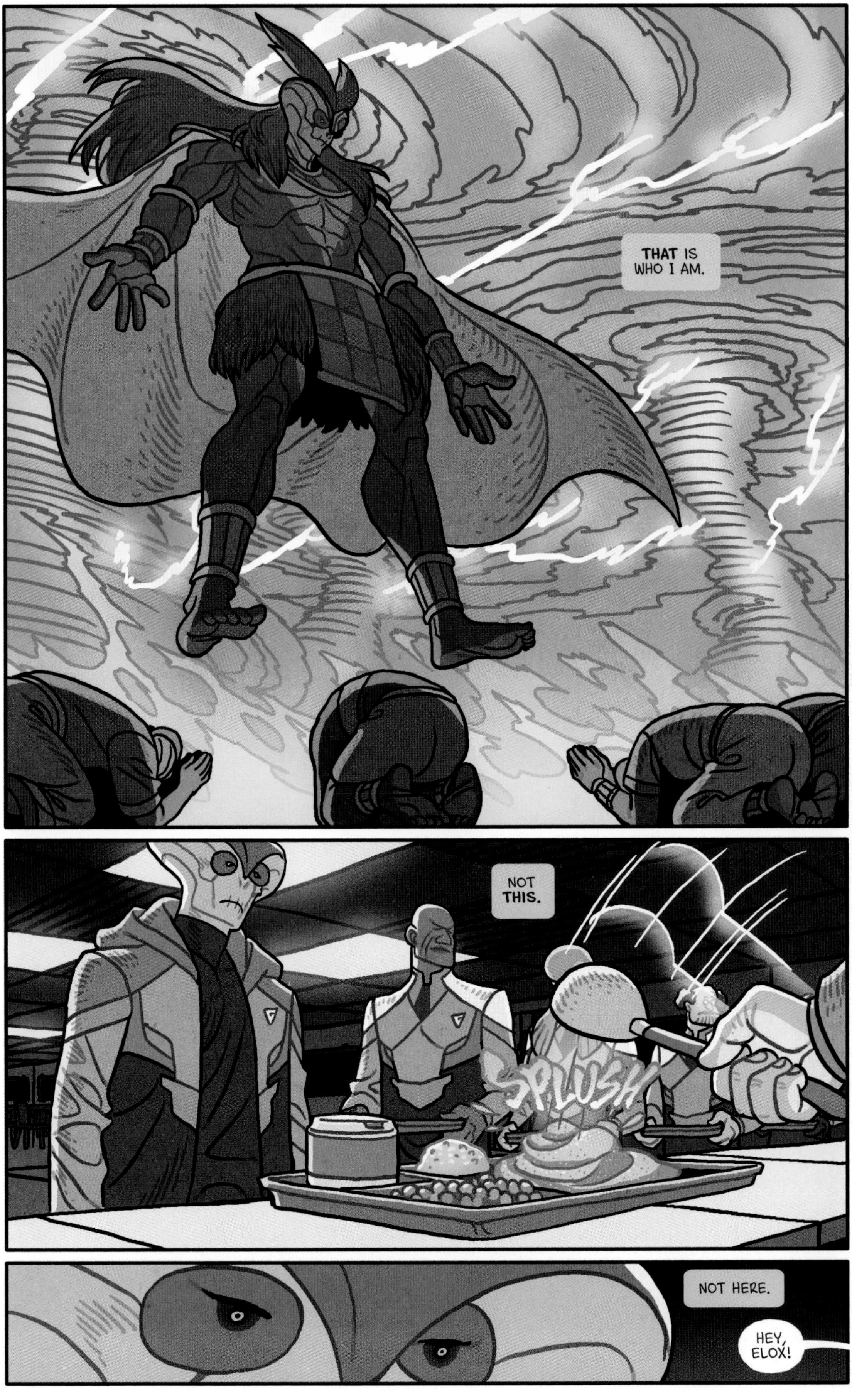
THAT IS
WHO I AM.
NOT
THIS.
SPLUSH
NOT HERE.
HEY,
ELOX!

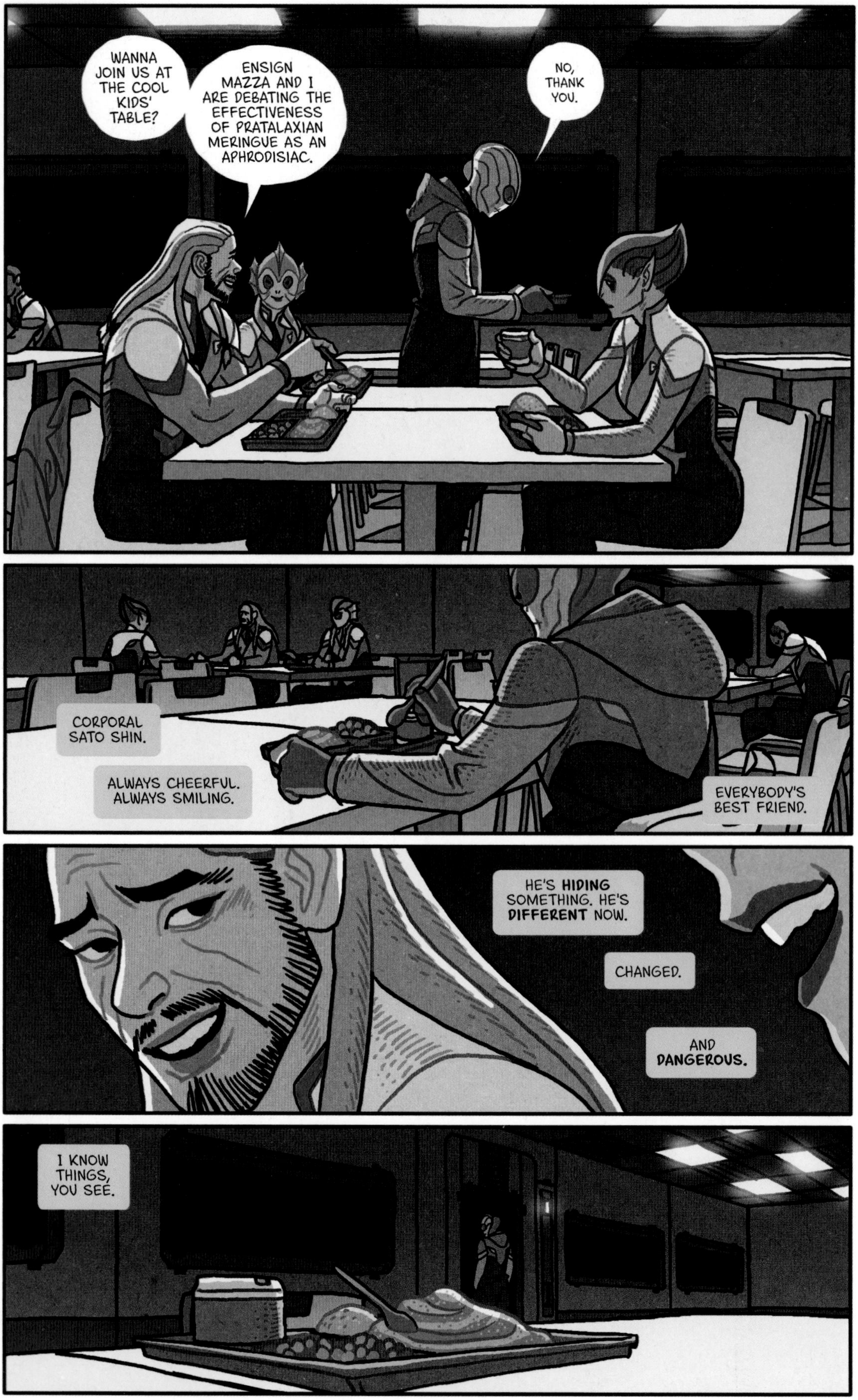
WANNA JOIN US AT THE COOL KIDS' TABLE?
ENSIGN MAZZA AND I ARE DEBATING THE EFFECTIVENESS OF PRATALAXIAN MERINGUE AS AN APHRODISIAC.
NO, THANK YOU.
CORPORAL SATO SHIN.
ALWAYS CHEERFUL. ALWAYS SMILING.
EVERYBODY'S BEST FRIEND.
HE'S HIDING SOMETHING. HE'S DIFFERENT NOW.
CHANGED.
AND DANGEROUS.
I KNOW THINGS, YOU SEE.

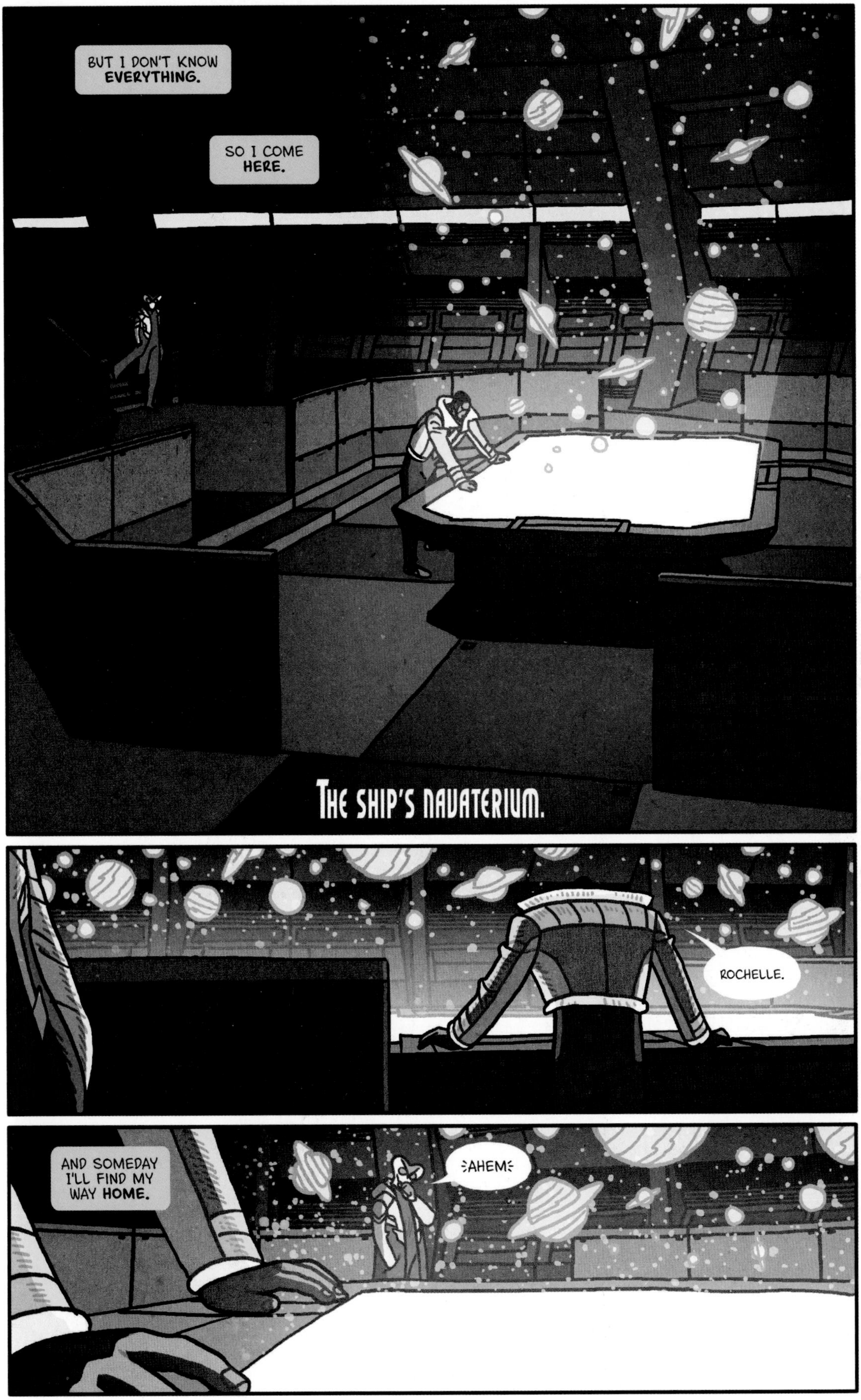
BUT I DON'T KNOW EVERYTHING.
SO I COME HERE.
THE SHIP'S NAVATERIUM.
ROCHELLE.
AND SOMEDAY I'LL FIND MY WAY HOME.
AHEM

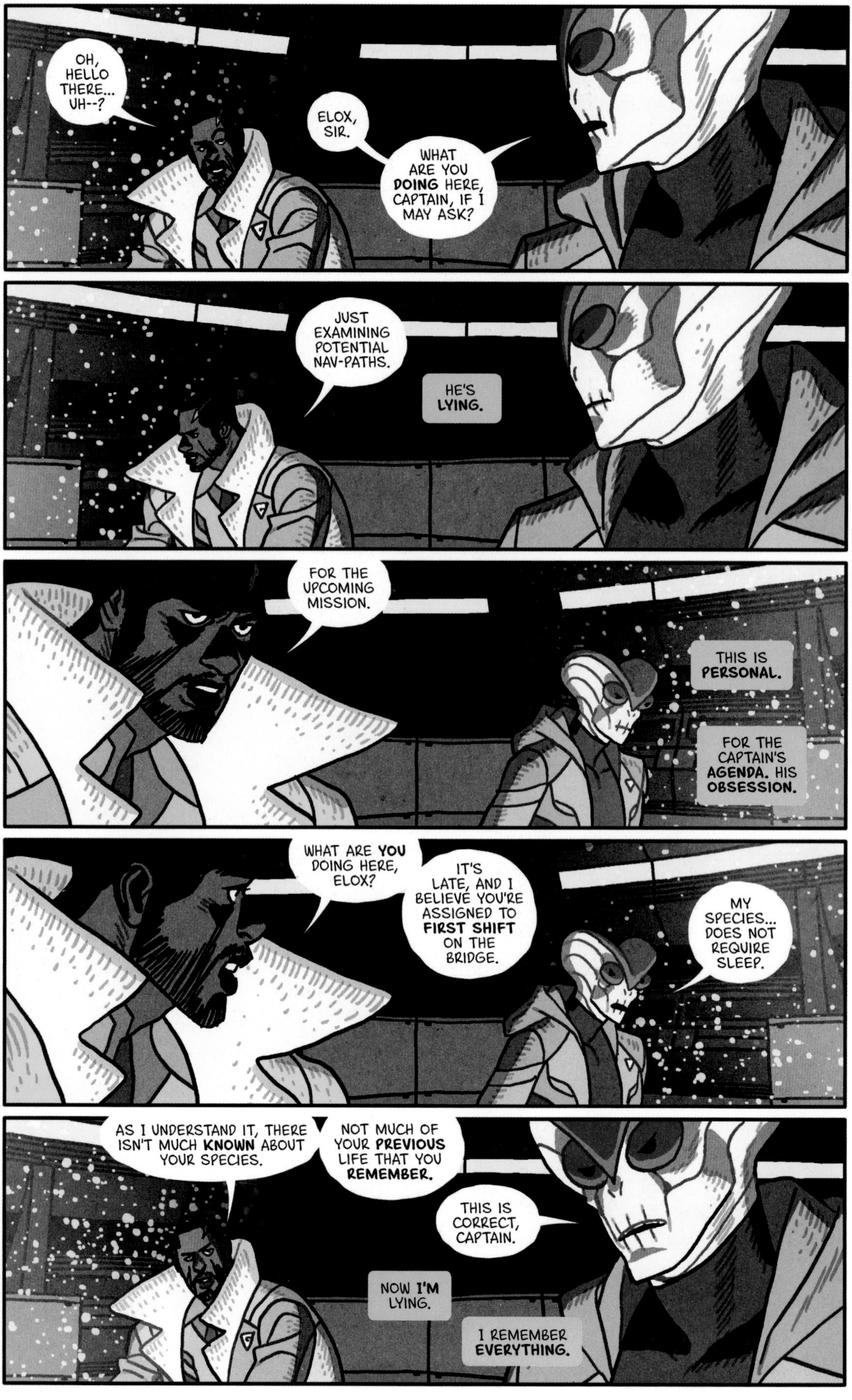
OH, HELLO THERE... UH--?
ELOX, SIR.
WHAT ARE YOU **DOING** HERE, CAPTAIN, IF I MAY ASK?
JUST EXAMINING POTENTIAL NAV-PATHS.
HE'S **LYING.**
FOR THE UPCOMING MISSION.
THIS IS **PERSONAL.**
FOR THE CAPTAIN'S **AGENDA.** HIS **OBSESSION.**
WHAT ARE **YOU** DOING HERE, ELOX?
IT'S LATE, AND I BELIEVE YOU'RE ASSIGNED TO **FIRST SHIFT** ON THE BRIDGE.
MY SPECIES... DOES NOT REQUIRE SLEEP.
AS I UNDERSTAND IT, THERE ISN'T MUCH **KNOWN** ABOUT YOUR SPECIES.
NOT MUCH OF YOUR **PREVIOUS** LIFE THAT YOU **REMEMBER.**
THIS IS CORRECT, CAPTAIN.
NOW **I'M** LYING.
I REMEMBER **EVERYTHING.**

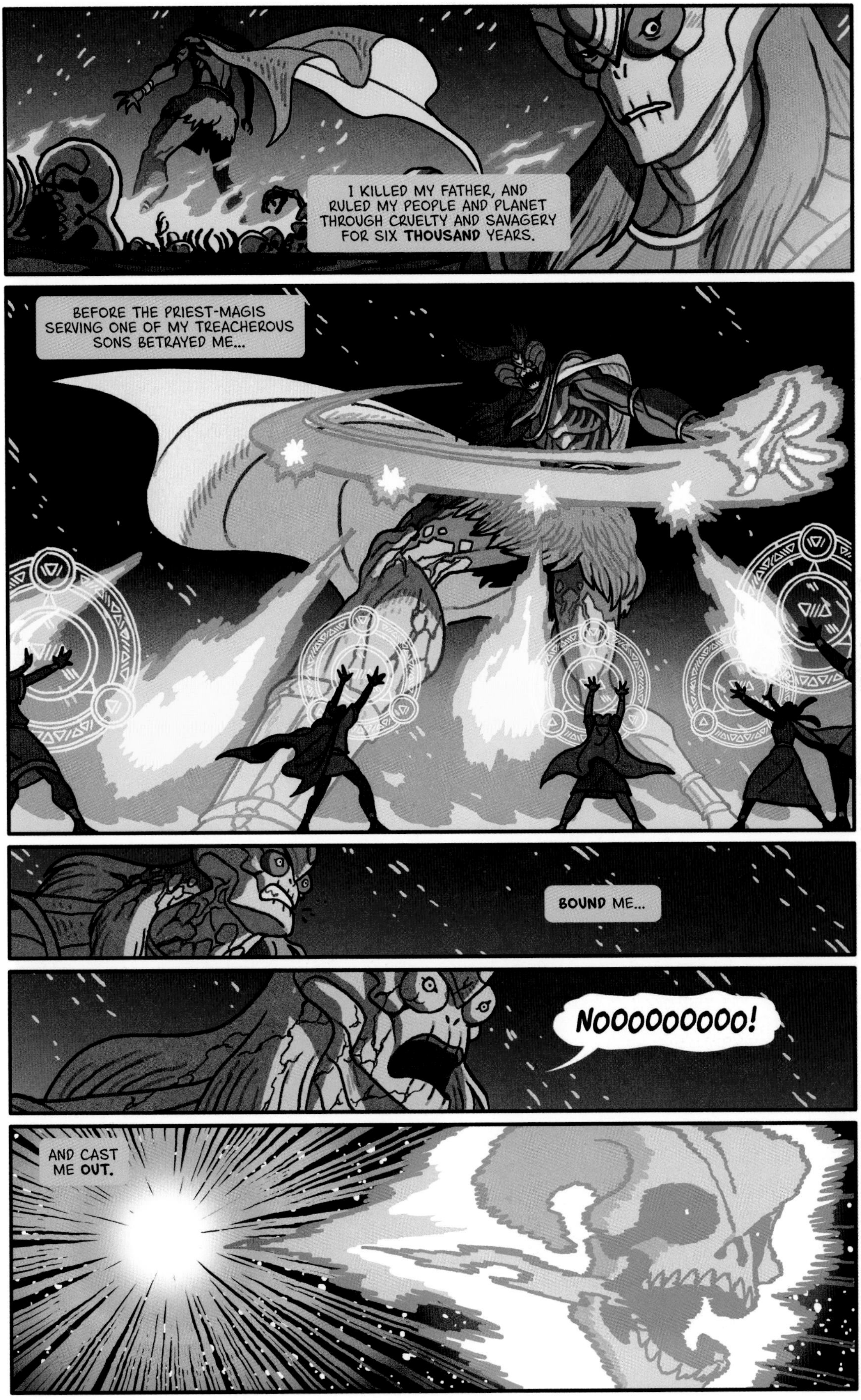

I KILLED MY FATHER, AND RULED MY PEOPLE AND PLANET THROUGH CRUELTY AND SAVAGERY FOR SIX THOUSAND YEARS.
BEFORE THE PRIEST-MAGIS SERVING ONE OF MY TREACHEROUS SONS BETRAYED ME...
BOUND ME...
NOOOOOOOOO!
AND CAST ME OUT.

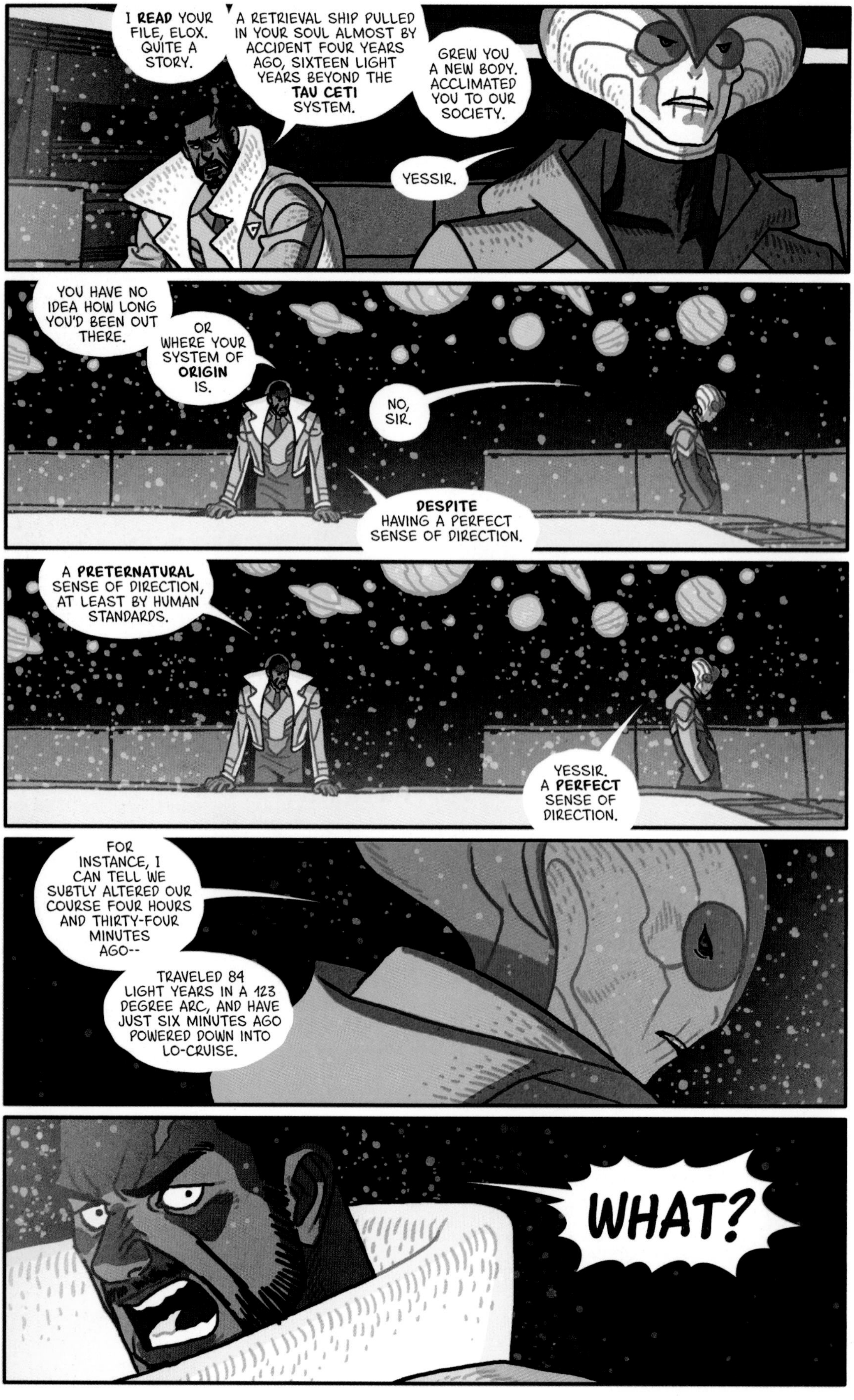
I READ YOUR FILE, ELOX. QUITE A STORY.
A RETRIEVAL SHIP PULLED IN YOUR SOUL ALMOST BY ACCIDENT FOUR YEARS AGO, SIXTEEN LIGHT YEARS BEYOND THE TAU CETI SYSTEM.
GREW YOU A NEW BODY. ACCLIMATED YOU TO OUR SOCIETY.
YESSIR.
YOU HAVE NO IDEA HOW LONG YOU'D BEEN OUT THERE.
OR WHERE YOUR SYSTEM OF ORIGIN IS.
NO, SIR.
DESPITE HAVING A PERFECT SENSE OF DIRECTION.
A PRETERNATURAL SENSE OF DIRECTION, AT LEAST BY HUMAN STANDARDS.
YESSIR. A PERFECT SENSE OF DIRECTION.
FOR INSTANCE, I CAN TELL WE SUBTLY ALTERED OUR COURSE FOUR HOURS AND THIRTY-FOUR MINUTES AGO--
TRAVELED 84 LIGHT YEARS IN A 123 DEGREE ARC, AND HAVE JUST SIX MINUTES AGO POWERED DOWN INTO LO-CRUISE.
WHAT?

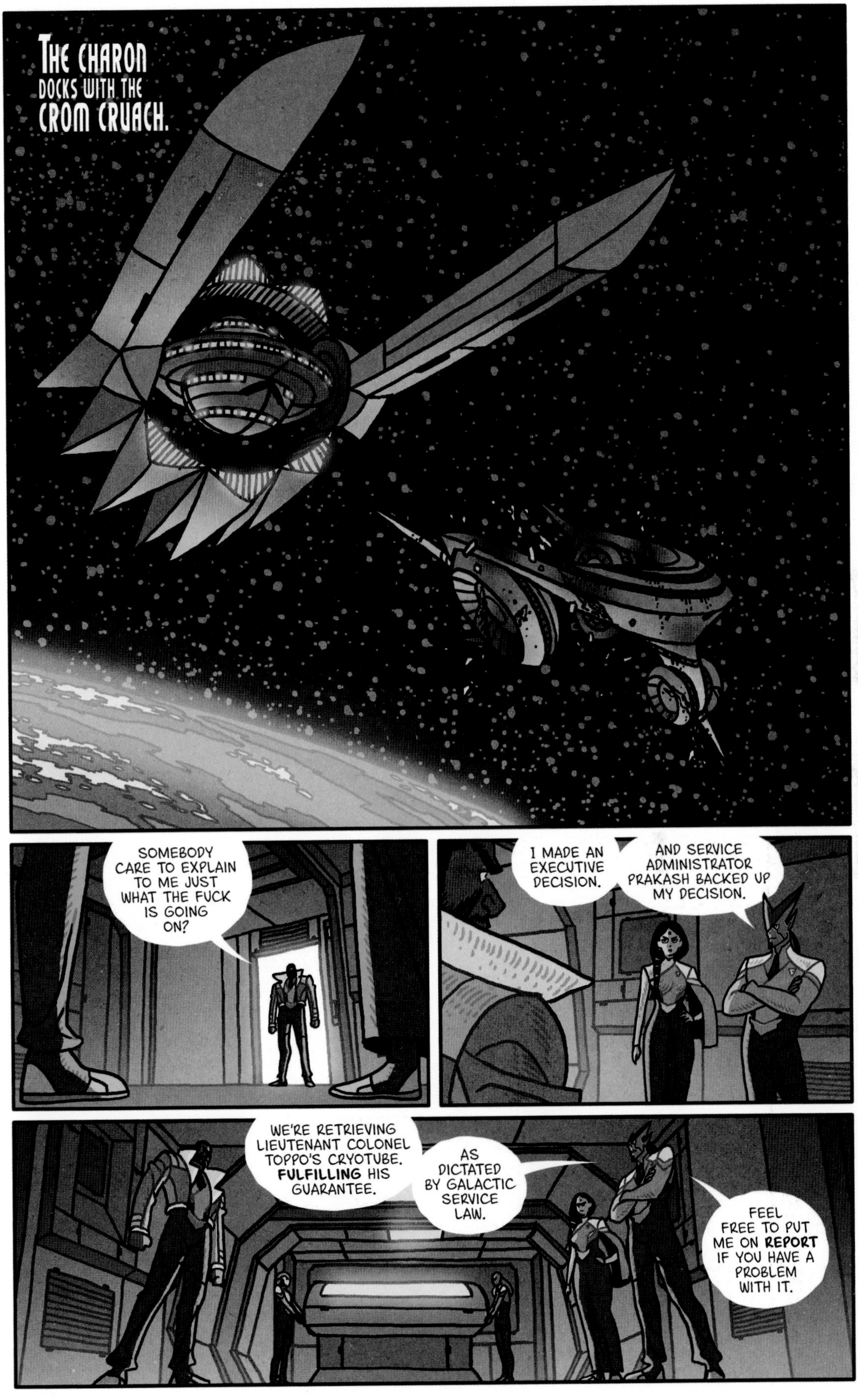
THE CHARON DOCKS WITH THE CROM CRUACH.
SOMEBODY CARE TO EXPLAIN TO ME JUST WHAT THE FUCK IS GOING ON?
I MADE AN EXECUTIVE DECISION.
AND SERVICE ADMINISTRATOR PRAKASH BACKED UP MY DECISION.
WE'RE RETRIEVING LIEUTENANT COLONEL TOPPO'S CRYOTUBE. **FULFILLING** HIS GUARANTEE.
AS DICTATED BY GALACTIC SERVICE LAW.
FEEL FREE TO PUT ME ON **REPORT** IF YOU HAVE A PROBLEM WITH IT.

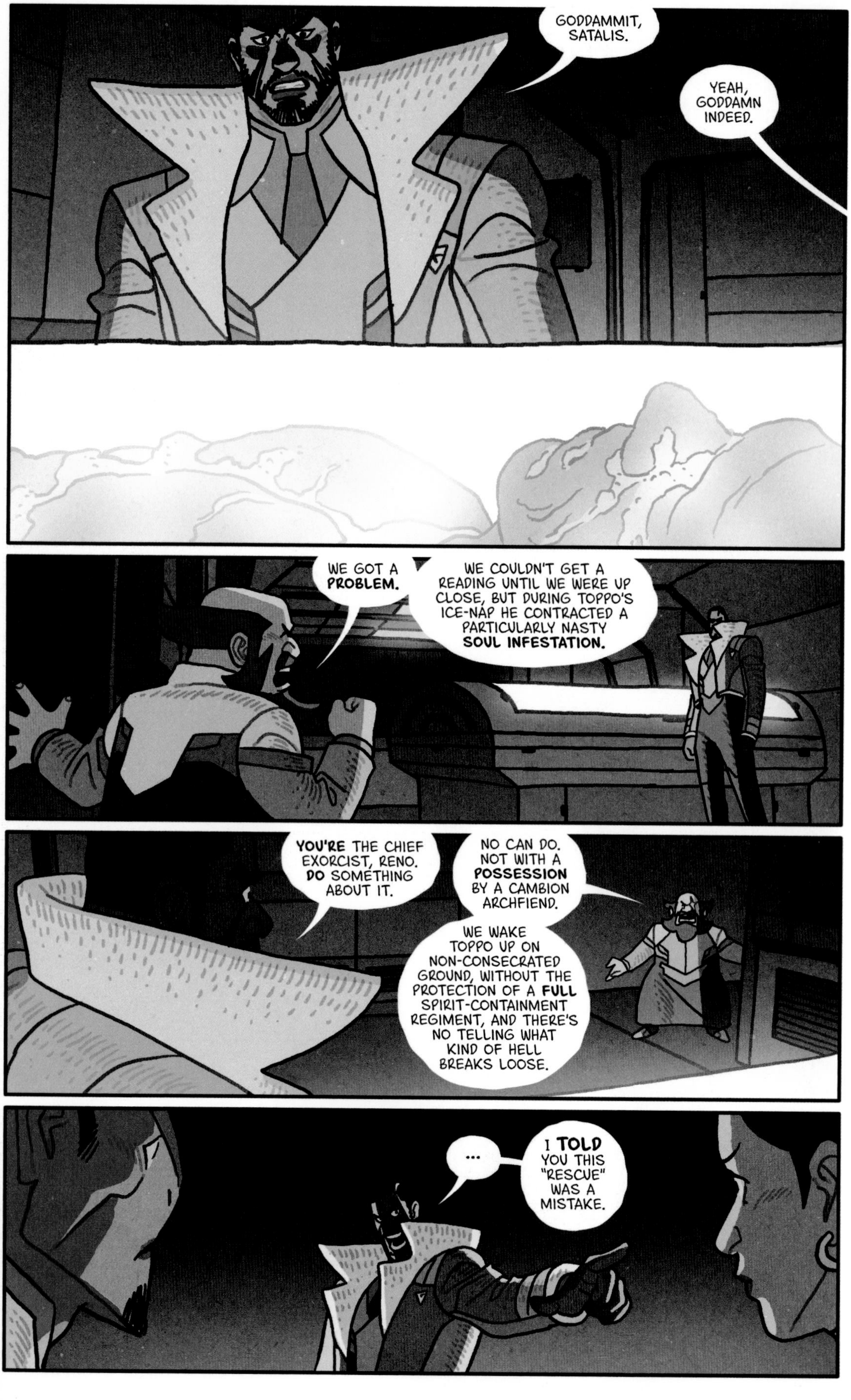
GODDAMMIT, SATALIS.
YEAH, GODDAMN INDEED.
WE GOT A **PROBLEM.**
WE COULDN'T GET A READING UNTIL WE WERE UP CLOSE, BUT DURING TOPPO'S ICE-NAP HE CONTRACTED A PARTICULARLY NASTY **SOUL INFESTATION.**
YOU'RE THE CHIEF EXORCIST, RENO. **DO** SOMETHING ABOUT IT.
NO CAN DO. NOT WITH A **POSSESSION** BY A CAMBION ARCHFIEND.
WE WAKE TOPPO UP ON NON-CONSECRATED GROUND, WITHOUT THE PROTECTION OF A **FULL** SPIRIT-CONTAINMENT REGIMENT, AND THERE'S NO TELLING WHAT KIND OF HELL BREAKS LOOSE.
...
I **TOLD** YOU THIS "RESCUE" WAS A MISTAKE.

AND SO CAPTAIN RIGG ORDERED **THE CHARON** TO BE REROUTED TO **ORCUS-6** FOR TRANSFER OF THE CRYOTUBE--

A DETOUR HE ANGRILY AND REPEATEDLY INFORMED US WOULD PUT US ANOTHER **SIX** DAYS OFF-SCHEDULE.

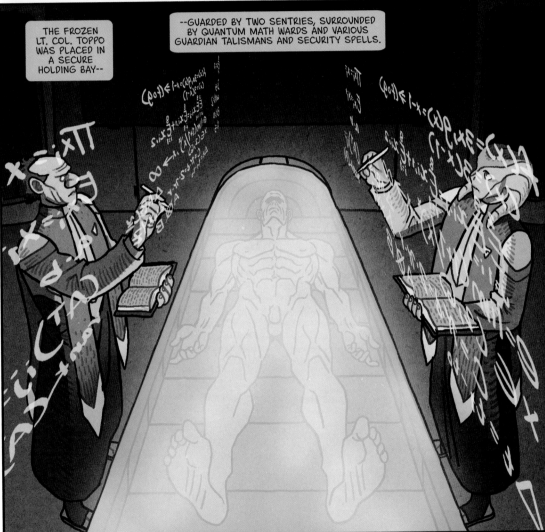

THE FROZEN LT. COL. TOPPO WAS PLACED IN A SECURE HOLDING BAY--

--GUARDED BY TWO SENTRIES, SURROUNDED BY QUANTUM MATH WARDS AND VARIOUS GUARDIAN TALISMANS AND SECURITY SPELLS.

I WAS ON THE BRIDGE WORKING MY NAVIGATION SHIFT WHEN IT HAPPENED.

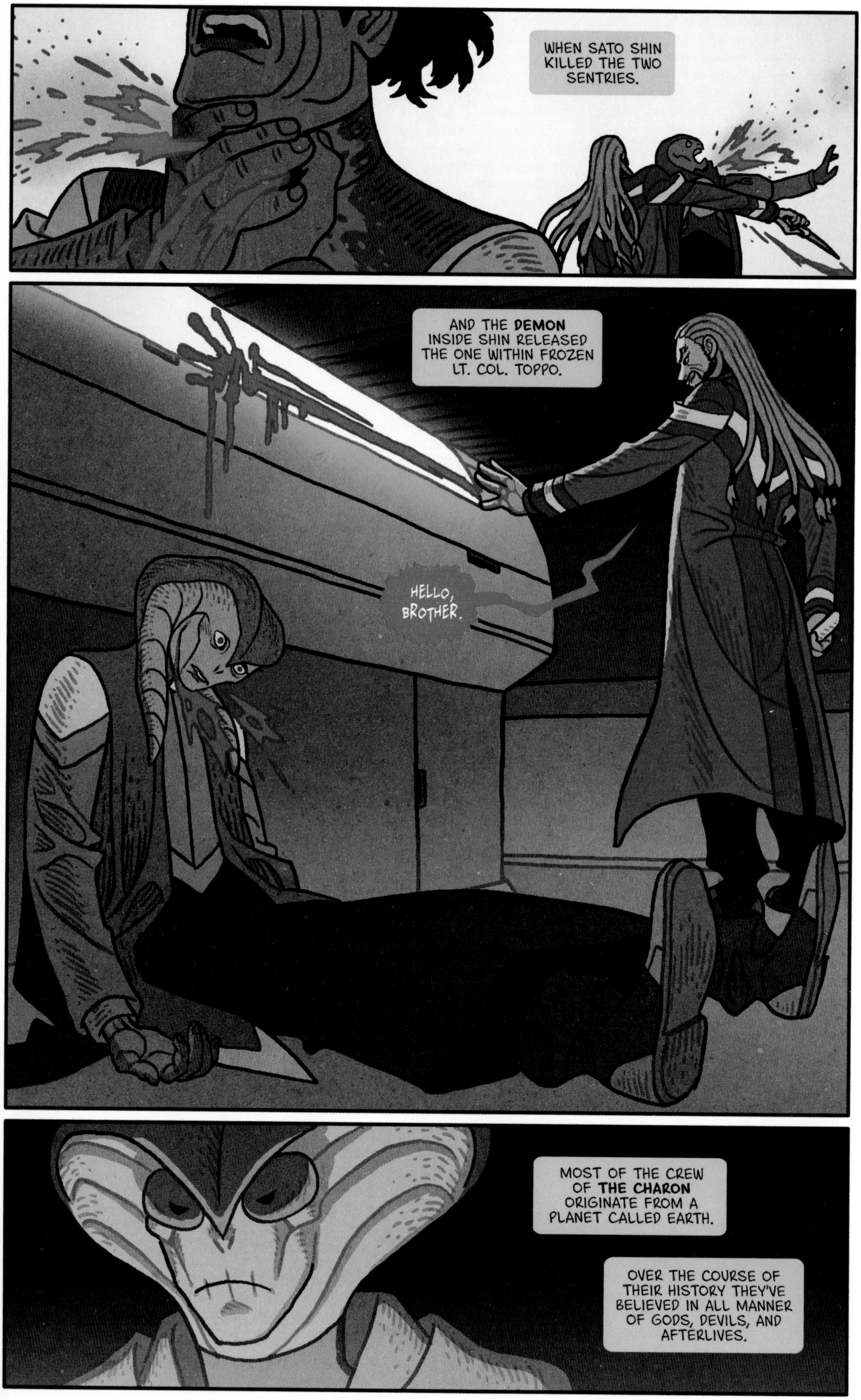
WHEN SATO SHIN KILLED THE TWO SENTRIES.
AND THE DEMON INSIDE SHIN RELEASED THE ONE WITHIN FROZEN LT. COL. TOPPO.
HELLO, BROTHER.
MOST OF THE CREW OF THE CHARON ORIGINATE FROM A PLANET CALLED EARTH.
OVER THE COURSE OF THEIR HISTORY THEY'VE BELIEVED IN ALL MANNER OF GODS, DEVILS, AND AFTERLIVES.

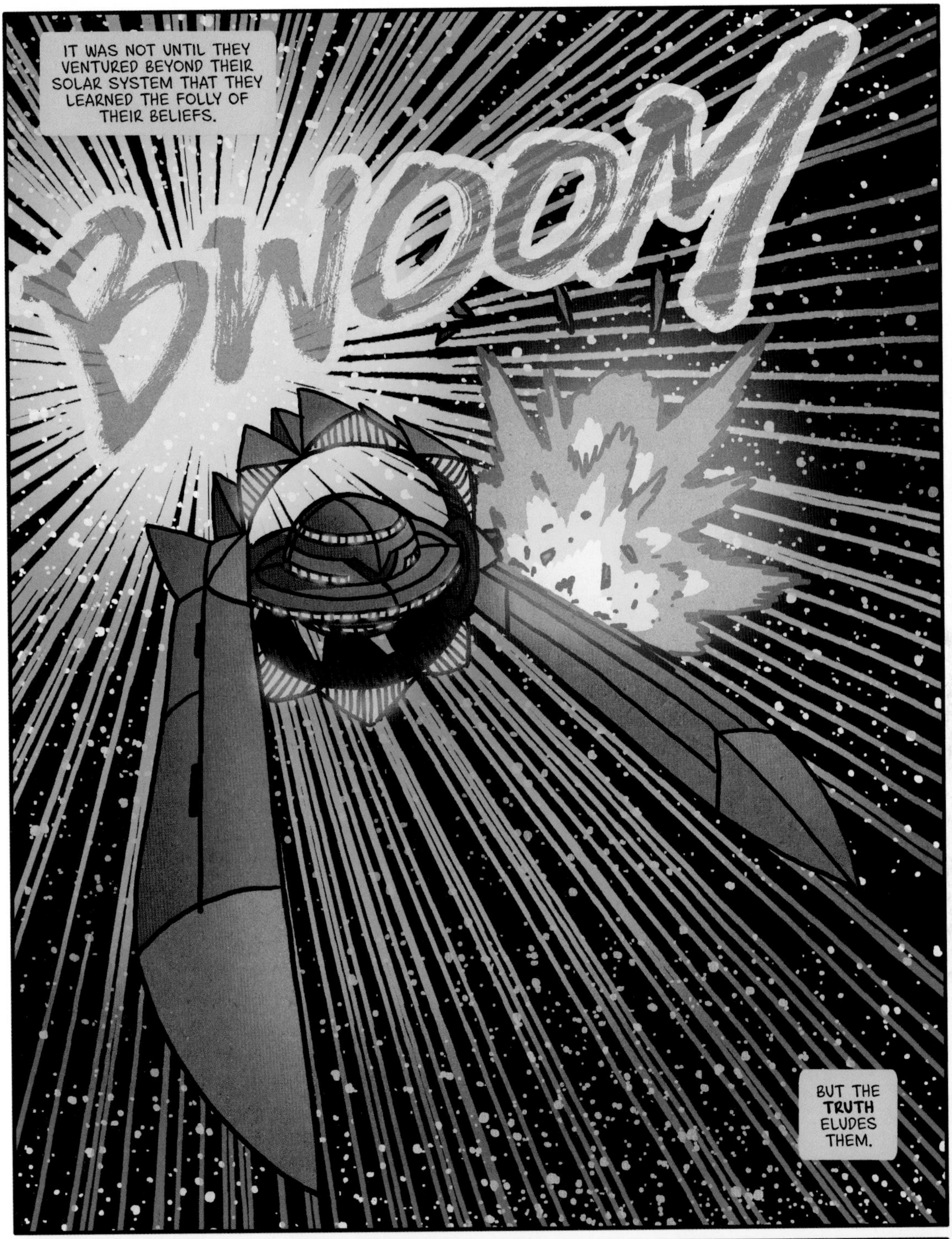
IT WAS NOT UNTIL THEY VENTURED BEYOND THEIR SOLAR SYSTEM THAT THEY LEARNED THE FOLLY OF THEIR BELIEFS.
BWOOM
BUT THE TRUTH ELUDES THEM.

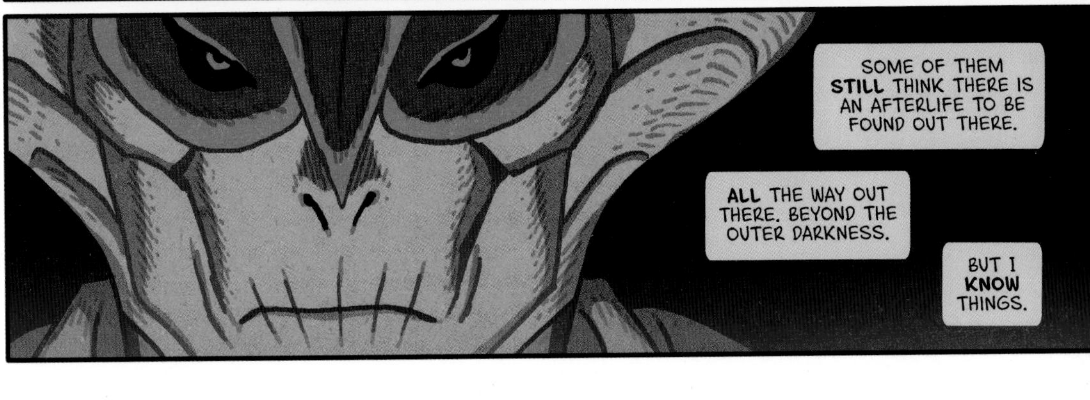
SOME OF THEM STILL THINK THERE IS AN AFTERLIFE TO BE FOUND OUT THERE.
ALL THE WAY OUT THERE. BEYOND THE OUTER DARKNESS.
BUT I KNOW THINGS.

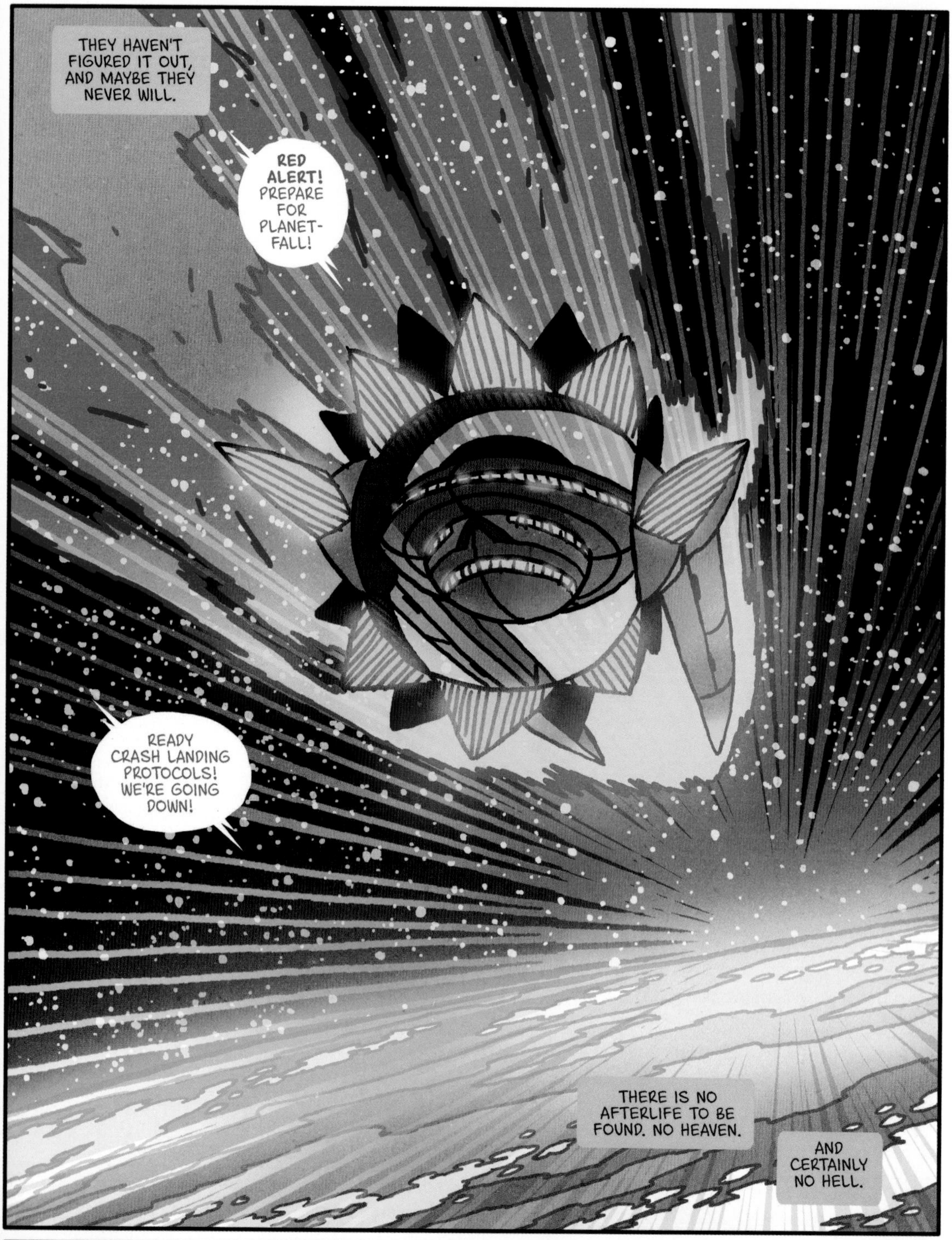
THEY HAVEN'T FIGURED IT OUT, AND MAYBE THEY NEVER WILL.
RED ALERT! PREPARE FOR PLANET-FALL!
READY CRASH LANDING PROTOCOLS! WE'RE GOING DOWN!
THERE IS NO AFTERLIFE TO BE FOUND. NO HEAVEN.
AND CERTAINLY NO HELL.

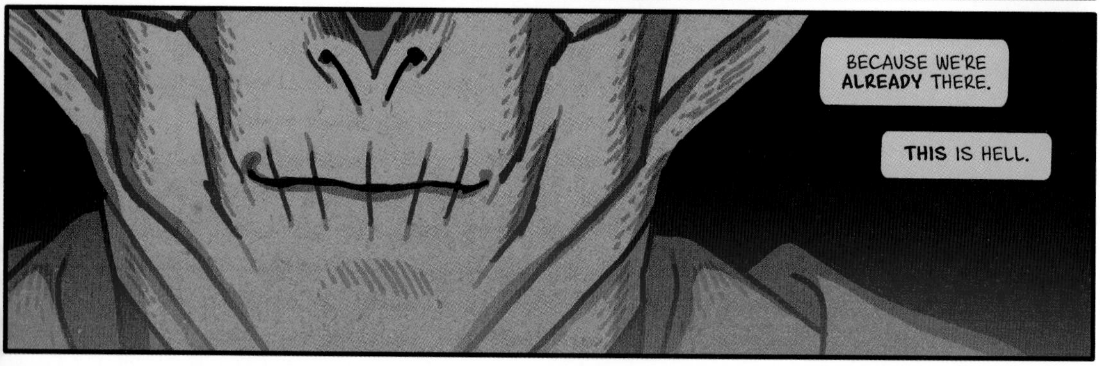
BECAUSE WE'RE ALREADY THERE.
THIS IS HELL.

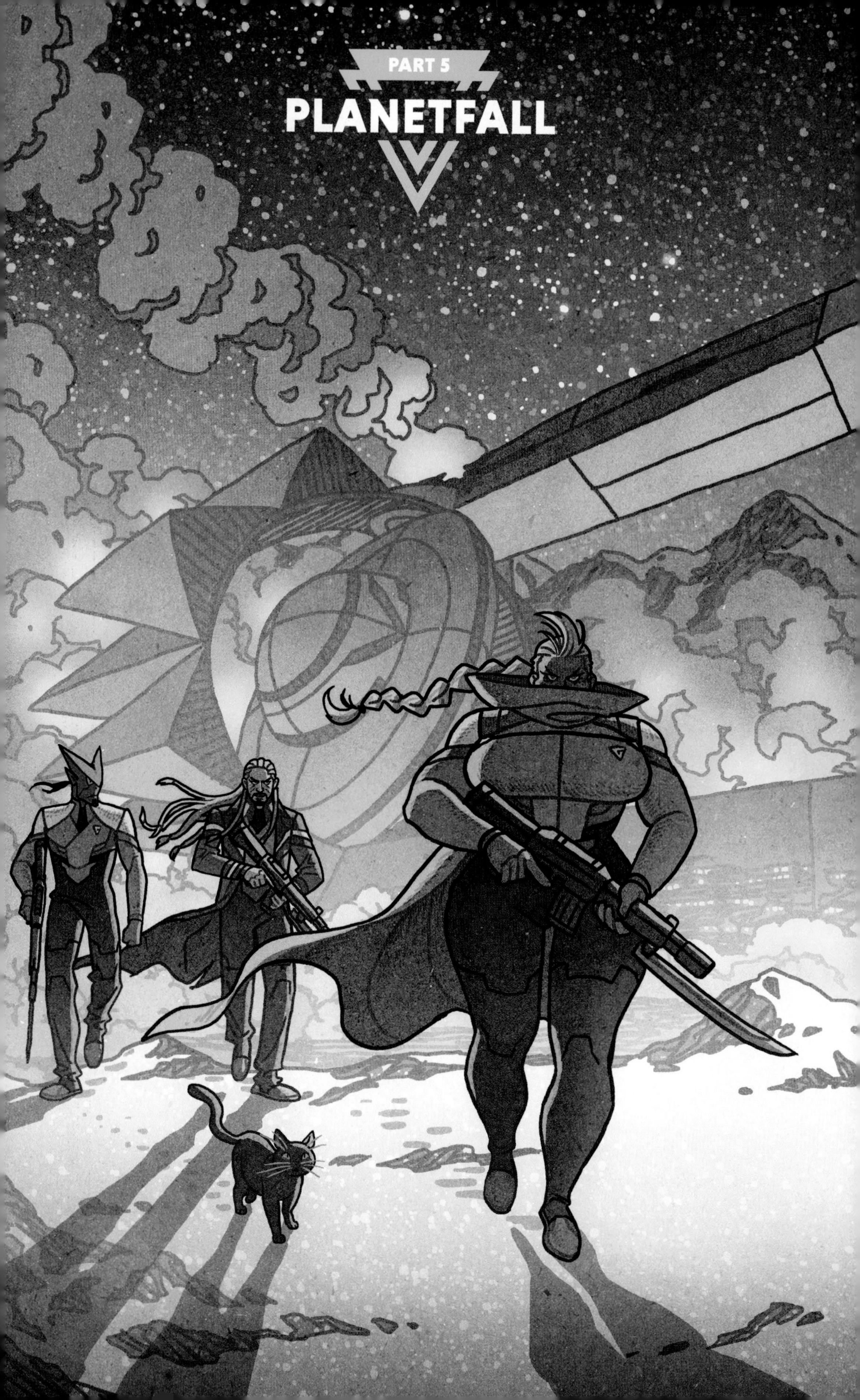
PART 5
PLANETFALL

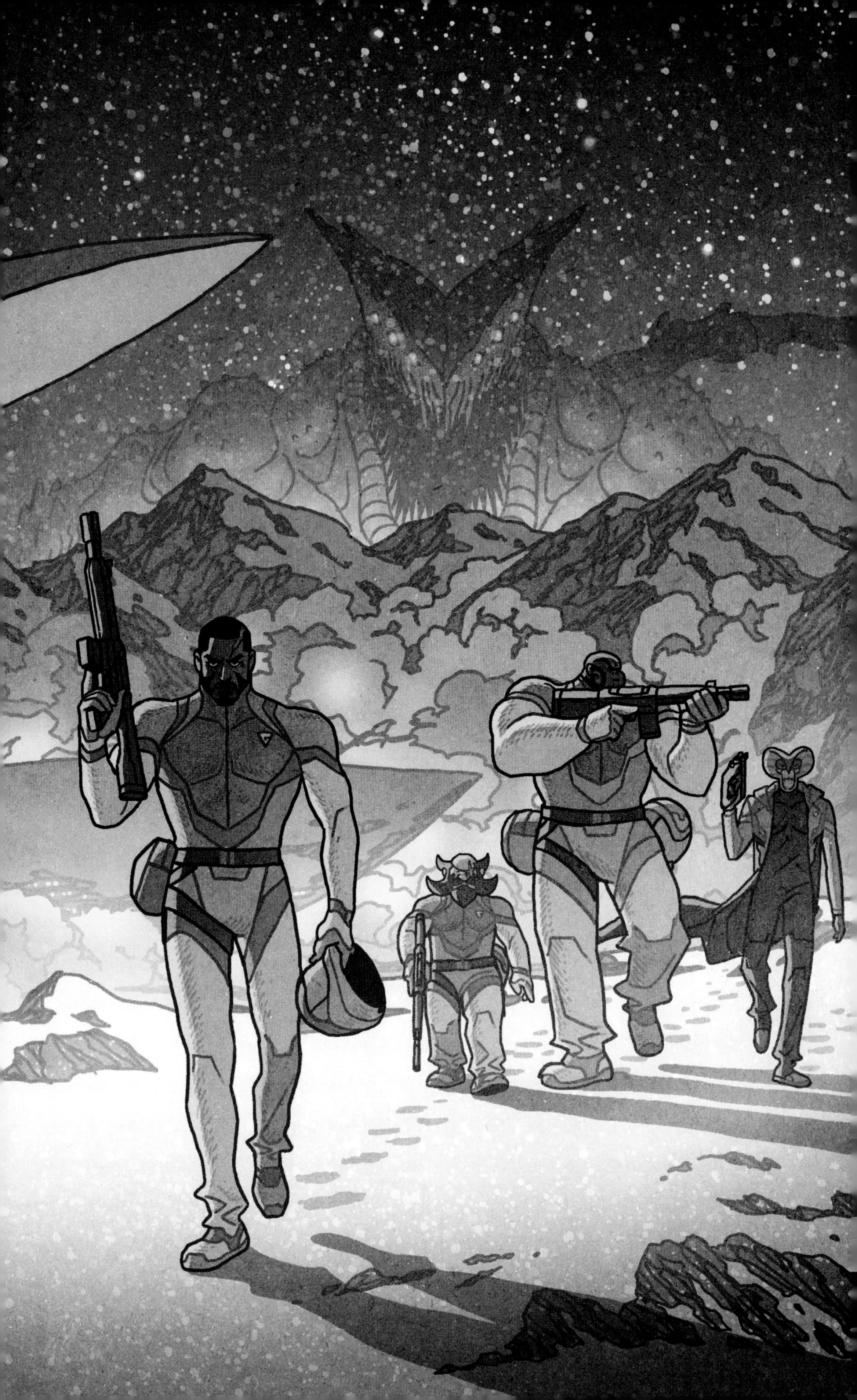

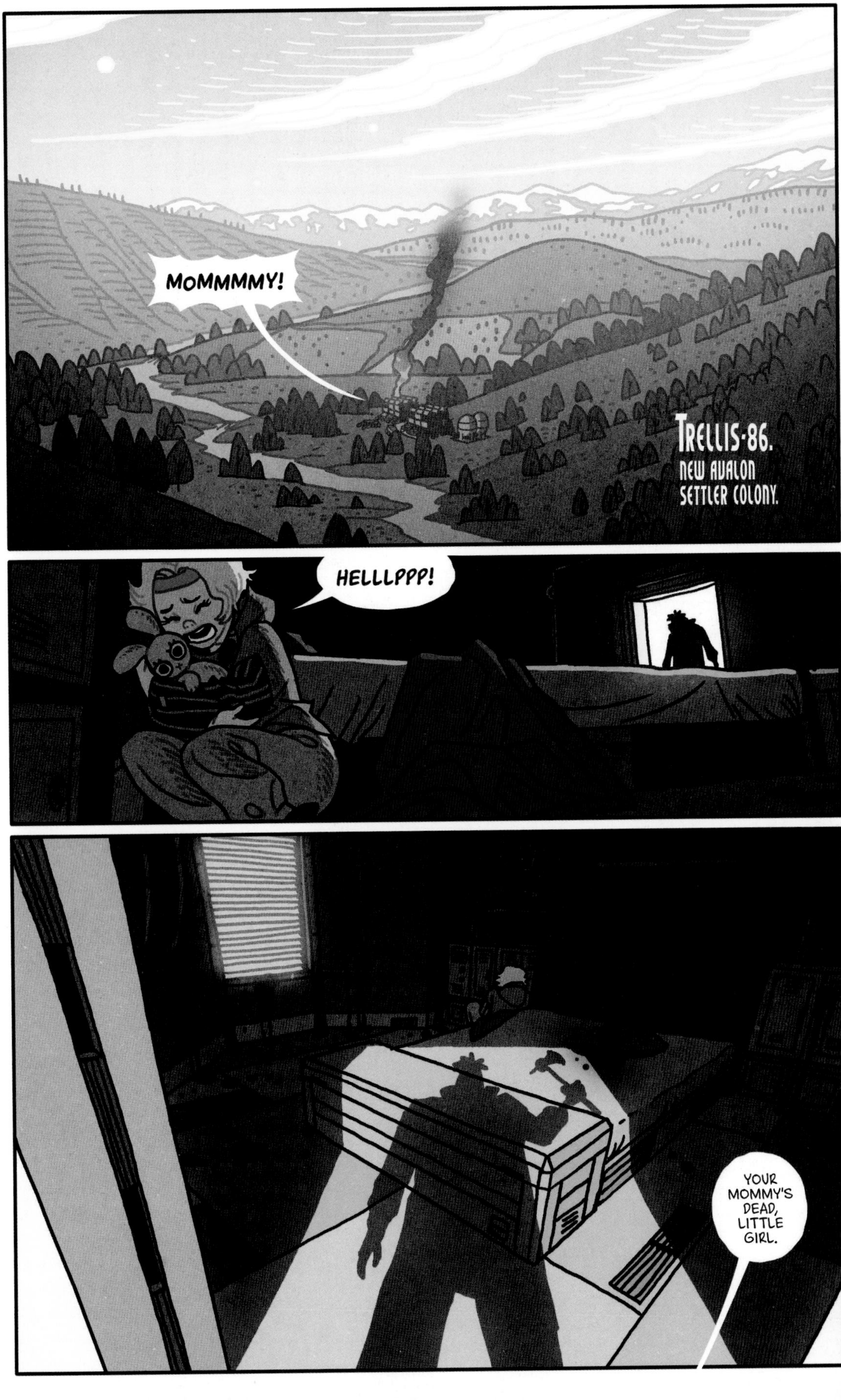
MOMMMMY!
TRELLIS-86.
NEW AVALON SETTLER COLONY.
HELLLPPP!
YOUR MOMMY'S DEAD, LITTLE GIRL.

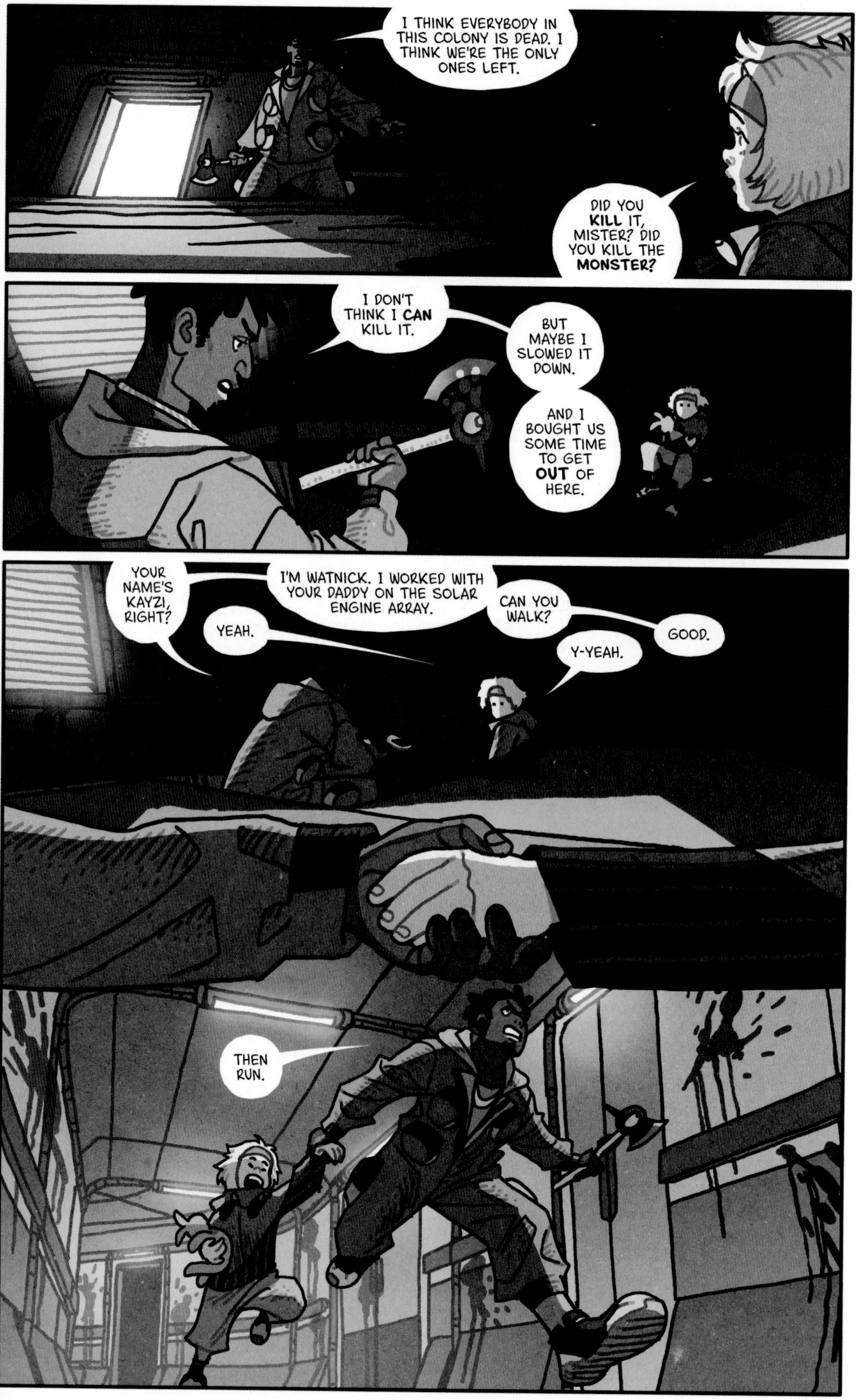

I THINK EVERYBODY IN THIS COLONY IS DEAD. I THINK WE'RE THE ONLY ONES LEFT.
DID YOU **KILL** IT, MISTER? DID YOU KILL THE **MONSTER?**
I DON'T THINK I **CAN** KILL IT.
BUT MAYBE I SLOWED IT DOWN.
AND I BOUGHT US SOME TIME TO GET **OUT** OF HERE.
YOUR NAME'S KAYZI, RIGHT?
YEAH.
I'M WATNICK. I WORKED WITH YOUR DADDY ON THE SOLAR ENGINE ARRAY.
CAN YOU WALK?
Y-YEAH.
GOOD.
THEN RUN.

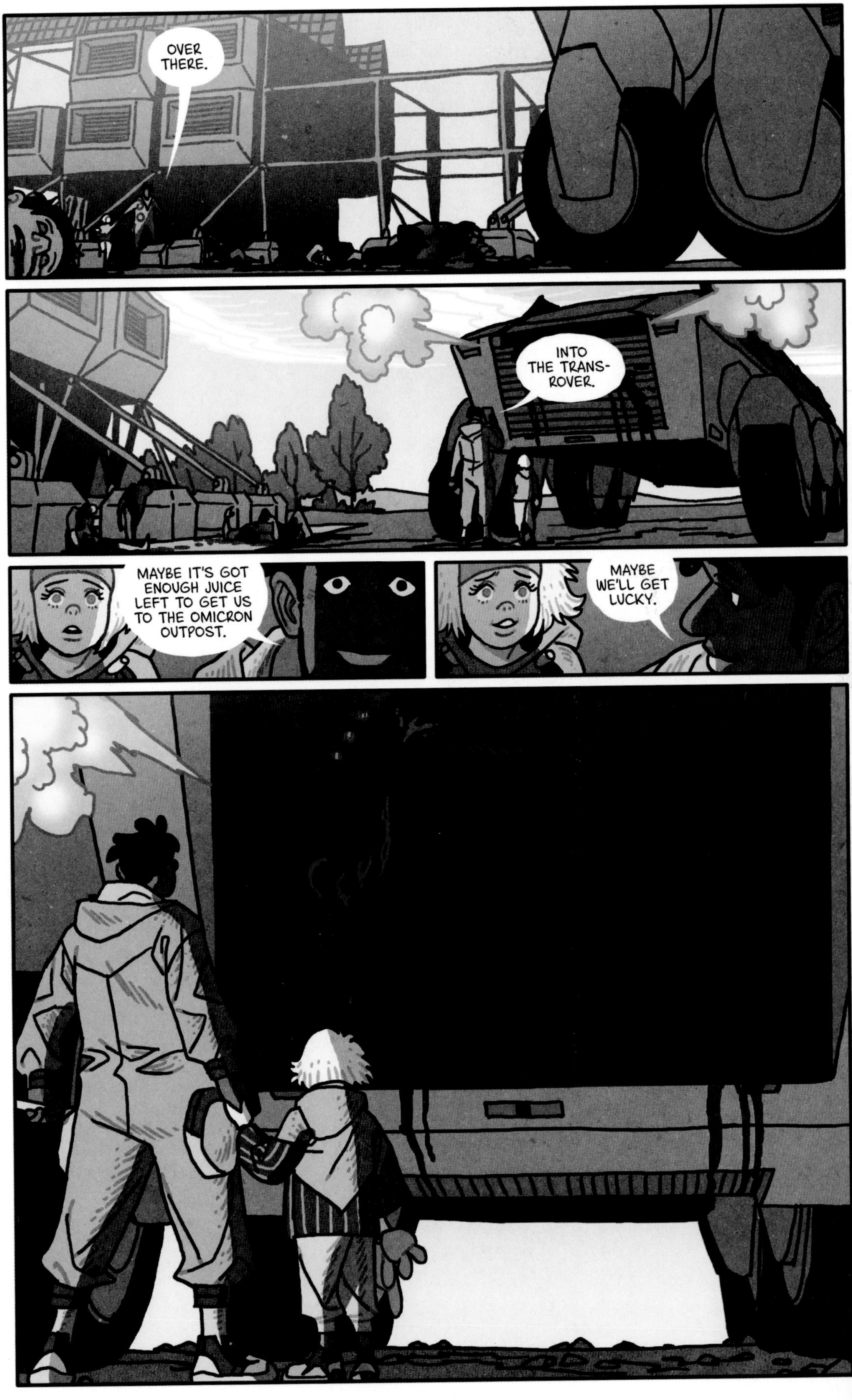
OVER THERE.
INTO THE TRANS-ROVER.
MAYBE IT'S GOT ENOUGH JUICE LEFT TO GET US TO THE OMICRON OUTPOST.
MAYBE WE'LL GET LUCKY.

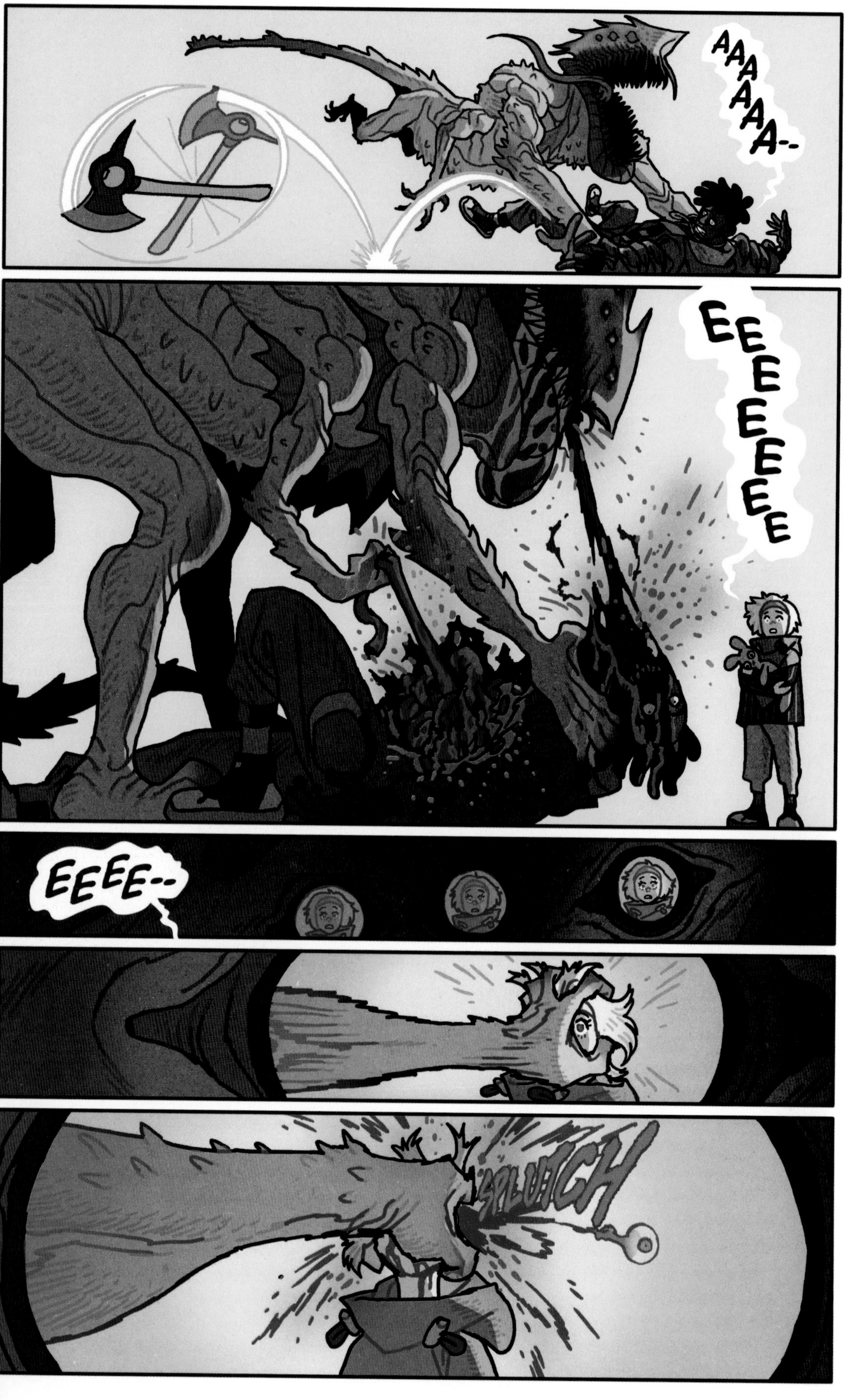
AAAAAA--
EEEEEEE
EEEE--
SPLUTCH

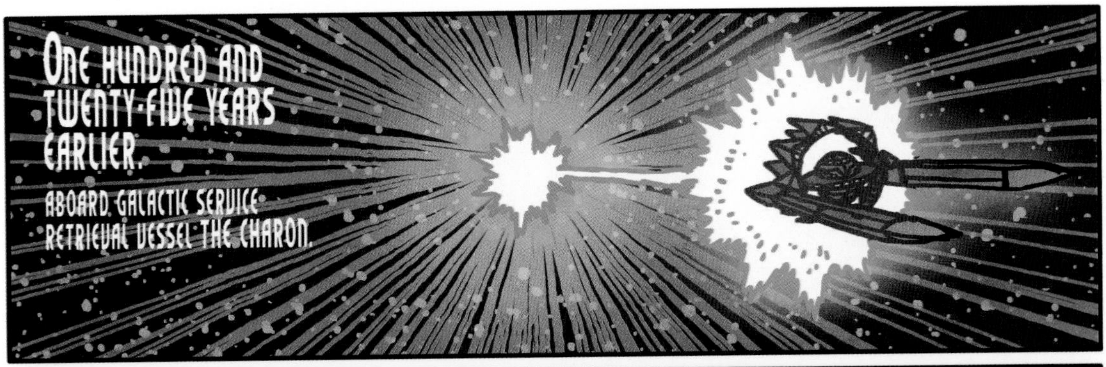
ONE HUNDRED AND TWENTY-FIVE YEARS EARLIER.
ABOARD GALACTIC SERVICE RETRIEVAL VESSEL THE CHARON.

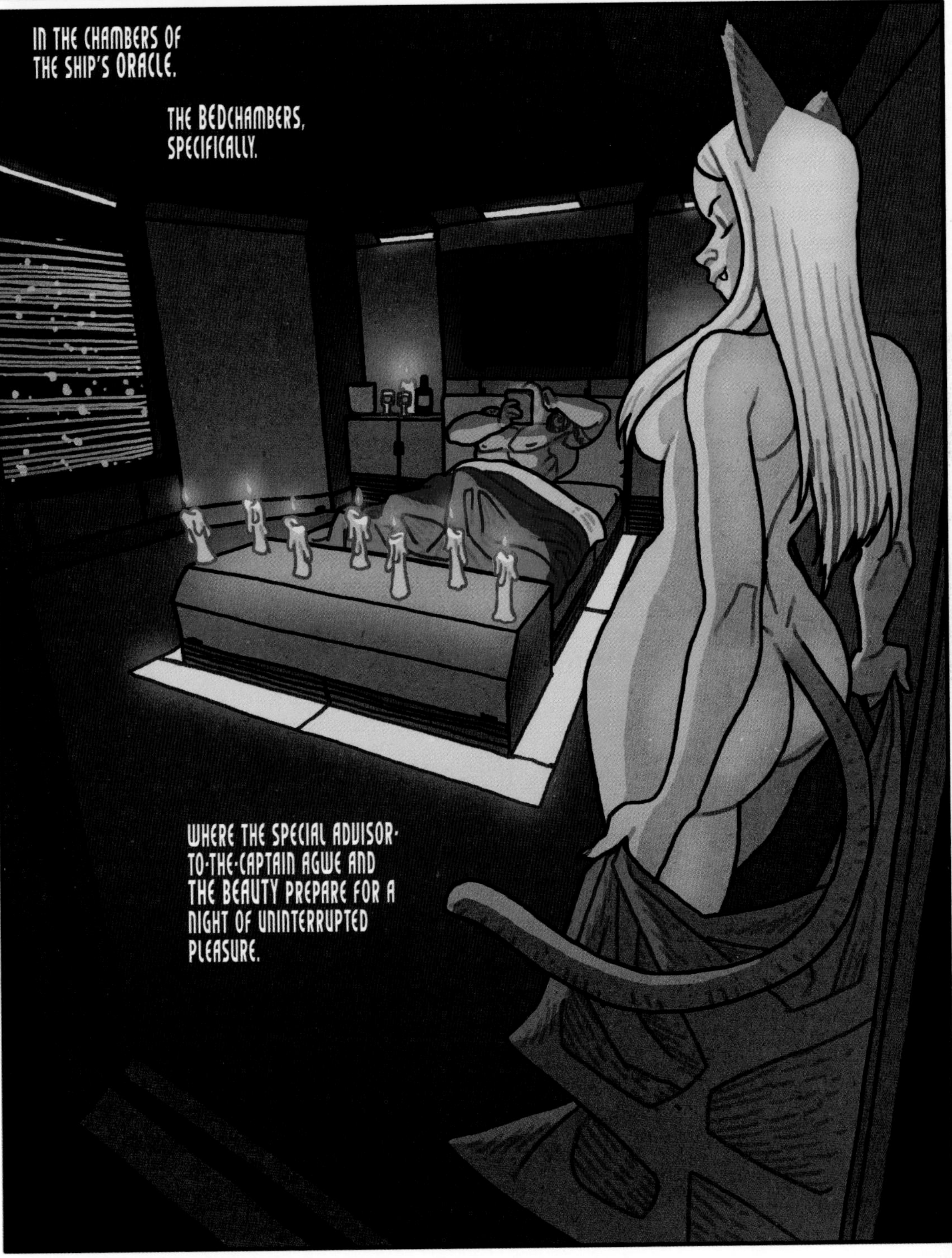
IN THE CHAMBERS OF THE SHIP'S ORACLE.
THE BEDCHAMBERS, SPECIFICALLY.
WHERE THE SPECIAL ADVISOR-TO-THE-CAPTAIN AGWE AND THE BEAUTY PREPARE FOR A NIGHT OF UNINTERRUPTED PLEASURE.

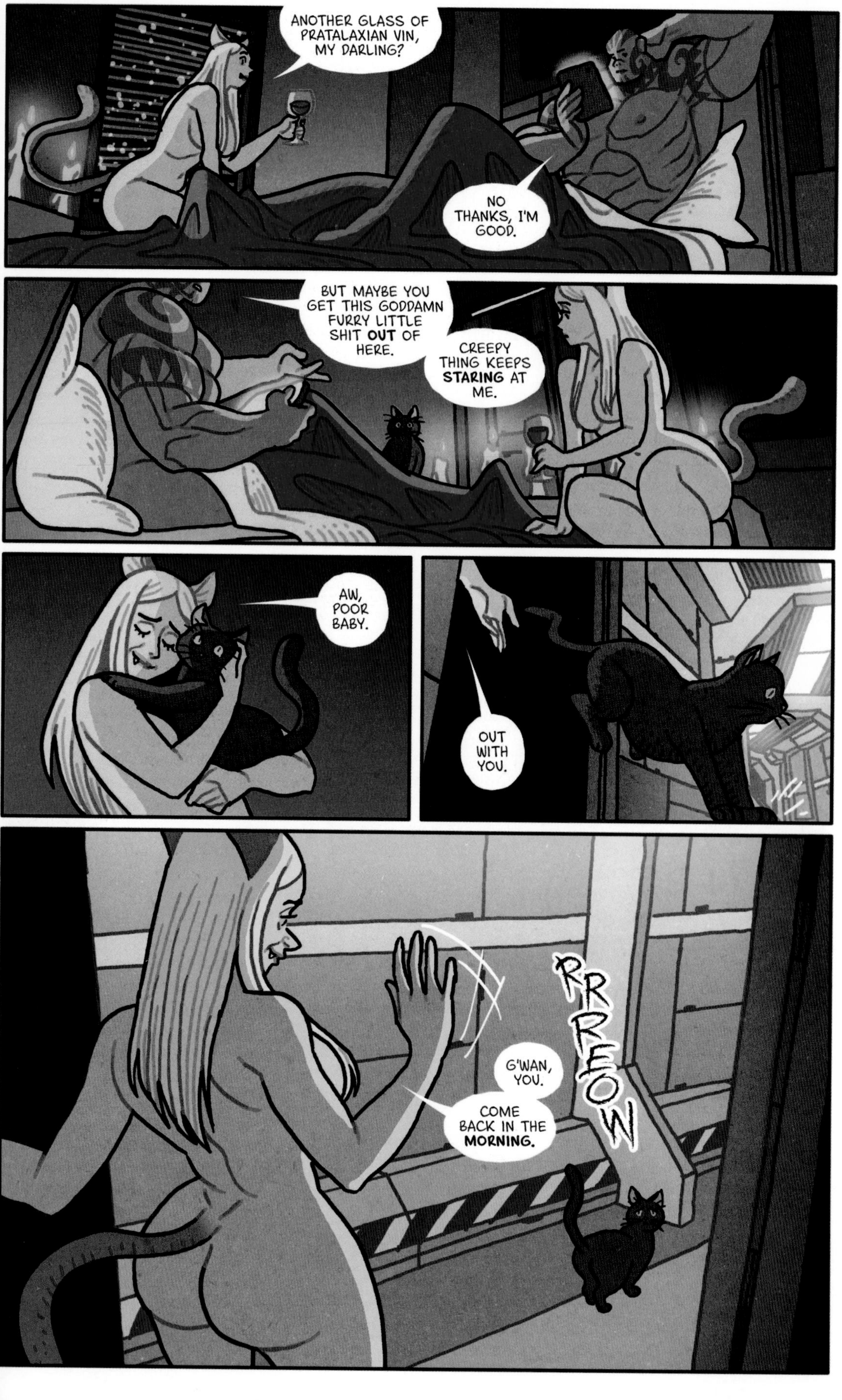
ANOTHER GLASS OF PRATALAXIAN VIN, MY DARLING?
NO THANKS, I'M GOOD.
BUT MAYBE YOU GET THIS GODDAMN FURRY LITTLE SHIT **OUT** OF HERE.
CREEPY THING KEEPS **STARING** AT ME.
AW, POOR BABY.
OUT WITH YOU.
RRREOW
G'WAN, YOU.
COME BACK IN THE **MORNING.**

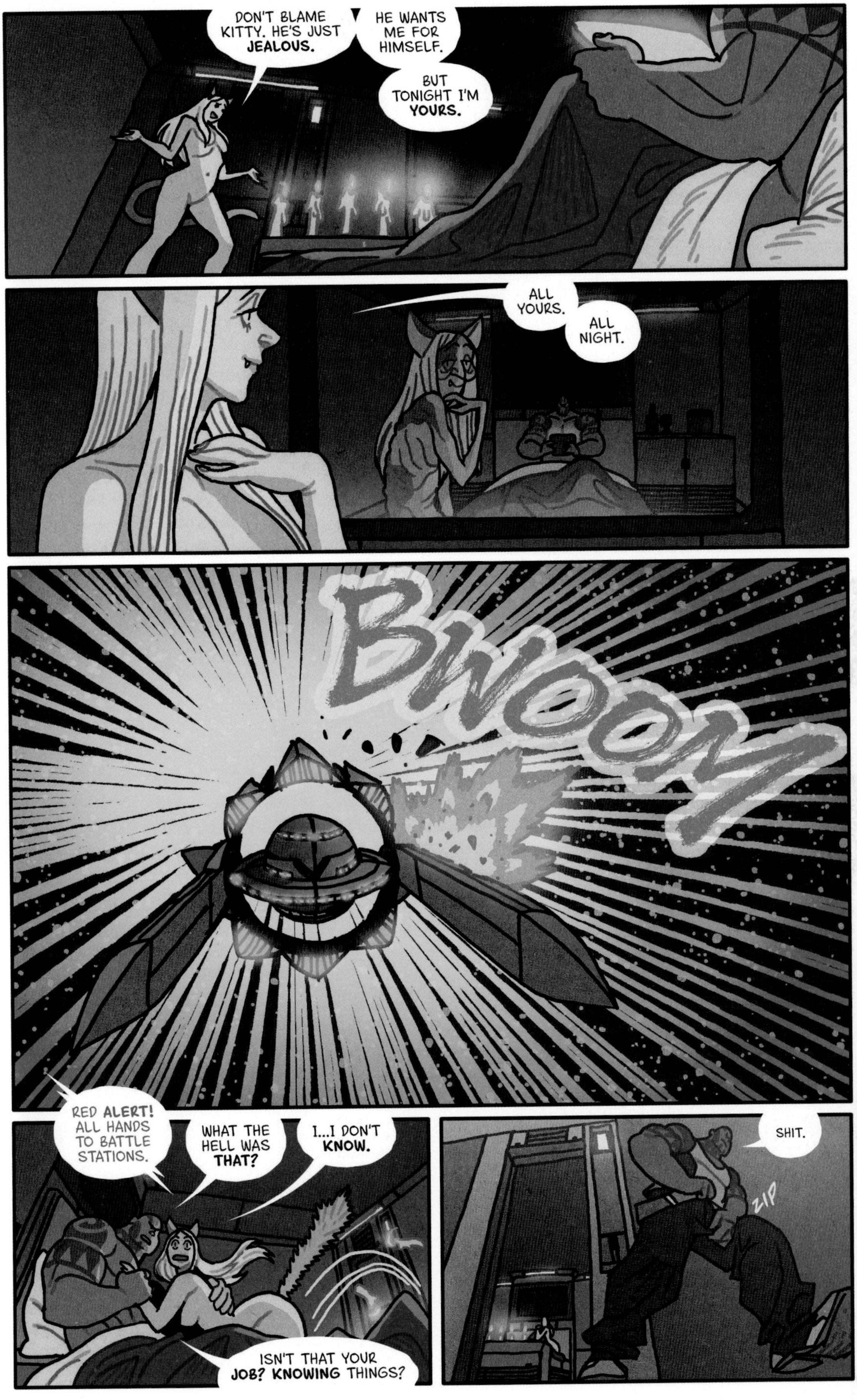
DON'T BLAME KITTY. HE'S JUST **JEALOUS.**
HE WANTS ME FOR HIMSELF.
BUT TONIGHT I'M **YOURS.**
ALL YOURS.
ALL NIGHT.
BWOOM
RED **ALERT!** ALL HANDS TO BATTLE STATIONS.
WHAT THE HELL WAS **THAT?**
I...I DON'T **KNOW.**
ISN'T THAT YOUR **JOB? KNOWING** THINGS?
SHIT.
ZIP

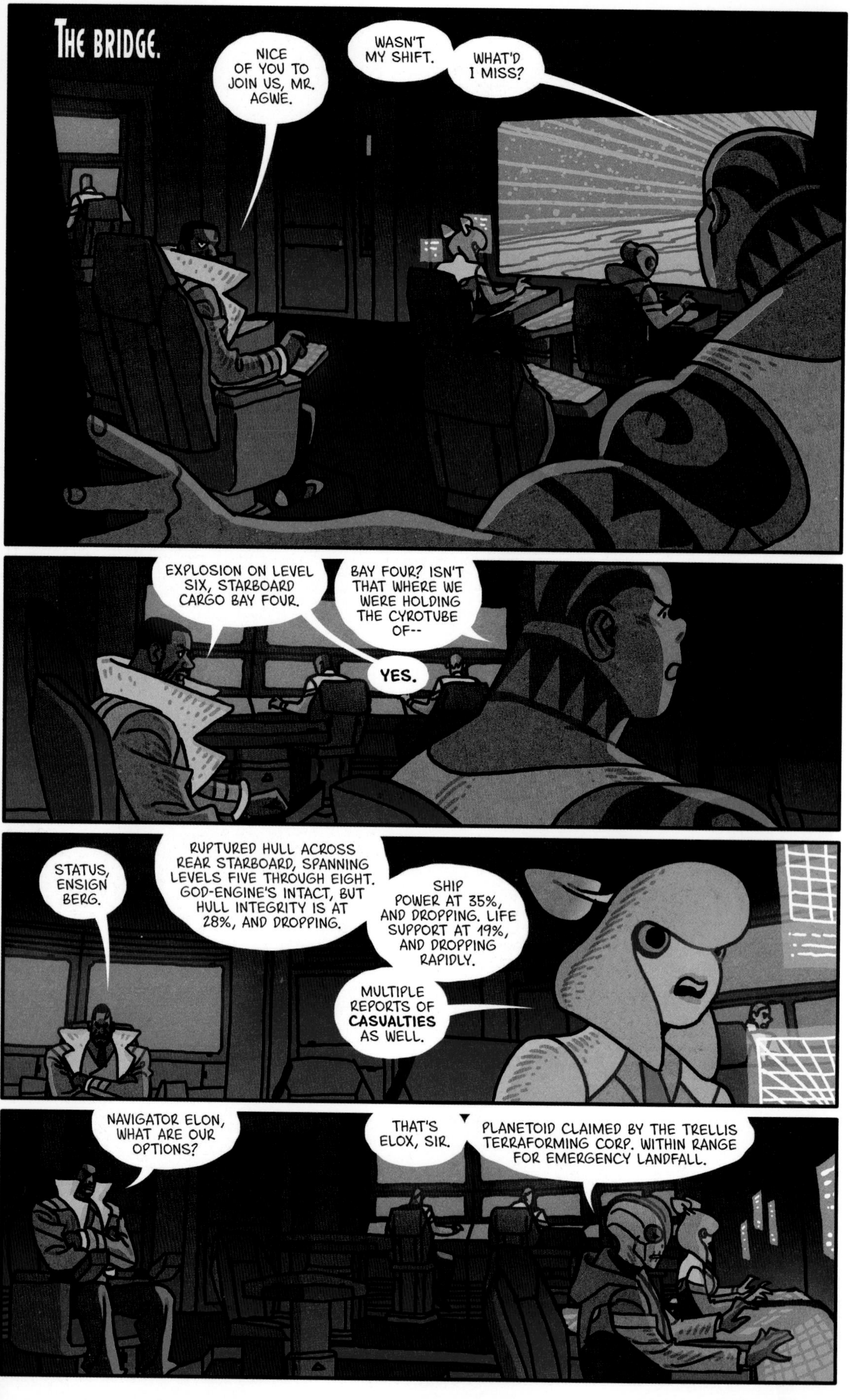
THE BRIDGE.
NICE OF YOU TO JOIN US, MR. AGWE.
WASN'T MY SHIFT.
WHAT'D I MISS?
EXPLOSION ON LEVEL SIX, STARBOARD CARGO BAY FOUR.
BAY FOUR? ISN'T THAT WHERE WE WERE HOLDING THE CYROTUBE OF--
YES.
STATUS, ENSIGN BERG.
RUPTURED HULL ACROSS REAR STARBOARD, SPANNING LEVELS FIVE THROUGH EIGHT. GOD-ENGINE'S INTACT, BUT HULL INTEGRITY IS AT 28%, AND DROPPING.
SHIP POWER AT 35%, AND DROPPING. LIFE SUPPORT AT 19%, AND DROPPING RAPIDLY.
MULTIPLE REPORTS OF CASUALTIES AS WELL.
NAVIGATOR ELON, WHAT ARE OUR OPTIONS?
THAT'S ELOX, SIR.
PLANETOID CLAIMED BY THE TRELLIS TERRAFORMING CORP. WITHIN RANGE FOR EMERGENCY LANDFALL.

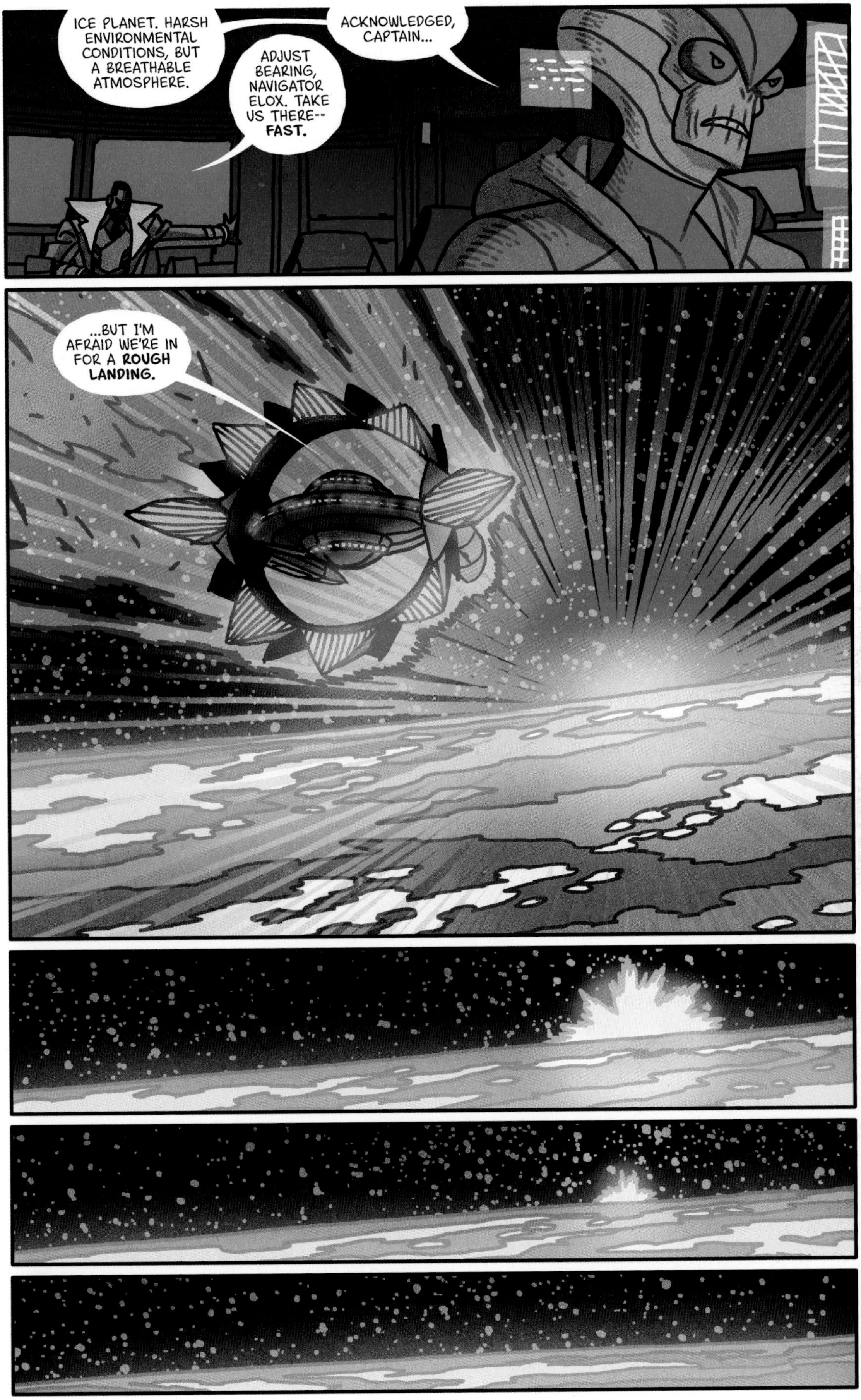
ICE PLANET. HARSH ENVIRONMENTAL CONDITIONS, BUT A BREATHABLE ATMOSPHERE.
ADJUST BEARING, NAVIGATOR ELOX. TAKE US THERE-- **FAST.**
ACKNOWLEDGED, CAPTAIN...
...BUT I'M AFRAID WE'RE IN FOR A **ROUGH LANDING.**

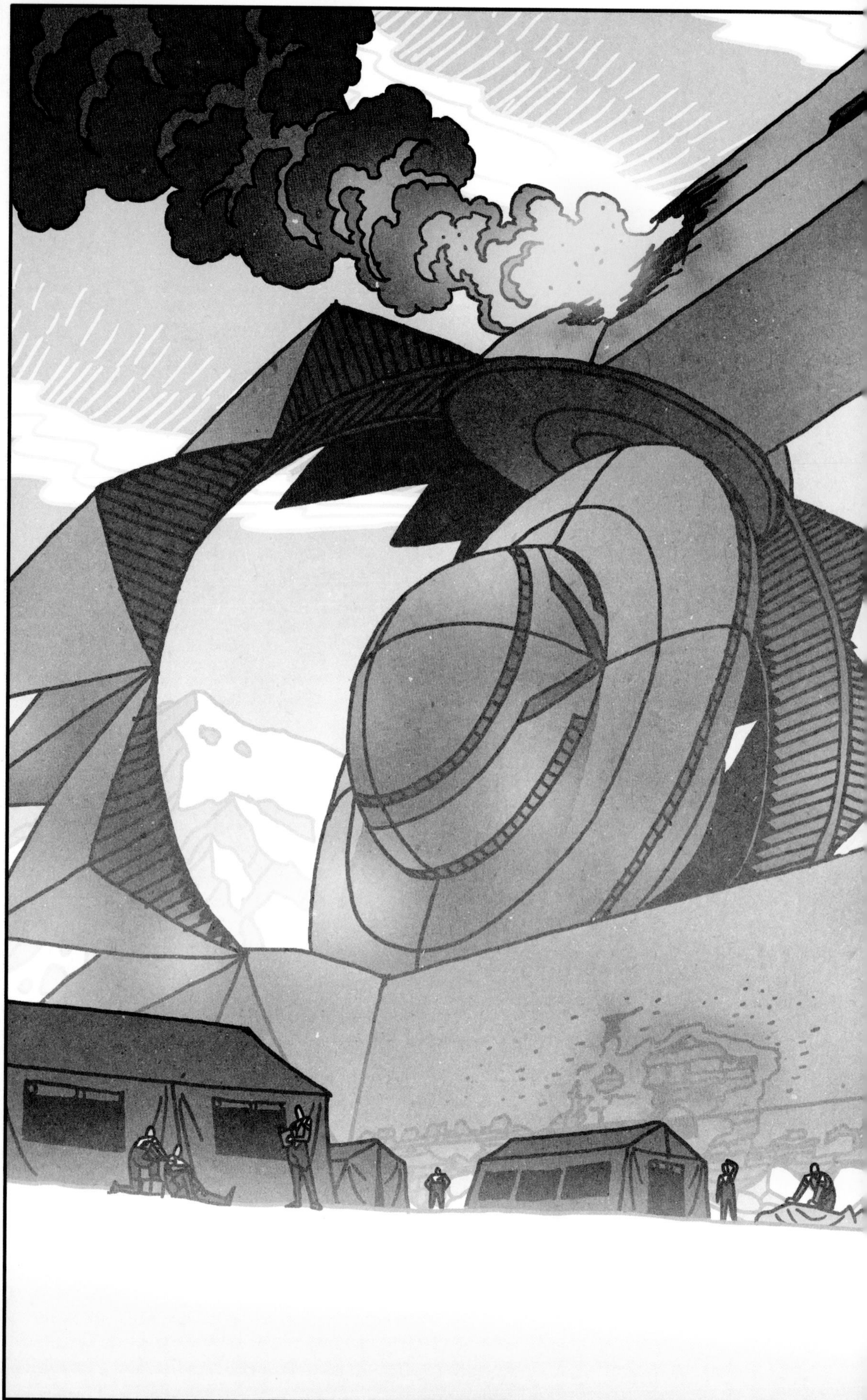

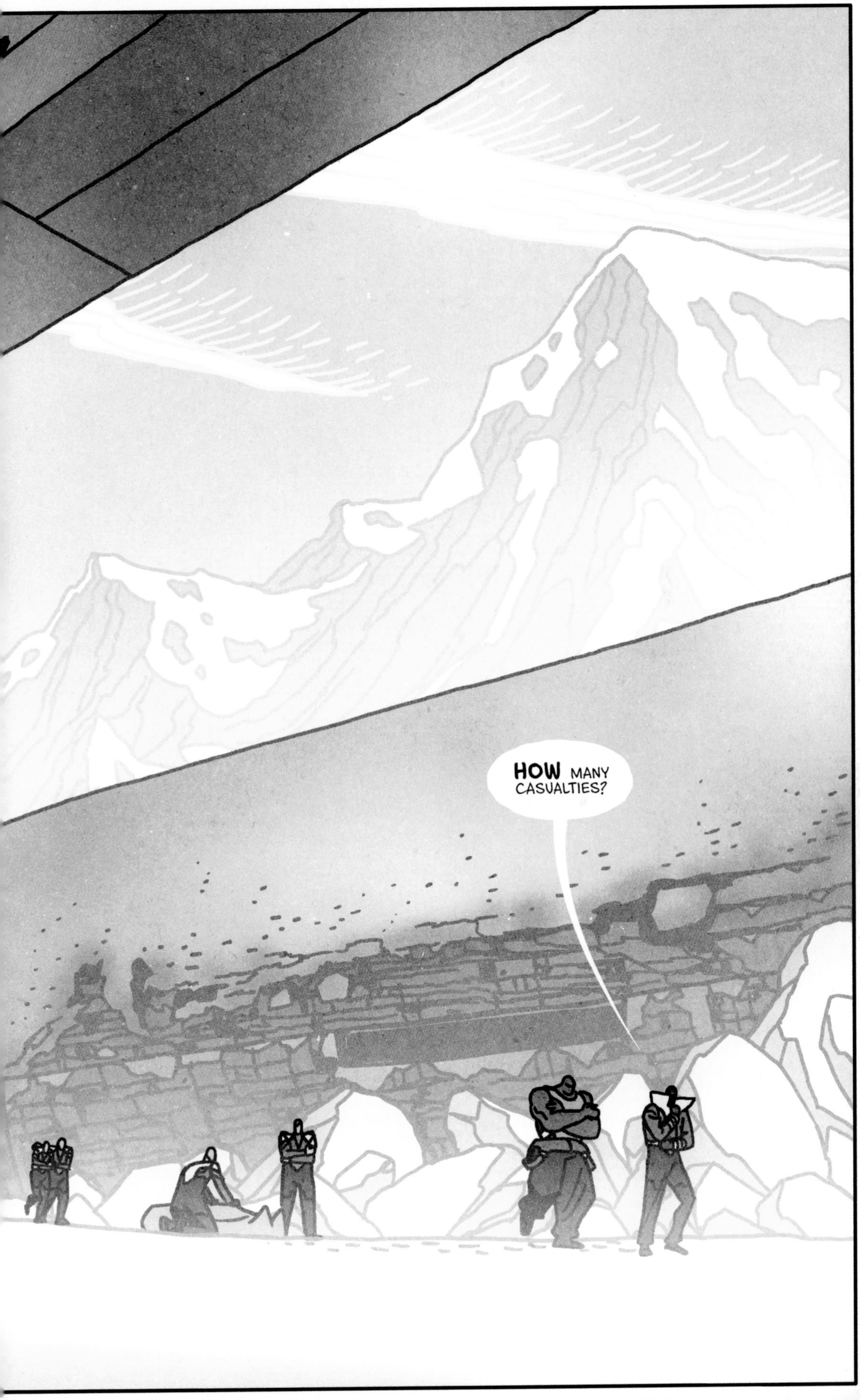
HOW MANY CASUALTIES?

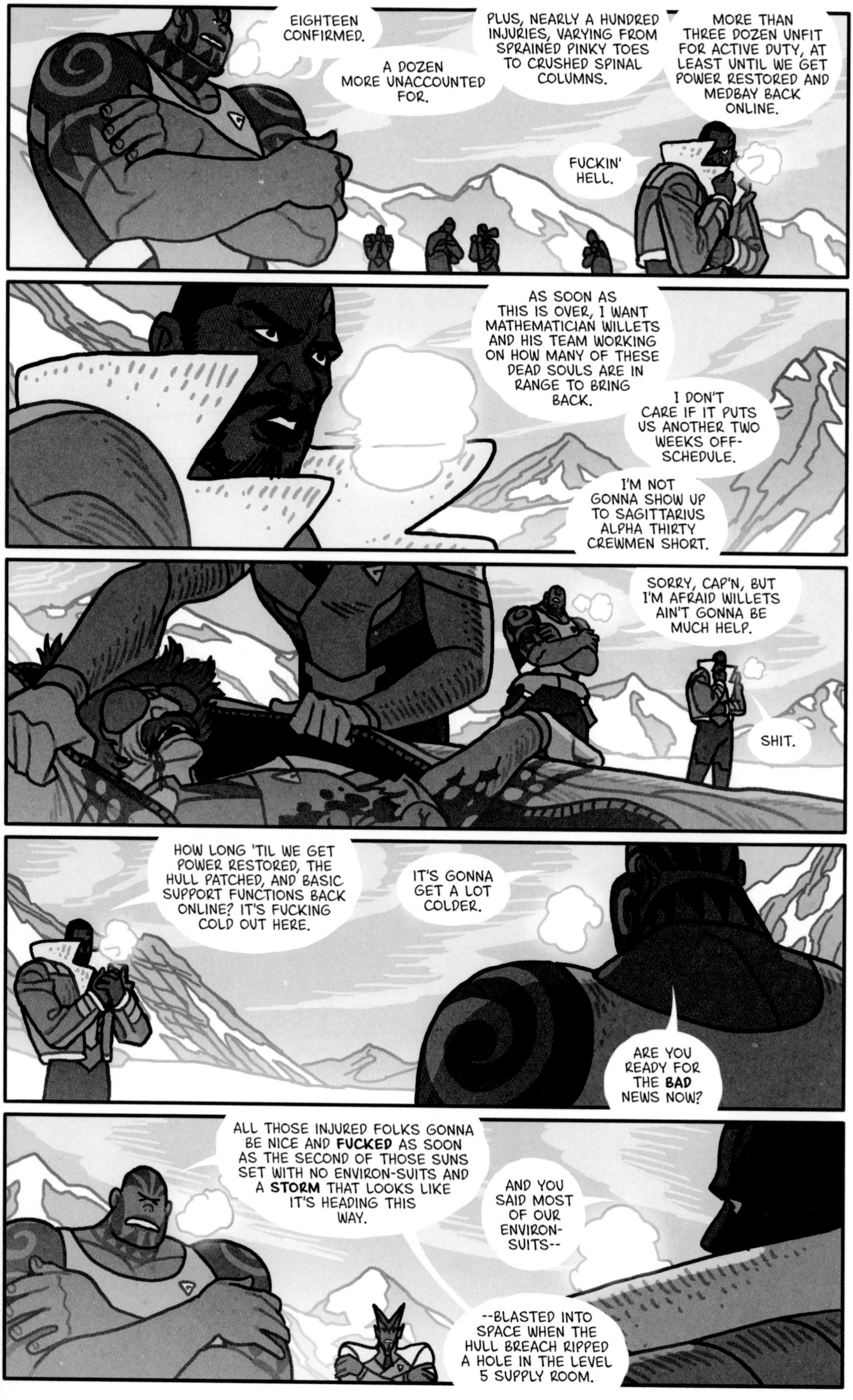
EIGHTEEN CONFIRMED.
A DOZEN MORE UNACCOUNTED FOR.
PLUS, NEARLY A HUNDRED INJURIES, VARYING FROM SPRAINED PINKY TOES TO CRUSHED SPINAL COLUMNS.
MORE THAN THREE DOZEN UNFIT FOR ACTIVE DUTY, AT LEAST UNTIL WE GET POWER RESTORED AND MEDBAY BACK ONLINE.
FUCKIN' HELL.
AS SOON AS THIS IS OVER, I WANT MATHEMATICIAN WILLETS AND HIS TEAM WORKING ON HOW MANY OF THESE DEAD SOULS ARE IN RANGE TO BRING BACK.
I DON'T CARE IF IT PUTS US ANOTHER TWO WEEKS OFF-SCHEDULE.
I'M NOT GONNA SHOW UP TO SAGITTARIUS ALPHA THIRTY CREWMEN SHORT.
SORRY, CAP'N, BUT I'M AFRAID WILLETS AIN'T GONNA BE MUCH HELP.
SHIT.
HOW LONG 'TIL WE GET POWER RESTORED, THE HULL PATCHED, AND BASIC SUPPORT FUNCTIONS BACK ONLINE? IT'S FUCKING COLD OUT HERE.
IT'S GONNA GET A LOT COLDER.
ARE YOU READY FOR THE **BAD** NEWS NOW?
ALL THOSE INJURED FOLKS GONNA BE NICE AND **FUCKED** AS SOON AS THE SECOND OF THOSE SUNS SET WITH NO ENVIRON-SUITS AND A **STORM** THAT LOOKS LIKE IT'S HEADING THIS WAY.
AND YOU SAID MOST OF OUR ENVIRON-SUITS--
--BLASTED INTO SPACE WHEN THE HULL BREACH RIPPED A HOLE IN THE LEVEL 5 SUPPLY ROOM.

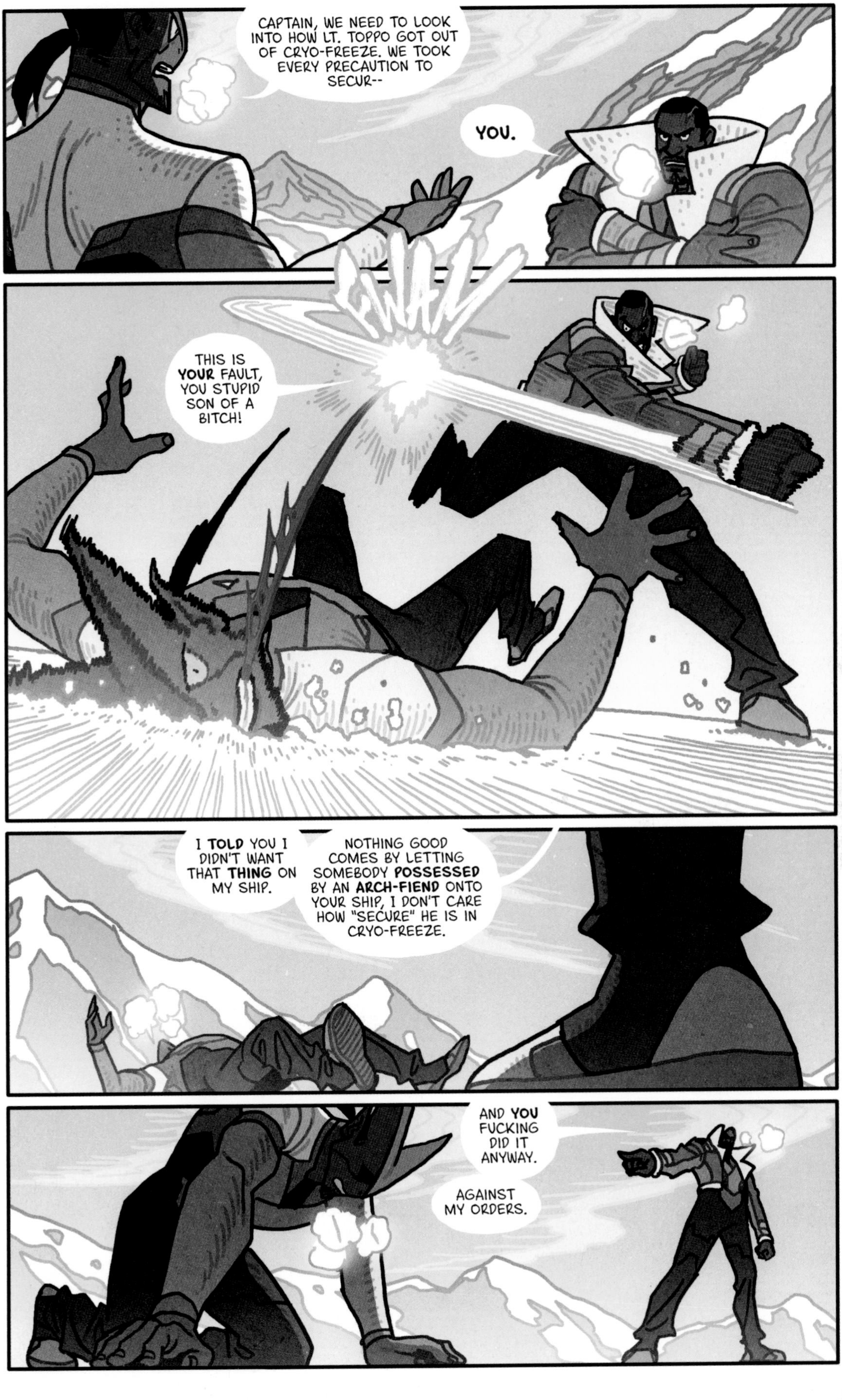
CAPTAIN, WE NEED TO LOOK INTO HOW LT. TOPPO GOT OUT OF CRYO-FREEZE. WE TOOK EVERY PRECAUTION TO SECUR--
YOU.
THIS IS YOUR FAULT, YOU STUPID SON OF A BITCH!
I TOLD YOU I DIDN'T WANT THAT THING ON MY SHIP.
NOTHING GOOD COMES BY LETTING SOMEBODY POSSESSED BY AN ARCH-FIEND ONTO YOUR SHIP, I DON'T CARE HOW "SECURE" HE IS IN CRYO-FREEZE.
AND YOU FUCKING DID IT ANYWAY.
AGAINST MY ORDERS.

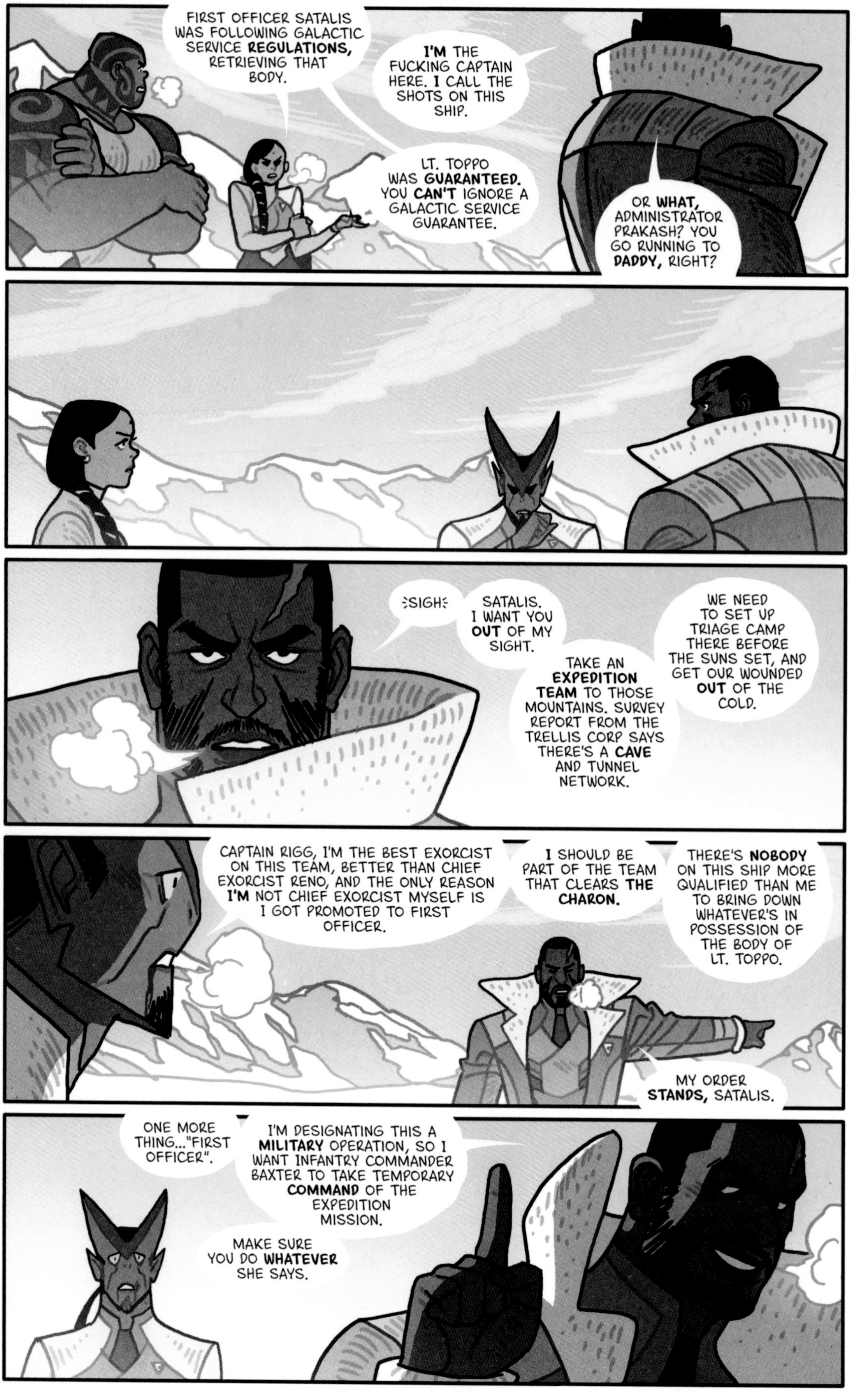
FIRST OFFICER SATALIS WAS FOLLOWING GALACTIC SERVICE **REGULATIONS,** RETRIEVING THAT BODY.
I'M THE FUCKING CAPTAIN HERE. I CALL THE SHOTS ON THIS SHIP.
LT. TOPPO WAS **GUARANTEED.** YOU **CAN'T** IGNORE A GALACTIC SERVICE GUARANTEE.
OR **WHAT,** ADMINISTRATOR PRAKASH? YOU GO RUNNING TO **DADDY,** RIGHT?
SIGH
SATALIS. I WANT YOU **OUT** OF MY SIGHT.
TAKE AN **EXPEDITION TEAM** TO THOSE MOUNTAINS. SURVEY REPORT FROM THE TRELLIS CORP SAYS THERE'S A **CAVE** AND TUNNEL NETWORK.
WE NEED TO SET UP TRIAGE CAMP THERE BEFORE THE SUNS SET, AND GET OUR WOUNDED **OUT** OF THE COLD.
CAPTAIN RIGG, I'M THE BEST EXORCIST ON THIS TEAM, BETTER THAN CHIEF EXORCIST RENO, AND THE ONLY REASON **I'M** NOT CHIEF EXORCIST MYSELF IS I GOT PROMOTED TO FIRST OFFICER.
I SHOULD BE PART OF THE TEAM THAT CLEARS **THE CHARON.**
THERE'S **NOBODY** ON THIS SHIP MORE QUALIFIED THAN ME TO BRING DOWN WHATEVER'S IN POSSESSION OF THE BODY OF LT. TOPPO.
MY ORDER **STANDS,** SATALIS.
ONE MORE THING..."FIRST OFFICER".
I'M DESIGNATING THIS A **MILITARY** OPERATION, SO I WANT INFANTRY COMMANDER BAXTER TO TAKE TEMPORARY **COMMAND** OF THE EXPEDITION MISSION.
MAKE SURE YOU DO **WHATEVER** SHE SAYS.

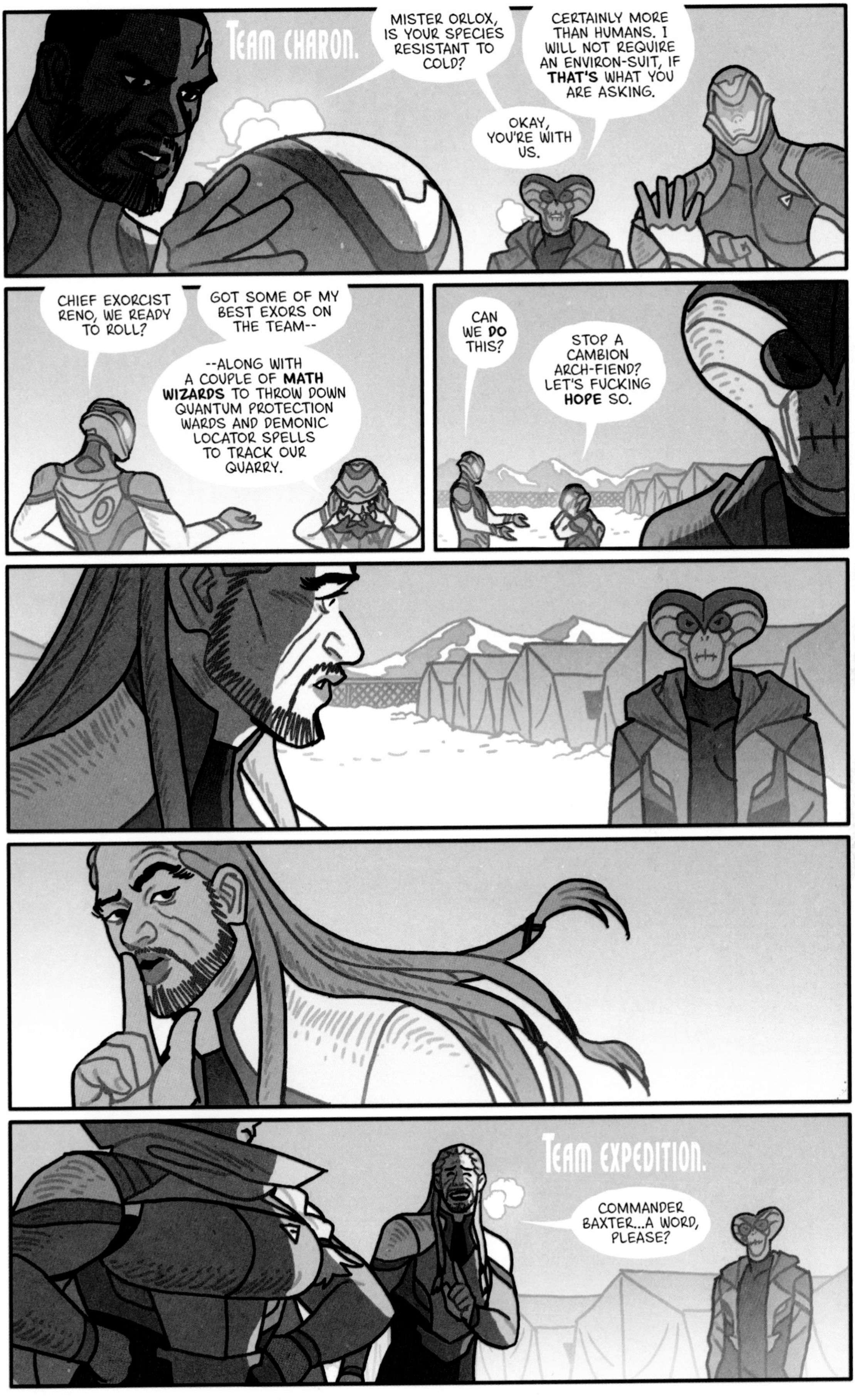
TEAM CHARON.
MISTER ORLOX, IS YOUR SPECIES RESISTANT TO COLD?
CERTAINLY MORE THAN HUMANS. I WILL NOT REQUIRE AN ENVIRON-SUIT, IF THAT'S WHAT YOU ARE ASKING.
OKAY, YOU'RE WITH US.
CHIEF EXORCIST RENO, WE READY TO ROLL?
GOT SOME OF MY BEST EXORS ON THE TEAM--
--ALONG WITH A COUPLE OF MATH WIZARDS TO THROW DOWN QUANTUM PROTECTION WARDS AND DEMONIC LOCATOR SPELLS TO TRACK OUR QUARRY.
CAN WE DO THIS?
STOP A CAMBION ARCH-FIEND? LET'S FUCKING HOPE SO.
TEAM EXPEDITION.
COMMANDER BAXTER...A WORD, PLEASE?

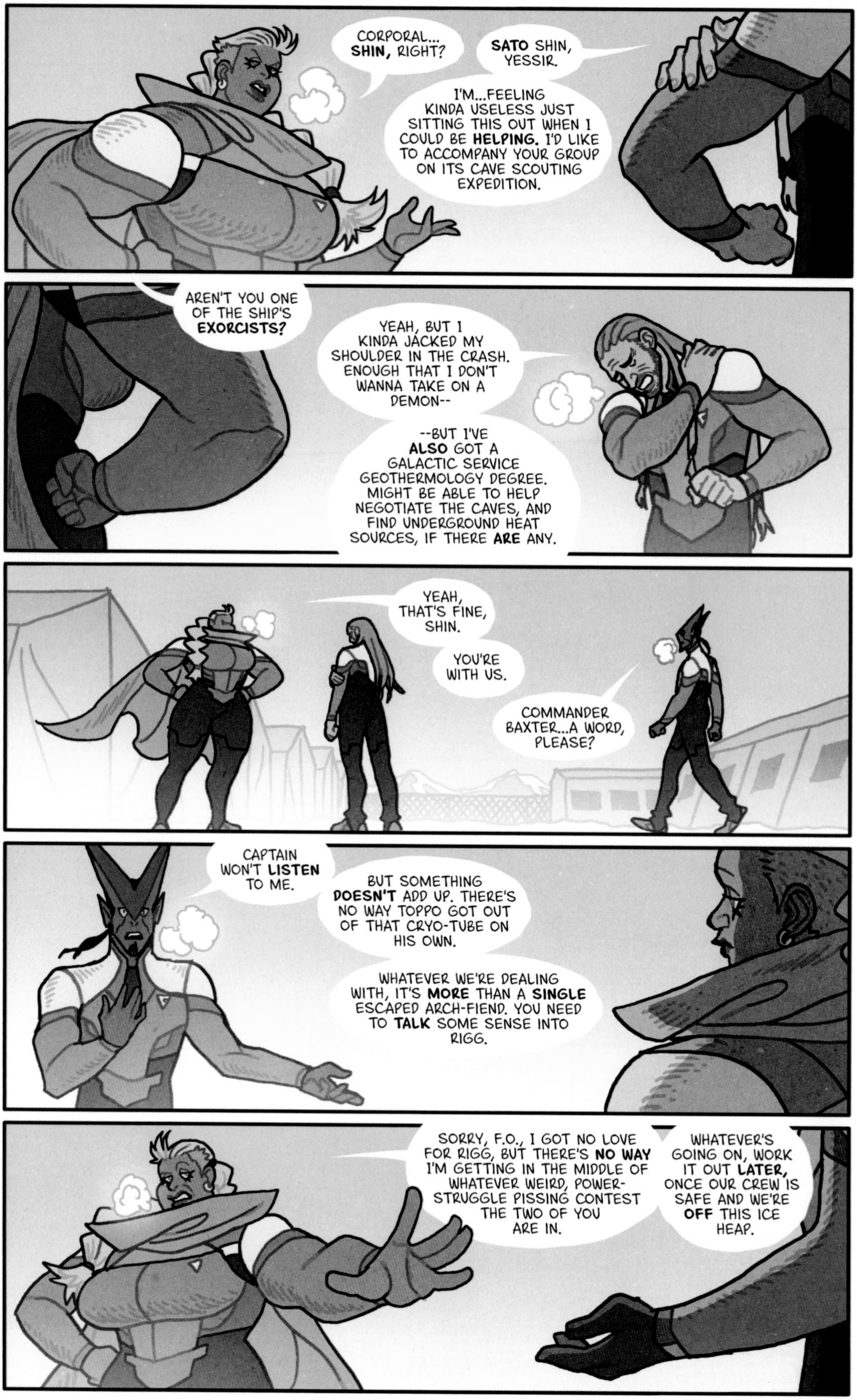
CORPORAL... **SHIN,** RIGHT?
SATO SHIN, YESSIR.
I'M...FEELING KINDA USELESS JUST SITTING THIS OUT WHEN I COULD BE **HELPING.** I'D LIKE TO ACCOMPANY YOUR GROUP ON ITS CAVE SCOUTING EXPEDITION.
AREN'T YOU ONE OF THE SHIP'S **EXORCISTS?**
YEAH, BUT I KINDA JACKED MY SHOULDER IN THE CRASH. ENOUGH THAT I DON'T WANNA TAKE ON A DEMON--
--BUT I'VE **ALSO** GOT A GALACTIC SERVICE GEOTHERMOLOGY DEGREE. MIGHT BE ABLE TO HELP NEGOTIATE THE CAVES, AND FIND UNDERGROUND HEAT SOURCES, IF THERE **ARE** ANY.
YEAH, THAT'S FINE, SHIN.
YOU'RE WITH US.
COMMANDER BAXTER...A WORD, PLEASE?
CAPTAIN WON'T **LISTEN** TO ME.
BUT SOMETHING **DOESN'T** ADD UP. THERE'S NO WAY TOPPO GOT OUT OF THAT CRYO-TUBE ON HIS OWN.
WHATEVER WE'RE DEALING WITH, IT'S **MORE** THAN A **SINGLE** ESCAPED ARCH-FIEND. YOU NEED TO **TALK** SOME SENSE INTO RIGG.
SORRY, F.O., I GOT NO LOVE FOR RIGG, BUT THERE'S **NO WAY** I'M GETTING IN THE MIDDLE OF WHATEVER WEIRD, POWER-STRUGGLE PISSING CONTEST THE TWO OF YOU ARE IN.
WHATEVER'S GOING ON, WORK IT OUT **LATER,** ONCE OUR CREW IS SAFE AND WE'RE **OFF** THIS ICE HEAP.

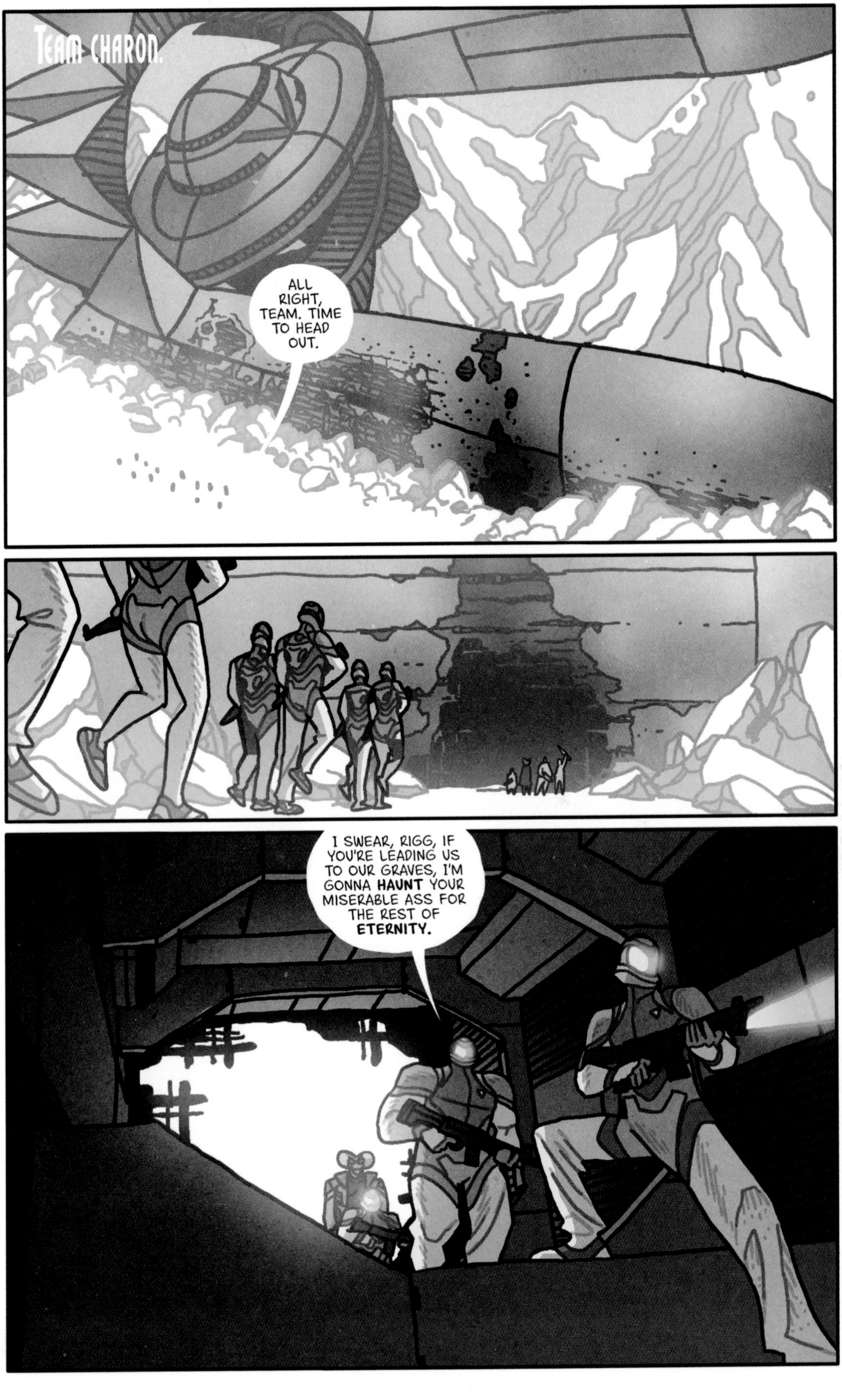
TEAM CHARON.
ALL RIGHT, TEAM. TIME TO HEAD OUT.
I SWEAR, RIGG, IF YOU'RE LEADING US TO OUR GRAVES, I'M GONNA **HAUNT** YOUR MISERABLE ASS FOR THE REST OF **ETERNITY.**

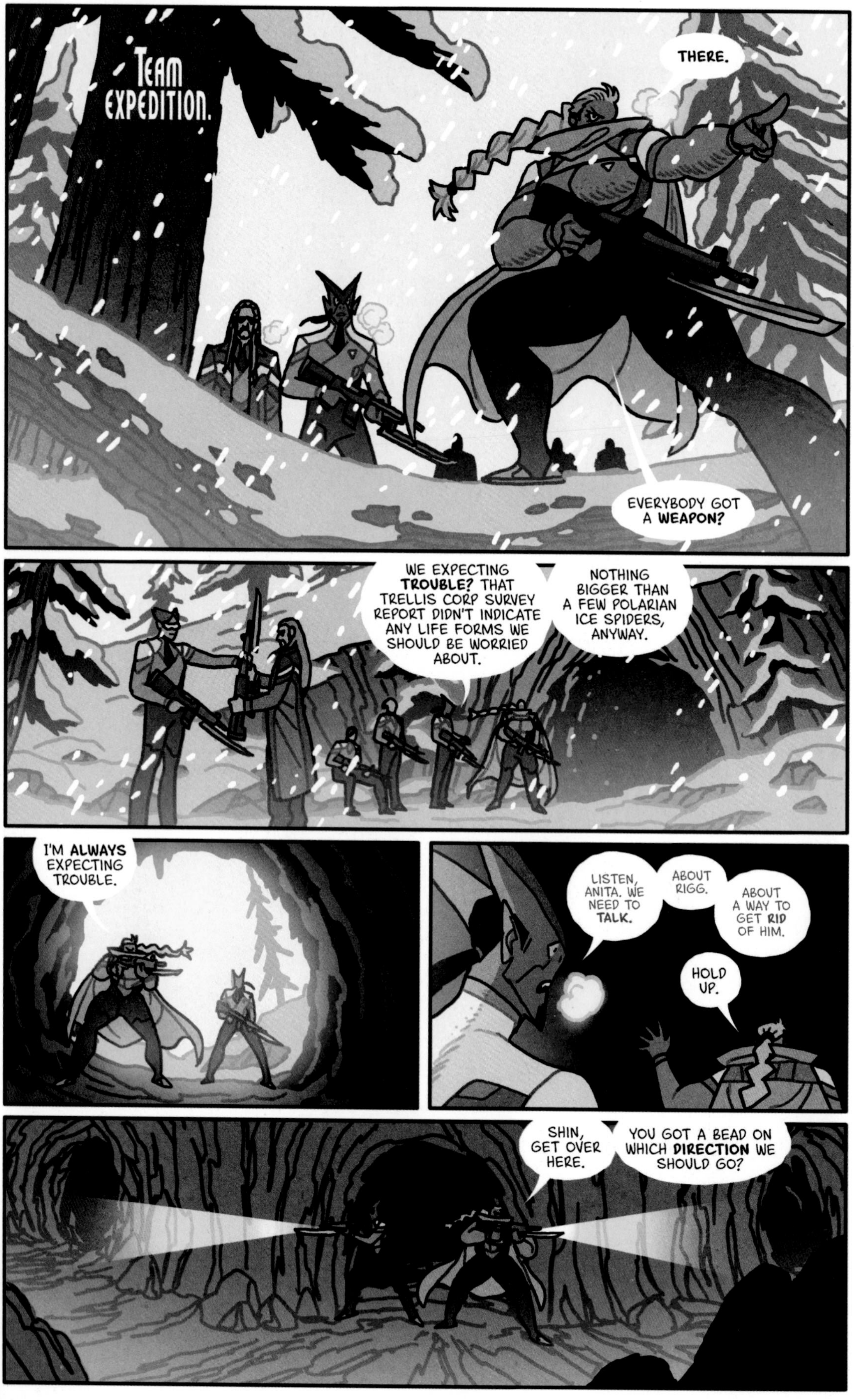
TEAM EXPEDITION.
THERE.
EVERYBODY GOT A WEAPON?
WE EXPECTING TROUBLE? THAT TRELLIS CORP SURVEY REPORT DIDN'T INDICATE ANY LIFE FORMS WE SHOULD BE WORRIED ABOUT.
NOTHING BIGGER THAN A FEW POLARIAN ICE SPIDERS, ANYWAY.
I'M ALWAYS EXPECTING TROUBLE.
LISTEN, ANITA. WE NEED TO TALK.
ABOUT RIGG.
ABOUT A WAY TO GET RID OF HIM.
HOLD UP.
SHIN, GET OVER HERE.
YOU GOT A BEAD ON WHICH DIRECTION WE SHOULD GO?

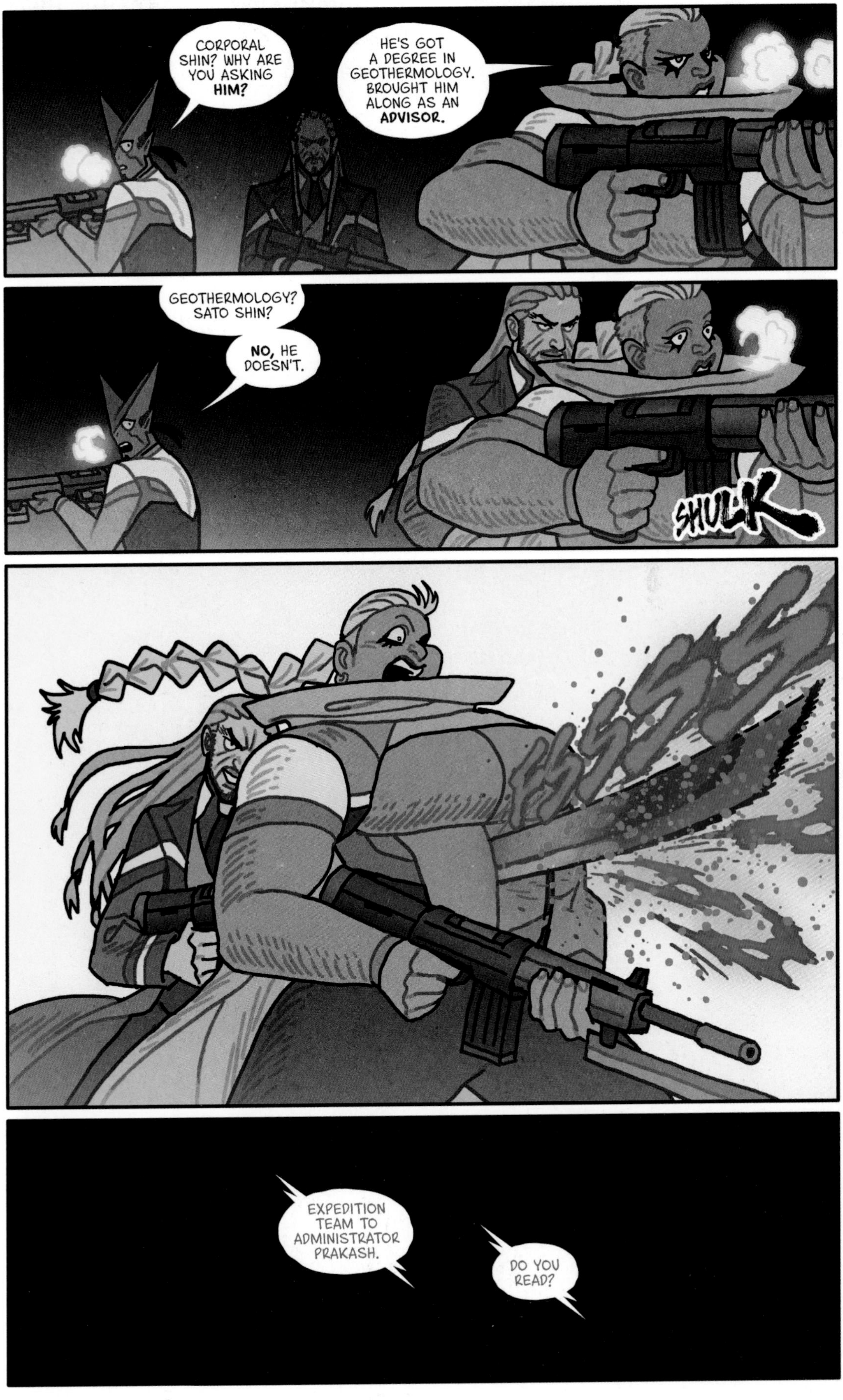
CORPORAL SHIN? WHY ARE YOU ASKING HIM?
HE'S GOT A DEGREE IN GEOTHERMOLOGY. BROUGHT HIM ALONG AS AN ADVISOR.
GEOTHERMOLOGY? SATO SHIN?
NO, HE DOESN'T.
SHULK
FSSSSS
EXPEDITION TEAM TO ADMINISTRATOR PRAKASH.
DO YOU READ?

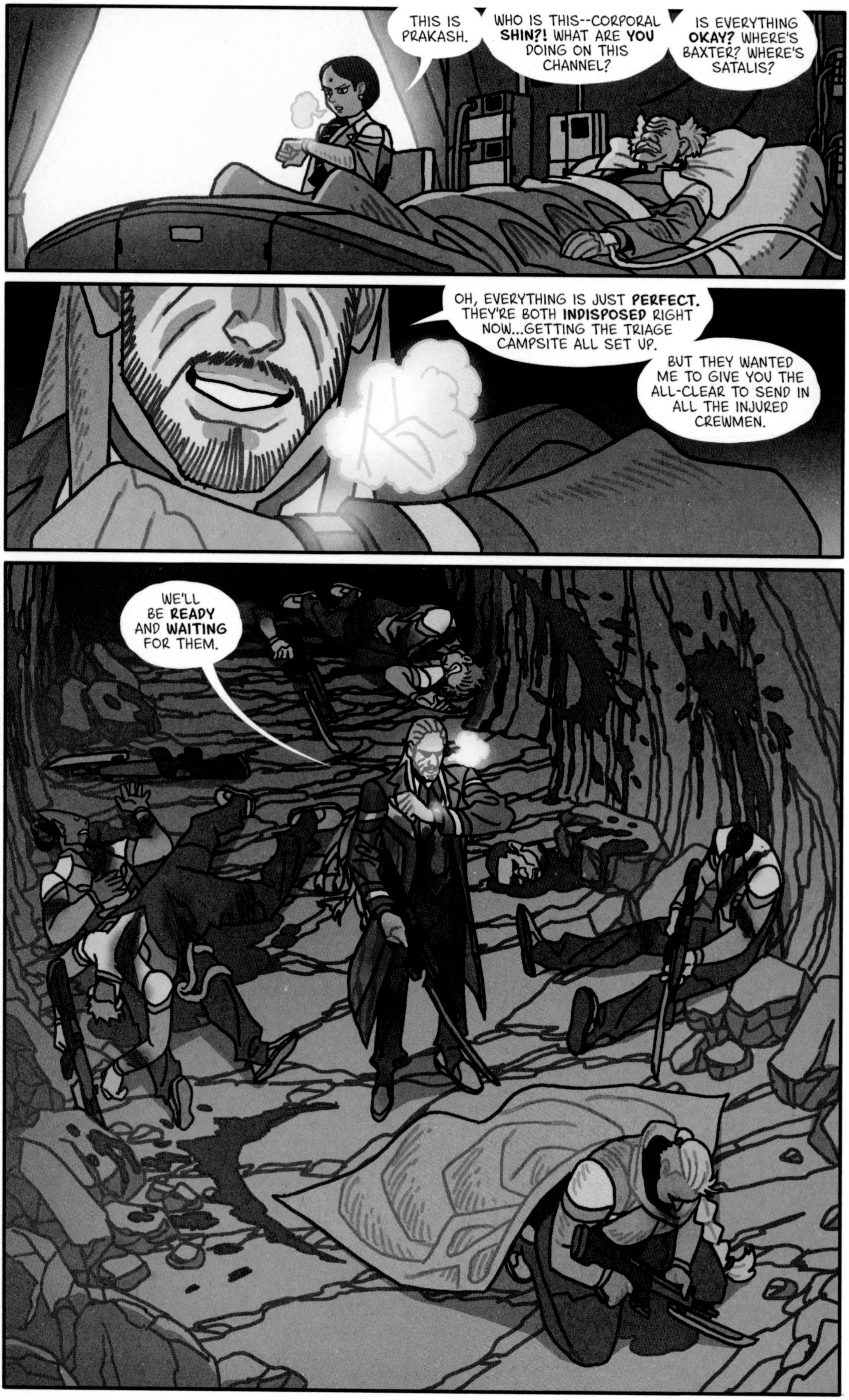
THIS IS PRAKASH.
WHO IS THIS--CORPORAL SHIN?! WHAT ARE YOU DOING ON THIS CHANNEL?
IS EVERYTHING OKAY? WHERE'S BAXTER? WHERE'S SATALIS?
OH, EVERYTHING IS JUST PERFECT. THEY'RE BOTH INDISPOSED RIGHT NOW...GETTING THE TRIAGE CAMPSITE ALL SET UP.
BUT THEY WANTED ME TO GIVE YOU THE ALL-CLEAR TO SEND IN ALL THE INJURED CREWMEN.
WE'LL BE READY AND WAITING FOR THEM.

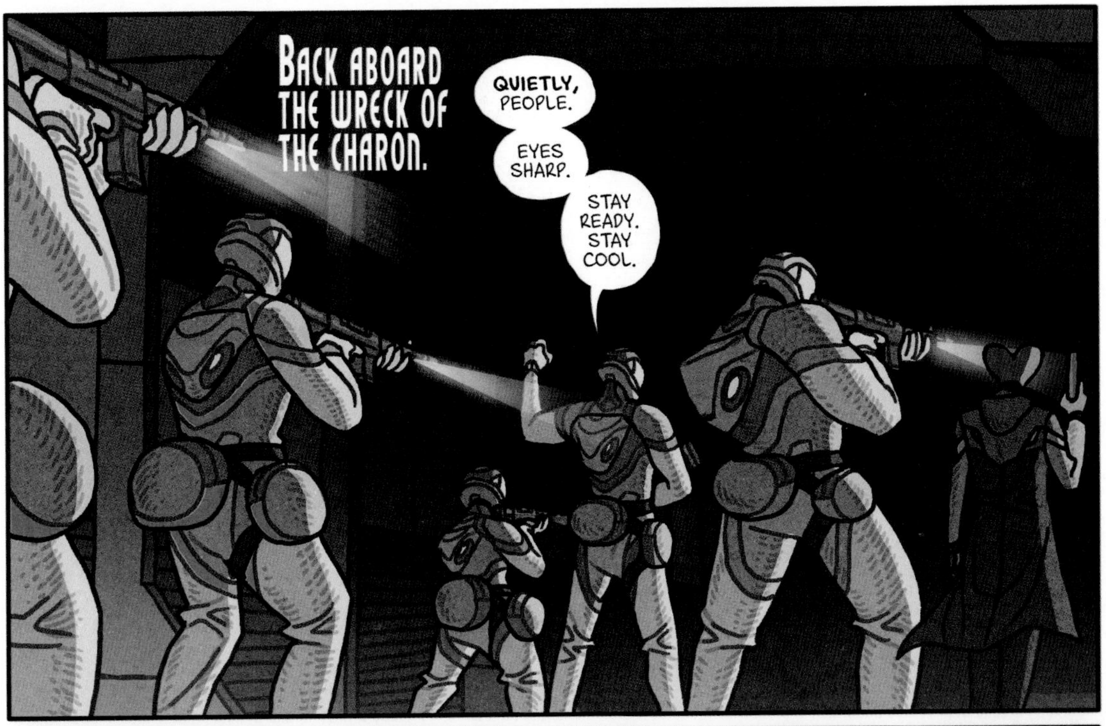
BACK ABOARD THE WRECK OF THE CHARON.
QUIETLY, PEOPLE.
EYES SHARP.
STAY READY. STAY COOL.

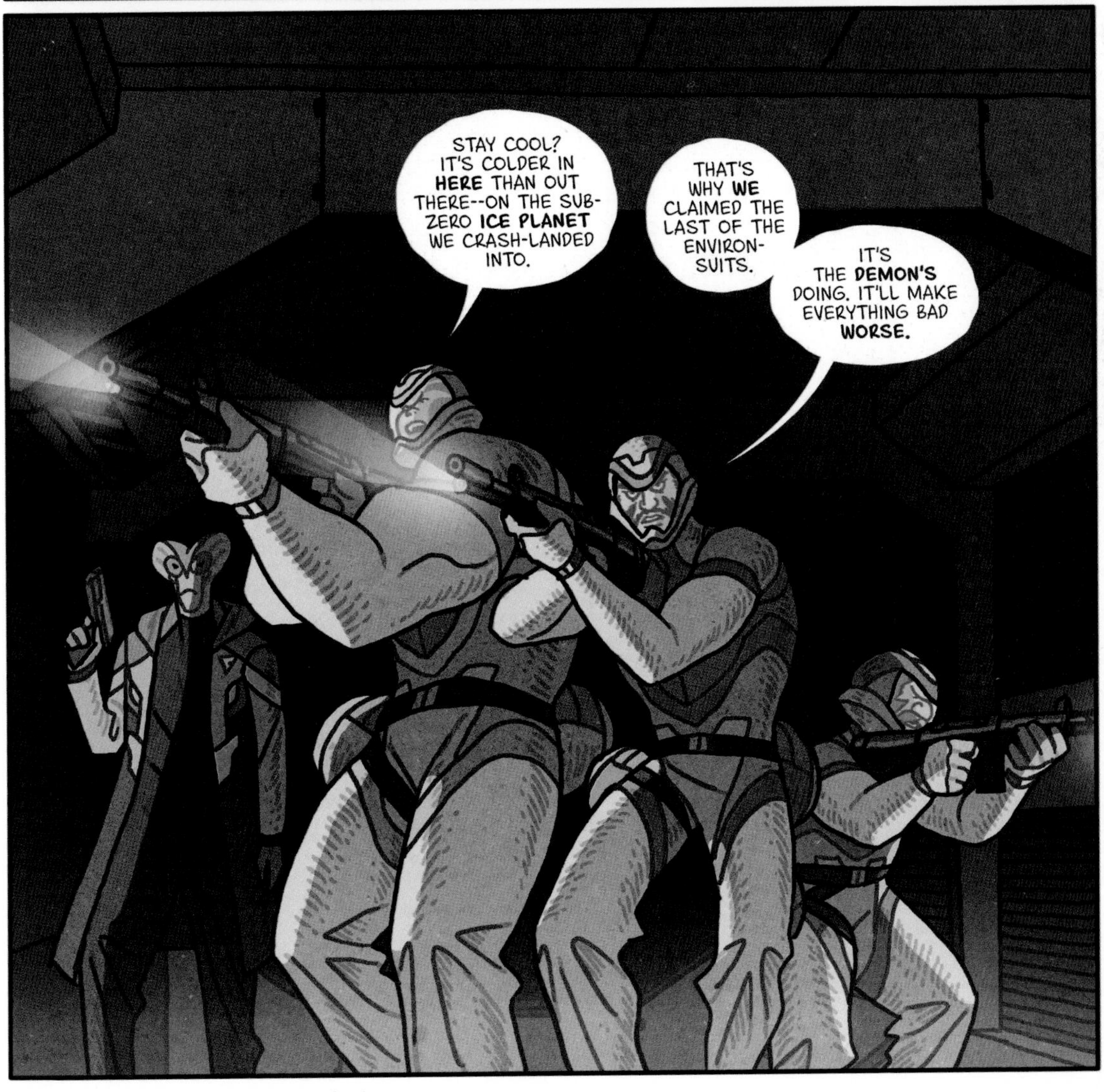
STAY COOL? IT'S COLDER IN HERE THAN OUT THERE--ON THE SUB-ZERO ICE PLANET WE CRASH-LANDED INTO.
THAT'S WHY WE CLAIMED THE LAST OF THE ENVIRON-SUITS.
IT'S THE DEMON'S DOING. IT'LL MAKE EVERYTHING BAD WORSE.

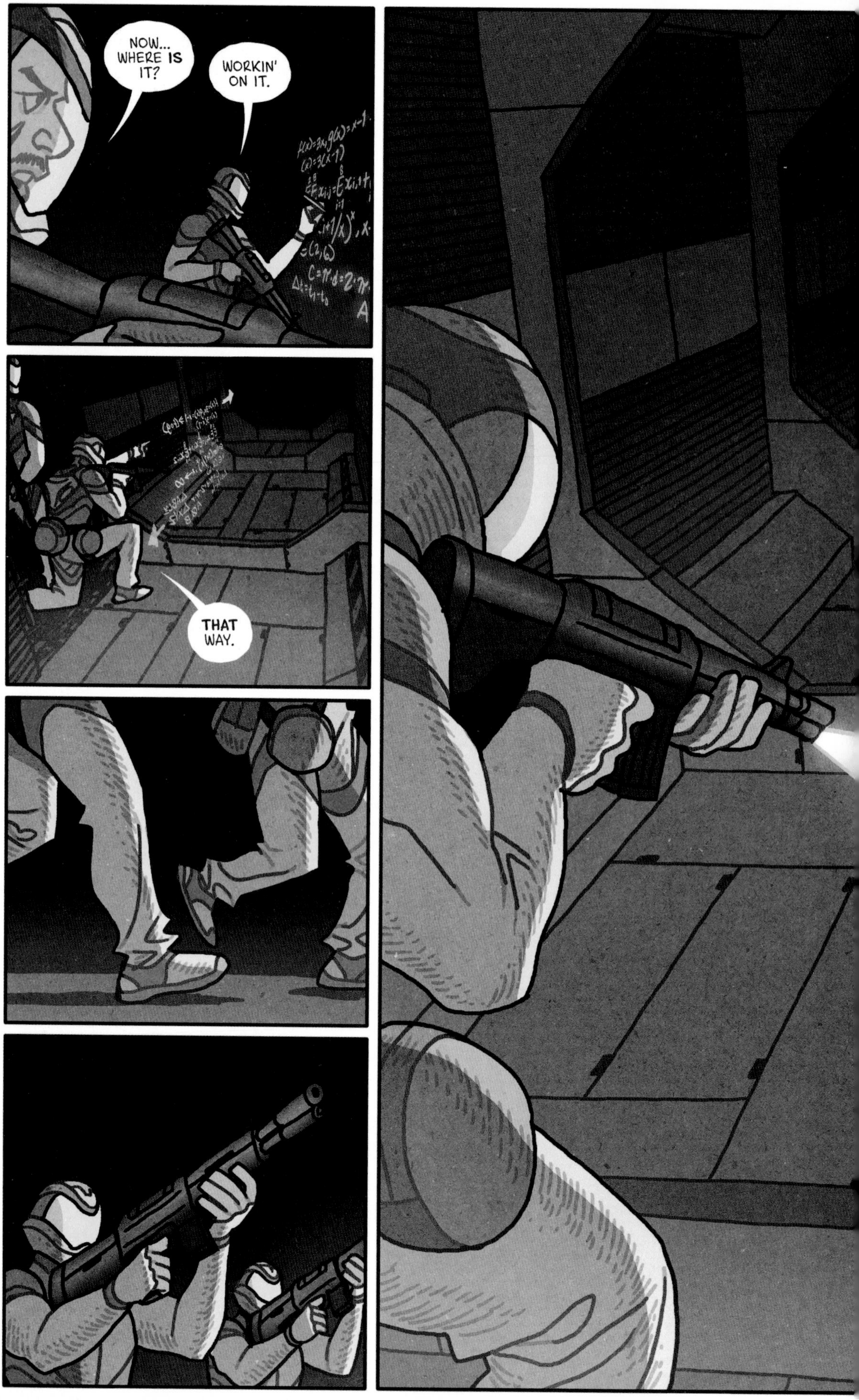
NOW... WHERE IS IT?
WORKIN' ON IT.
THAT WAY.

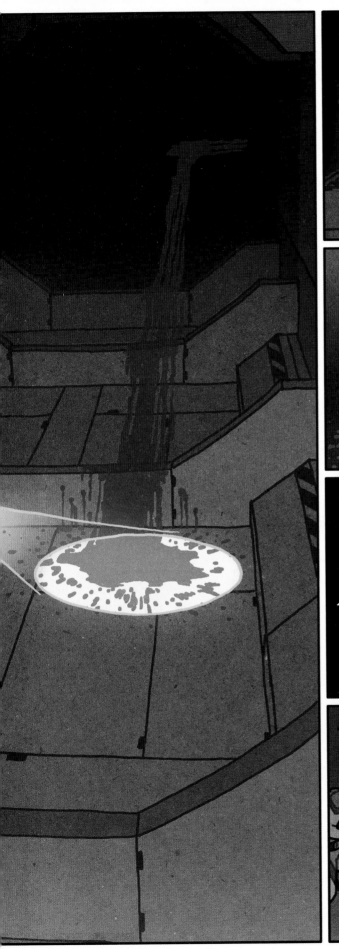

PRIVATE MORRIS. ONE OF THE ONES UNACCOUNTED FOR, RIGHT?

NOT ANYMORE.

POOR BASTARD.

THUMP

THUMP

YOU **HEAR** THAT?

UP AHEAD.

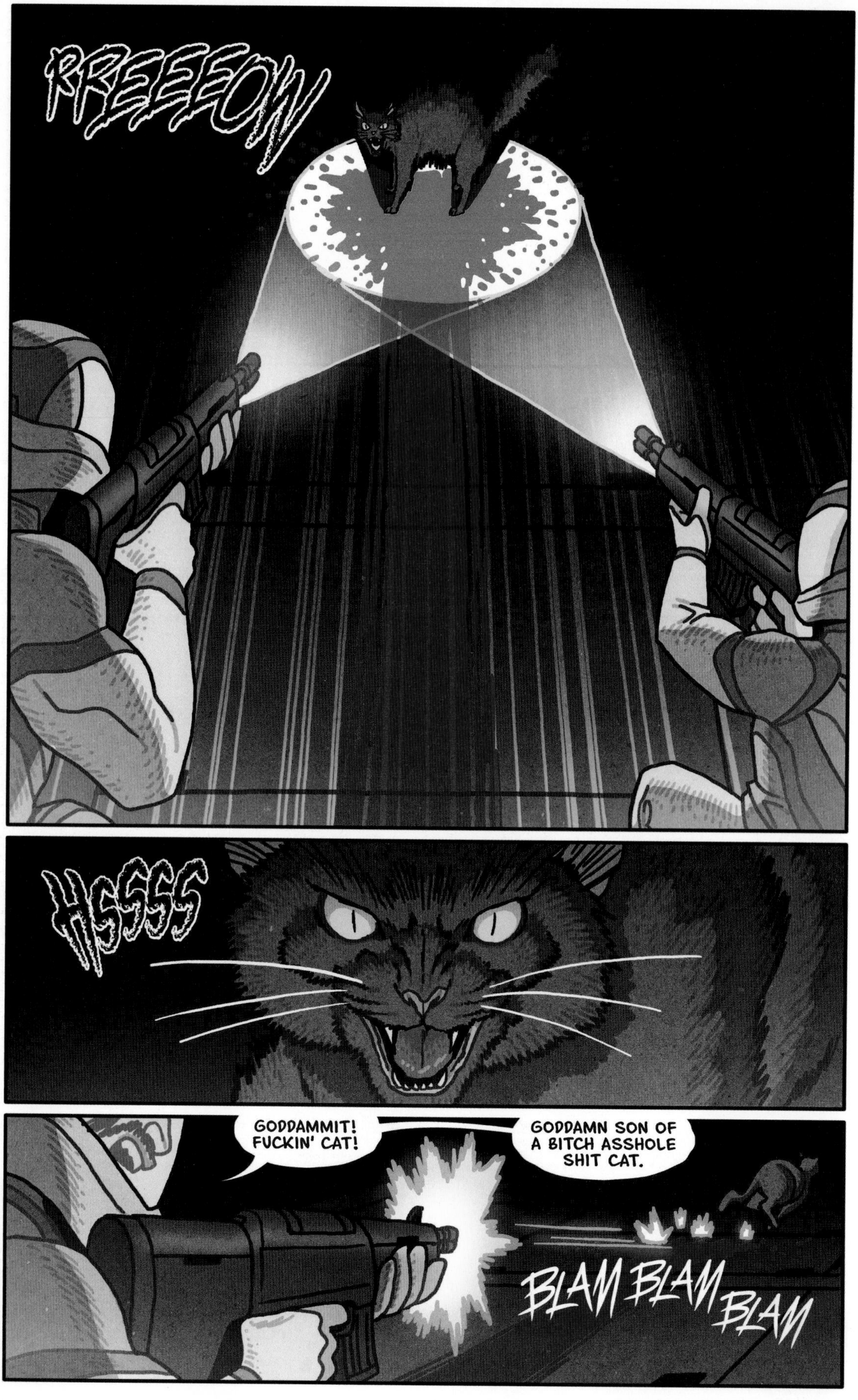
RREEEOW
HSSSS
GODDAMMIT! FUCKIN' CAT!
GODDAMN SON OF A BITCH ASSHOLE SHIT CAT.
BLAM BLAM BLAM

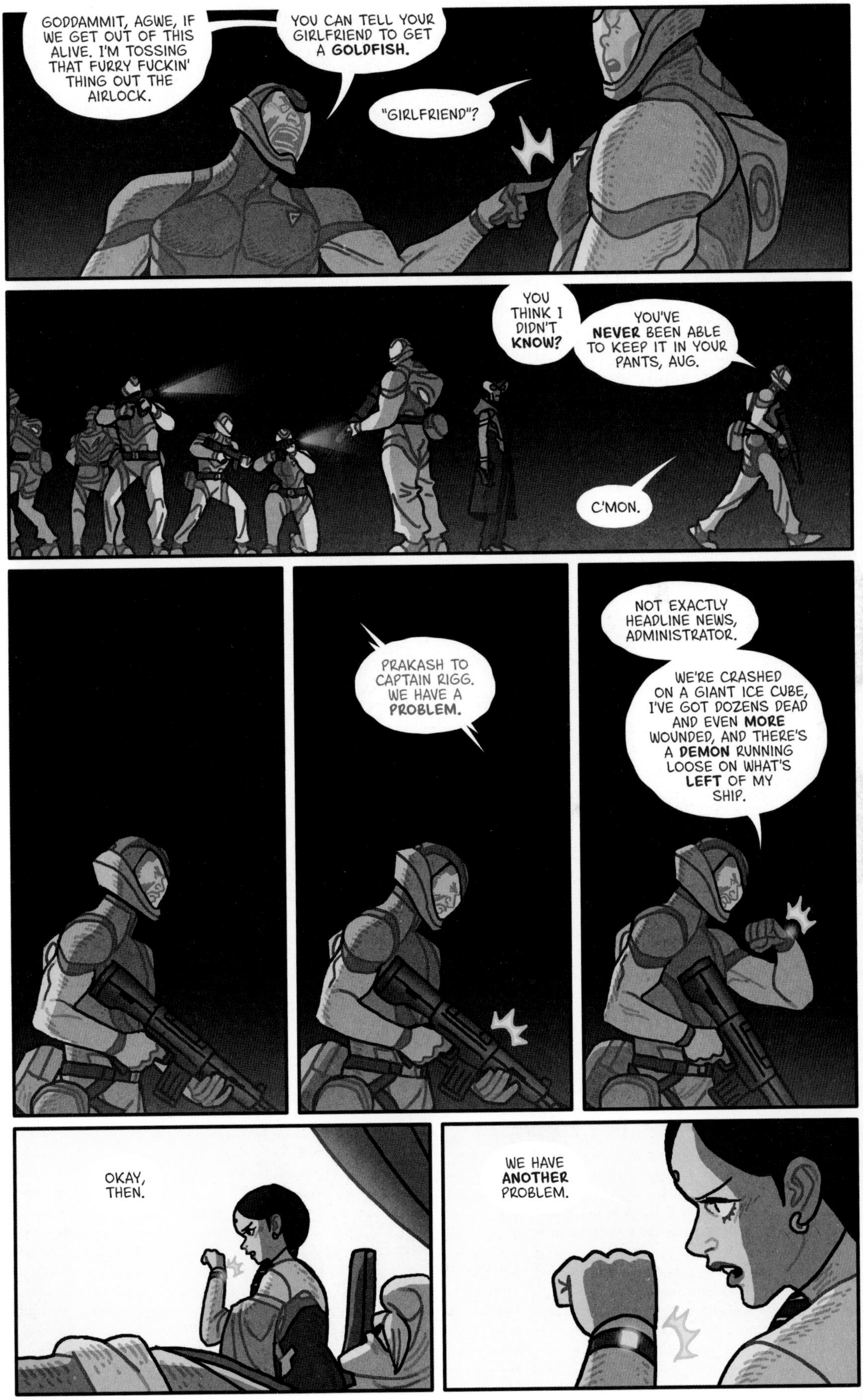
GODDAMMIT, AGWE, IF WE GET OUT OF THIS ALIVE. I'M TOSSING THAT FURRY FUCKIN' THING OUT THE AIRLOCK.
YOU CAN TELL YOUR GIRLFRIEND TO GET A **GOLDFISH.**
"GIRLFRIEND"?
YOU THINK I DIDN'T **KNOW?**
YOU'VE **NEVER** BEEN ABLE TO KEEP IT IN YOUR PANTS, AUG.
C'MON.
PRAKASH TO CAPTAIN RIGG. WE HAVE A **PROBLEM.**
NOT EXACTLY HEADLINE NEWS, ADMINISTRATOR.
WE'RE CRASHED ON A GIANT ICE CUBE, I'VE GOT DOZENS DEAD AND EVEN **MORE** WOUNDED, AND THERE'S A **DEMON** RUNNING LOOSE ON WHAT'S **LEFT** OF MY SHIP.
OKAY, THEN.
WE HAVE **ANOTHER** PROBLEM.

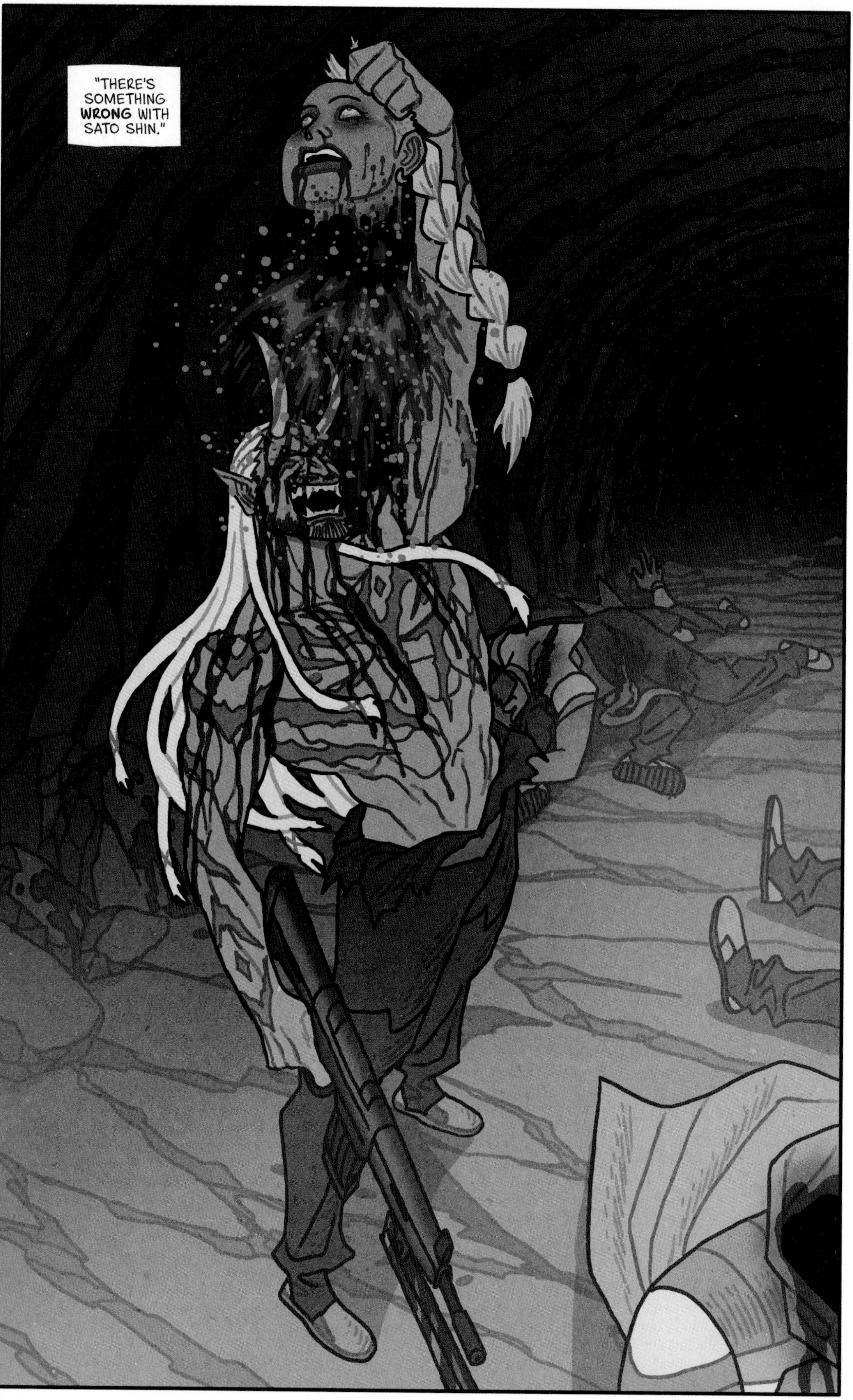
"THERE'S SOMETHING WRONG WITH SATO SHIN."

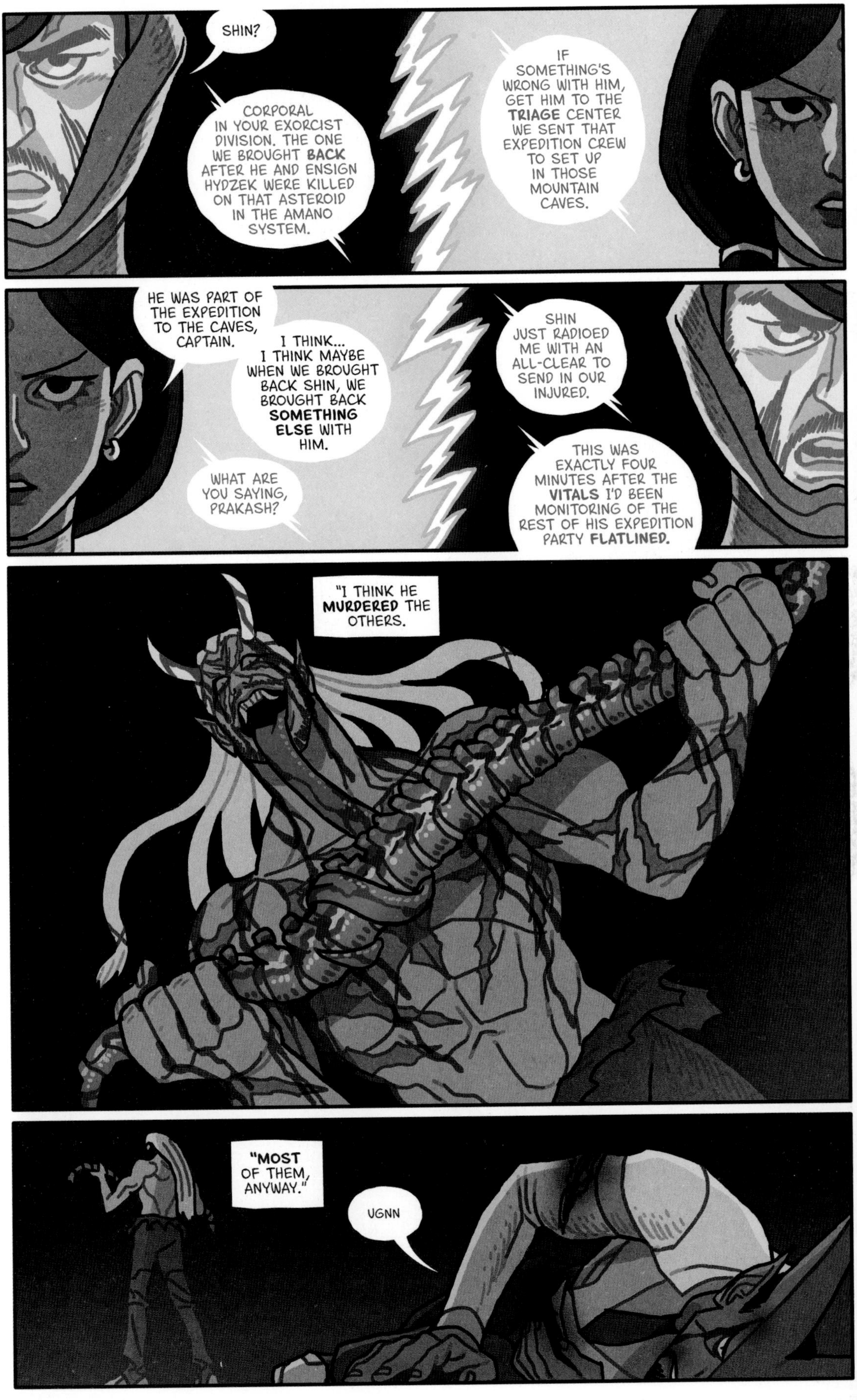
SHIN?
CORPORAL IN YOUR EXORCIST DIVISION. THE ONE WE BROUGHT **BACK** AFTER HE AND ENSIGN HYDZEK WERE KILLED ON THAT ASTEROID IN THE AMANO SYSTEM.
IF SOMETHING'S WRONG WITH HIM, GET HIM TO THE **TRIAGE** CENTER WE SENT THAT EXPEDITION CREW TO SET UP IN THOSE MOUNTAIN CAVES.
HE WAS PART OF THE EXPEDITION TO THE CAVES, CAPTAIN.
I THINK... I THINK MAYBE WHEN WE BROUGHT BACK SHIN, WE BROUGHT BACK **SOMETHING ELSE** WITH HIM.
WHAT ARE YOU SAYING, PRAKASH?
SHIN JUST RADIOED ME WITH AN ALL-CLEAR TO SEND IN OUR INJURED.
THIS WAS EXACTLY FOUR MINUTES AFTER THE **VITALS** I'D BEEN MONITORING OF THE REST OF HIS EXPEDITION PARTY **FLATLINED.**
"I THINK HE **MURDERED** THE OTHERS.
"MOST OF THEM, ANYWAY."
UGNN

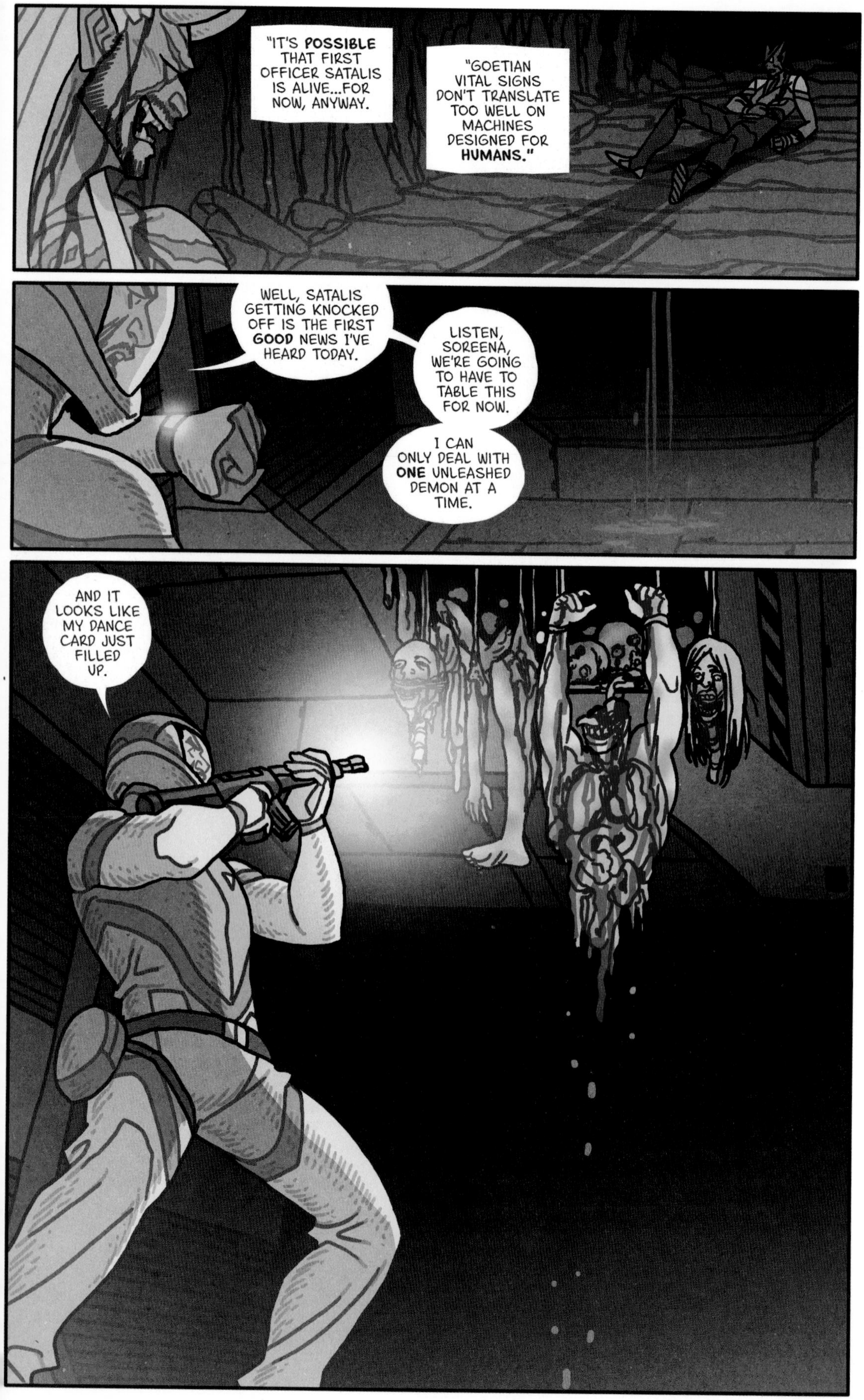
"IT'S **POSSIBLE** THAT FIRST OFFICER SATALIS IS ALIVE...FOR NOW, ANYWAY.
"GOETIAN VITAL SIGNS DON'T TRANSLATE TOO WELL ON MACHINES DESIGNED FOR **HUMANS.**"
WELL, SATALIS GETTING KNOCKED OFF IS THE FIRST **GOOD** NEWS I'VE HEARD TODAY.
LISTEN, SOREENA, WE'RE GOING TO HAVE TO TABLE THIS FOR NOW.
I CAN ONLY DEAL WITH **ONE** UNLEASHED DEMON AT A TIME.
AND IT LOOKS LIKE MY DANCE CARD JUST FILLED UP.

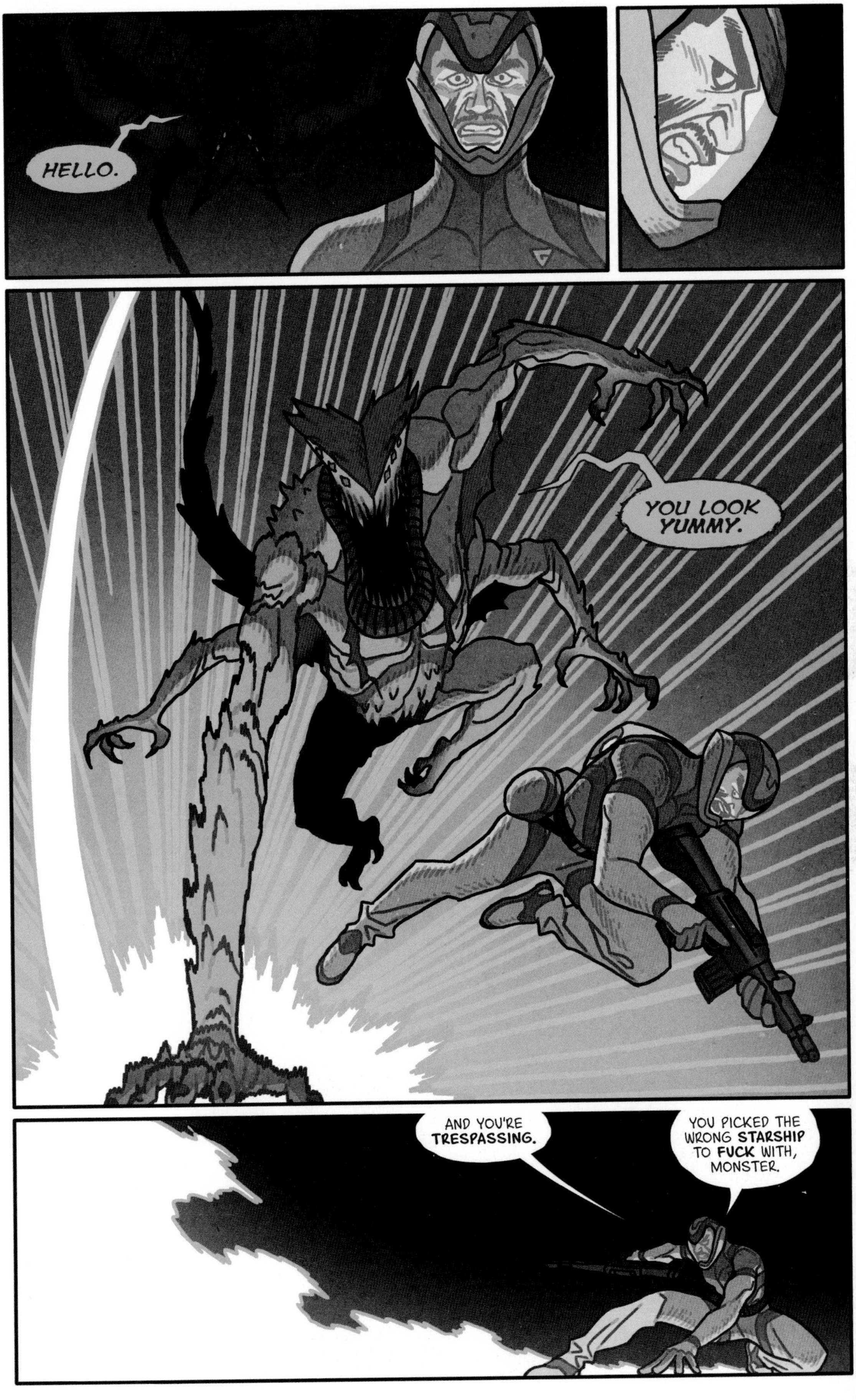
HELLO.
YOU LOOK YUMMY.
AND YOU'RE TRESPASSING.
YOU PICKED THE WRONG STARSHIP TO FUCK WITH, MONSTER.

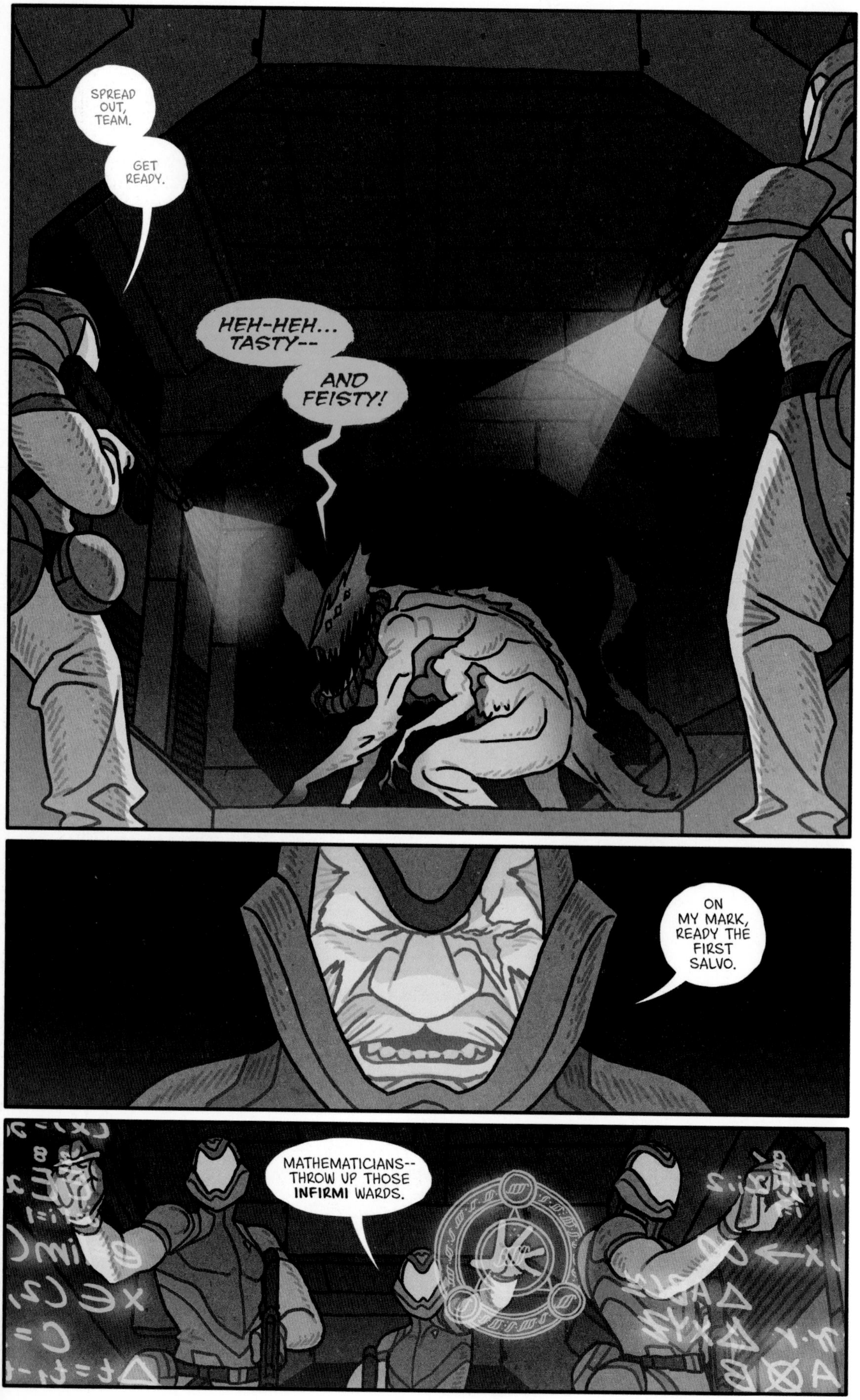
SPREAD OUT, TEAM.
GET READY.
HEH-HEH... TASTY--
AND FEISTY!
ON MY MARK, READY THE FIRST SALVO.
MATHEMATICIANS-- THROW UP THOSE **INFIRMI** WARDS.

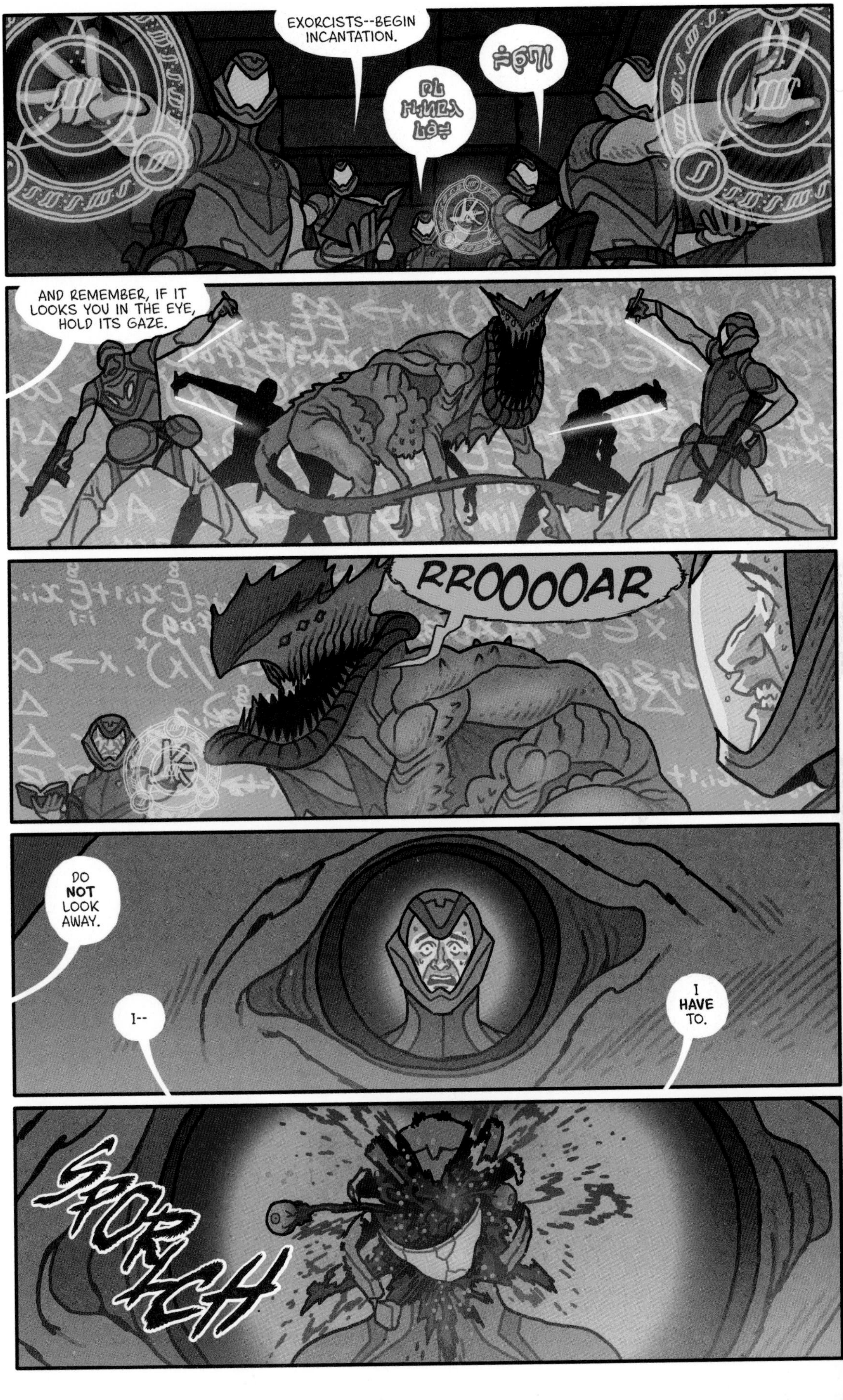
EXORCISTS--BEGIN INCANTATION.
AND REMEMBER, IF IT LOOKS YOU IN THE EYE, HOLD ITS GAZE.
RROOOOOAR
DO **NOT** LOOK AWAY.
I--
I **HAVE** TO.

BLAM
BLAM
BLAM
YOU FUCKIN' ABOMINATION.
HURRHHH
YOU'RE NOT HURTING IT, RIGG.
NO, BUT IT FEELS GOOD TO TRY.
NOW...WHILE ITS ATTENTION IS ON ME.

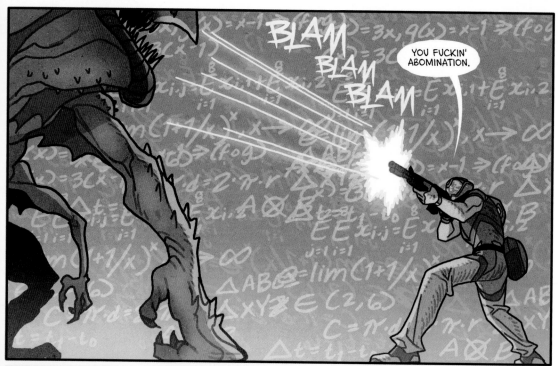

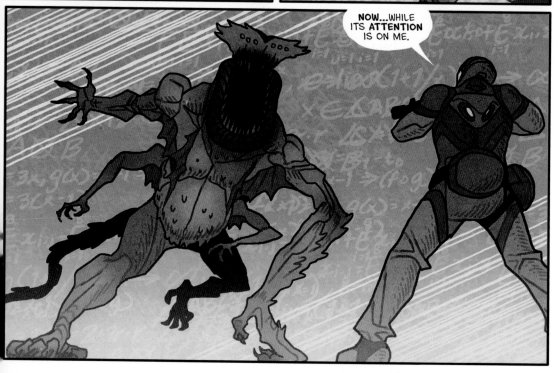

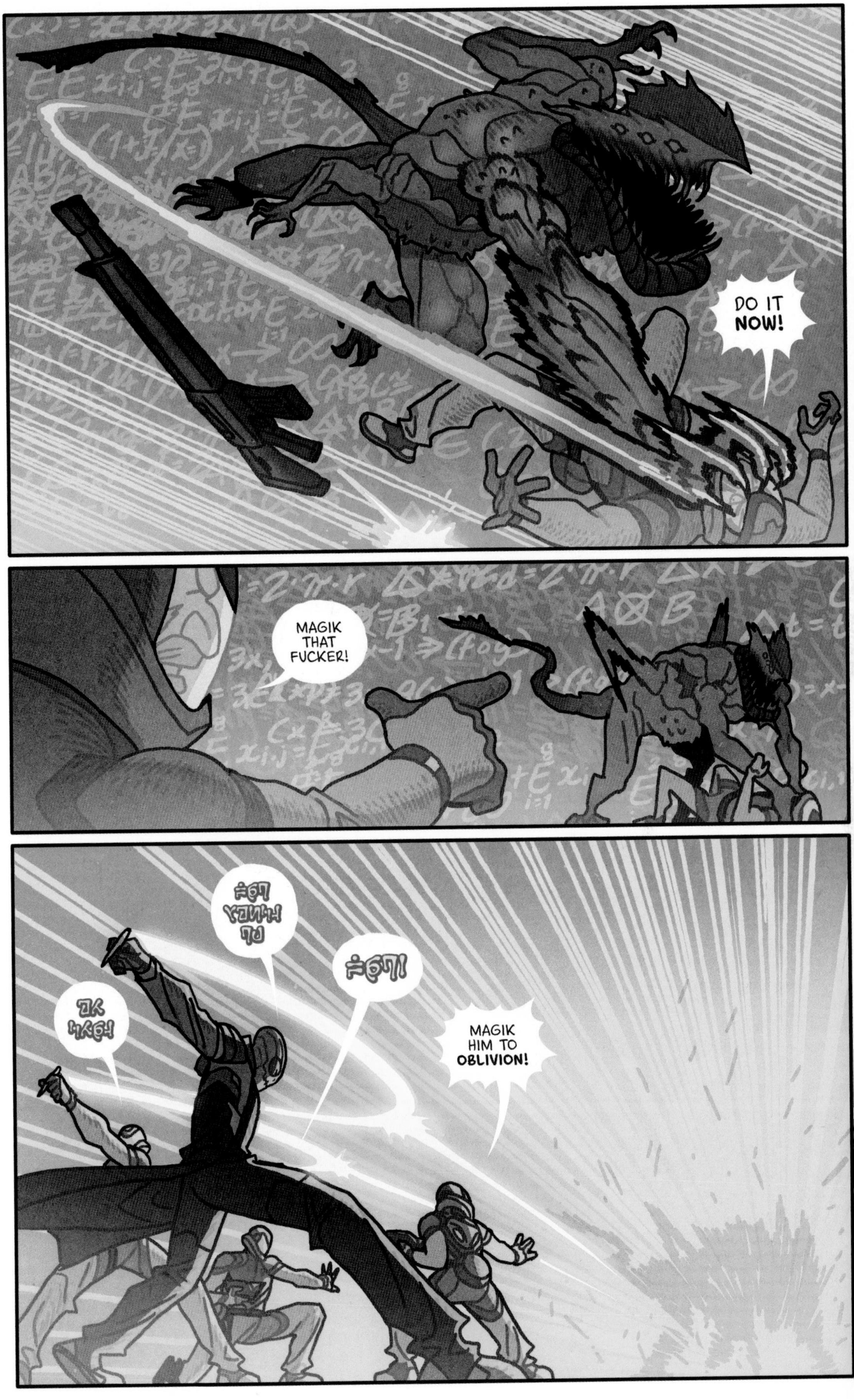
DO IT NOW!
MAGIK THAT FUCKER!
MAGIK HIM TO OBLIVION!

IT'S DONE.

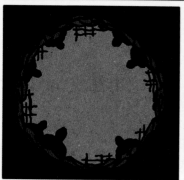

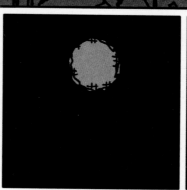

Soon.

CHALK UP ONE FOR THE GOOD GUYS, ADMINISTRATOR.

BE CAREFUL WITH THAT CONTAINER. BIG NASTY IN THERE.

AND MAKE SURE IT'S JETTISONED INTO THE NEAREST SUN ONCE WE'VE GOT THE CHARON AIRBORNE.

THERE'S NOTHING IN THAT BOTTLE, RIGG.

HEH.

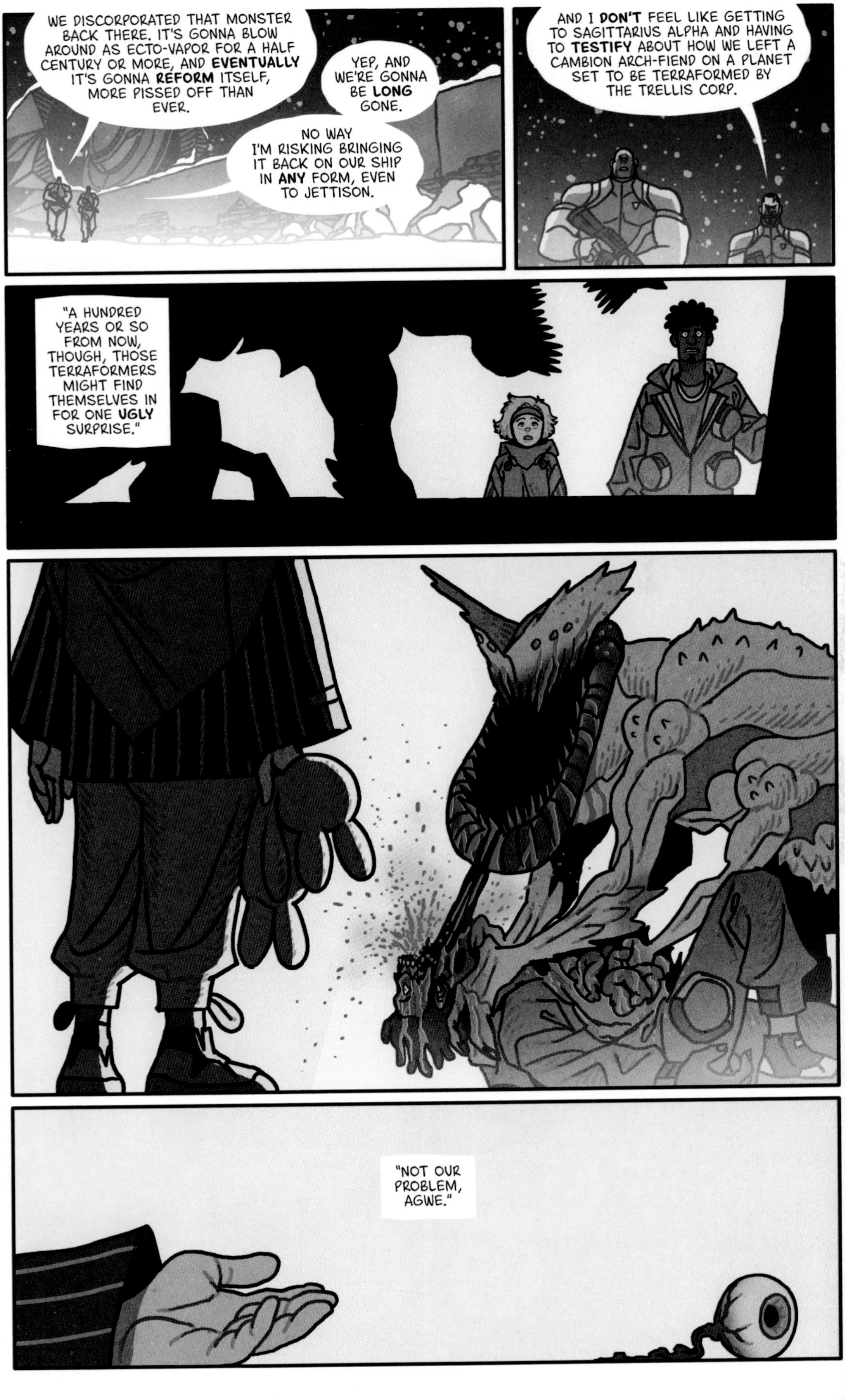
WE DISCORPORATED THAT MONSTER BACK THERE. IT'S GONNA BLOW AROUND AS ECTO-VAPOR FOR A HALF CENTURY OR MORE, AND **EVENTUALLY** IT'S GONNA **REFORM** ITSELF, MORE PISSED OFF THAN EVER.
YEP, AND WE'RE GONNA BE **LONG** GONE.
NO WAY I'M RISKING BRINGING IT BACK ON OUR SHIP IN **ANY** FORM, EVEN TO JETTISON.
AND I **DON'T** FEEL LIKE GETTING TO SAGITTARIUS ALPHA AND HAVING TO **TESTIFY** ABOUT HOW WE LEFT A CAMBION ARCH-FIEND ON A PLANET SET TO BE TERRAFORMED BY THE TRELLIS CORP.
"A HUNDRED YEARS OR SO FROM NOW, THOUGH, THOSE TERRAFORMERS MIGHT FIND THEMSELVES IN FOR ONE **UGLY** SURPRISE."
"NOT OUR PROBLEM, AGWE."

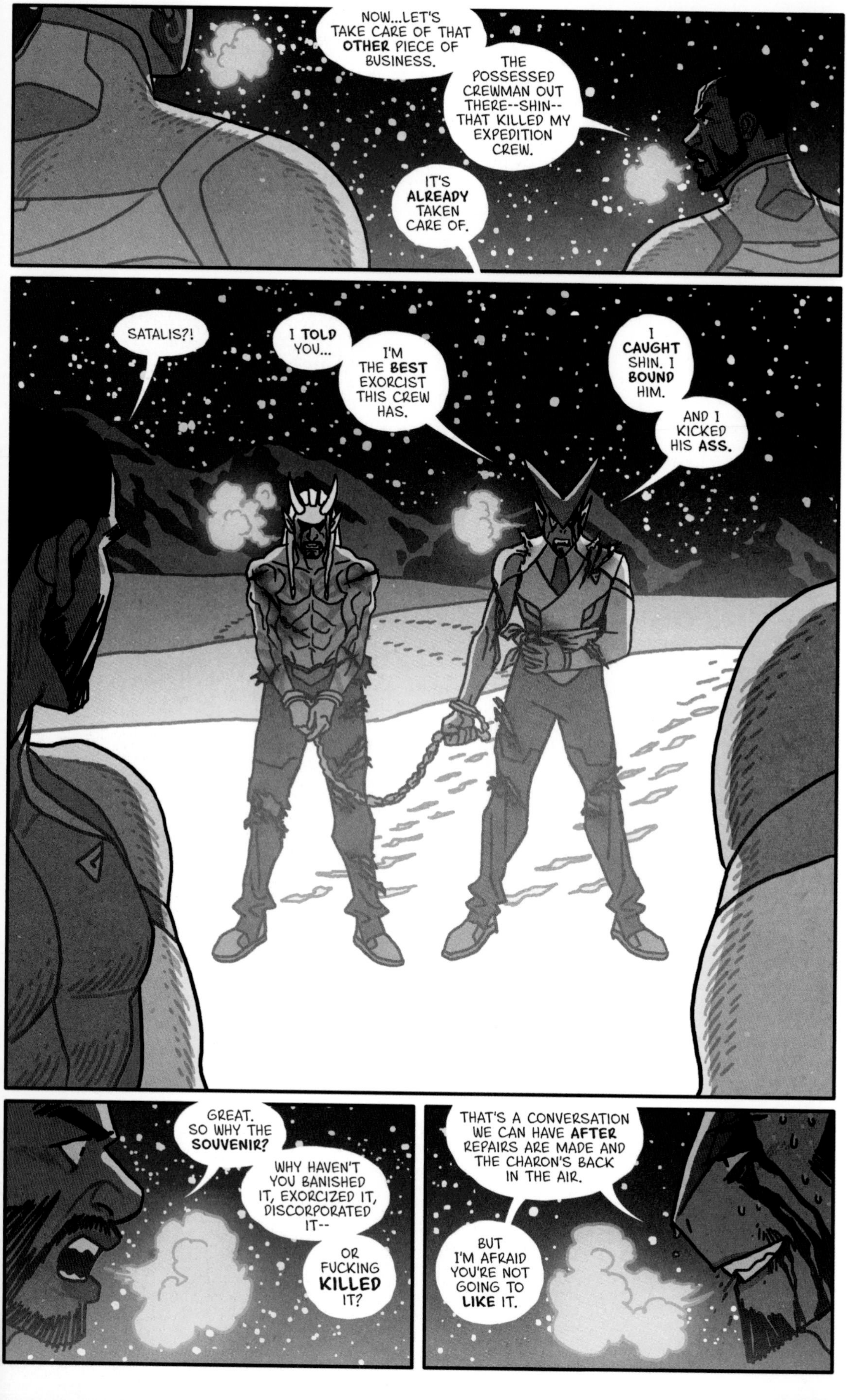
NOW...LET'S TAKE CARE OF THAT **OTHER** PIECE OF BUSINESS.
THE POSSESSED CREWMAN OUT THERE--SHIN--THAT KILLED MY EXPEDITION CREW.
IT'S **ALREADY** TAKEN CARE OF.
SATALIS?!
I **TOLD** YOU...
I'M THE **BEST** EXORCIST THIS CREW HAS.
I **CAUGHT** SHIN. I **BOUND** HIM.
AND I KICKED HIS **ASS.**
GREAT. SO WHY THE **SOUVENIR?**
WHY HAVEN'T YOU BANISHED IT, EXORCIZED IT, DISCORPORATED IT--
OR FUCKING **KILLED** IT?
THAT'S A CONVERSATION WE CAN HAVE **AFTER** REPAIRS ARE MADE AND THE CHARON'S BACK IN THE AIR.
BUT I'M AFRAID YOU'RE NOT GOING TO **LIKE** IT.

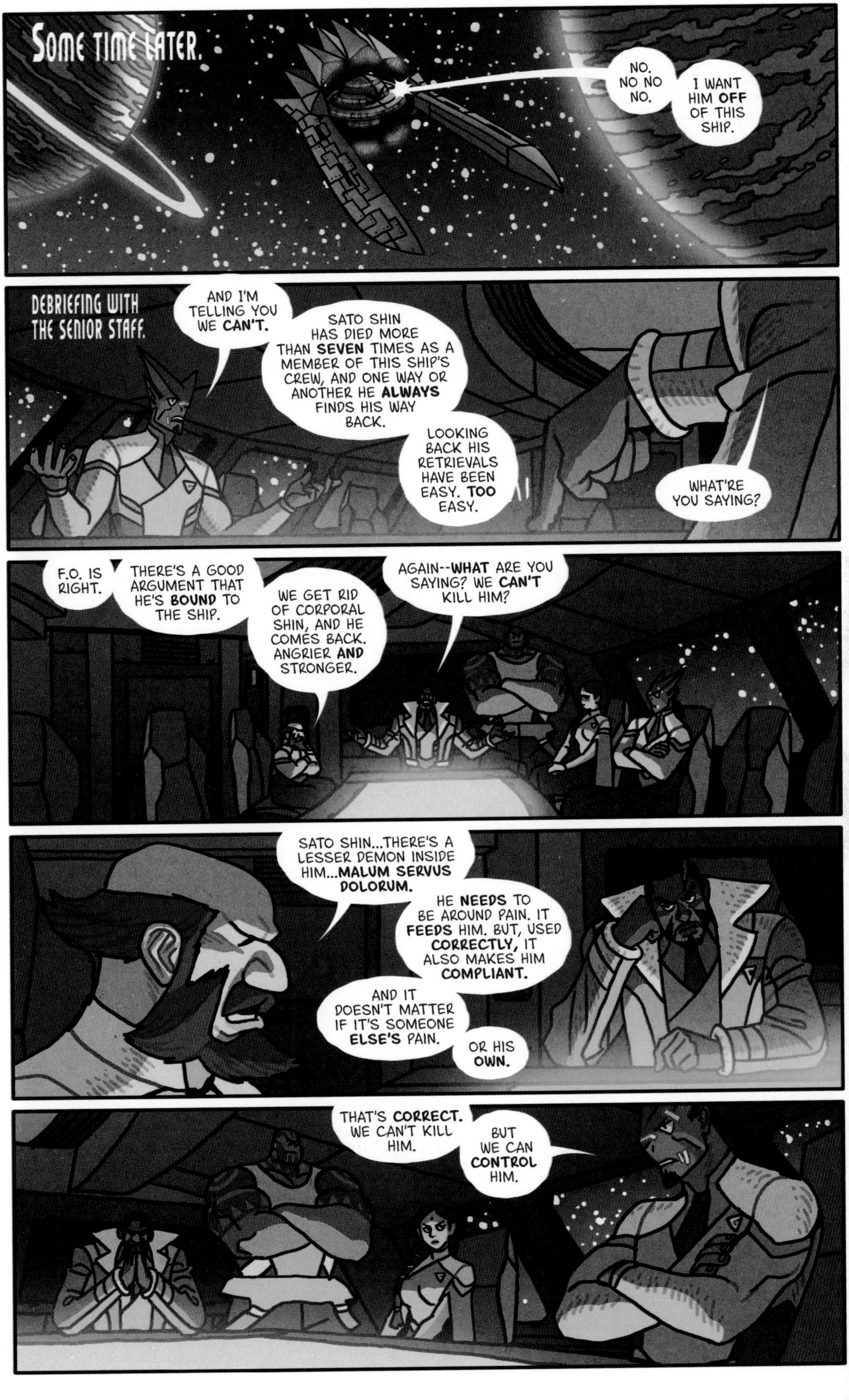
SOME TIME LATER.
NO. NO NO NO.
I WANT HIM OFF OF THIS SHIP.
DEBRIEFING WITH THE SENIOR STAFF.
AND I'M TELLING YOU WE CAN'T.
SATO SHIN HAS DIED MORE THAN SEVEN TIMES AS A MEMBER OF THIS SHIP'S CREW, AND ONE WAY OR ANOTHER HE ALWAYS FINDS HIS WAY BACK.
LOOKING BACK HIS RETRIEVALS HAVE BEEN EASY. TOO EASY.
WHAT'RE YOU SAYING?
F.O. IS RIGHT.
THERE'S A GOOD ARGUMENT THAT HE'S BOUND TO THE SHIP.
WE GET RID OF CORPORAL SHIN, AND HE COMES BACK. ANGRIER AND STRONGER.
AGAIN--WHAT ARE YOU SAYING? WE CAN'T KILL HIM?
SATO SHIN...THERE'S A LESSER DEMON INSIDE HIM...MALUM SERVUS DOLORUM.
HE NEEDS TO BE AROUND PAIN. IT FEEDS HIM. BUT, USED CORRECTLY, IT ALSO MAKES HIM COMPLIANT.
AND IT DOESN'T MATTER IF IT'S SOMEONE ELSE'S PAIN.
OR HIS OWN.
THAT'S CORRECT. WE CAN'T KILL HIM.
BUT WE CAN CONTROL HIM.

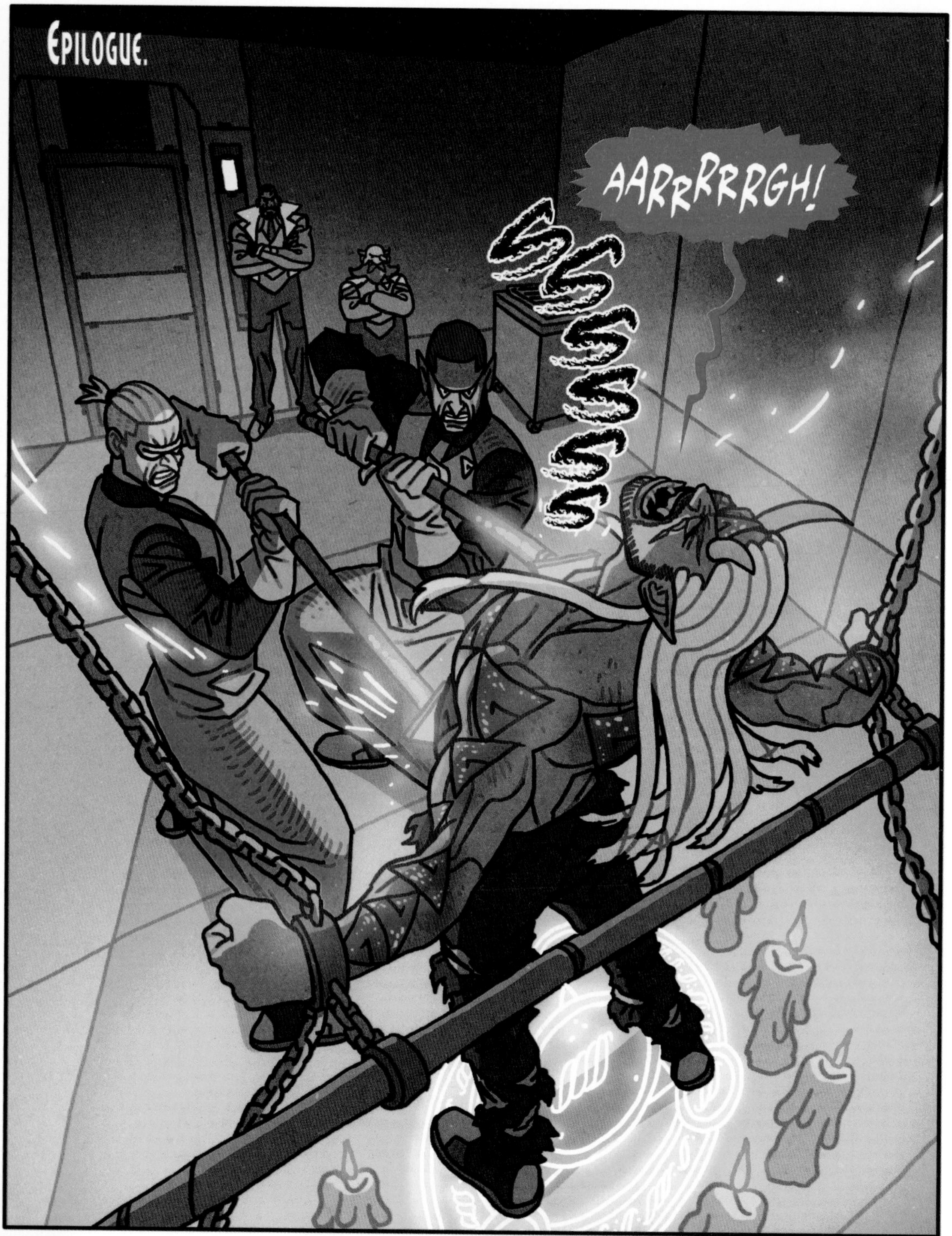
EPILOGUE.
AARRRRRGH!
SSSSSSSS

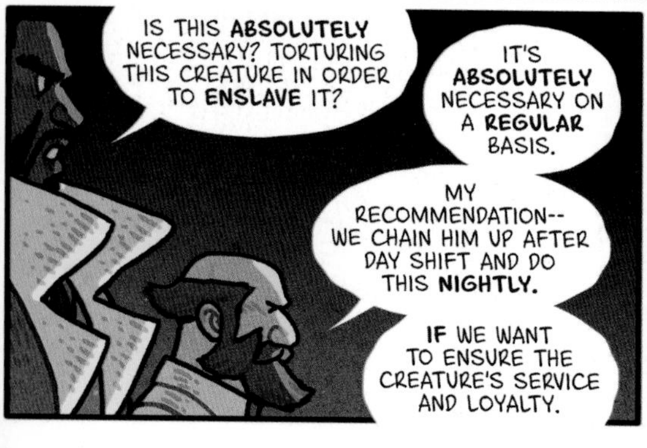
IS THIS ABSOLUTELY NECESSARY? TORTURING THIS CREATURE IN ORDER TO ENSLAVE IT?
IT'S ABSOLUTELY NECESSARY ON A REGULAR BASIS.
MY RECOMMENDATION-- WE CHAIN HIM UP AFTER DAY SHIFT AND DO THIS NIGHTLY.
IF WE WANT TO ENSURE THE CREATURE'S SERVICE AND LOYALTY.

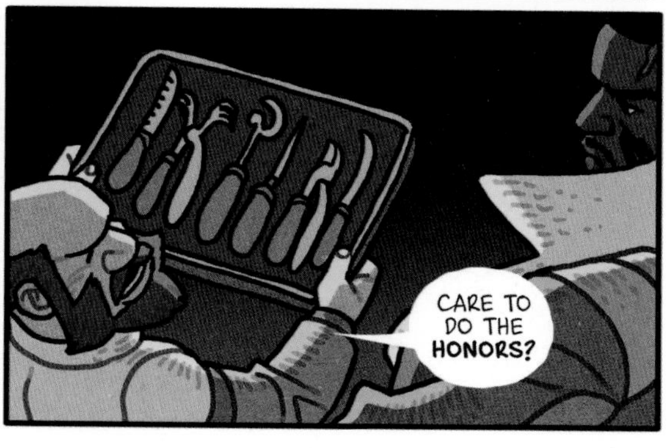
CARE TO DO THE HONORS?

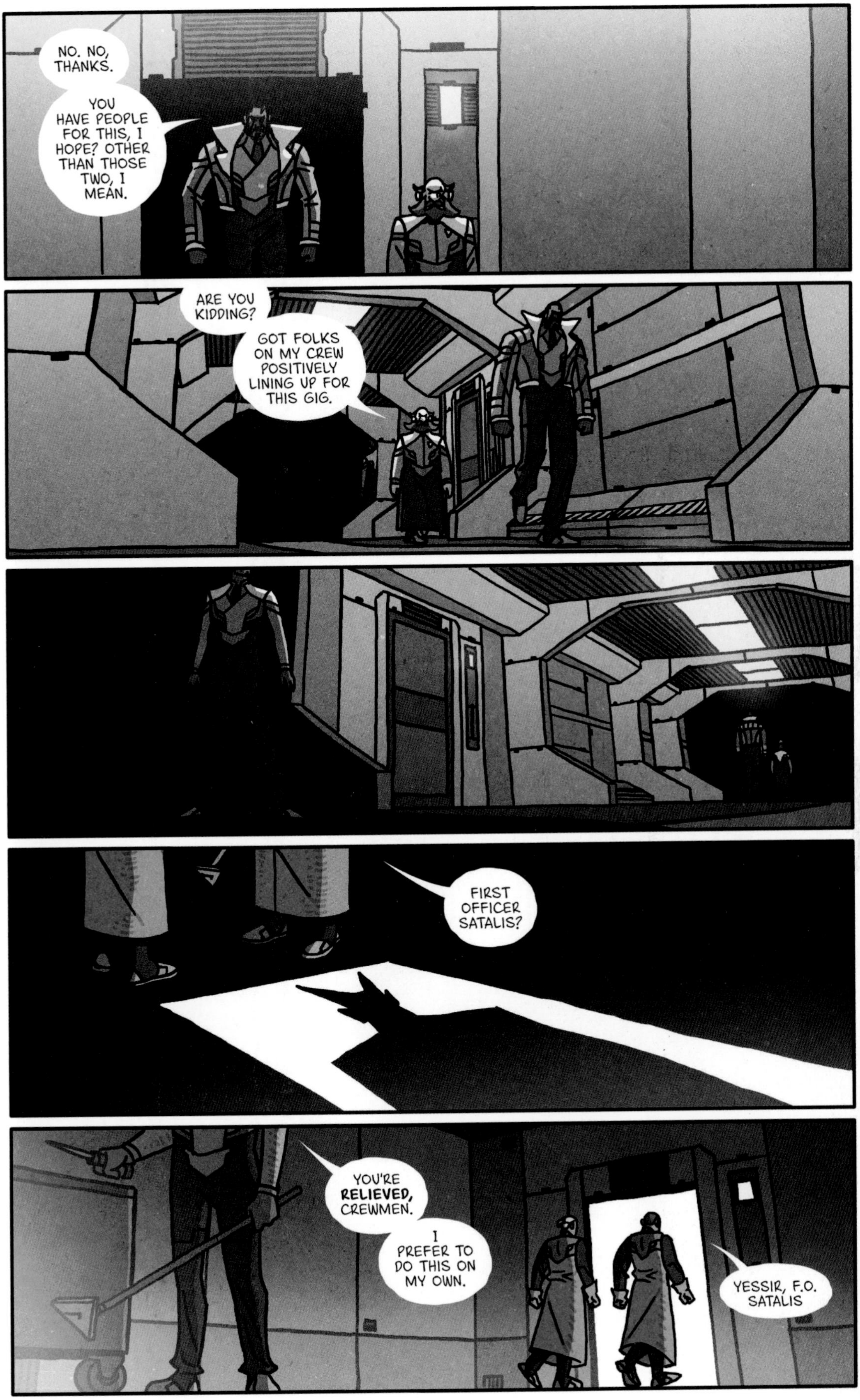
NO. NO, THANKS.
YOU HAVE PEOPLE FOR THIS, I HOPE? OTHER THAN THOSE TWO, I MEAN.
ARE YOU KIDDING?
GOT FOLKS ON MY CREW POSITIVELY LINING UP FOR THIS GIG.
FIRST OFFICER SATALIS?
YOU'RE **RELIEVED,** CREWMEN.
I PREFER TO DO THIS ON MY OWN.
YESSIR, F.O. SATALIS

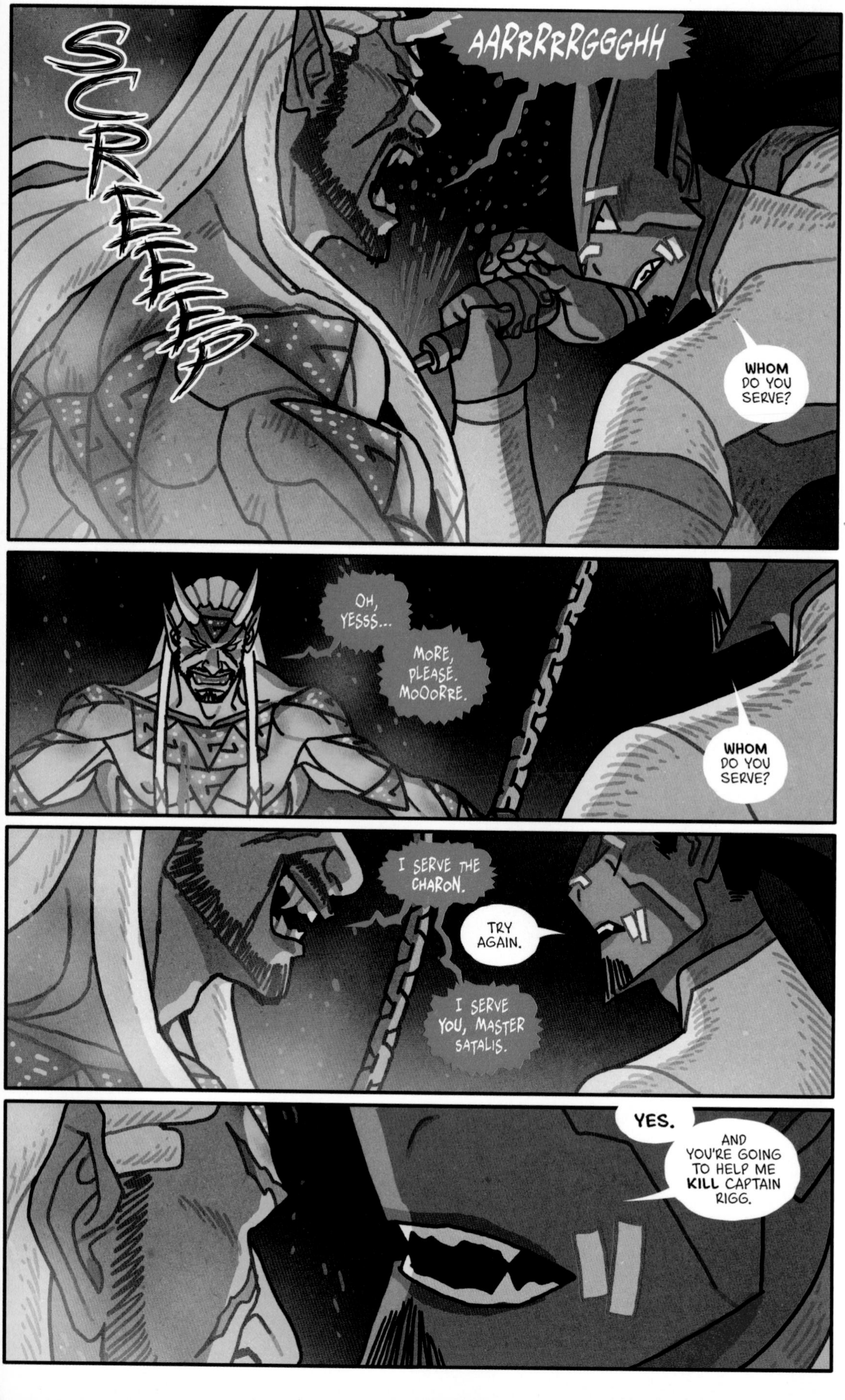
SCREEEEP
AARRRRRGGGHH
WHOM DO YOU SERVE?
OH, YESSS...
MORE, PLEASE. MOOORRE.
WHOM DO YOU SERVE?
I SERVE THE CHARON.
TRY AGAIN.
I SERVE YOU, MASTER SATALIS.
YES.
AND YOU'RE GOING TO HELP ME KILL CAPTAIN RIGG.

TO BE CONTINUED

CHARON PERSONNEL &

JOSHUA RIGG
SHIP CAPTAIN

AGWE
CAPTAIN'S ADVISOR

ALASTOR SATALIS
FIRST OFFICER

SOREENA PRAKASH
SHIP ADMINISTRATOR

MALONA HYDZEK
ENSIGN

SATO SHIN
CORPORAL

THE CRONE
SHIP ORACLE

KITTY
SHIP ORACLE'S FAMILIAR

COMBATANT RECORD

BAXTER
INFANTRY COMMANDER

MALACHI RENO
CHIEF EXORCIST

WILLITS
LEAD MATHEMATICIAN

ZAPHUS
CHIEF MORTICIAN

ELOX
SHIP NAVIGATOR

THE DRYX
THE ENEMY

GALLU
SHIP'S GOD-ENGINE

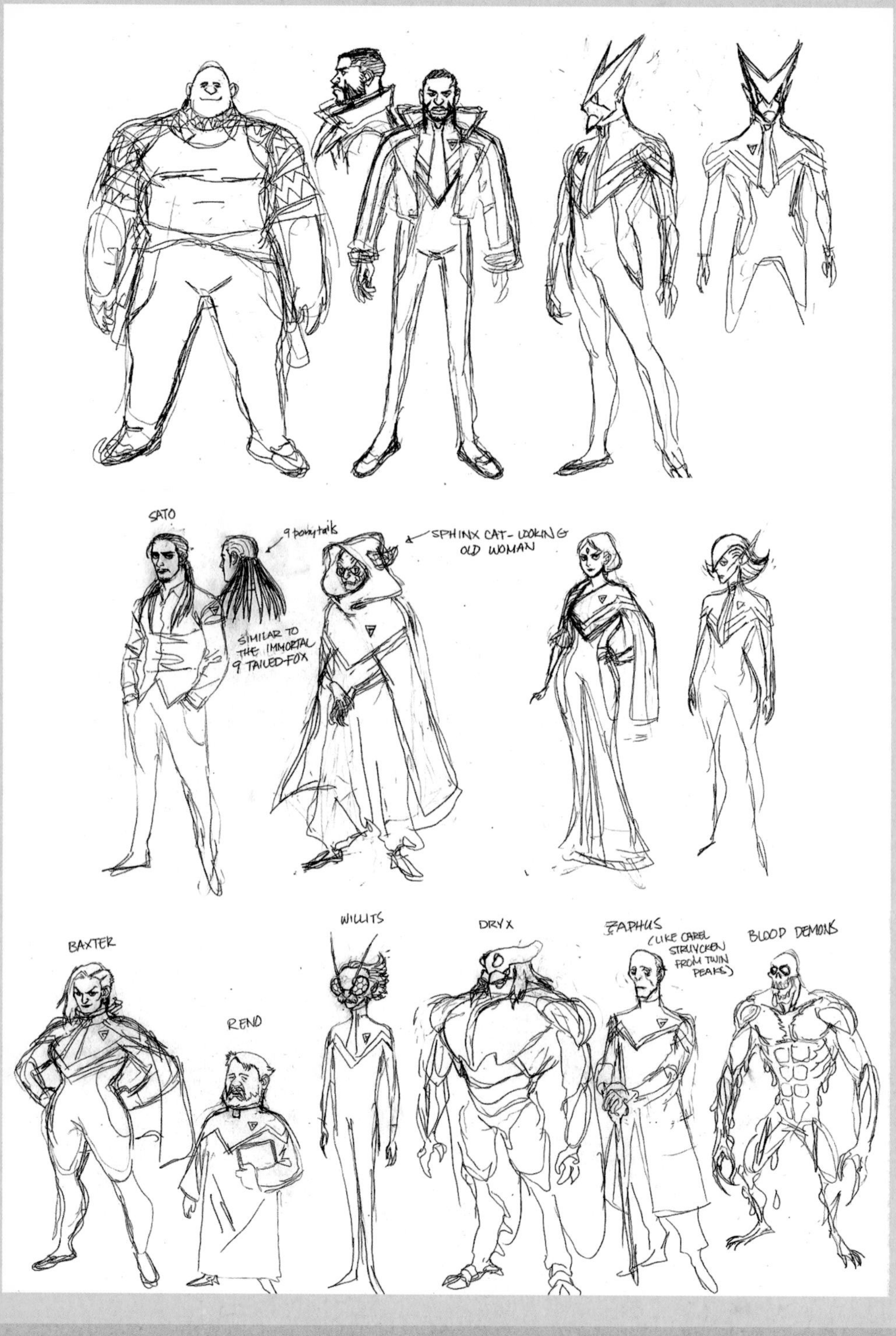
SATO
9 pony tails
SPHINX CAT-LOOKING OLD WOMAN
SIMILAR TO THE IMMORTAL 9 TAILED-FOX
BAXTER
RENO
WILLITS
DRYX
ZAPHUS (LIKE CAREL STRUYCKEN FROM TWIN PEAKS)
BLOOD DEMONS

CHARACTER SKETCHES

EARLY CONCEPT LOG

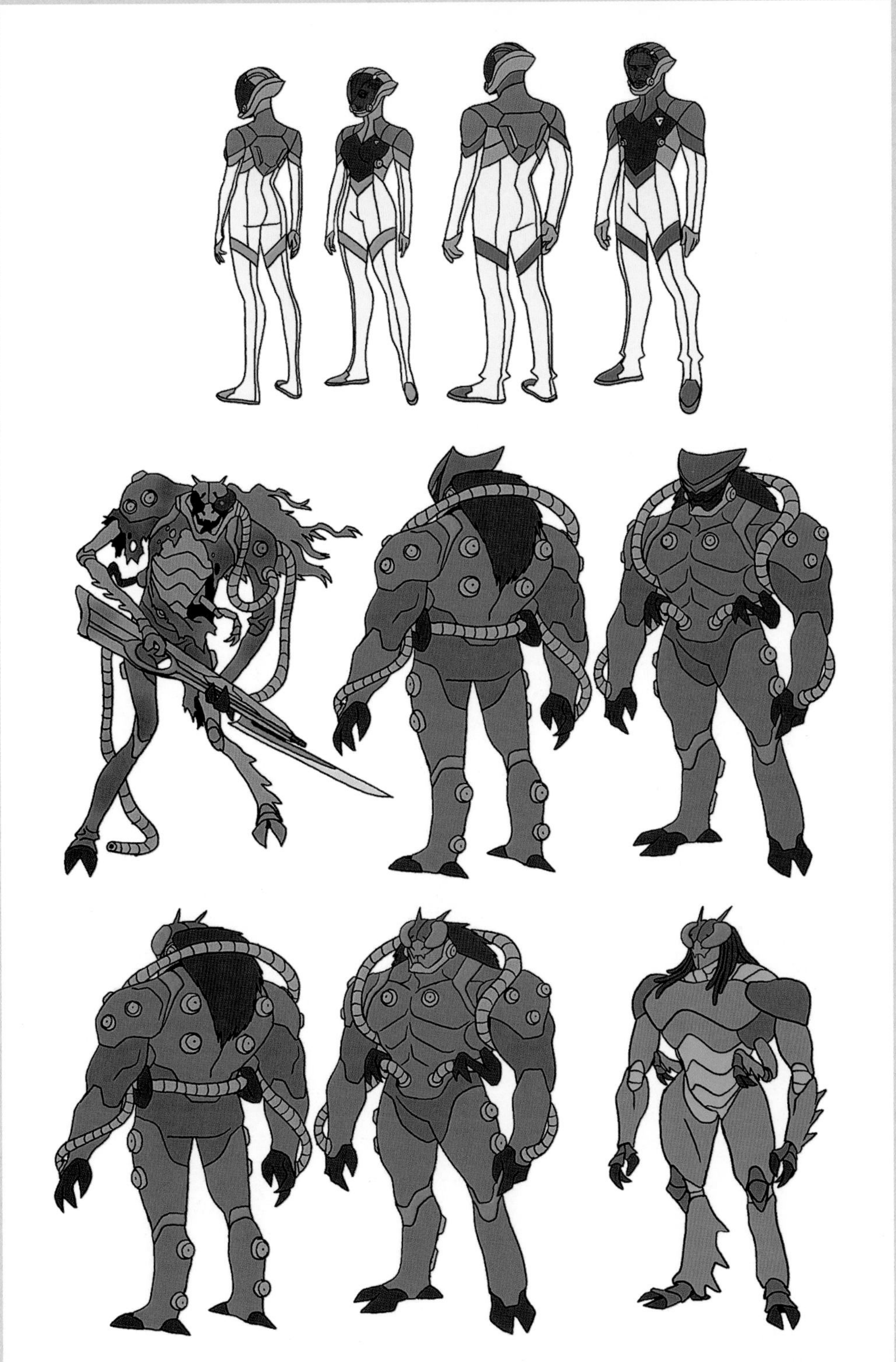

COLOR PASS / TURNAROUNDS

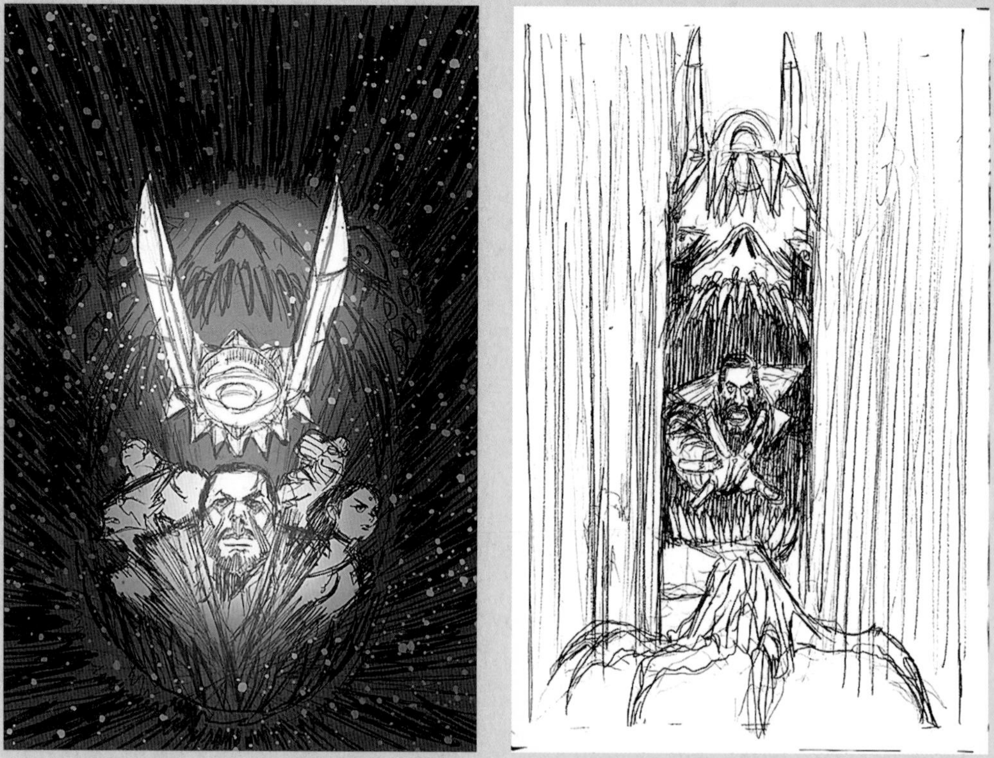

COVER #1 SKETCHES

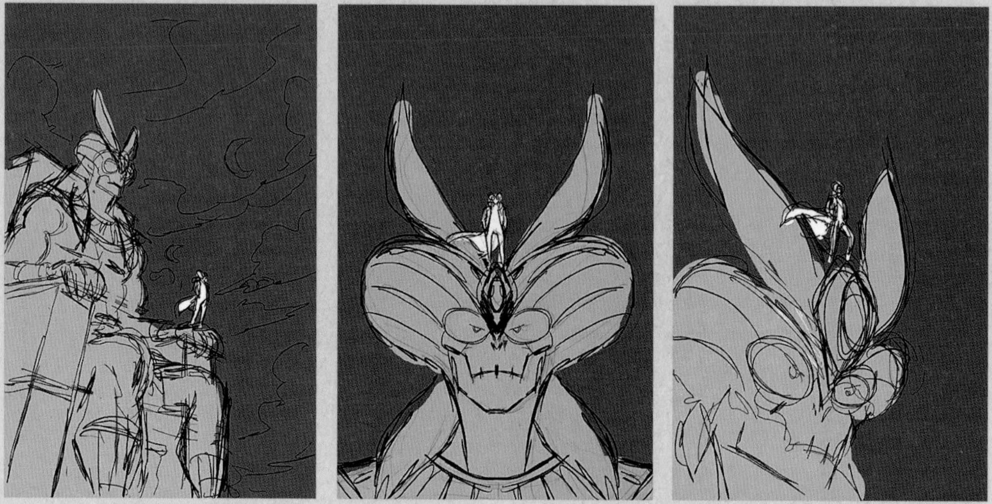

COVER #4 SKETCHES

EARLY CONCEPT LOG

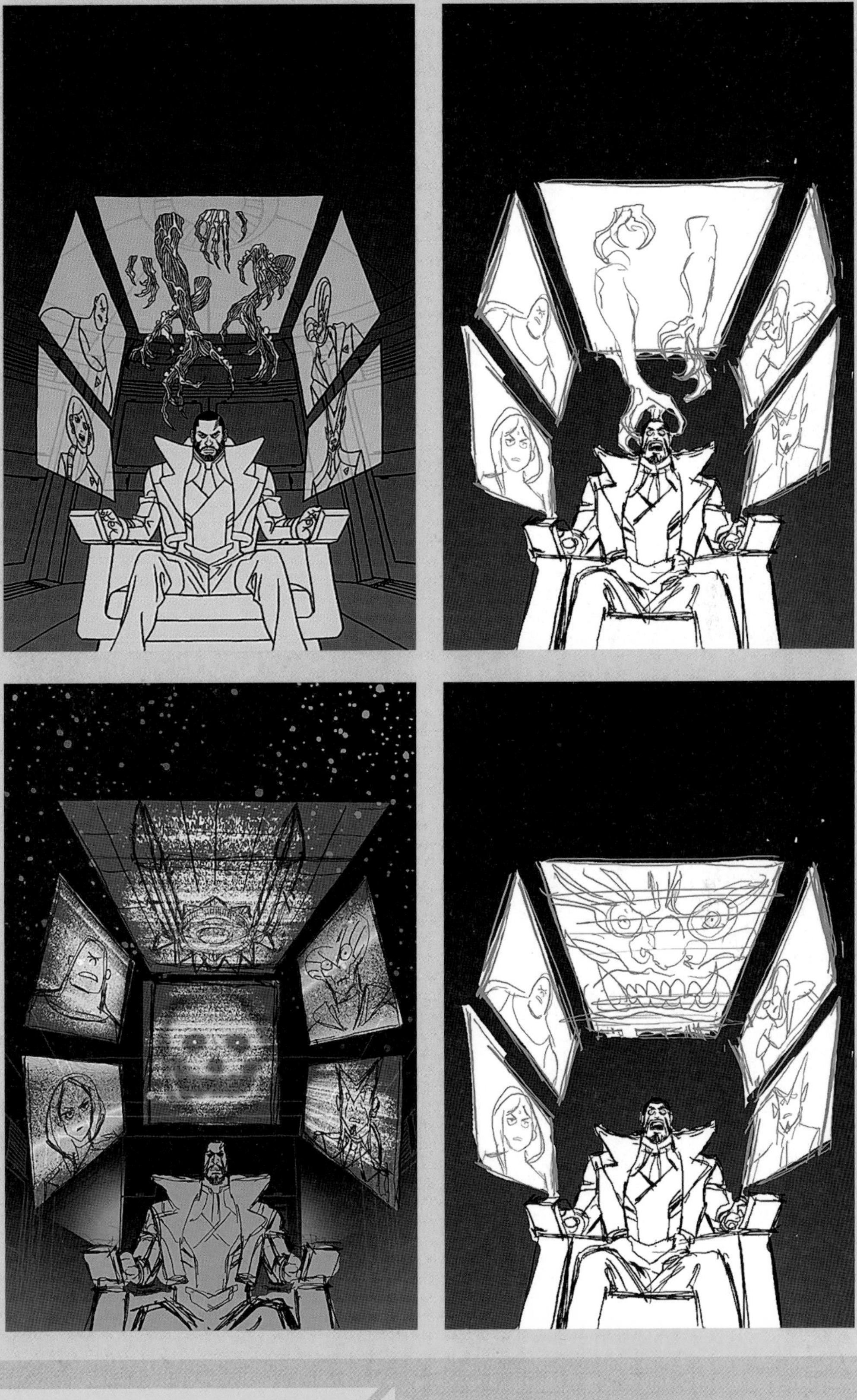

COVER #2 SKETCHES

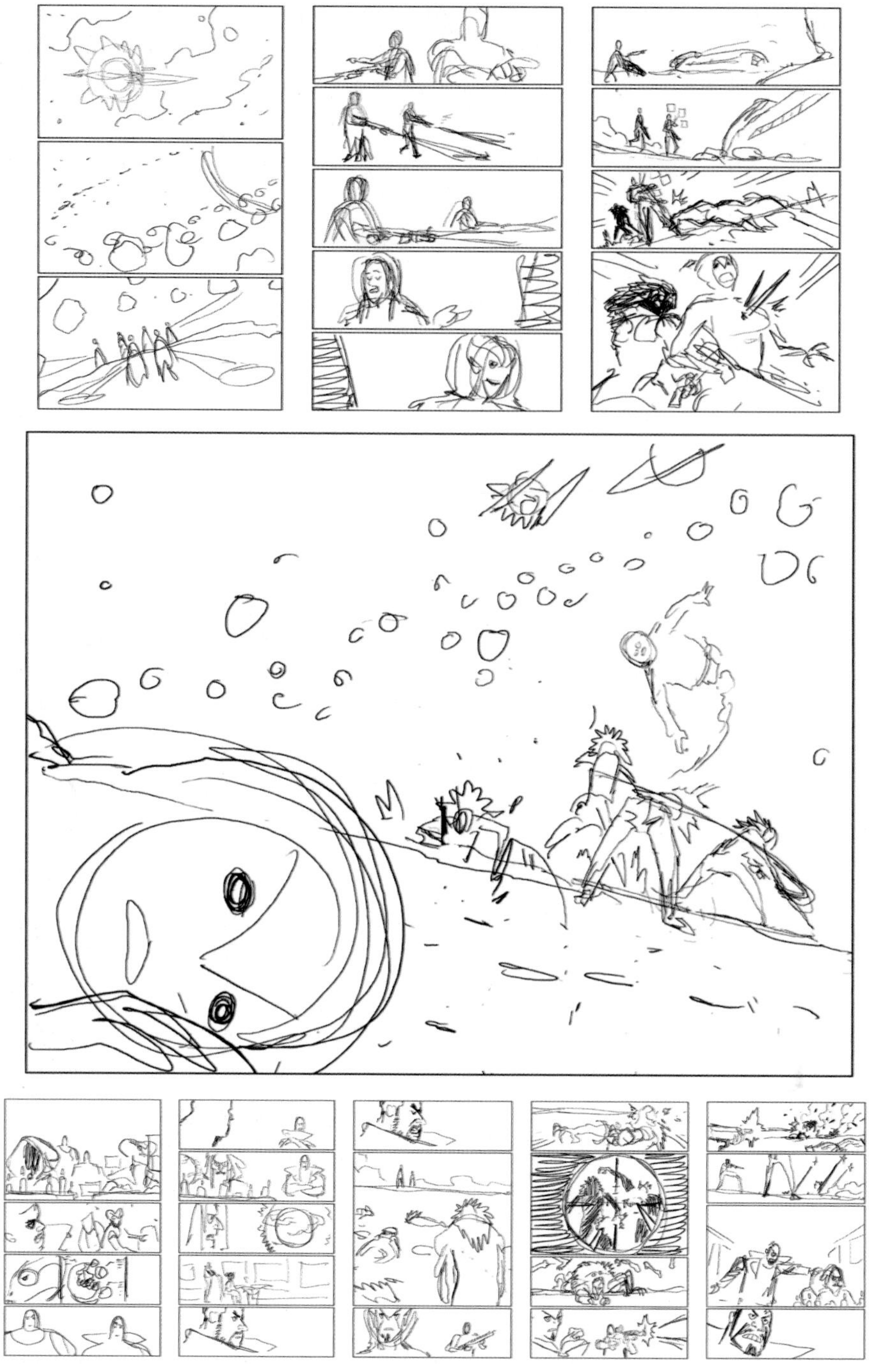

ISSUE #3 THUMBNAILS

EARLY CONCEPT LOG

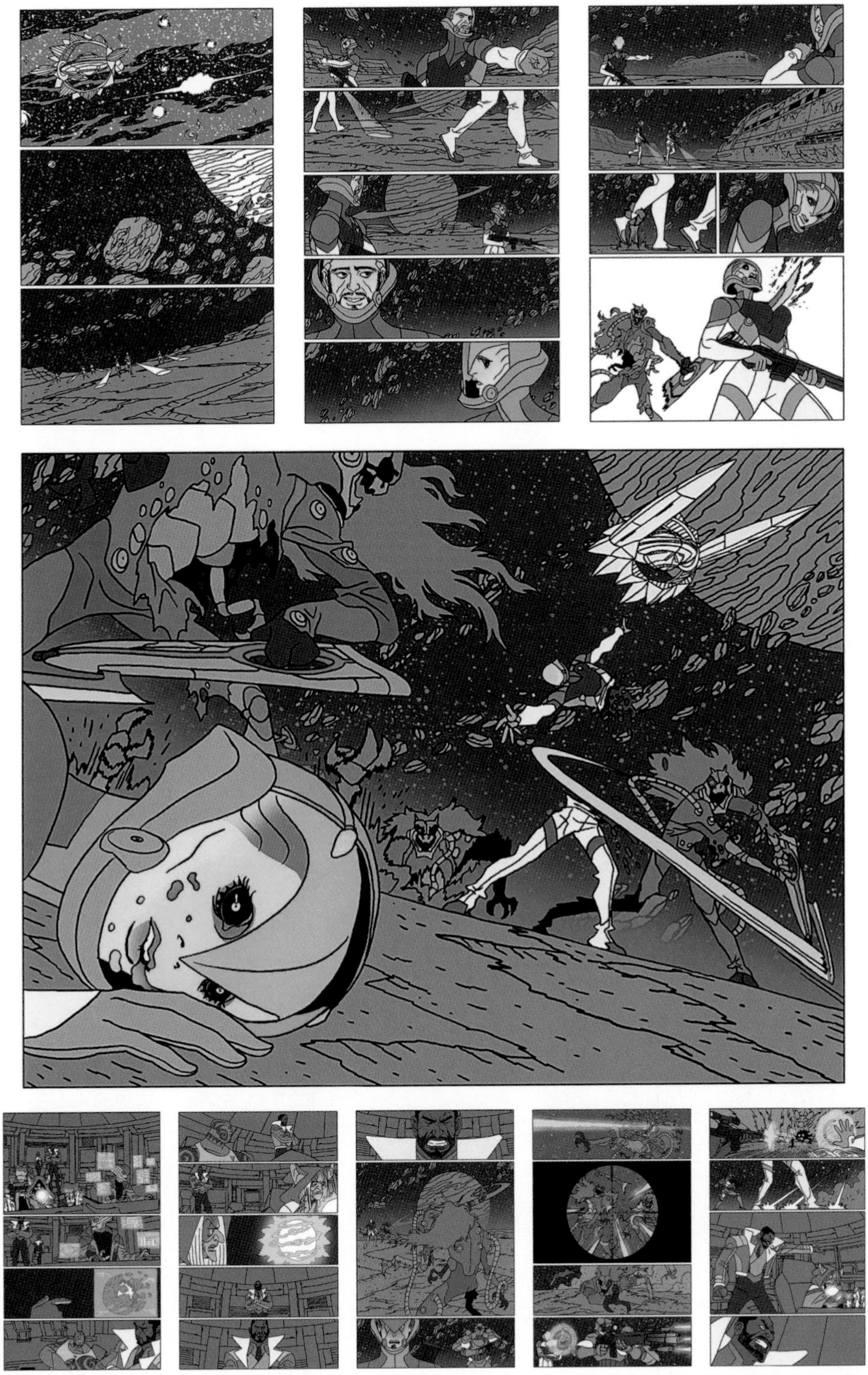

ISSUE #3 COLOR PASS

FOR MORE TALES FROM ROBERT KIRKMAN AND SKYBOUND

ROBERT KIRKMAN
LORENZO DE FELICI
ANNALISA LEONI
OBLIVION SONG
CHAPTER TWO

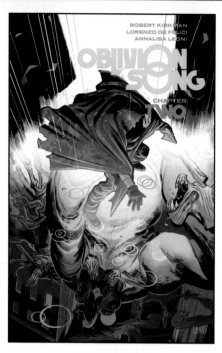

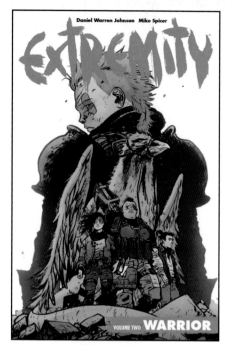

CHAPTER ONE
ISBN: 978-1-5343-0642-4
$9.99

CHAPTER TWO
ISBN: 978-1-5343-1057-5
$16.99

Daniel Warren Johnson Mike Spicer
EXTREMITY
VOLUME TWO WARRIOR

VOL. 1: ARTIST TP
ISBN: 978-1-5343-0242-6
$16.99

VOL. 2: WARRIOR TP
ISBN: 978-1-5343-0506-9
$16.99

BIRTHRIGHT
BLOOD BROTHERS

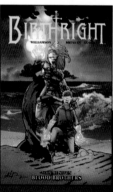

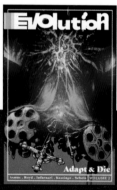

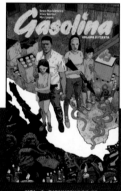

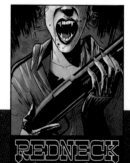

VOL. 1: HOMECOMING TP
ISBN: 978-1-63215-231-2
$9.99

VOL. 2: CALL TO ADVENTURE TP
ISBN: 978-1-63215-446-0
$12.99

VOL. 3: ALLIES AND ENEMIES TP
ISBN: 978-1-63215-683-9
$12.99

VOL. 4: FAMILY HISTORY TP
ISBN: 978-1-63215-871-0
$12.99

VOL. 5: BELLY OF THE BEAST TP
ISBN: 978-1-53430-218-1
$12.99

VOL. 6: FATHERHOOD TP
ISBN: 978-1-53430-498-7
$14.99

VOL. 7: BLOOD BROTHERS TP
ISBN: 978-1-5343-1053-7
$14.99

EVOLUTION
Adapt & Die
VOLUME 2

VOL. 1: ORIGINS OF A SPECIES TP
ISBN: 978-1-5343-0656-1
$16.99

VOL. 2: ADAPT & DIE TP
ISBN: 978-1-5343-0878- 7
$16.99

Gasolina

VOL. 1: BIENVENIDOS TP
ISBN: 978-1-5343-0506-9
$16.99

VOL. 2: FIESTA TP
ISBN: 978-1-5343-0864-0
$16.99

REDNECK

VOL. 1: DEEP IN THE HEART TP
ISBN: 978-1-5343-0331-7
$16.99

VOL. 2: THE EYES UPON YOU TP
ISBN: 978-1-5343-0665-3
$16.99

VOL. 3: LONGHORNS TP
ISBN: 978-1-5343-1050-6
$16.99